KABOOM!

Diane —
Keep that
good music
coming!!!

Brian
Adams

OTHER BOOKS BY BRIAN ADAMS

Love in the Time of Climate Change

KABOOM!

Brian Adams

GREEN WRITERS PRESS

Brattleboro, Vermont

Printed in the United States

10 9 8 7 6 5 4 3 2 1

The author gratefully acknowledges permission
to quote lines from the following song lyrics from
John Prine, "Paradise," *John Prine*, 1971.

Green Writers Press is a Vermont-based publisher whose mission
is to spread a message of hope and renewal through the words
and images we publish. Throughout we will adhere to our
commitment to preserving and protecting the natural resources
of the earth. To that end, a percentage of our proceeds will
be donated to environmental activist groups. Green Writers Press
gratefully acknowledges support from individual donors,
friends, and readers to help support the environment
and our publishing initiative.

Giving Voice to Writers & Artists Who Will Make the World a Better Place
Green Writers Press | Brattleboro, Vermont
www.greenwriterspress.com
Follow the author: brianadamsauthor.wordpress.com

ISBN: 978-09962676-6-3

PRINTED ON PAPER WITH PULP THAT COMES FROM FSC-CERTIFIED FORESTS, MANAGED FORESTS
THAT GUARANTEE RESPONSIBLE ENVIRONMENTAL, SOCIAL, AND ECONOMIC PRACTICES BY
LIGHTNING SOURCE. ALL WOOD PRODUCT COMPONENTS USED IN BLACK & WHITE, STANDARD
COLOR, OR SELECT COLOR PAPERBACK BOOKS, UTILIZING EITHER CREAM OR WHITE BOOKBLOCK
PAPER, THAT ARE MANUFACTURED IN THE LAVERGNE, TENNESSEE PRODUCTION CENTER ARE
SUSTAINABLE FORESTRY INITIATIVE® (SFI®) CERTIFIED SOURCING.

Climb the mountains and get their good tidings. Nature's peace will flow into you as sunshine flows into trees. The winds will blow their own freshness into you, and the storms their energy, while cares will drop off like autumn leaves.

—JOHN MUIR, *Our National Parks*, 1901

KABOOM!

Prologue

IT WAS JUST MY LUCK. The moment the cell door closed I got my period. Perfect timing or what?

"Excuse me!" I yelled out. "I have a medical emergency here!"

Silence. No response.

"Hello!" I yelled again. "I'm having issues!" I tried rattling the bars the way they do in the movies when convicts want to cause trouble or create a diversion for a jailbreak or something sinister like that. But the only sound my rattling made was a pathetic squeak. Kind of like the sound that one of Auntie Sadie's goats makes when you rub its butt.

Still no response.

I raised my voice in that shrill, high-pitched, girly-girl way that I find so annoying when other girls do it.

"Anyone home? I'm kind of bleeding here! Somebody do something!"

Finally, after what seemed like forever, the jailer dude came shuffling around the corner. His hair was all askew, his uniform wrinkled, his eyes puffy and swollen. He looked exhausted.

"What's a girl gotta do to get a tampon around here?" I asked, forcing a smile and attempting to inject a little humor into the situation. Given the circumstances, this was probably not the smartest thing to say.

The jailer glared at me with his tired eyes, wheezed a breath in and out, turned, and silently shuffled away, once again making himself as scarce as boobs on a rooster. I was left alone to bleed in peace.

All things considered, it had been quite a day. I had skipped out on school and chained myself to a logging truck at the bottom of Mount Tom. Our mountain. Our sacred mountain. The mountain the coal company wanted to blow the top off of. The police had come, arrested me, and dragged me away.

And now, here I was hours later, bleeding to death in jail.

And that wasn't even the highlight! The absolute best part, the crowning moment of my day, actually my entire life, was when my boyfriend told me, for the very first time, that he loved me.

"I love you," he had said. "I love you so much!"

Me! He said he loved *me*!

Awesome or what?

1

I LIVE IN GREENFIELD, WEST VIRGINIA. The heart of Appalachia.

Greenfield is a coal mining town in a coal mining state. You were either a miner, related to a miner, or worked in a place supported by miners. Take the coal out of Greenfield and it's hard to imagine there'd even be a town.

And if Coal is King, then the crown prince is the high school mascot—the Greenfield High Coal Miner.

The Miner is always a prince, never a princess. Girls need not apply. It is, as my Auntie Sadie says, the way of the world.

"Why can't I be The Miner when I get to high school?" my little sister Britt asked one day.

"'Cause you're a girl," Sadie said.

"So what? Being The Miner would be fun!"

"In case you hadn't noticed, you don't have a penis," I told her. "Give it up."

Little sisters! Jeez!

Being the mascot is the sweetest thing you can possibly be at our school. The position to die for. Sure, there are the head cheerleader and the captain of the football team and "Miss Coal Greenfield," but they're *nada*, nothing, tiny goat turds compared to "The Miner"—our high school mascot.

Auditions for the job are beyond intense. It's like running for mayor. Or even president. The whole town comes out to watch the show. Bookies lay odds on the favorite, miners bet like mine owners, fortunes are won and lost. Okay—maybe I'm exaggerating a little bit here, but it *is* quite the scene.

Auntie Sadie told me a great story about the classic mascot incident in town. "The Year of the Scam" as folks in Greenfield still call it.

"Bill Mayrose was the manager of the bank back then," Sadie said, sucking in her breath. "Oh my goodness, was he a looker!"

There are two types of men in Auntie Sadie's world: lookers and snookers. The lookers are hot and the snookers are not. Auntie Sadie has been on the lookout for a looker for as long as I can remember, without any success. Sadie is on the plus side of 300 pounds and she has a lazy eye and perpetual eczema that envelopes her face. Much as I love her, it's going to have to be some sort of special looker to take a second look at her.

"That Bill Mayrose was something else!" Auntie continued. "He thought he was God's gift to the world, that man. Lord above, not only was he a looker but he had more money than a sow has nipples."

"What's that, like ten dollars?" Britt asked. She was twelve and a know-it-all. Britt the Twitt.

"Quiet, child!" Sadie continued. "Don't interrupt. Now, Mayrose had a little bit of a boy who put the ook in snook. As spoiled as Prince William's child, that kid was.

"So, when that dweeb Alex, Bill Mayrose's runt of the litter, got to be a senior in high school, Mayrose goes off and bribes the high school principal to choose his son as the mascot. Bribes him! And not some dipshit little tweedly kind of bribe but a big respectable bribe like the mine owners give to the politicians at the statehouse."

"How much?" Britt asked.

"Six figures, rumor has it."

"Auntie, that's like a hundred thousand dollars," Britt protested. In her defense, neither of us ever quite knew how much of Sadie's stories to believe.

Sadie rolled her eyes (as much as she could with an uncooperative lazy eye) and gave me a wink. I punched Britt in the arm. After all, a good story, true or not, should never be interrupted.

"Child, may I continue?" Sadie asked.

Britt sighed, nodded her head, and rubbed her arm.

"Anyway, that boy was no more mascot material than that three-legged goat of mine. Lord knows, even the goat smelled better. Cutting to the chase, somebody caught wind of the scam and squealed. They say the snitch was one of Bill Mayrose's flings, some sleaze that did payroll for American down at the mine."

American is the name of the company that owns and operates the coal mine in Greenfield.

"Evidently he had dumped her a few weeks before and now it was payback time," she went on. "The mascot scam was the biggest thing to hit this town since the mine cave-in at ol' Number 3 in '97. The whole town got their knickers into such a knot you couldn't drive down Franklin Street without running over someone sobbing and flailing their arms and shouting out obscenities. Good gracious me, you would've thought the mine had shut down, the way the poopoo hit the propeller!"

"What happened then?" Britt asked.

"The high school principal resigned and snuck off in the middle of the night. Bill Mayrose fled town with barely his shirt on his back."

Sadie sat back in her chair and fanned herself with a bag of Cheetos. She ate them obsessively and had convinced herself that they satisfied all of the major food groups. My guess was that at least half of her 300 pounds were Cheeto flavored.

"Bill Mayrose," she sighed, picking at her eczema, which was even more red and flushed than usual. "Whew! I wonder whatever happened to that man. For all his faults he was quite the looker."

"What happened to his kid?" Britt asked.

"Ha! Funny you should ask. He still lives here. Not only that, he's gone on to become one of the bosses down at the mine!"

"Is there a moral to this story?" I asked.

"Darlings," Sadie said, closing her good eye and letting the lazy one do its thing. "I hate to clue you in, but when it comes to coal there's nothing moral about it!"

2

AT THE END OF MAY, auditions are held for next year's high school mascot and the town goes absolutely bonkers. It's pretty much the highlight of the year, which tells you something about our town.

Everyone shows up. Everyone. People who left Greenfield years ago and vowed never to set foot in town again, come hell or high water, are sucked back in for the big event. Rumor has it that one year even Bill Mayrose came sneaking back in, disguised as a woman.

A television station down in Charleston finally got wind of it. Now every year they send a TV crew to video the finalists and interview the winner. You'd think we'd be the laughingstock of the whole state, the whole country, the way we hyperventilate and salivate and gyrate and practically have a conniption fit about the whole thing. But no. We've become a tourist attraction. A destination site. *Wild Wonderful West Virginia*, the tourist magazine put out by the state, went so far as to feature us in an article last year and now lists the audition as one of their must-see events.

Last spring, when I was a freshman, Ashley got the idea of silk-screening T-shirts that read "I was there! Greenfield High School Mascot Auditions 2015." Below that was a picture of a hillbilly coal miner jumping up and down with a jug of whiskey in one hand and a banner that said "Go Greenfield!" in the other. Pretty sick. Conjuring up every stereotype that urban folk have of us Appalachia coal people.

Ashley is my best friend. She always has been and she always will be. I've known her forever.

Anyway, the T-shirt idea was a huge hit. We set up a stand outside the gym and sold out in three hours. Fifty T-shirts at ten bucks each. You do the math. We made a fortune.

We're planning on doubling or even tripling our output next year, maybe branching out into coffee mugs and onesies for the little ones.

Ashley has already come up with a thousand different designs, some of which are really offensive, some pretty lame, and others amazing. We're even thinking of having people vote for the best one. Sort of like *The Voice* on TV. Only not.

The Greenfield High mascot for this school year is Marc Potvin. All bow down to the chosen one.

Poor Ashley. She's obsessed with Marc Potvin. She has as much chance with him as I do with Kevin Malloy, Marc's best bud. Which is absolutely none. They're both seniors. They're both hot. They're both super-popular.

And Ashley and I are, well, not.

They're senior sensations.

We're sophomore slugs.

"Better a slug than a slut!" Auntie Sadie said when I moaned to her about my cruel, cruel fate.

"That's helpful!" I said. "Such fabulous choices."

The closest that Ashley has gotten to Marc was when she accidentally-on-purpose dropped her science book and, stooping to pick it up, accidentally-on-purpose touched one of her boobs to Marc's knee.

I was standing next to Ashley by her locker.

"Score!" Ashley silently mouthed to me, pumping her fist.

Ashley is the master of drive-bys. That's what we call it when you accidentally-on-purpose touch a guy with your boob.

Ashley's goal is to do a drive-by on every hot guy in the entire school by Christmas. She's already up to nineteen and it's only the third week of class.

"You're a perv," I told her.

"Takes one to know one," she said.

Ashley goes so far as to plan her drive-bys in advance. She rehearses every move as if she were contemplating robbing Bill Mayrose's bank.

My drive-bys are all accidental. Like the time I fell on top of Sean McKenzie when we were playing volleyball in gym.

"Cyndie, that was no drive-by!" Ashley argued. "That was just a spaz move. You can't count it!"

"Count it?" I groaned. "I'll be in therapy for years trying to forget it!"

When I was lying there on top of him he reached around and fondled one of my boobs. A quick "grab-and-go" as the boys call it. Embarrassing. Humiliating. If Sean McKenzie had been a looker it would have been one thing, but hot he was not.

Now, if I had fallen on top of Kevin Malloy? That would be a different story! Definite fodder for one of those late-night thinkabouts.

Lately Ashley has been starting off each day recounting her last night's thinkabout. That's our code word for touching ourselves. Not just touching but, you know, touching touching.

As in down-there touching. "Mining the muff," as we say in Greenfield.

There's not the minutest smidgeon of a detail that I don't know about Ashley's life—whether I like it or not, whether I want to know it or not, I know it. I could write a book. Two or three volumes. Not that there is really all that much to write about. After all, we live in Greenfield, for goodness sake.

Ashley is the master of WTMI, way too much information.

"Oh my God, Cyndie," Ashley gushed as we were walking to school yesterday. "I had the best one *ever* last night! Starring Marc and me down by the river."

"What else is new," I said.

"Anyway," Ashley continued. "I was wearing that new pink bikini I showed you and he had on a Spongebob Swimsuit and one of our T-shirts! It was so hot!"

"Wait!" I said, stopping in the middle of the road we were crossing and causing a car to swerve to avoid us. "You had a thinkabout featuring Spongebob and our drunken miner?"

"Stop!" Ashley giggled. "It was Marc. He is such a looker!"

While we make up most of our own terms—or Ashley/Cyndie–speak, as we call it—we occasionally steal one of the sweet ones from Auntie Sadie.

"Anyway, the good stuff came when the suit came off and he started in on me!"

The rest of the walk consisted of Ashley's spirited mono-logue, recounting in explicit detail exactly what "starting in on her" meant.

As I said, even from a BFF it was WTMI.

Speaking of thinkabouts, here's an incredibly embarrassing story:

Last weekend I was in the middle of a wonderful one and Britt walks in on it. No knocking. No warning. She just waltzes right on into my room.

I was off in la-la land and didn't even have time to take my fingers out of my you-know-what.

Britt stopped dead in her tracks, sucked in her breath, took one look at me, and dropped a whole bowl of popcorn on the floor.

"What are you doing?" she yelled.

"What does it look like I'm doing, twit?" I yelled back. "Ever heard of knocking? Ever heard of the right to privacy? Get out of my room! Now!" I threw a pillow at her.

"Dad!" Britt yelled down the stairs. "Cyndie is masturbating!"

Oh my God! When I got my hands on that girl there was going to be a master *beating*!

Why did my mother have to have a second child?

3

ASHLEY AND I reserve our thinkabouts for our bedrooms, but we do some of our best thinking on Mount Tom.

Mount Tom is our mountain. It's the mountain that we can bike to when we want to get away from the world and the crazies and my twit of a sister and Ashley's mother, who drives her insane. It's the mountain we go to when we just want to be by ourselves.

We made a path to the top of the mountain that no one else knows about—no one, except for Ashley and me and

Tom himself, and he's not talking 'cause he's long dead and gone.

It's our special, sacred place.

Mount Tom was named—surprise, surprise—for Tom, some old-time miner who, back in the day, came tromping up here looking for his lost pig, tumbled off the cliff, broke his neck, and died. Why folks didn't come up with a more imaginative name than Mount Tom is beyond me. I mean, really, think of the possibilities! Ashley and I once spent an entire afternoon dangling our legs over the edge of the cliff on top and renaming the place.

"Lost Pig Peak."

"Porky's Revenge."

"Tumbling Tom's."

We knew every maple, beech, ash, and birch on that mountain like the back of our hands. We'd gone so far as to name some of the larger and taller trees. We called them our great-grandfathers and great-grandmothers and they stood guard in a sacred grove and watched over the two of us and didn't allow anyone else up there. Just Ashley and me. The chosen two.

We bow to them whenever we pass by and I swear that sometimes, particularly on wild, wonderful, windy days, they bow their branches low to the ground right back at us.

If you think all trees look the same, think again. Each tree, even trees from the same species, are as different from each other as you are from me. Their shape, their bark, their leaves, their flowers, their seeds . . . all different. Just like people.

I suppose that if an alien race of tree creatures landed their space ship on planet earth and examined us humans, at first glance they'd think we were all identical. "Seen one, seen them all," they'd tell each other, and they'd hightail it back home so as not to miss *Roots* or *Sesame Tree* or whatever else was on must-see Tree TV. But if they hadn't been in such a rush, if they took the time to look, to really look, they'd notice how special each one of us humans really were.

Same thing with the trees on Mount Tom.

There's Sugar Daddy, a giant sugar maple that we once thought of tapping for the yummy sap locked inside, but the thought of driving a stake into his mapley heart was way too much to bear. Six of us holding hands would barely circle his studly hulkiness.

There's Bradley Beech, named after Bradley Cooper, the movie star, whom Ashley has a thing for. Once, in a brief moment of weakness, Ash and I were on the verge of carving our names and "BFF" deep into his smooth, gray bark. She had her pocketknife out and open and had just found the perfect spot, when—*BAM!* Down plummeted a gnarly branch from the canopy that landed with a thud right next to us. A message from the forest nymphs. A big STOP! sign sent from the tree goddess above. We caught our breath, looked at each other, and put the knife away forever.

There's Sadie's Twin, an enormous black cherry with bark that looks like crispy, burnt potato chips, kind of resembling Auntie Sadie's skin after a super-bad outbreak of her eczema.

But our hands-down favorite is She, a fabulous white ash with leaflets that turn deep purple in the fall. Leaflets as purple as the eggplants that grow like weeds in Auntie Sadie's garden. Leaflets as purple as the varicose veins that bulge out so frighteningly on Auntie Sadie's enormous thighs.

Ashley is super-attached to that particular white ash tree. They do, after all, share a name. Whenever we walk by it, Ashley wraps her arms around it and gives the tree a big ol' bear hug and a wet, smoochie, tongue-on-bark kiss. It's really cute, in a somewhat weird and kinky kind of way.

Sometimes, when we can't decide what is true and what isn't, or why the world is the way that it is, or why boys do what boys do, or why zits just happen to pop out at all the wrong moments, or why whenever you wear a really cute short skirt it always seems to get caught in your underwear after you pee and you don't know it until people point and laugh, we stop and we sit and we ask She.

And She answers. She whispers to us with the rustling of her leaves. She replies with the groaning of her trunk as she sways majestically in the breeze. She is full of tree wisdom. She is the sage of the forest. And what She says is always the truth, the whole truth, and nothing but the truth, so help me goddess of the wild and wonderful West Virginia woodlands.

To be honest, Mount Tom is more like a mountain wannabe than a real mountain. It doesn't take that long to climb to the top. But once you get there, there is a little cliff overlook and a ledge that the two of us can just barely squeeze out onto and we can sit back and look out over the entire holler where Ash and I live. It's an incredible view. It's like the whole world is ours; the houses, the school, the stores. Even the Evangelical church with its pointy steeple.

Neither Ashley nor I are churchgoers in the traditional sense. My father is a born-again American Civil War reenactor and spends most of his Sundays fighting holy battles that took place 150 years ago. Ashley's mother is way too hungover on Sunday mornings to even think about getting her sorry ass up and out of bed and dragging Ash anywhere.

So off we go to the top of Mount Tom. It's our church. Our temple to the gods and goddesses.

We make our way to the top and we sit on the edge of the world and we get a good heavy dose of that old-time religion.

And, like I said, it's where we do some of our best thinking.

It was on top of Mount Tom where we first thought to divide the world of boys into four kingdoms.

"I think," Ashley said as we made a catapult from a beech branch and shot nuts out over the edge of the world, "that Auntie Sadie is on to something. She's got her 'lookers' and her 'snookers,' right?"

"Your point?" I asked.

"We need a system, too. To rate the boys."

"Why not just use hers, like we always have?"

"No way! We must have our own. We must!"

After a few hours of incredibly brilliant brainstorming, this is what we came up with:

- *Kingdom Number One: Losers.* Boys such as Sean McKenzie, whose only redeeming quality was keeping us awake in English with his farting or zit popping or falling out of his chair whenever he fell asleep, which happened at least four times every class. One time Mr. Cooper, the science teacher, kicked him out of lab because he sneezed too much.

- *Kingdom Number Two: Untouchables.* Those hotties way over our heads. Worthy of starring in a think-about, total priorities for drive-bys, but not real life potential. I mean, let's face it, there are certain guys whom you know it's never going to happen with so you might as well not even go there, whether you're obsessed with them or not. The Marc Potvins and the Kevin Malloys of the world.

- *Kingdom Number Three: Friends.* Hanging-out with material. Fun to make fun of, good to copy homework off of, useful to bum rides from if they can drive, but nothing more. Kids like Sam Walker who liked to fish and Jason Berring who ran track.

- *Kingdom Number Four:* The most important category. The one that required endless analysis, intense intellectual thought, perpetual contemplation, and ongoing late-night angst: Possibilities. Hotties within the realm of reality. Ashley kept insisting that Marc Potvin really did belong in this category but she was just dreaming.

The kingdoms are fairly fluid. A boy could start off one week as a friend, plummet in the polls to Kingdom One following some stupid incident or obnoxious comment, and then magically redeem himself by the end of the week with a single glance in our direction or a flick of his hair or a million other tiny, almost imperceptible things and wind up right smack-dab at the top of Kingdom Four.

We've pretty much got every boy in the school ranked, except for the freshmen who, as everyone knows, don't really even count as people. The notable exception is Dan Felton, who has been held back a grade so many times he must be in his midtwenties and, while not the brightest lamp in the mine, is way, way hot.

The third week in September we stayed after school and helped Mr. Cooper clean his lab, and he scored us a sweet job collecting tickets at one of the high school home football games. We didn't get paid but we did get in free to the game and were allowed to eat as much as we wanted at the food stand. Even though it was crap food, it was *free*, which made it *awesome!*

As an added bonus, we got to watch Marc Potvin do his mascot thing with his miner's helmet and his oversized overalls and his inflatable shovel which he used to whack other mascots in the head with, much to the delight of the crowd. As unattractive as all that sounds, Ashley would still pant and drool and feel faint and get totally loopy.

Anyway, being the ticket takers at the game gave us an up-close-and-personal look at all the boys from other towns. As we ripped their tickets and handed the stubs back to them we yelled out their numbers on the Boy Scale.

"I got three Ones," I called out to Ashley as guys with zits bigger than footballs came shuffling up to me.

"Lucky you!" Ashley laughed. "But take a lookie at two o'clock. Incoming Fours. A whole flock of them!"

When one of the hotties handed Ashley his ticket, she accidentally-on-purpose dropped it, scoring a sweet drive-by as she stood back up.

"*Ka-ching!*" Ashley said, pumping her fist and turning around to drool at their swaying rear ends.

Most of the time—in fact, 99.9 percent of the time—Ashley and I agreed on which kingdom the boys belonged. But when we disagreed, the sparks would fly. Once she didn't talk to me for six whole hours, close to seven, because I simply suggested the possibility of demoting Mark Potvin from a hottie to a loser.

"Are you *nuts*?" Ash exclaimed, her pupils dilating in disbelief. "I mean, are you completely crazy?"

Of course, Ashley had been home sick the day last year when Mark Potvin had downed a six-pack of soda and was practicing belching the ABC's, and halfway through the letter G he had gagged and threw up all over my locker. It even got into those little vent openings they have so if you forget your gym clothes over the weekend the fumes don't build up to the point that the whole place explodes. I swear I can still smell it when I open the locker door.

"Marc Potvin?" Ashley cried again. She was visibly shaking. Her eyes were rolling back in her head. She looked like she was ready to speak in tongues, the way they do in those evangelical churches.

"A loser? That guy is so hot I get heartburn just saying his name!"

"Ashley. I hate to tell you, but heartburn is a bad thing," I said.

"Then heart*freeze*. Whatever."

"Then why don't you go barf on his locker? Maybe that'll turn him on and then the two of you can go behind the bleachers and do it!"

That got her panties in a twist.

Like I said, we didn't speak for hours.

Moral of the story: there are certain boys on the list you absolutely don't mess with; Marc Potvin clearly being one of them.

Auntie Sadie says it's rude and disrespectful to rate guys.

"How would you feel if the boys kept lists of you girls?" she asked.

"Earth to Sadie!" I said. "Of course boys do! The only difference is they only have two categories. Those who don't and those who do."

Sadie sighed. "I guess some things never change," she said.

"Anyway," I continued. "You're just jealous because our system is so much more sophisticated than yours. All you've got are hotties and snotties."

"Lookers and snookers," Auntie Sadie corrected.

"Whatever. We've taken the system to a whole new level."

Auntie Sadie took a moment to digest this before seeing the wisdom of our ways.

"And how do *you* rate?" she asked.

"On the boy's scale? Jeez, Sadie! Please! You know I'm not that kind of girl! Anyway, I thought you were down on lists. I thought you said they were rude and disrespectful!"

"They are. But I'm curious to know whether or not there's a boy out there worth his weight in cornfield beans. Any guy in this town who's not out of his cotton-pickin' mind is going to rate you a hottie!"

"Are you kidding?" I said. Pleased as I was with the compliment, anything Auntie Sadie said was highly suspect. I could do no wrong in her eyes. Childless herself, she was my surrogate mother. Had been since my mother, Sadie's sister, died when I was five.

According to her I was God's gift to the universe. I could poo in my pants and she'd label it a Rembrandt.

"Anyway," I continued, "how am I supposed to know? On Ashley and my scale I'm sure I'd rate a One. Or at best a Three."

To refresh your memory, Ones were losers and Threes were almost as bad: dreaded friends.

Auntie Sadie scowled and spat out chewing tobacco juice, making a pool of yuck on the ground. "One plus three equals four, darling. Which is what you are. H-O-T Hot! If I was a guy I wouldn't be able to keep my hands off you. Which, God knows, they'd better or I'll kick their butts from here to kingdom come!"

I don't know which image was more terrifying: Auntie Sadie as a guy, all lazy-eyed, eczema-scarred 300 pounds of him with his hands all over me? Or Sadie safely guarding my virginity for the rest of eternity, hunting down and literally crushing any Possibility that came within shouting distance.

"We're screwed!" I said to Ashley. "With Sadie as protector we'll never get asked out! Undatables! Forever doomed to wither on the Friend vine!"

"No way!" Ashley said. "We don't get asked out because we're Twos. Untouchables!"

I shook my head and laughed.

"We're so hot, boys don't think they have a snowball's chance in hell of scoring with us," Ashley continued. We were on our way to school and Ashley had stopped in the middle of the road to adjust the padding in her bra to make her boobs stick out a little bit more.

"Are they even?" Ashley asked.

"Are what even?"

"Number one and number two! Who do you think? I swear to God, number two's getting tinier by the second. I'm fifteen years old and I'm already shrinking!"

Ashley was obsessed with boob number one being bigger than boob number two. I'd measured them dozens of times but she was still fixated on the unevenness issue. Once she pilfered a magnifying glass from Mr. Cooper's class and had me spend all of lunch in the girl's room stall searching for a millimeter of difference. Of which—surprise, surprise—there was absolutely none.

If someone had walked in on us, our chances of making it with a guy would have plummeted from zero to around negative five thousand.

"Oh my God!" Ashley exclaimed, stopping dead again in the middle of the road. "I've just had an epiphany!"

Epiphany was Ashley's favorite word of the week. She used it about a thousand times a day. She had had more epiphanies this week than Sean McKenzie, supreme ruler of the Kingdom Ones, had zits.

"We have to come up with a master plan. We have to bring ourselves back down to Earth. We have to show the boys that, even though we're goddesses, rock stars, out-of-this-world babes, total catches, we're still just girls. Girls with wants. Girls with needs. Girls with desires!"

"Girls who are not flattened road kill!" I yelled, dragging Ashley to the side of the road as two of the top high school losers in their beat-up pickup truck almost ran us over.

"Are you sure they're even?" Ashley asked, fiddling with her boobs while ignoring the obscenities hurled in our direction. "Number two seems to be riding awfully high today! God they look good, though, don't they?"

Even with all of her concerns about her boobs, low self-esteem was not one of Ashley's issues. Reality, yes.

Self-esteem, no.

4

SCHOOL WAS SCHOOL. Generally a royal pain-in-the-ass, but it was where the boys were and I got to hang out with Ashley and there was constant drama, so it was tolerable.

Most of the teachers were either sadists or morons, counting the days until their retirement. Most had given up on us, operating under the assumption that we were all a bunch of meth-smoking, moonshine-drinking, trailer-trash hillbillies that would never amount to a pile of coal slickens, so why bother expending any intellectual energy even trying to shove the tiniest morsels of knowledge into our miniscule heads?

Particularly for us girls. In the eyes of most West Virginia guys, we were already barefoot and pregnant, good for serving up lunch at the diner or, better yet, working the stripper pole at the "gentlemen's club" in Charleston.

I learned absolutely nothing in most of their classes. In fact, some teachers were so god-awful that you came out knowing less than when you went in. Their classes were a vast, intellectual black hole that zapped all the creativity and thirst for knowledge right out of you. They were like cerebral vampires, sucking out brains rather than blood, and without any of the undead's redeeming sex appeal.

Case in point: algebra with Mr. Livingston.

I had begun the year knowing a thing or two about equations and variables and formulas and crap like that. In fact, I even kind of liked the stuff. There was some sort of sanity in math: rules were rules. There was a definite right and wrong. It was clear-cut, comforting, no mushy gray areas of doubt or confusion. If I paid attention, I got it.

"You're, like, a brain!" Ashley said whenever I'd let her copy my homework. "You're, like, a math goddess. You'll probably grow up and marry Einstein."

"Einstein's dead!" I told her.

"What?" she exclaimed. "When did that happen? God, I don't go online for half a day and things go from pudding to poop!"

Anyway, Mr. Livingston was the king of the horrid vampires. He had something wrong with his nose and obsessively scratched and yanked on it, oblivious as to how pathetic and totally gross it was. His knowledge of math seemed rudimentary at best, and, though I'm no math whiz, even I could catch the constant incorrect equations he put up on the board.

By the end of the third week of class I could barely add single digit numbers anymore.

"You poor child!" Auntie Sadie sympathized. "I had Mr. Livingston when I was a sophomore. He was about a hundred years old then! I thought he'd be dead by now. Does he still pick his nose?"

"Ugh!" I said, gagging. "It makes me want to puke!"

Auntie Sadie let out a deep sigh. "When that man dies they'll probably stuff his body and prop him up in front of the class with his finger still stuck deep inside his snotlocker!"

"Yeah!" I said, laughing. Auntie Sadie could be quite the hoot. "Who knows, that way I might even learn some math!"

English class was not much better.

Ashley and I only survived that shit show by designing a comic book featuring the daily crime-fighting adventures of Diaper Lady, aka Mrs. Osgood, the English teacher. She was one of those old bags with blue hair and a puffy, crumpled look, with a butt three sizes too big that stuck out at an incredibly awkward angle as if she had on an adult diaper. Maybe even two. This was not unlikely, given the nasty way she smelled. Her comic-book superpower was her ability to lift up the hem of her skirt and stop criminal evil doers dead in their tracks with her Super Stink.

There was one exception to the Evil Teacher Club: Mr. Cooper, the science teacher.

That man could teach.

Granted, he was nothing to look at. He was pencil thin, with a shocking matt of uncontrollable, frizzly gray hair that leapt out every which way. Very Einsteinish. He'd comb it fastidiously during class, which only made matters worse.

"Left your finger in the light socket again?" Ashley asked him.

He laughed and laughed.

You could say crap like that to Mr. Cooper. He acted like a human being.

Mr. Cooper worshiped all things science. While most of the other teachers seemed content just to torture us and make our lives as miserable as possible, Mr. Cooper cared. He actually wanted us to learn.

He was in love with what he taught. His body, all 100 pounds of it, would start to twitch and tremble at the mere mention of some exotic marsupial in New Zealand or a newly discovered orchid in Vietnam. If you correctly defined his "science word of the day," he'd leap out of his seat, shout "Hallelujah!" or "Praise the Lord!" and flap his hands in the air, twirl and wiggle his way up to you, and give you a high five. He'd shout and perspire and pace and then stop dead in his tracks in the middle of the classroom, close his eyes and go into a semi-trance while he quoted Rachel Carson or John Muir or Aldo Leopold or some other long-dead environmentalist as if he were reciting the Sermon on the Mount.

Mr. Cooper would have us make up songs about endangered species. Ashley and I did this lame rap on the black rhinoceros and from his reaction you'd have thought we'd saved the world.

"Again!" he cried, clapping his hands and bouncing up and down like a four-year-old. "Sing it again!"

Mr. Cooper would sometimes forget that we were sophomores and juniors with a few slacker seniors thrown in and he'd treat us like first graders, but no one seemed to mind.

"Criss-cross applesauce!" he'd shout when one of us got out of our seats to poke or prod or pinch the kid sitting in the next seat over. It was usually Peter Rosnick or Charley Robinson or Michael Dabbs, ADHD boys incapable of sitting still for more than forty-five seconds. Boys, frankly, who should still be back in the first grade. Criss-cross applesauce meant sit the hell down, cross your arms and your legs, keep to yourself and stop annoying other people. The boys would hang their heads, grin, shuffle back to their chairs, cross their arms and their legs, and lamely try to keep still for another minute or two.

Other teachers would scream and curse and scream some more. Not Mr. Cooper. All Mr. Cooper had to do was say "criss-cross."

In the middle of lab, when he wanted our attention he'd climb on the top of his desk, clap his hands three times, and shout, "One-two-three—eyes on me!"

We were all supposed to stop what we were doing, clap our hands twice, and shout back to him, "One-two—eyes on you!" And then make circles with our fingers and put them over our eyes like we were staring out of binoculars. Pretty lame, but it always seemed to work.

True story:

Once, in the middle of the frog dissection lab, Ashley forgot she was still holding the poker she had her poor frog's ovaries stuck onto when Mr. Cooper yelled, "One-two-three!" Ashley clapped her hands and the ovaries went flying clear across the room and nailed one of the sweeter sophomore boys, *splat*, right between his eyes. Perfect shot!

"Ashley!" the boy cried out, wiping off the frog eggs dripping down his goggles. "You've lost your female thingy!"

Poor Ashley. She turned five thousand shades of red. Redder than the strawberry poison-dart frog from Costa Rica that Mr. Cooper had only minutes before shown us a Power Point picture of. Redder than the Vidal Sassoon Pro Series Vibrant Red Hair Color dye that Ashley had secretly dumped into her hair in the back of Walmart when we were in the seventh grade, mistaking it for the Vidal Sassoon Pro Series Dark Cool Blonde Color dye she had meant to use. So red that if she blushed any harder I was afraid her face would fall off.

When Mr. Cooper was on one of his tirades, pacing back and forth, waxing eloquently about coral reefs or laughing hyenas or some such natural wonder, he would comb and recomb his hair in hyperspeed fast motion. He'd comb his hair and then he'd take out one of those disposable flossers and floss his teeth. Seriously. Right in front of the class.

Combing and then flossing and all the while talking and gesticulating wildly and pacing back and forth.

Weird or what?

"I'd like to play poker against that man!" Ashley said.

"What are you talking about?" I asked.

"Mr. Cooper. Think of the money you could make. Any time he had a decent poker hand he'd take out the comb and the flosser. He wouldn't be able to help himself. You'd be able to read him like a book. I could retire on my winnings!"

One of Ashley's major goals in life was to make it big and retire early. Like at seventeen. Although something told me that selling Greenfield High School mascot T-shirts and playing Texas hold 'em with Mr. Cooper wasn't exactly going to do it.

There was another awesome thing about Mr. Cooper: he swore in class. He'd call politicians "bastards" and "sons of bitches." If he didn't like our homework he'd call it "a piece of shit."

Every so often a student's parents would get their panties in a wad and go bitching to the principal about his ungodly language and demand that Mr. Cooper learn to hold his tongue.

"They can go to hell!" we heard Mr. Cooper yell to the principal following one parental complaint.

We liked Mr. Cooper. We liked him a lot. We liked him so much that Ashley and I would surf the 'Net in order to bring him late-breaking news of weird science, just to witness his orgasmic reaction. Doing something like that for other teachers was unimaginable.

"Mr. Cooper!" Ashley yelled from the back of the classroom. "Do you know army ants make nests out of their own bodies?"

Mr. Cooper lurched spastically, spilled his pile of papers onto the floor, and immediately launched into a spirited monologue on the wonder of colonial insects.

I started sophomore year frankly not giving a goat's turd about science. I had always thought of science as boring as hell, totally devoid of meaning.

What did it have to do with my life? Nothing, as far as I could tell. I couldn't care less about the subject.

And then came Mr. Cooper, or Coop as we called him behind his back.

He was like the Pied Piper of Hamelin, leading us unsuspecting kids from the "science sucks" side of town, never to return. He was like the minister they brought in for the revivals at the Souls' Haven Evangelical Church, but instead of the word of God he filled us up with the gospel of nature and the religion of science.

Even some of the brain-dead back-row boys whose fathers cooked crystal meth and beat the crap out of them would stay awake and pay attention in class and occasionally, just occasionally, go so far as to even ask a question.

"He's like a rock star," Ashley said about Coop. "A god."

"Wait a minute!" I said. "I thought that was us?"

"Oh yeah," Ashley said. "Whoops!"

5

My father is obsessed with the American Civil War, or as some of the folks down here call it, the War of Northern Aggression. Bizarre as it seems, there are lots of folks down here who still seem to be fighting it.

Bert Stanmere, one of the classic senior stupids and a real piece of work, has a Confederate flag on the antennae of his truck that he almost ran us over with and a bumper sticker with the catchy slogan "Hear My Rebel Yell!" Whatever the heck that's supposed to mean. Once, when we were leaving school through the parking lot, Ashley flicked his flag with her middle finger. We didn't see him sitting in the front seat smoking cigarettes with his equally stupid sidekick, Michael Mead.

"Hey!" he yelled, opening the door. "What the hell do you think you're doing?"

I just about jumped out of my skin, I was shaking so hard. Bert Stanmere, with his tattoos and his mohawk, was one scary dude. A total One on the guy scale, aka Loser, but a hulky, bulky, frightening Loser.

Before I could apologize and whisk us off to safety, Ashley had to go and open her big mouth.

"Hey!" she yelled back, standing her ground, staring him down, one hand on her hip and the other giving yet another middle-fingered flick to his flag. "Why don't you get the hell over it? The North won the war. Deal with it, asshole!"

Then we ran like the mine was about to collapse.

"One of these days you're going to get us killed, Ash!" I said, practically peeing my pants.

"Until then," Ashley yelled back, "keep on running!"

Anyway, back to my father. He is an American history professor at the community college in Charleston and knew more about the Civil War than any other man living or dead. Ask him about something that was happening in 2015 and he was totally clueless. Ask him about something that happened in 1864 and he knew every intimate detail down to the color of the buttons on a Union colonel's britches.

With no wife to rein him in, our "vacations" are endless explorations of Civil War battlefields. It wasn't until I was about ten that I realized there were even other vacation destination possibilities. I had just assumed that all kids did what we did, and I felt totally ripped off when I found out that those lucky-duckies with enough money went to places like Six Flags or Disneyworld or the beach or someplace sweet like that.

Last summer, for the millionth time, we were being dragged around the battlefield at Bull Run when my father leapt onto a cannon.

"This is sacred ground!" he cried out.

"Get down, Dad!" Britt and I pleaded. "Please! Get off the cannon!"

It was humiliating. Beyond embarrassing. Tourists looked at him like he was a crazy man and backed away. Others thought he was part of the show and took pictures. One kid even asked him for his autograph.

The really pathetic part was that this was not an unusual occurrence. As soon as we get off the main road and turn the corner into yet another Civil War battlefield in Virginia or Tennessee or Pennsylvania or whatever state we're in, my father goes off into one of his trances. He leaves the present and becomes part of the past. To him, it isn't 2015. It really isn't. It's the 1860s and the height of the American Civil War.

"Charge!" my father hollers, stopping the car in the middle of the road and leaping over a stone wall, imaginary rifle in his hand and fury in his eyes. Britt and I have to beg some anxious park ranger to cut my father a little bit of slack and not drag him away to the loony bin.

Fortunately (or not), after so many repeat performances in the same battlefields, the park personnel have gotten to know him. Some are amused by his antics, some annoyed, but as long as he doesn't harm anyone they let him go off and do his thing, no matter how clinically insane it seems to be. I could tell they felt sorry for Britt and me.

"Where's your mom?" a park ranger once asked us while we were touring the battlefield in Petersburg, Virginia, and my father was screaming obscenities at General Burnside for totally botching the Battle of the Crater during the siege of 1864. "Wouldn't you be more comfortable hanging out with her?"

I gave the ranger the evil eye.

"My mommy is dead!" Britt said, taking her thumb out of her mouth while still holding tightly to Mister Wiggins, her stuffed bunny. She was five at the time.

That shut him up.

The most embarrassing moment of my life happened at Gettysburg when I was thirteen. We were on a pilgrimage to that battlefield and my father was pacing back and forth, staring out over the distant cornfield at the Triangle, past the split-rail fences to the far line of distant woods, waiting for the assault of General Pickett and his men. It was a hot August afternoon in 2012, but in my father's head it was the early morning of July 3, 1863—the last day of the battle of Gettysburg, the "High-Water Mark of the Confederacy," the beginning of the end for the South.

Joy of all joys, at that very moment I got my period for the first time.

I was standing there, anxiously watching my father, hoping he didn't do anything too embarrassing, when suddenly I looked down and my white shorts were stained a brownish red.

"*Aiieee!*" I screamed in total panic. "I'm bleeding!"

My father, in a frenzy, came running up, took one look at me, and went off the deep end.

"You've been shot!" he cried, scooping me into his arms. "My daughter's been shot! The attack is on! The Confederates are advancing! Fall back, you fools!" he yelled to a crowd of elderly tourists that had just gotten off a park bus. "Fall back!"

Wild-eyed and practically frothing at the mouth, my father plowed into them, knocking some blue-haired woman with a walker flat on her ass.

It was total mayhem. The old folk thought it was a terrorist attack or something. They were practically climbing over each other, frantically trying to get back on the effin bus. I was wailing, "I'm bleeding! I'm bleeding!" My father was shouting, "Fall back! Fall back! Bring up the 69th Regiment! Give 'em hell, boys!" Poor Britt had been grabbed by the tour guide and whisked onto the bus for safety.

In the nick of time, a park ranger (female, thank God) came running up and straightened out the whole ridiculous mess. She brought me back to park headquarters, gave me a five-minute lesson on feminine hygiene, hooked me up with a couple of pads and a pair of shorts from the lost-and-found, and returned me to my father, who, somewhat chagrined and at least temporarily back in the present, was still apologizing to the blue-hair he had bowled over.

"My daughter is menstruating!" he proudly announced to the entire bus. "For the first time! Right here at Gettysburg! Right here at the pivotal point of one of the greatest battles ever fought. Who would have thought?"

The whole tour bus erupted into applause.

If I could have crawled under a rock and died right then and there amongst the corpses of the 50,000 Yankees and Rebels, I would have gladly done it.

6

Lots of fathers have hobbies. They hunt. They fish. They go to football games.

Not my father.

Embarrassing as it is, my father has gone beyond simply dragging us to Civil War battlefields to becoming a full-fledged American Civil War reenactor. That means he dresses up as a Confederate brigadier general and plays Civil War make-believe on weekends. It's a hobby for history buffs with issues.

Sad. Pathetic. But, unfortunately, true.

It's sort of like a cult. There should be laws against it.

I used to hate with a passion being dragged to battle reenactments with my father. Sometimes it seemed like every damn weekend we were off fighting the Civil War. I'd be bored to tears, with my only amusement being tormenting Britt and making her cry and fighting with her like Yanks and Rebels.

Once I pissed Britt off so much that she sprinted through the field of battle to tell on me to my father. Dodging soldiers in the middle of an intense Confederate charge she clung to my father, whimpering and sniffling and droning on and on about what a meanie I was.

"Daddy!" Britt whined. "Cyndie told me I'll never get boobs!"

"Have you no decency!" my father shouted back, not to Britt but to the attacking Union infantryman, expertly blocking the fake bayonet thrust with his officer's broad sword.

"Have you lost any shred of compassion!" he screamed again, his eyes shooting sparks, his voice booming even louder than the artillery fire from the opposite ridge.

"Have you no humanity? There are civilians on the field! For the love of God, man! Civilians!"

The Union soldier, lying on the ground with my father's officer boot planted firmly on his chest, burst out laughing.

I thought it pretty funny myself, but evidently my father and Britt did not.

•

And then, just like that, everything changed.

Everything.

It was the third weekend in September. A bright beautiful West Virginia beginning-of-fall day. There I was stuck at a Civil War reenactment at the Trans-Allegheny Haunted Lunatic Asylum. Yup. You heard that right. A Civil War reenactment at a historic 1900s lunatic asylum that is supposedly haunted. I am seriously not making this crap up.

It's a major living-history event, the highlight of West Virginians' Civil War reenactment year, the day reenactors have circled in red on their Civil War calendar and salivated over for months. There are tents and bayonet drills and storytelling and cooking demonstrations and a fashion show and old-time music and a mock battle and all kinds of crap like that.

Like I said, these people are obsessed.

Whenever I'm dragged, kicking and screaming, to these moronic events I either waste my time picking on Britt or I hide away where no one can see me obsessively texting Ashley and reading trash magazines and eating fattening crap food and pretending that I have nothing to do with the modern-day lunatics and their clinically insane antics.

But, for some crazy, unfathomable reason, for that one event, on that one day, I had succumbed to intense pressure and let myself be persuaded by Auntie Sadie to actually partake in the madness.

I was cursed with a family of reenactors, Auntie Sadie having fallen under their evil cult spell as well. Not as a soldier, though she could have kicked ass at that one. The Union lines wouldn't stand a chance with Auntie Sadie marching toward them. At the mere sight of her hulk they'd have broken ranks, reenactment or no reenactment, and bolted screaming for the hills.

Auntie Sadie played the part of a Civil War nurse in a frontline operating room. She had gone so far as to take a ten-week class on Civil War medicine.

The lengths people went for this crap!

One of the other reenactment nurses in Sadie's posse was getting married that weekend. Sadie said she had no one else but me to staff her stupid Civil War operating room.

"You've got to be kidding!" I laughed when Sadie asked if I'd sub in.

"Please!" Sadie begged. "I'm desperate!"

"You want me to wear a Civil War hoop skirt?"

"Liza has a perfect one you can borrow. She's just your size. You'll look beautiful!"

"Yeah, right!" I scoffed. "I'll look like one of the lunatics from the asylum. And I'm supposed to do what?"

"Play the part of a nurse in camp. You'll have fun!" Sadie said.

"Fun?" I grumbled. "Fun? How about torture! Just the thought of this makes me want to stab myself in the boobs with a bayonet. Oh my God, Sadie, what if someone saw me?"

Auntie Sadie, teary-eyed, got all pouty and laid down the guilt trip, droning on and on about "all the things I do for you" and "since your mother died" and "I ask this one tiny little favor, but no. . . ."

Eventually I caved. I had no choice. I begged and pleaded for Ashley to go with me, but she refused.

"You know I'd take a bullet for you," she said. "A real bullet. Not some lame Civil War reenactment thingy. I'd lay down my life for you. I'd do anything. You know I would. Just not this!"

"Thanks a bunch, Ash."

So I went. Not willingly, but I went.

The hoop skirt she made me wear was far from sweet. It took a series of gymnastic moves to get into and it looked totally absurd. It consisted of an actual bunch of different-sized hoops fastened together with the skirt on top. The hoops were smaller at the hips and got progressively bigger and bigger as they descended down to the ground like an upside-down ice cream cone. Evidently it was all the rage back in the day. I couldn't fathom why. I felt like a manikin in a cage.

And it wasn't even historically accurate. Auntie Sadie was fond of telling the tourists a gruesome story about why Civil War nurses didn't wear hoop skirts like most of the other fashionable women. Hospital aisles were evidently so narrow that women wearing those skirts couldn't walk without catching their hoops on all sorts of things. One nurse who didn't get the hoop skirt memo caught hers on the bed of one poor, wounded soldier. The sudden jolt ripped open his wound and he bled to death. Imagine that! You survive four years of the bloody hell of the Civil War only to die from some nurse's hoop skirt! Bummer.

Anyway, the grounds of the haunted lunatic asylum were packed. There were thousands of folks crawling all over the place. Tourists from across the country were taking selfies next to their snotty, whiny kids. I spent most of the time sitting in a big tent that was supposed to be a battlefield operating room, bored out of my skull, scratching and fanning myself because my hoop skirt was so damn hot and uncomfortable. Endlessly answering questions about Civil War surgical procedures, which I knew absolutely nothing about. Sadie had given me a tutorial but, frankly, I couldn't give a damn. Whenever Sadie wasn't around I'd just make crap up.

"Jahoobie," I replied, answering a tourist's question about anesthesia, using the lame slang word that Ashley and I used to call our boobs. I emphasized my point by emphatically waving around a fake wooden leg that would be strapped to an amputee's knee.

"They'd give them Jahoobie and WHACK, off they'd go amputating an arm or a leg or whatever they felt like without even a whimper from the dude on the table. Not a whimper! WHACK!"

"Jahoobie?" the tourist asked again, his eyebrows arching up.

"Google it!" I answered, brandishing the wooden leg menacingly, knowing I'd never see him again. "WHACK!"

The Saturday afternoon of the big event there was a mock battle in "Asylum Field" behind the historic buildings. My father was in a wicked foul mood. Stonewall Jackson, the general in charge, had demoted him from a brigadier general to a lowly cadet, one step below a private, and put someone else in command of his division. This was the result of an unfortunate episode a month and a half earlier when my father, caught up in the heat of the battle and the thrill of the charge, had screwed everything up royally during another reenactment.

At the "Battle of the Pines," tourists had paid five bucks each to watch a mock battle. It was staged to sway this way and that with heavy losses on each side. It was to last about an hour, which was just about the attention span of most tourists. They wanted their money's worth, but nothing more.

At the time, my father was the commanding officer of the 4th Division, 6th Regiment of the Army of Northern Virginia. His detachment was supposed to creep around the edge of the woods, get ambushed by a Union regiment, and retreat into the orchard. Then the battle was to continue with a Union charge.

Yeah, right. As if that was really going to happen.

Stonewall Jackson obviously did not know my father.

Lapsing into one of his time-warp-seizure-thingies, there was no way Dad was going to fall for this ambush crap. Fifteen minutes before the battle was even supposed to begin, my father came charging with his troops out of the forest.

"Yee-haw!" he screamed, forgetting his officer status and unleashing the infamous rebel yell.

The Union troops were totally unprepared. They were sitting around chatting it up and hadn't even picked up their guns. They were stunned when my father's regiment came bursting through, taking no prisoners, shooting them down as they sat. Within five minutes the battle—or rather, the massacre—was over.

Stonewall Jackson was pissed. Really pissed.

"Damn it, General!" Jackson railed. "I told you to sit tight! You were supposed to be the ambushee, not the ambush*er*!"

"Sir!" my father said saluting him. He was sopping wet with perspiration and still had a wild look in his eyes. "With all due respect, I saw an opening and I took it! I had a responsibility to my troops!"

"Sir!" barked Stonewall, saluting back. "Are you a total and complete moron? The battle was over in five minutes. Five minutes! The damn Yankees hadn't even loaded their rifles. None of the artillery even got off a shot! People have been waiting on lawn chairs for hours and most of them missed the entire thing because they were either at the concession stand getting a damn beer or waiting in line at the porta-potties to take a piss. We do not have a bunch of happy campers out there! They want their damn money back!"

Poor dad. Not a great day on the battlefield. He won the battle but kind of lost the war.

•

Anyway, back to the lunatic asylum.

Saturday afternoon was beautiful. The sky was a deep Union blue with a couple of sweet Confederate gray clouds marching in and out like puffs of cannon smoke. Behind the fields, the lunatic asylum's turrets and cupolas and spires and towers stared down approvingly. I could just imagine the ghosts of crazed inmates peering through the ancient windows, cheering on the Blue or the Gray or whoever. I imagined those ghosts didn't really give a crap who won, as long as there was plenty of action with a healthy dose of total insanity thrown in. I imagined they were sitting around chuckling to themselves: "And they locked *me* up for being a lunatic? Seriously?"

With Auntie Sadie's blessing, I was allowed temporary reprieve from my post as lame nursing assistant to watch, along with a gazillion other tourists, the action on the battlefield. Not that I gave a crap, but if I had to spend another moment in the nurses' tent I was going to go as crazy as the lunatics. I borrowed a chair and sat up front with the rest of the crowd.

Reenacted battles are lightly choreographed. Generally speaking, the reenactors are given instructions by their commanding officers as to who is attacking whom when and from where and what the general flow of events is going to be. Regular soldiers are pretty much told to go with the flow.

And, of course, some of them have to make-believe die. Reenactment or not, it is, after all, war. The crowd demands it. And what is a battle without blood and guts and gore and the tragic death of young studs in the prime of their life?

There are three reasons soldiers die in a reenactment:

1. It is totally obvious. There are ten soldiers shooting right at you from point-blank range and, duh, your ass is dead. End of story.

2. You're told you'll fall at a certain place and at a certain time. Your commanding officer deals out cards to his troops and all the hearts have to stop beating at the first major volley at the ravine or at the line of trees or wherever. It's the luck of the draw. Wrong suit and sorry, Charlie—you're dead!

3. You're tired or you're hot or you tripped or the blisters from your boots are really bugging you or, if you're an old fart like most of the reenacting lunatics are, you're out of breath or sweating up a storm or your artificial hip or knee or name-another-part-of-your-body is acting up so why not just be dead? Why not just lie down in the comfort of the grass and look up at the beautiful blue and gray sky and thank your lucky stars that this is only a reenactment and not the horrible, bloody, insane shit-show that the American Civil War actually was.

On this particular Saturday afternoon, Confederate troops were to burst from the edge of the woods near the asylum road and charge the Union line occupying the hill.

It was really quite a sight. Britt and I were sitting to the side of the action, where we could see and hear the Rebel troops getting pumped and psyched, waving their Rebel flags and taunting the Union troops and jumping up and down in anticipation of the imminent charge.

They even had the cutest little marching band playing and the boys in gray, totally stoked, sang along with great gusto.

Our gallant boys have marched
To the rolling of the drums,
Shout, shout the battle cry of Freedom!
And the leaders in charge cry out,
"Come, boys, come!"
Shout, shout the battle cry of Freedom!

The obvious question to ask the Confederate soldiers was "Freedom for whom?" My father wasn't exactly marching on the side of the politically correct.

All I can say is, Thank God it was 2015!

Anyway, the big moment had finally arrived. The tourists were settled in their lawn chairs, fanning themselves and drinking soda and beer and snapping selfies and hooting and hollering like they were part of the action.

Their kids pointed fingers at each other or they waved around the toy guns they had bought in the tourist crap-trap tent, and they made "*POW POW POW*" sounds while running around in circles. I was still holding the wooden leg that I had been showing off to tourists, and one of the little snots actually asked to borrow it for a rifle.

"No effin way!" I said. "This is mine. Get your own damn gun!"

All the while I was thinking to myself, *I missed staying over at Ashley's and watching crap reality TV shows all day for this?*

The Confederate line moved out from the row of trees and took a deafening volley from the Union troops. A bunch of the older, fatter slackers fell immediately but the rest of the Army of Northern Virginia, shoulders back, heads held high, bravely marched on.

They have laid down their lives
On the bloody battle field,
Shout, shout the battle cry of Freedom!
Their motto is resistance—
"To tyrants we'll not yield!"
Shout, shout the battle cry of Freedom!

Suddenly Britt gave me a shove.

"Look!" she squealed.

"What?" I exclaimed, jumping back. I had been distracted by a total stud of a tourist sitting in the front row, some guy in his late teens chugging beers who looked straight out of a Hollywood action flick with his shirt off and his man on.

"It's Kevin!" Britt whispered.

"Who?"

"Kevin! Kevin Malloy from your school!"

Oh my God! She was right! There he was, sure as shooting, just a hundred yards in front of me, marching at the head of the line singing ridiculously loud and totally off key with his gun slung loosely over his shoulder and his longish hair spilling out of his Confederate cap. It was Kevin! Kevin the god. Kevin the Untouchable!

"What's he doing here?" I whispered back to Britt. Britt was only in the seventh grade but, as much as I couldn't stand her, she did know everything. She had the skinny on every kid in Greenfield from K to 12. She was like a walking encyclopedia of the local who's who. A few months earlier some high-schooler had actually Facebooked her to make sure some girl was single before he asked them out.

"You didn't know?" Britt said, rolling her eyes at me. "He joined Dad's regiment! He's Private Kevin."

There was another withering volley from the Union troops, and the Confederate line staggered and fell back.

Kevin Malloy, now Private Kevin, pivoted, spun in place, groaned loud enough for the world to hear, sank to his knees, groaned once more and fell to the ground.

So young!

So brave!

So hot!

So dead!

The rest of the Confederate line reformed, and marched on to the raucous cheering of the lawn chair warriors.

Kevin was one of a dozen dead soldiers a few hundred feet away from us. I could see them breathing but doing their best not to move, although one kept sneezing and another one's cell phone went off, much to the laughter of the crowd.

And then, all of a sudden, Private Kevin gave a rebel yell, leapt up, and began dancing in place.

"Yee-haw!" Kevin screamed.

"No fair!" Studly Man yelled, waving his bottle of Bud. "You're dead!"

Kevin didn't care. He was dancing. Crazy dancing. It was like an old-time fiddle tune was playing in his head. His feet were clogging every which way and his arms were slapping and flailing.

"You're dead, dude!" Studly the heckler yelled out again. "You're done!"

Then Kevin started running toward the crowd of tourists. Sprinting and yelling, still flailing and slapping. With a shock, the crowd realized the reason. He was surrounded by a swarm of yellow jackets and they were stinging the crap out of him. Private Kevin had fallen on a nest of stingers. Enough to raise him from the dead!

"Yee-haw!" Kevin yelled again, his hat off, his eyes wild, his face contorted in pain.

The audience scattered. People were screaming. Lawn chairs and coolers tipped over, beer spilled, and children were dragged away as Kevin came rip-roaring through the crowd.

Britt had split but, not the quickest in the reflex department, I remained frozen in place, glued to my chair, totally mesmerized. Kevin plowed into me, knocking me over and falling right on top of me.

Still grasping the wooden leg, I started whacking Kevin with it. I was doing my best to go after the yellow jackets, but my aim wasn't the best and I delivered a crushing blow or two to Kevin's eye and jaw.

WHACK WHACK WHACK! went the peg leg.

BOOM! crashed the artillery firing from Lunatic Asylum Ridge.

"*Yee-haw*," Kevin cried, writhing on top of me.

It was, as they say, a rather awkward moment.

•

Smoke from the battlefield was still thick in the air, but Kevin was being brought back from the dead in Sadie's tent. He really did look like he had been through the wars.

His uniform was ripped, the back of his neck was one mass of swollen bites, and he had a black eye and a split lip from being beaten with the wooden leg.

"Sorry about that," I apologized for the fiftieth time. Auntie Sadie was putting some sort of salve on his bug bites.

"Apologize?" Kevin said. "No way. You saved my life!"

I blushed.

"Seriously," he continued. "I thought I was dying for real. Those things are nasty! Did you get stung?"

"Are you kidding?" I answered. "It would take more than a yellow jacket to get into this skirt!"

Kevin squinted at me through swollen eyes.

"Wait a minute," he asked. "Don't you go to my school?"

"I do," I answered, flattered that he recognized me.

"You're like . . . what . . . in ninth grade or something?"

"Tenth," I said. "And you're like . . . what . . . a senior?" As if I didn't know. He was Kevin Malloy—Marc the Mascot's best friend, for crying out loud. Everyone knew which grade he was in.

"Only if I survive this!" Kevin moaned as Sadie squirted salve on his neck.

"Cyndie," Sadie said, handing me the tube of aloe cream she had been using. "Take over for me while I go get more ointment."

Relieved that I could stand behind Kevin so he wouldn't see even more blushing, I continued to put the cream on his neck. Even covered with stings and with his face tattered and torn, he was, as Auntie Sadie would say, definitely a looker. Blondish brown hair, a little too long, curled down over his ears. Tall, built, but not weird-body-builder-freak-show way, sparkly eyes. And fortunately, even after repeated blows with the wooden leg, all of his teeth were still there.

I did my best to manage my breath so as not to gasp or sigh or faint or do something else to further humiliate myself. There was a strong wind blowing and it threatened to lift my hoop skirt up and carry it away with me still in it. I was having a hard time keeping my feet on the ground.

Other than that one awkward incident in gym class, I had never been this close to a guy. I was literally breathing down his neck.

"It looks like there's another bite underneath your shoulder," I lied, hoping beyond hope he might actually take off his shirt.

Of course, wouldn't you know it, just then Britt shows up.

"Hi Kevin," she says, not batting an eye.

"Hey, Britt," Kevin said. "You're here, too?"

For goodness sake, Kevin knew my little sister?

"After how Cyndie messed you up, you're still letting her touch you? Ewww!" Britt said, a shocked look on her ridiculous face.

I reached for the wooden leg and took a swing at her.

"Sorry!" Britt huffed. "I was just saying!"

"Don't!" I replied, shooting her my best evil eye. "Out. Now. Go find Sadie!"

Britt stuck her tongue out at me and scooted out the tent flap.

"PITA!" I said, rolling my eyes and continuing to swab Kevin's neck while peering down his shirt.

"Huh?"

"My little sister. Pain In The Ass."

Kevin laughed. I kept swabbing.

"Mmmm . . . ," he purred. "That feels good. A little to the right."

Believe me, I was more than happy to oblige.

All too quickly, Sadie and Britt (curse them!) came bustling back in and Auntie took over as nurse. It wasn't too long before Kevin was well enough to rejoin the living and reconnect with his regiment.

"Well," he said, grinning through his swollen mouth. "Gotta run. It's been real. And seriously, thanks again. Cute skirt by the way! You look hot!"

For the millionth time I blushed.

"See you at school?" he asked.

"I'll be the one with the peg leg," I replied.

Ahhh! Why do I say the things I do? Why couldn't I come out with "In your dreams" or "If you're lucky" or something classic like that. "I'll be the one with the peg leg?" Really?

But he had talked to me. Kevin Malloy had actually talked to me!

7

THERE WAS AN OLD COAL MINE halfway up to the top of Mount Tom, about a hundred yards off the trail we had made. You could only get there by crawling on your hands and knees through a dark green and mysterious tunnel of rhododendrons, which made for a perfect hidden entrance. Ashley and I had discovered it when I threw her shoe into the tangled mass after she had told me for the hundredth time how much bigger her boobs were than mine.

The mine was exactly one of those sketchy places that parents continually warned us kids to stay away from. Scary stories at sleepovers or Halloween nights always had the witch or the vampire or the zombie or the death-eater or whoever was the latest and greatest evil-doer sneak out of an abandoned coal mine just like the one we had discovered. It was there that they dragged pathetic, kicking-and-screaming little girls and boys and roasted them alive and sucked out their brains and picked their bones clean with their nasty, crooked teeth.

True story:

In third grade this kid named Gabby Glonski had been fooling around in an old abandoned mine down near the Green River, and the wooden support structures suddenly collapsed and trapped her inside. Totally trapped! Can you imagine? No food, no water, completely dark—a kid's worst nightmare!

Fortunately, her little brother was playing nearby and saw the whole thing go down. He skedaddled out of there and got help, and it took half the town six hours to dig her out, but they did it. To this very day Gabby still can't go into a dark room, and she sleeps with a light on and stays away from any tight places like elevators and closets and even basements.

But Ashley and I loved our mine. It had that sweet mixture of taboo and danger and secrecy. It wasn't very big, with a horizontal shaft that extended only about fifteen feet, with rotting timbers that propped up the ancient roof, and with roots of the trees above sending tangled shoots down into the dark. We figured it was one of those classic family mines that some old-timer, maybe even ol' Tom himself, had dug out ages ago, using the coal to heat his house and cook his food. A thick black seam of coal still glistened from the walls.

We made up endless stories about Tom creeping in here with his pigs and making moonshine in his mine. Maybe he had had a nip or two too many and that was why he plummeted off the cliff and broke his neck. Or maybe his pigs had gotten into the sweet stuff and pushed him over. Maybe the mine was even haunted!

Ashley and I had scavenged a couple of raggedy old cushions and a cloudy mirror from the town dump and had schlepped them all the way up there to decorate our "living room." We'd light candles in the corners of the mine and we'd talk and talk and talk. It was there that we had made our pact to be best friends forever, Lord willing and the Green River don't rise, and pricked our fingers to seal the promise with our very own blood on the wall of coal. It was there where we swore to keep our mine secret from everybody. It would be our mine, just ours, forever and ever. And it was there where we kept our "ridiculous jar," a beat-up old cookie tin stuffed with scraps of paper documenting every lame thing we had done that year. Every year on New Year's Eve, we opened the jar and read all our antics out loud and laughed our fool heads off.

I had just put in a new ridiculousness summarizing the peg leg escapade.

"You sure he said 'hot'?" Ashley asked for the five zillionth time. "Rather than 'cute skirt, by the way. NOT!'"

"Ashley. For the love of Tom, this is the most important thing anyone has ever said to me in my entire life. You better believe I'd remember it. Word for word!"

Ashley and I had been pouring over the Incident at the Haunted Lunatic Asylum for over two hours. Candlelight flickered on the coal walls, illuminating the blood on my cuticles that I had bitten to bleeding trying to decipher the true meaning behind what Kevin had said to me.

"I mean, you were hot, right? It was, like, 5,000 degrees that day. And that hoop thingy would have kept you warm even at 20 below. You sure that's not what he meant?"

"Ashley!" I exclaimed.

"Sorry. It's just that nothing like this has ever happened to us before. We're in uncharted territory here!"

It gave me great comfort to hear Ashley use the words *us* and *we*. If I had to figure this out alone I'd be totally effed.

"I don't know," I sighed. "He was probably just playing with me."

"Maybe not. You had just saved his life, for crying out loud. Even if it did mean permanent facial disfigurement and probable brain damage!"

"Thanks, Ash."

"Any time. So . . . he was really lying on top of you?"

"Right on top. It seems as though the only way I'm ever going to get anything is either by falling on a guy or having him fall on me. First Sean McKenzie in gym and now Kevin Malloy on the battlefield."

"Well, look on the bright side. You're lucky. You had an actual guy on top of you. I've never gotten anything."

I laughed.

"But, you know, he's right," Ashley said.

"What do you mean?"

"You really are hot!"

"Humph!"

"Girl, don't *humph* me! You are! You really are. If I was a guy I would totally date you!"

I snuggled up closer to her, feeling her warmth in the coolness of the mine, and put my arms around her.

"I'd date you, too!"

"Too bad we aren't lesbians," Ashley sighed.

"It would be so much easier," I sighed back.

8

STILL SITTING IN OUR SECRET MINE, and with the Mystery of the Lunatic Asylum still unresolved, we were about to call it a day and head for home when I heard something.

I caught my breath and grabbed Ashley's hand as I strained my ears.

Voices!

There were voices in the distance. Voices getting closer.

"Did you hear that?" Ashley whispered.

"Shhh!" I whispered back.

Voices! Men talking. Two, then three of them. They were coming up the mountain, getting nearer and nearer, their voices growing louder. They stopped uncomfortably close to the hidden entrance to our mine.

Ashley was squeezing me so hard I could barely breathe. I had to pinch her arms to get her to release her stranglehold. The pounding of both our hearts drowned out the conversation the men were having.

Who would possibly be tramping around up here? On our mountain? Outside our mine? We had never before seen hide nor hair of anyone up here, not a single soul.

I was frightened. The only thing I could think of was that these were crystal meth cooks looking for a place to do their dirty work and set up a methamphetamine lab. It scared the crap out me. That stuff was bad news. Guys like that, if they knew you knew what they were up to, could do serious damage.

Ashley and I were frozen in place at the far end of the mine, trying to mask the fear in our breath. You know how when you're trying to be quiet, really quiet, all sorts of things happen that make your body want to scream out? Suddenly

I had to cough, I had to sneeze, I had to pee so bad I thought I would wet myself. But I just clung to Ashley and closed my eyes and hoped to hell that neither of us would have a heart attack.

The voices continued up the mountain and out of earshot.

"Shit!" Ashley whispered.

"Double shit!" I whispered back.

"Who do you think they are?" Ashley whispered.

"Meth cooks! Who else could they be? If they find us we're dead!"

"Raped and then dead!"

"Beaten, raped, and then dead!"

"Enough!" Ashley said in a low voice, pinching me. "What do we do? They went up the mountain. What goes up must come down."

"Shit!" I whispered.

"Double shit!" Ashley whispered back.

West Virginia was the crystal-meth-lab capital of the universe. Guys went into the woods and set up methamphetamine labs and cooked up this whacked-out illegal drug that screwed you up big time. People used it to stay awake, to amp up their energy, to increase their alertness. Guys at school would brag that they were "Breaking Bad" and could stay hard for days on meth.

The only thing I saw were guys hard *up*—twitchy, depressed, psychotic, toothless with meth mouth, and crazy as hell. They were like the witches/vampires/zombies/death-eaters all rolled into one.

Not only was the drug illegal and awful, but it was also dangerous to make and the toxic waste from meth labs totally screwed up the environment.

Kingdom Number One was way too kind a category for a guy on crystal meth. The typical high school loser was a king compared to a meth head. They deserved a ranking all to themselves. A special place in boy hell. A total zero.

We waited a few more minutes and, hearing nothing, snuck out of our mine and made like the wind. We knew every tree, every boulder, every twist and turn on Tom. Once we got going there was no stopping us. It would take way more than a gang of meth heads to catch us.

At the bottom of the mountain, near where we had stashed our bikes and where the road took a turn toward the river, there was a truck parked. There was nobody in it.

Emblazoned on its side were the words "American Mining Company."

Ashley and I pedaled for home like the death-eaters themselves were on our tails.

9

WE TOSSED OUR BIKES ON THE LAWN and collapsed (me in the fetal position) on my living room couch. Dad was still at work. Britt was at her circus arts practice at the community center.

I was shaking. My legs were thumping so hard they were cramping up. I was hyperventilating and dizzy, on the verge of a Looney Tune (as Ashley referred to my periodic moments of insanity).

"Stop shaking!" Ashley demanded. "You're driving me crazy!"

"I can't. I can't stop!"

Ashley leaned over and pulled my hair, something she used to do a lot in kindergarten. Once she even got kicked out of school for it. Old habits die hard.

"Ouch! Ashley, stop!"

"Stop shaking and I'll stop pulling!"

"God, Ashley, who do you think those dudes were? Meth heads?"

"Meth heads don't flag trees to advertise where they're cooking!"

"What are you talking about?"

"Didn't you see? When we were running down the hill? The trees had red flags on them. Those guys were marking the trees."

The only thing I had seen when we running down the hill were the shadows of three crystal-meth-crazed, death-eating hillbillies hot on our trail. Everything else was a faded blur.

"And didn't you see the truck?" Ashley asked. "American Mining Company. Meth heads don't advertise. Not that way."

"Why would someone mark the trees on Mount Tom?" I asked.

"I don't know," Ashley replied, her voice deep and guttural, growling like a barrel full of bears. "But Tom will curse us if we don't find out!"

•

My mother died of breast cancer ten years ago, when I was five and my little sister Britt was two. I don't have many memories of Mom, but one that is ingrained in my brain is curling up in her lap and being read to for hours and hours.

My mother was a great reader. She'd do all the story characters' voices in a crazy, mixed-up, wonderful way. She'd get so animated that she'd put me and the book down and hop around the room, flailing her arms and flinging back her tangled mass of jet-black hair as she acted out some zany scene. Sort of like Mr. Cooper, only not.

Once, when I must have been around four, in the middle of a Curious George the Monkey story she leapt off the top of the couch and hit her head on a lamp, which came crashing down on top of her. The bulb splintered into a million tiny pieces, sparkling like the candlelit walls of coal in Tom's Mine.

"Do it again!" I giggled, clapping. "Do it again!"

I remember that like it was yesterday.

Here's another good memory:

One of my favorite picture books was *Custard the Dragon* by Ogden Nash. I can still see Mom, prancing about the room, singing,

Belinda was as brave as a barrel full of bears,
And Ink and Blink chased lions down the stairs,
Mustard was as brave as a tiger in a rage,
But Custard cried for a nice safe cage.

Ink was a kitten. Blink was a mouse. Mustard was a little yellow dog. And Belinda was the little girl in the story.

"You're just like Belinda!" my mother would tell me, wrapping me up in her arms and smothering me with kisses. "My brave little girl. My barrel full of bears!"

I think about that a lot.

Too bad what Mom said about me is totally untrue.

Ashley is Belinda, Ink, Blink, and Mustard all rolled into one.

I, on the other hand, am Custard. I don't have a brave bone in my body.

•

"Don't make me go back up there!" I whimpered, my legs still vibrating uncontrollably. I scanned the living room, desperately searching for that nice, safe cage.

"Wait a minute!" Ashley said. "That's our mountain, Cyndie. Nobody messes with our mountain!"

I tried to channel Belinda but all that came through was Custard.

10

ASHLEY AND I BEGAN with Auntie Sadie, because my father was worthless in these situations. The only current events he kept up with were the dates for Civil War reenactments. Once I asked him who the president of the United States was and he said Lincoln. Seriously. Abraham Lincoln, for goodness sake! And I think he actually meant it.

Ashley's parents were off-limits as well. She had vowed never to speak to them again after they grounded her for getting caught sneaking into the boys' locker room for a lookie at Marc the Mascot. The vice principal had called her parents and expressed concern about her "inappropriate behavior."

"You know, Ashley," I told her. "That was not your finest hour. Occasionally parents actually have a point. Now, if you had listened to me . . ."

"If I had listened to you I wouldn't have seen Marc the Mascot with his pants down. The way my life is going, that may be as far as I ever get with a guy."

"Yeah, but . . ."

"Butt is right. You should have seen *his*! I'm telling you, Cyndie, life is short. You gotta get what you can get when you can get it."

"Yeah, and that's working really well for you, isn't it?" I said. "The only thing I get is whacking a guy covered in yellow jackets with a wooden leg. The only thing you get is getting caught peeping in a skuzzy locker room. I don't really think that's what they mean by getting it!"

"Which is why we need to get to the bottom of who's trespassing on our mountain!"

Which made absolutely no sense at all, but, nonetheless, off we went to seek guidance from Auntie Sadie.

"That's none of your concern who's marking those trees, girls," Sadie said after we told her what had happened, leaving out certain details like our hideout in our secret mine. "You best just stay away and mind your own beeswax."

"It is too our concern!" I countered. "It's our mountain!"

"Darlings. Number one: it is not your mountain. Number two: you know perfectly well we got two things worth selling in our part of the world. Trees and coal."

"Three if you count crystal meth," Ashley replied.

Auntie's lazy eye stopped its wandering and stared right at her.

"Like it or not, girls, that's what we got. Trees and coal. Coal and trees. Think about it. What would Greenfield be like without them?"

"Ummm ... green?" Ashley answered.

Sadie threw the end of a carrot she was fixing for a salad and hit Ashley in the nose.

"Don't be smart with me, girls! How many of your friend's parents work for American Coal Company? Huh? How many? Who do you think pays for those nice little houses they live in? Who do you think puts all that good food on their table? And Cyndie, don't you forget for a minute that my husband and your granddaddy, God rest their souls, were both miners. We don't go biting off the hand that feeds us, girls. We just don't. You're both fifteen years old. You should know that by now!"

"But why would a mining company mark trees?" I asked.

"The only reason you mark a tree is to cut it down," Sadie said.

Ashley and I practically jumped out of our skins.

"My best guess is that the company knows there's coal up there. And if there's coal, you're damn sure the mining company's gonna get their dirty hands all over it. They're most likely marking trees to cut them down and build a road to a new mine. We all know that what the mining company wants, the mining company gets. That's the way of the world, girls. Always has and always will be. Deal with it!"

This was not exactly the answer we were looking for.

"Shit!" Ashley said as we stormed out of Sadie's house and sat on the stoop and sulked.

"Double shit!" I seconded.

"It's times like these that I could really use a cigarette."

"What are you talking about? You don't even smoke!"

"Yeah. But if I did, this is exactly the moment when I would."

There were times when Ashley imagined her life as a Hollywood movie. Her inner director would ask, "What would my star actress do in a similar situation?" and Ashley would go for it. It was what got her into trouble sometimes. Case in point: her doing the Peeping Tom thing in the boys' locker room.

Never a dull moment with Ashley. It was one of the things I loved about her.

And also one of the things that scared the crap out of me.

11

"I SWEAR," ASHLEY SAID ANGRILY, "if they so much as touch a twig on her branch there's going to be hell to pay!"

Keeping our eyes and ears open and looking over our shoulders every millionth of a second, we had gone back to Mount Tom the next day after school. Following the line of trees marked with bright red flags led us straight up to our sacred grove. We stopped dead in our tracks.

There She was, wrapped tightly, looking like a big ol' Christmas present. A red flag around her trunk and another one flapping in the breeze on her lowest branch.

She. Our beloved white ash. A marked tree.

Cutting down trees on someone else's mountain had never bothered me. I mean, I had never really thought about it before. It was like, "Yeah, whatever."

Auntie Sadie had been right. Coal and trees. Trees and coal. Logging in Greenfield was a way of life, just like mining.

But there were trees, and there were *trees*. These were not your ordinary, run-of-the-mill, cut-'em-&-truck-'em trees.

These were *our* trees.

Sugar Daddy.

Bradley Beech.

Sadie's Twin.

She.

Ashley was sitting with her arms around the massive furled trunk of the white ash, her cheek pressed against the ridged, diamond-like pattern of her bark. It was like she was hugging her mother, something I had never seen her do in real life.

I had no idea how to age a tree but I knew that white ash was old. Not just old but ancient. A true sage of the forest. You could feel it. Nothing could grow that enormous, that wrinkled, that ashy gray, and not have seen a lot of years go by. I imagined that She was here when Lincoln really was the president, when West Virginia seceded from its sister state and split off to join the Union.

Think of all of the stories She had to tell.

Ashley reached into the backpack she was wearing and brought out a pair of scissors.

She stood up and with one single motion cut the marker flag that was strangling the white ash.

The red flag fluttered to the ground.

"One down" she said, stashing the flag in her pack. "One down and lots more to go."

She stood up and held out the scissors.

"Ready?" she asked.

I froze. I looked into Ashley's eyes and I saw that Hollywood director look. A half-squint steely look that made me shudder. A look that was not to be messed with. A look that changed everything.

My mind raced with all sorts of conflicting thoughts cascading down my brain like the Green River does after a heavy rain.

What was the wise thing to do here?

If it's illegal, does that make it wrong?

Did I really want to co-star in Ashley's movie?

I was Custard, for crying out loud. Not Belinda. This was not my thing.

"Ready?" Ashley asked again.

There are times, even when they are happening, that you know are really important. Times that define you.

Once, when Ashley and I were in middle school, this girl JoJo Phippen had teased Ashley for a week about not having boobs.

"Flattie!" she taunted. "Boobless!"

Ashley was furious. We snuck over to the girl's house late one night with a carton full of eggs to throw at her window.

"This'll teach her," Ashley said. "She'll see whose boobless now!"

"Ready?" Ashley asked.

"No!" I said. "No, I am not."

Flat-chested or not, we snuck back home, leaving the windows unegged.

This time, on Mount Tom, I was still sitting on the ground. The wind had picked up and the ash leaves, so many of them, too many to count, were sashaying in the breeze. I looked at Ashley. She had one arm propped against the tree, and the other one holding out the scissors. I had never seen her so serious.

"Ready?" Ashley asked for the third time.

I stood up, took the scissors from Ashley, gave the bark of She a playful pinch, bowed to her three companions, and continued up the mountain.

12

In history class we learned that Rosa Parks wasn't some tired old woman who, on a whim one day in 1955, refused to give up her seat in the front of the Alabama bus to a white man and sparked the entire civil rights movement. That's the story the media came up with. The truth was that Rosa Parks had been active in civil rights for years. Her refusal to give up her seat was no random action. She knew what she was doing.

When Ashley and I cut down every flag on every tree from the road at the bottom of Tom right up to the tippity-top, we didn't have a clue. I thought that we had gone back to Tom just to check out the flags on the trees, and I didn't even know that Ashley had brought along a pair of scissors. She had thrown them into her back pack at the last moment, along with some gum, a few candles, and a brand-new bottle of sparkling "Made for Me Pink" nail polish.

Ours was not exactly a well-planned act of conscience. We were not exactly the Rosa Parks of Mount Tom.

We just went and did it.

If we had thought about it, if we had discussed the pros and cons, if we had listened to the advice from Sadie or my father or whomever, those flags would not have come down.

And everything, everything would be different.

But there we were, sitting in Tom's Mine, with the candlelight playing on the walls of coal, painting our toenails and counting the flags from Ashley's backpack.

"Seventy-two," Ashley said. "Not bad for an afternoon's work."

We had cut down one hundred and seventy-two flags on one hundred and seventy-one trees. She was the only one who had the distinction of a twofer. It had been a breezy day but I swear to wild, wonderful West Virginia that every time we cut down one of those flags, each and every tree shook and swayed and bowed to us.

Even after talking to Sadie, we still didn't know exactly who had flagged those trees, or why they were flagged. We assumed it was American Coal Company but we didn't know for sure. We just knew that they had to come down.

It was as simple as that.

"You know," I said, holding Ashley's big toe still while I polished the edges, "I almost wish those guys *had* been meth heads. Meth heads don't go around cutting down trees."

"Yeah. They just go around robbing and shooting people."

We both sighed, ears open to any sounds from the outside.

"What now?" I asked.

"You still have my left little toe to do. And you missed a spot on the middle one."

"No," I said. "I mean what now about this?" I held up the bundle of red flags.

"I don't know," Ashley said. "Something tells me we haven't seen the last of those guys."

I took a deep breath and blew on Ashley's toes. The smell of the polish and the flickering of the light on the pile of flags made my eyes water. That and knowing that that nice safe cage to crawl into didn't exist. It never had existed and it never would.

"Do you think we did the right thing?" I asked.

"Do you think we had a choice?" Ashley answered.

I took off my shoes and socks, handed Ashley the bottle of nail polish, and put my toes in her lap.

13

"THERE HE IS!" Ashley said, poking me. We were in between classes and Kevin Malloy was walking down the hall straight toward us.

"Say something!" Ashley whispered.

"Shhh!" I whispered back.

He was getting closer.

We had been doing the stalk and gawk all week in school, and Ashley and I had Kevin's schedule down pat. We knew which hallway he'd walk down when. Ashley had convinced me that the time had arrived to get serious.

I had practiced clever pickup lines all morning.

"Where's your yellow jacket?" I could ask him.

Or: "Back off. I've got more wooden legs where that one came from."

Or: "Hey there, Private. Still got the zingers from the stingers?"

And now, here he was, directly in front of me. In the flesh. Ashley gave me one more pinch.

"Hey!" Kevin said. "It's the girl who almost killed me! Or was it saved my life? I can't remember!"

"S'up," I managed to say.

"You doing battle this weekend?" Kevin asked, referring to yet another upcoming reenactment.

I tried to speak but my mouth was ice and the words froze. I could only nod.

"Leave the leg at home," Kevin said. "One concussion is enough!"

I smiled. At least I think I smiled. It may have been more of an awkward grimace. It's hard to smile with a frozen face.

"Later," Kevin said.

"S'up," I said.

"Well," Ashley said, trying to be supportive. "That went well."

"Stop, Ashley. That was a total disaster and you know it. 'S'up'? That's all I could say. 'S'up'? He probably thinks I'm a special-needs student."

Ashley put her arm around me. "Chill, Cyndie. It went great! He, like, asked you out!"

"He did not ask me out!"

"Sure he did! He asked if you were going to the Civil War thingy!"

"That was not an ask! And 's'up' was definitely not an answer!"

"Well, look on the bright side," she said. "At least you didn't beat the crap out of him!"

"S'up," I said. "I mean, stop. I mean, whatever!"

14

"Coop—I mean, Mr. Cooper?"

Ashley and I had stayed after school to help him clean up after a particularly messy water-quality lab.

"To what do I owe the distinguished honor and profound pleasure of the presence of my two star students on this beautiful Tuesday afternoon?" Mr. Cooper asked. "Clearly, cleaning up this hazardous-waste dump, this Superfund site, this orgy of scientific chaos is not, I imagine, high on your list of pleasurable activities. And I don't quite recall giving you a detention."

Mr. Cooper had never given detention to anyone. Ever. It was not in his repertoire.

And what he said about us being his star students was not exactly the truth.

I was doing well in his class. Really well. I enjoyed science, just like I enjoyed math. And, also like math, there was something comforting in the way the natural world worked. Comforting and beautiful. There were patterns and relationships, form and function that all made sense to me. Everything was connected to everything else and it all fit together like the squares on the old quilts my mother had inherited from her parents and her grandparents.

Unlike the rest of the world. If you looked at what went on in the rest of the world, it sucked. Totally sucked. If you paid attention to the news, the rest of the world seemed to be spiraling out of control, without direction or meaning.

I had never been one to pay attention to life outside Greenfield. I didn't watch TV news. I didn't read the paper. I didn't even glance at the headlines as I scrolled down Yahoo. I went online for the latest in celebrity gossip, music videos, and fashion advice, but that was about it. The rest of the world seemed distant and irrelevant, nothing that had anything to do with me. So why bother?

But this last week Britt had become obsessed with the story of terrorists beheading an American hostage in the Middle East. She was making me watch the evening TV news with her night after night. It was tortuous. Terrifying. Drone strikes in Pakistan. Genocide in Syria. Starvation and poverty and climate change and endless war. And now, icing on the cake, terrorists go and behead this do-gooder aid worker. I mean, the dude goes all the way across the world to try to do the right thing and he gets his head lopped off. Down comes the sword. *BAM!* Off with his head. The entire thing was recorded on video for the whole world to watch.

We were learning about metaphors in English, and the hostage-beheading thing seemed to me a perfect one for the screwy state of the world. I wrote about it in English class for an assignment, leaving out the obvious connection to

Mount Tom, and Diaper Lady had actually seemed to like it. She had written "Well done. Interesting," on the top. Who would have thought?

Anyway, while I did well in class, Ashley . . . well . . . let's just say Ashley struggled. While she could be thick sometimes, she sure wasn't stupid. Far from it. She was absolutely the most brilliant person I knew. Let's put it this way. She just didn't see school as a high priority.

As feisty as she was, she seemed dangerously close to plummeting into the West Virginia sexist stereotype. The one that demoted us girls to second-class citizens, good for going up the stripper's pole and down on guys, but not much else.

You didn't need school for those things.

Ashley rarely handed in work. She never cracked a book. She just didn't seem to think that school mattered. If it weren't for me forcing her to occasionally study for an exam she'd still be languishing in the seventh grade.

Even if I had to become a coal miner, her sorry ass was going to pass, damn it. There was no effin way I was going to move up a grade without her.

"I don't see the point!" Ashley would say, exasperated when I told her she had to memorize the chemical equation for photosynthesis.

"I mean, seriously, who really gives a crap? I'm not saying photosynthesis isn't awesome. It's *totally* awesome! If She does it then it must be way cool. But really, why bother regurgitating back the CO_2 and the H_2O and whatever comes next in the correct order? Isn't it enough just to know that plants and trees do it? I mean, doesn't it take away from the great mystery of life if you understand too many of the details? I don't want to lose sight of the trees for the forest!"

"Think of all the advances civilization would have made with logic like that," I said to Ashley, although, after watching the news for a week, *advances* and *civilization* did not exactly seem like words that fit together. It reminded me of the quote that we learned in history class from the great leader of Indian independence, Mahatma Gandhi. When asked what he thought of Western civilization, Gandhi replied, "I think it would be a good idea."

Anyway, you get the point. Mr. Cooper calling us his "two star students" was not exactly the God's truth.

Of course, if you asked Ashley who Jay-Z was dating or what color Taylor Swift's favorite panties were, her mouth would be stuck in overdrive for hours.

School smart or not, I did love my Ashley.

•

"We were wondering what you know about Mount Tom?" Ashley asked Mr. Cooper.

Mr. Cooper knew everything about the natural world. From A to Z, aardvarks to zooplankton, Mr. Cooper knew it all.

And he knew everything about Greenfield as well. He was born and bred here.

"Inbred," he liked to say. "It's what gives me my outstanding good looks and my peculiar sense of humor."

He was not only our go-to science guy but the town historian as well. Unlike Mr. O'Shansky, our tenth-grade history teacher, who I seriously doubt even knew that West Virginia was actually a state.

"Mount Tom." Mr. Cooper sat down on the top of his disaster of a desk and immediately knocked a random beaker onto the floor. He kicked the broken glass to the side with his shoe.

"Nice example of an igneous intrusion," he said. He reached into his pocket and pulled out one his disposable flossers and began flossing his teeth, that bizarre habit we had grown fondly accustomed to.

Mr. Cooper always looked like crap except for his teeth, which were impeccable.

"What about the forest there?" I asked.

"Oaks, oaks, and more oaks, as I recall," he said.

"With a few beeches, maples, cherries, and ashes thrown in," Ashley added.

Mr. Cooper stopped in mid-floss, his eyebrows arched, and he stared at Ashley.

"Very good, young lady. Very good."

"So why would they flag the trees there?" I asked.

"Why would who flag the trees?"

"The mining company. American Mines."

Mr. Cooper's eyebrows arched again.

"What the hell!" he said, flossing furiously. "American Mining Company? Marking trees on Mount Tom?"

"Yup," we said in unison.

"Bastards! Sons of bitches! I didn't expect this for another year or two."

"Expect what for another year?" Ashley asked.

Mr. Cooper scowled and extended the flosser into the depths of his cavernous mouth. We waited while he diligently worked on the bottom left row of teeth.

"Two years ago Ian McGreggor sold Mount Tom to American. He didn't want to do it, but that man was deeper in debt than a one-legged miner. Mount Tom had been in his family since before Christ. He once told me that Tom was his great-great-granddaddy, though if you gave Ian McGreggor a drink or two he was liable to tell you just about anything. With that man it was hard to separate the beef from the bullshit."

That was one thing we loved about Mr. Cooper. His inability to self-edit. Words would flow from behind his flosser that had no business in a high school classroom.

Once, on Mr. Cooper's birthday, the principal had presented him with a roll of duct tape.

"What's this for?" Mr. Cooper asked.

"To seal your lips," the principal answered. "It will keep you employed and me off the phone with irate parents."

"Shall I leave the flosser in or out?" Coop asked.

Everyone laughed.

"So what is American planning on doing with the mountain?" I asked. Ashley and I were holding our breaths.

"Blow the top off of it!" Coop said, practically spitting with rage.

"Seriously," Ashley said. "What are they going to do?"

Mr. Cooper took his flosser out of his mouth and crossed his heart with it.

"I kid you not," he said. "Believe me, I wish I was."

"Blow its top off?" I asked, incredulous.

"Mountaintop removal!" Mr. Cooper scowled, once again flossing furiously. "Clear cut every oak, beech, ash, maple, and cherry. And then blow the top of that mountain to kingdom come! Coal is king and that mountain is a palace of it. And the cheapest way in is to blast through the gates!"

15

BACK IN THE DAY there was only one way to mine coal. Dig a hole in the ground, prop the mine open with wooden beams and support structures, and get the coal out. By hand. By mule. By train. By truck. Whatever it took.

It was dirty. It was dangerous. Sadie's husband, my Uncle Nelson, died in the collapse of Mine Number 3. It took them two weeks to dig his body out.

My granddaddy Lewis died of black lung disease. He inhaled so much coal dust that his lungs turned from pink to black. Not a good thing if you're a lung.

Uncle Nelson died before I was born. But I remember Granddaddy Lewis, coughing and spitting and barely able to speak a sentence he was so short of breath. He died when I was ten.

Factors of five are evil. My mother ten years ago, my granddaddy five years ago, and now, Mount Tom.

Coal mining has always been dangerous and unhealthy but at least the mountain was left above the mine and there were jobs. After all, duh, it takes coal miners to mine coal. A mountain of 'em. The Greenfield American Three Mine had been producing for decades. It reopened after the collapse, and now close to half the town was employed working the mine. As I said before, take the mine away from a mining town and there isn't a lot left.

"Bastards!" Mr. Cooper roared. "They'll stop at nothing to get what they want! They want to blow the mother up!"

Coop had worked himself into such a furious frenzy that the flosser had flew to the floor and joined the broken beaker in the corner of the room. Spittle was frothing from Coop's mouth like one of those rabid dogs on Animal Planet, wild and crazed and needing to be put down before they did some serious damage.

"Sons of bitches!" he hissed.

We had never seen Mr. Cooper like this before. Pissed? Yes. Annoyed? Most definitely!

But never anything like this.

•

Mountaintop removal.

It was all the rage here in West Virginia. And, come to find out, had been for years.

Who knew? Obviously, not Ashley and me.

Picture this:

A beautiful mountain, blanketed in green. A West Virginian quilt of trees, trees, and more trees. The who's who of the forest hopping and scurrying and flying and buzzing and bounding from tree to awesome tree.

Nature. Awesome nature. A feast for the eyes. A sanctuary for the soul. A temple to the gods.

Always had been and always would be.

Until now.

Until this.

Mountaintop removal. Blow the top off of the mountain.

I know. I know. It sounds like some really lame action flick where a bunch of terrorist dudes cross the border and sneak into the country and start blowing shit up before Will Smith or Dwayne Johnson or Vin Diesel come and beat the crap out of them.

But that's what the coal companies do. They cut down all the trees on the top of a mountain, lay down tons of dynamite, and then—*KABOOM*! Hundreds of vertical feet on the summit of a mountain are blown sky high.

Gone. Just like that. Goodbye, paradise. The top of the mountain blasted apart. And all the rock and debris dumped to the side, burying streams and valleys.

It's like taking that forested quilt, that fabric of life, and tearing the middle right out of it. Rip out the heart. Rip out the soul.

To the company it makes perfect sense. Why hire a bunch of locals to dig, dig, and then dig some more when you can just cut to the quick and blow the whole thing up? It's much easier that way. Take the miner out of mining. More bucks for the bang.

Of course, like Comedy Central said, keep it up and they'll just have to call us 'billies, because there won't be any more hills left to put us on.

This had been going on for years throughout Appalachia. Years. Mount Tom wasn't going to be the first to lose his head. Coal was king and the emperor had a fierce appetite for beheadings.

How could I not have known this?

Sadie had told us that you don't bite the hand that feeds you.

But what about the hand that holds the sword that chops off the head?

•

You know the ads you see on TV where there's this happy little family sitting on the couch, reading or playing games or just plain snuggling together? I know it's just an ad. I know it's setting the mood to get us all gooey and mushy inside so we'll rush off and buy some worthless piece of crap that we don't need and we don't even want and we clearly can't afford.

But those ads work for me. I like them.

I remember sitting on the couch just like that happy little family. Sitting on the couch with my mom and my dad and little Britt thinking that nothing bad could ever happen to us. Nothing. That grown-ups would take care of everything and the world was a safe and wonderful place where only princesses and unicorns and cute little puppies played, happy as a catfish in Green River muck, not a care in the world.

And then my mom died. I was five. I didn't have a clue as to what death was and I remember, night after night, waiting for her to come back home from wherever she was and tuck me in and kiss my forehead and read me a story or sing me this lullaby by Deanna Coleman:

Well I love my baby
sweet and fair
you've got the sky in your eye
the sun in your hair
I rock you to sleep most every night
and sing you this song
while I hold you tight.

There are nights where I still lie awake, waiting for my mom. Waiting for my bedroom door to open. Waiting for the hallway light to illuminate the shadows of her jet-black hair and her face and her smile. Waiting for her to kneel by my bed and pull the covers up tight under my chin and kiss me lightly on my forehead.

The night after Mr. Cooper told us what they were planning to do to Mount Tom was one of those nights.

I lay awake and waited. All night long. And Mom never came.

I'd have to say that up until that very moment I'd really thought that grown-ups had it more or less figured out. That they had it together. That I was safe in their hands.

Even growing up with a dead mom and a slightly crazed dad and a twit of a sister, I was happy. I didn't worry about the world. Call me silly. Call me naïve. Call me whatever you want, but that's how I felt.

What a difference a week makes.

Watching the news with Britt and being force-fed the terrifying images of the world as it was had been bad enough.

And now this.

They were going to cut a road to the top of Tom and then clear-cut the rest. Cut down every tree on the top of the mountain. Every tree. And then blow the top off of the mountain to get at the coal inside!

This was definitely not having it together. This was definitely not figuring it out.

This. Was. Horrible.

16

WE WERE BACK IN OUR MINE on Mount Tom. I was brushing Ashley's hair and totally failing once again to pull off a decent French braid.

"So," I asked. "What are we going to do?"

"Give up, I guess," Ashley said.

"Give up? Are you kidding me? Just like that? Give up?"

I was stunned. This wasn't like Ashley. She was more stubborn than a drunken mule. Once she got an idea in her head, no matter how outrageous or ridiculous it was or what a potential shit-show, talking her down was next to impossible.

"I can't believe you, Ashley!" I said, incredulous.

"What's not to believe?" she replied. "Ouch. You're pulling my hair!"

"Sorry." I eased up on the braid. "I mean quitting right now. It's so not you!"

"What's it have to do with me?" Ashley asked. "I mean, don't get me wrong, Cyndie, but this wasn't even my idea. You're the one who saw it in *Teen Vogue*."

"*Teen Vogue*? What are you talking about?"

"Seriously, I appreciate the effort and all. I really do. And please, please, don't you ever stop brushing my hair. But after the thousandth time I just don't think the French braid thing is going to fly. It just isn't. No offense, but a hair braider you're not. Harebrained, yes. Hair braider, no."

Relieved, I let out a laugh that echoed through the mini-mine.

"Wow!" I said. "I thought you meant . . ."

"Saving Mount Tom? Give up on that? *Puh-lease!* Who do you think I am? Who do you think we are!"

Whew! If Ashley had bowed out of the battle there'd be no fight. There was no way I could do this alone. Without her—no me.

And without us—no Tom.

I felt the pull of Belinda the Brave. Not a-barrelful-of-bears brave, not even a bucketful, but at least I could feel her presence.

French braid or not, we were not going to let Tom go down without a fight.

•

We both agreed that we needed allies. There was strength in numbers. It was like the old saying, "It takes a village to save a mountain," or something like that.

"The meth heads," Ashley said. "That's who we need on our side. If they're cooking meth on the mountain then they probably care as much about Tom as we do! If we had them in our camp, American would back the hell off in an instant. Nobody messes with those dudes!"

As previously noted, methamphetamines were as common in Greenfield as Confederate flags on pickup trucks. Kids would even do stand-up comedy about it in the lunchroom.

"How many meth heads does it take to change a light-bulb?" one joke went. "Four. One to hold the bulb and three to smoke until the room spins."

Very funny.

Not.

I mean, don't get me wrong; Ashley and I had certainly done our share of putting the S in *Stupid* when it came to alcohol. Like the last time we raided her parents' stash of booze. The results were not pretty.

"*Arggg!*" Ashley moaned, hugging the toilet bowl and blurfing up the last of the Cheetos along with an unhealthy amount of Southern Comfort (from that day forward known as Southern Discomfort). "Somebody shoot me!"

"Remind me why we thought this was fun?" I slurred, sitting on the edge of the bathtub, both feet on the floor, desperately battling the spins while I held her head as she heaved and heaved again.

Another piece of paper for the ridiculous jar. Although that was way more stupid than ridiculous.

Half the kids at school get trashed every Friday and Saturday night. The bottle heads brag endlessly about how much they drink and how totally wasted they get. They even have a party spot down near the river they call "Heaver's Holler." On weekends you can do the Jesus thing and walk on water, it's so thick with puke there.

Between the meth heads, the bottle heads, and the be-headers, it's enough to make you lose your head.

"I'm not so sure about the meth-head strategy," I said to Ashley. "I can't see it bringing a whole lot of people over to our side."

"We might be surprised," Ashley said. "Half the town seems to be in on the action. Those folks probably have their own lobbyists down at the statehouse!"

"How about we put them in the maybe column?" I said. "To be revisited at a later date. As in never."

"Humph!" Ashley said. "Okay. How about Shannon Sullivan's two brothers who just got back from Afghanistan? Maybe we could get them to place land mines all around Mount Tom. I heard they did that kind of stuff over there. They could mine Tom so American can't!"

"Awesome!" I said. "That's a fab idea. We'll blow up the effin mountain so the mining company doesn't! Destroy Tom in order to save it! Works for me!"

Ashley humphed again. "Okay, Miss Smarty Pants. If my ideas suck so bad, why don't you come up with something?"

"I think we should tell Mr. Cooper about what we did. With the flags and stuff. See what he thinks the next steps are."

"Are you kidding?" Ashley said. "Favorite teacher or not, he'll turn us in. He'll go straight to the police. We'll be in jail by sundown."

"No way. Coop won't tell."

"He will."

"He won't."

"He will," Ashley said. "He has to. He's like a mandated reporter or something."

"That's for child abuse, not for saving trees."

"This is abuse. Worse than abuse. It's like rape. It really is. They're going to cut down all the trees on Mount Tom. *Our* mountain. That would be bad enough. But then they're going to blow it up! Can you believe it? Blow it up!"

An article had just come out in the local paper detailing American's mountaintop removal plans. The reporter who had interviewed the mine owners hzadn't thrown one hard-ball question at them. Instead, the article read like a glowing review of a Taylor Swift album, for God's sake, giving the impression that somehow after Tom had lost his head he'd be even more handsome than before.

Ashley paused and wiped her face on my shirt. I was feeling a little teary-eyed myself.

"I mean, if you cut down the trees they grow back, right?" Ashley continued. "But if you blow the top off of the mountain where are they going to grow? Huh? Where? If that's not abuse, if that's not rape, then I don't know what is! Mr. Cooper should be turning *them* in, not *us*."

We grew quiet, listening to the soft rustle of a light rain on the rhododendrons outside our mini-mine and thinking about how unfair it all was.

I just wanted to go back to painting Ashley's toenails and talking about boys. I wanted to finally figure out how to French braid her hair. I wanted to know that our mountain and our trees and our sanctuary would always be safe and that there was nothing that could ever come and screw it all up and turn it into such a colossal mess. I wanted to not know what I now knew and go back to how it all was before.

But that wasn't going to happen. Once you know, you know. There was no unlearning the truth. There was no turning back.

But seriously, who were we kidding? We were fifteen, for goodness sake! And girls! Given how folks down here felt about females, what could we possibly do to stop American from blasting Mount Tom into oblivion? Did we actually think we had a chance in a bazillion years of stopping them? I mean, really. Why even try if we were doomed to fail?

It was like going after a Number Two: an Untouchable. What was the point?

"Changing the subject," Ashley said. "Any new ideas on how we're going to snag you Kevin Malloy?"

17

Saving the world or not, life does go on. There were other things equally worthy of obsession.

Namely (duh!) boys. One specific boy to be exact.

Civil War reenactments had abruptly ceased to be a PITA. What with Kevin Malloy proudly marching with the Army of Northern Virginia, I was counting down the seconds to the next battle.

"What's up with you?" Britt asked. "You actually want to go?"

It was Saturday and we were heading up to Maryland to annihilate the Army of the Potomac.

"Well," I said. "You know how it makes Dad happy to have us there. And Auntie Sadie needs my help again."

"Since when did you ever care about making Dad happy?" Britt asked.

"Well, you know ... I mean ... like ..." It was hard to speak in the grip of a full-body blush.

Britt stared hard at me.

"Wait a minute!" she said. "You can't fool me! There's something else going on here. It's that boy, isn't it? The one you attacked! Kevin Malloy!"

Ouch! Outed by the little sister! And this from a twelve year-old?

And all of it was true. Unintentional or not, I had touched an Untouchable. Since the moment he had fallen on top of me at the Haunted Lunatic Asylum and I had whacked him half to death with the peg leg, I was having a hard time getting that boy out of my head.

If Mr. Cooper had, with all of his scientific know-how, at that very moment dissected my head and computed the percentage of my brainpower devoted to matters of critical importance, he would have come up with the following statistics:

- 2 percent to the English essay due Monday, a character analysis of Hester Prynne in *The Scarlett Letter*, a book I hadn't yet cracked a page of.

- 3 percent to breathing, blood circulation, eating, drinking, peeing, pooping, and all other essential bodily functions.

- 21 percent to my personal appearance, with particular emphasis on the terrifying nest of zits that circled my chin. Ashley told me about some pill she saw advertised on the 'Net that boasted a lifetime guarantee of no more acne after you used it. Imagine that! Joy of joys! A pimple-free life! The only drawback was that your kids would get birth defects and your liver would fail and you'd get a bunch of other unpleasant and potentially catastrophic medical conditions that all pretty much sucked. As tempting as the offer was, I decided to stick with my Clear Proof Acne Treatment Gel, which not only promised to unclog my pores and remove excess oil but also swore to prevent embarrassing breakouts and future flare-ups, and to leave my skin feeling sexier. Not that you'd know it from looking at my zit goatee.

- 31 percent to Satan and Company and the destruction of Mount Tom.

- 43 percent to Kevin Malloy.

"I don't understand why the English essay ranks so high?" Ashley asked me. "It seems to me that all of that valuable mental energy could be much better spent focusing on Kevin."

•

Before the incident at the Haunted Lunatic Asylum, Kevin Malloy was about as untouchable as they came. I had seen him at school roaming the halls but he was a senior, for goodness sake, and best friends with Marc the Mascot, one of the populars. He was firmly entrenched as a Number Two. There had been no need to go there.

But now, wonder of wonders, I had another chance to redeem myself from the awkward spaz move at school and get up close and personal. He wasn't just Kevin the senior, he was Private Kevin in the 3rd Division, 7th Regiment of the Army of Northern Virginia.

"What's gotten into you, young lady?" Auntie Sadie asked. "A week ago I had to drag you here by the hoops on your skirt. Now you're frothing at the bit for a go at it!"

Once again, a blush. A sort of Neiman Marcus Bordeaux Lust nail polish kind of blush, the one that Ashley lusted over, the one brighter than a deep plum but more intense than standard red. Just like it said on the bottle.

I was once again decked out in the Christmas-tree look of the hoop skirt borrowed from one of Sadie's friends. The same one that Kevin called cute, that he had said I looked hot in. If it ain't broke, why fix it?

And, once again, after a few hours of bullshitting tourists with Civil War nursing nonsense, I took leave of the field hospital so that I could have a front-row seat during the actual battle.

Battles were pretty much the same for every reenactment. There were a few subtle differences but for the most part they all kind of looked alike. One side charged. Everybody shot off cannons and guns and screamed like lunatics. The other side retreated or counterattacked or whatever. And, as always, much to the audience's delight, lots of tragic deaths for both the Blue and the Gray.

Meanwhile the tourists gawked and got hammered and cheered raucously while their kids ran around out of control, acting like little Yanks or Rebels and creating all sort of mischief and mayhem.

This particular reenactment's claim to fame was that it featured the 4th Artillery Regiment of the 2nd Maryland Volunteers. Their twenty-two Civil War–replica cannons were brought in by real live horses and they were now furiously firing on the advancing Confederates from atop the grassy knoll. Even if you didn't give a rat's ass about the Civil War or history or any of that stuff, it was still a sight to see. Twenty-two cannons firing away. Boom after boom after boom.

And there he was: Private Kevin. Marching into the thick of it. Guns blasting, cannons crashing, smoke wafting over his fallen comrades.

And still Kevin marched on.

Into the Valley of Death.

My hero!

When the Union artillerymen fired their cannon, they would use a rammer to drive home powder into the cannon breech. In real war it would have also driven down the cannonball, but (duh!) they left those out in the reenactments. The cannons were all bark and no bite. At least up until now.

A rammer was a long wooden stick with a round piece of wood at the end. Before discharging the cannon, you had to (duh again!) take the rammer out.

And here's where it got interesting.

In the heat of the battle, with the Confederate troops yee-hawing their rebel yells as they charged the grassy knoll, some

Union yahoo, half in the bag and zoned out in la-la land, forgot to take the rammer out of the cannon he was firing. Even without their balls, those cannons could sure get it up. The officer set fire to the fuse and the cannon shot out the rammer. It lazily arced into the air above the battle and the troops and the noise and the confusion and, like a drone strike, came down, you guessed it, slam-bang on Private Kevin's head.

Boom!

I had my gaze fixed on Kevin when down he went with a thud. Oblivious, his gallant comrades bravely marched on. With the smoke and the shots and the shouts and the booms, nobody seemed to have witnessed this tragedy but me.

"He's been hit!" I yelled from the sidelines. "Kevin's been hit!"

"Of course he has, sweetheart!" one of the tourists yelled back. "That's the whole point isn't it?"

Everybody laughed but me.

There was Kevin lying face down in the field and no one seemed to notice. Nobody.

Maybe he was dead! Not just play dead but real dead. As in *dead* dead!

It couldn't be true! Not to Private Kevin. Not to my Kevin! (Well, not really *my* Kevin, but I was already beginning to think of him that way. A girl can dream, can't she?)

I rushed out to save him.

Running through a field with a hoop skirt on is sort of like hopping backwards down an escalator. It really shouldn't be done. I must have wiped out about fifteen times before I finally made it to my fallen warrior.

As I was running I could hear the tourists cheer me on. They thought I was part of the act. Part of the reenactment.

"You go, girl!" someone yelled.

Kevin was still flat on his face, but even over the roar of the ongoing battle I could hear him moan.

"You're alive!" I shouted, relief flooding over me. "You're alive!"

Kevin rolled over and tried to sit up.

"Oh my God!" he said, rubbing the top of his head, cowering. "It's you again!"

"You're alive!" I cried again like a moron. "You're alive!"

"What did you do this time? Attack me from behind? One beating wasn't enough? Where's the peg leg?"

"No!" I tried to explain. "You were hit by the cannon."

"The cannon? I hate to clue you in, Sandy . . ."

"Cyndie."

"Sorry. Cyndie. Those cannons aren't real. This is just a . . ."

I held up the rammer for him to see.

"Some moron forgot to pull out in time!" I told him.

Kevin cracked a smile and continued to rub his head.

"Not a good idea," Kevin said. "You know what they say about sex and basketball. You always dribble before you shoot!"

There I was, sitting in the field of battle in my hoop skirt, helping Private Kevin recuperate from his near-death experience, with the battle still furiously raging around us, and he's making jokes about sex! About *sex*, for God's sake! We're surrounded by death and destruction and despair, and he's cracking sex jokes! To me!

"Nice skirt!" he said. "Very . . ."

"Basketball-like? With the hoop and all?"

Kevin laughed.

"Help me up, will ya?" he asked.

To the cheering of the crowd I put my arm around Kevin and we both staggered to our feet. Kevin doffed his Confederate cap to thunderous applause and limped back to the sidelines.

"I thought it was your head that got hit," I whispered.

"Shhh. Gotta play it up. We have them eating out of the palm of our hand."

Kevin waved again to the crowd. The tourists had all stopped watching the battle and were eagerly turned toward the two of us. As Kevin continued to lean on me with one arm while using the rammer as a crutch with the other, he suddenly turned and gave me a kiss. Not a peck-on-the-cheek kiss but a lip-to-lip wowzie. For the whole world to see! No tongue involved but still enough to make me go limp.

The crowd went wild. People were hooting and hollering. To thunderous applause we wandered our way back to the hospital tent. Somehow, as weak in the knees as I was, I managed to stay upright.

"Sorry about that," Kevin said after I settled him in on the field hospital cot and had placed an ice pack on the growing bump on his head.

"Sorry about what?" I asked.

"About the kiss. That was pretty inappropriate. I was just caught up in the moment."

Sorry about the kiss? Oh my God! Was he kidding? It was the greatest moment of my life!

"No need to apologize," I said. "It happens to me all the time."

"What?"

"The living dead are constantly all over me. I'm like a zombie magnet! They can't keep their mouths off of me."

"Wow," Kevin said. "Who knew?"

"Exactly. Anyway, the crowd loved it."

"They sure did. Evidently we made quite the couple."

Britt had come back bearing the news that we were the highlight of the reenactment. The hit of the show. A bunch of tourists came in wanting to take our picture. One little girl even asked me for my autograph. The event organizer wanted to know if we could schedule a repeat performance next year.

"It's pretty amazing that you didn't get seriously hurt!" I said to Kevin, still holding an ice pack to the bump. "I mean, that rammer was going five zillion miles an hour and came crashing right into your skull."

The Union artillery officer who had let loose the weapon of destruction had showed up at the nurse's tent and awkwardly begged Kevin's forgiveness.

"Dude," Kevin said. "That was, like, awesome. We're the talk of the town. Celebrities. And best of all, once again I got to be rescued by my hot nurse."

Blush, blush, and blush some more. I borrowed the ice pack to mop my brow.

"So," Kevin said after our adoring fans had finally left us alone. "We've got to stop meeting like this. First the smackdown with the peg leg, and now getting hammered with the rammer. And I thought the real Civil War was dangerous!"

I laughed.

God, Kevin was cute. He had these deep, dark brown eyes with girly-girl eyelashes that curled up forever. His unruly hair swept over the ice pack and cascaded down his ears and the back of his neck. Even the bump on his head was adorable.

And his lips. Oh my God. Thick, pouty, mischievous lips. Lips that had actually kissed mine. Even a totally fake just-for-show kiss was still a kiss.

"Next time I suggest substituting Marc the Mascot's miner helmet for the Rebel cap," I said. "Not exactly historically accurate but it'll keep you alive to fight another day."

"I don't know," Kevin said, looking up at me. "I'm sort of enjoying all the attention."

I was still fussing over the bump. Caressing was perhaps a better word. "Keep this up and you'll be getting even more," I said. "The first reenactment casualty. You'll be front page news of the *Civil War Times*. I might be a zombie magnet but you're a disaster magnet."

Kevin continued to stare at me.

"What are you, like, a junior?" he asked.

"Sophomore," I said.

"Oh yeah, right."

"What are you, like, a freshman?" I asked.

Kevin half laughed and half grimaced as I pressed down with the ice pack.

He reached out and shook my hand.

"Kevin," he said.

"Cyndie," I replied.

Neither of us let go for quite a while.

18

"He kissed you and then he held your hand?" Ashley asked.

"Cut it out, Ashley. It was a stage kiss and then we shook hands."

"Kids don't shake hands. That's totally lame. You might pound it. You might high five it. You might even wave. But no one shakes hands. No one."

"We shook hands," I repeated.

"You didn't shake hands. You don't make sex jokes, slip them the tongue, and then shake their effin hand. You just don't do it. He held your hand."

"It was a shake Ashley. And there was no tongue. I was there, remember?"

"No tongue?"

"No tongue."

"But definitely a hold."

"Stop!" I said.

We were back in Tom's Mine following another round of flag cutting. American had come back and marked the identical trees just as before. We had cut them all down. The flags, not the trees.

And we had also ripped down the signs that they had nailed up all along the road.

PRIVATE PROPERTY

NO TRESSPASSING

ANY DAMAGE TO THIS PROPERTY WILL RESULT IN

ARREST AND CRIMINAL PROCEEDINGS

AMERICAN COAL COMPANY

Once again, we hadn't really thought about it, we had just done it. We didn't have a plan. We hadn't even talked about it. It just seemed to be the thing we had to do. Part of what was expected. The new normal.

The whole way up the mountain it was a snip snip here and a snip snip there and down came the flags.

"Is it my imagination or are our little Tomsters a bit chattier than usual today?" Ashley asked as we cut down the last flag. We called the animals on Mount Tom "our Tomsters," and like the trees, we had even named a few of them.

There was Lady Gaga the barred owl, which we'd sometimes see at dusk, staring us down with her deep brown, almost black eyes and asking us, "Who cooks for you, who cooks for you all?" in her haunting hoot. She'd sit at her perch and twist her head round and round in that freakish way that owls do as if their necks were wind-up toys.

"If I could do that," Ashley said, "I'd join the circus and make a million."

There was Jay-Z the red squirrel, who'd chatter-rap nonstop as he raced back and forth across his old stone wall, hurling zingers at us fast and furious. It was unclear to Ashley and me if he did this because he was totally pissed or actually quite delighted to see us.

There was Taylor Swift, the whitetail deer that never stuck around long enough for a proper introduction but instead high-tailed it out of there—flight at first sight.

There were the Black Crows, TNTC (too numerous to count), that laughed at our every move as if we were the funniest effin things this side of Comedy Central.

I know, I know. It all sounds so juvenile and lame, so Walt Disneyish, as if we were third graders. But somehow, the act of giving them names made them all that more real to us. They weren't just animals. They were *our* animals. Our very own Tomsters.

There were a lot more of them as well. We couldn't see them, we couldn't even hear them, but we knew they were out there. We could feel their presence, watching our every move, eyes staring from behind the trunks of trees or camouflaged under leaf litter. Not staring at us in a creepy-stalker, horror-movie kind of way. Not like "better watch your backs girly-girls or you'll be breakfast, lunch, and dinner." But in a comforting "hey, welcome back" kind of way.

They knew we belonged here, too.

"It seems as though they approve," Ashley said.

"Approve of what?" I asked.

"Us cutting down the flags. Listen to them. It's like applause. It's like we're rock stars."

Ashley was right. The noise level was definitely ratcheted up a notch. With every cut flag it had seemed to grow louder and louder until the entire woods was a symphony of sound. Hoots and churs and grunts and caws. The Tomsters were twittering and tweeting the news to the whole wide world. "Go for it!" they were shouting.

"Do it!"

"Yes!"

The angst I had felt after the first time we had cut down the flags was still there. I was, once again, confused and uncertain. But there was much less hesitation this time.

My father was a great fan of an old-time folk musician named Pete Seeger who once said, "The world will be saved by a million little acts."

This was starting to feel like one of them.

"Do you think they look good?" Ashley asked.

"Of course they do," I replied.

"Seriously?"

"Duh! How could they not? They don't have flags on them anymore."

"Jeez, Cyndie," Ashley said, adjusting her bra. "I was talking about my boobs, not about the trees."

This was one for the ridiculous jar. Here we were trying to save the world, or at least our little portion of it, and Ashley was once again obsessing about her boobs.

"Chill, Ashley," I said. "If I had boobs like yours I'd think I'd have died and gone to heaven. If I was a guy or if I was into girls I wouldn't be able to keep my hands off of them. They're perfect. Quit your bitching. I mean, seriously, look at mine. I've got boy boobs."

"Haven't you been listening to a word I said?" Ashley asked. "That's the issue. That's the problem. I'm only fifteen and I'm already a C. If they don't stop growing I'll be flying past Z by the time I'm twenty!"

"I should be so lucky. Mine don't even make the alphabet! What comes before the letter A?"

"I'd so rather have yours than mine any day. Before too long I'm going to need an effin wheelbarrow to cart these things up this mountain."

"Let's just hope there'll still be a mountain to climb," I said.

"Anyway, you do too have boobs," Ashley said. "They're perfect for you. Totally hot. No wonder Kevin's all over you."

"Kevin's not all over me."

Ashley snorted.

"Anyway, can we please change the subject? If I hear one more thing about your boobs I'm going to take out these scissors and . . ." I waved them menacingly at her chest.

"Message received," Ashley said, removing her hand from under her top.

"So what are we going to do now?" I asked.

"About Kevin?"

"No, about Tom."

"Tom?" Ashley asked. "Tom who? You have another guy after you? Jeez, when it rains it pours!"

"*Mount* Tom, you moron!"

"Yeah. Right. Sorry. I have an idea."

"As long as it doesn't involve boobs I'm all ears," I said.

"A children's crusade," Ashley said.

"A what?"

"A children's crusade. I was thinking about this the other day in history. You know the thing they did in the Middle Ages in Europe where tens of thousands of kids marched to the Holy Land to convert everyone to Christianity. We could do the same thing."

"March to the Holy Land?"

"No! March on Mount Tom!"

"Thank God," I said. "That's way closer. But didn't they all die of disease and starvation and get sold into slavery or something?"

"Whatever," Ashley said. "And there was another children's crusade in the 1960s down in Alabama. A bunch of African American kids marching for civil rights."

I was impressed. Ashley had actually stayed awake in class!

"I hate to burst your bubble, but as I recall that didn't go down so well, either. Like fire hoses sprayed on the kids and police attack dogs and beatings and arrests and all sorts of crazy racist crap."

"My point exactly," Ashley said. "Think about it. What if we got everyone to march on American? What if the police brought out fire hoses and attack dogs and those of us who survived died of disease or starvation or got sold into slavery. I mean, seriously! It would be totally awesome. It would go viral on YouTube. There'd be no way they could blow up Tom after that!"

"Yeah. And you wouldn't have to worry about your boobs anymore either."

"Why not?"

"Because you'd be dead," I said.

"Or a slave."

"Either way, not exactly appealing choices!"

But I had to give her credit. It was an interesting idea. What if we got a whole bunch of us kids to march on American? There were kids who would do it. There were kids at school who cared. There were a lot who didn't, but there had to be a bunch who would be down for it.

And so, sitting in our mini-mine with the candles flickering inside and the animals frolicking outside, we began planning the Great Mount Tom Children's Crusade.

American had their corporate office right in the center of Greenfield, across from the Burger King, about a mile from the high school. We could make up banners and signs and slogans and get a petition and march right on up there and demand that they listen to us. We could get a bullhorn and sing and chant.

We were a bunch of kids, for crying out loud. It was our town. It was our mountain. They'd have to listen.

"I bet Kevin Malloy would come," Ashley said. "If you were up front and center with that hot hoop skirt, a banner, and a bull horn, there's no telling what might happen."

That sealed the deal.

The Great Mount Tom Children's Crusade was on.

19

WE AGREED THAT MR. COOPER was the go-to guy for support and advice on this one. We'd keep our mouths shut about cutting down the flags. It would be our little secret for now. But if we were to pull off a children's crusade, it would be good to have at least one adult in on the action.

"Maybe we should call it a young adult crusade," Ashley said. "I mean, seriously, look at the size of my boobs. I'm not exactly a child."

"Oh my God, here we go again!" I sighed. "And thanks, Ash. You always make me feel so much better about myself."

"We! I meant *we*! *Our* boobs! We're not children!"

"Boobs or no boobs, let's stick with the Children's Crusade. It rolls off the tongue much better. Plus, it packs a much more powerful punch. There's something about being a young adult that's kind of pathetic."

All week long in science class, Mr. Cooper had been on a tear about climate change. Humans burning fossil fuels—oil, gas, and coal—and pumping all those heat-trapping greenhouse gasses into the air and warming up the planet. His lectures were a cross between a rant and a sermon. He was combing and flossing and flossing and combing so obsessively I was getting anxious his hair would all fall out and his teeth would explode out of his gums. There he'd be, bald and toothless and still going off.

Mr. Livingston, the moronic math teacher that he was, had the stupidity to walk in on Coop in the middle of one of these tirades.

"Mr. Cooper!" Livingston said, his squirrelly face twitching away. "My students next door are extremely distracted by the volume of your voice. It is extremely difficult for young minds to concentrate when you continually shout out your opinions about controversial subjects. Do you mind, sir, turning it down a notch?"

"Turn it down?" Coop snorted, turning it up. "Turn it down? I'll give you 'turn it down'!" He threw back his head, closed his eyes, and howled like a coyote: "*Yip yip yip yow-ow-ow-ow!*"

Livingston, wild-eyed and trembling, backed away and skedaddled out of the classroom while Mr. Cooper glared at him like a wild animal.

"A D!" Coop howled, the coyote still possessing him. "That man gets a D! A D for Denier!"

No one had a clue what he was talking about.

"Most of you have Mrs. Osgood for English, correct?" Mr. Cooper asked, his voice regaining some degree of normalcy.

We all groaned, images of poopy diapers bringing on the gag reflex.

"And you're reading *The Scarlet Letter*?"

More groans.

"What did the character Hester Prynne wear on her dress?"

"An A," Ashley shouted. "A for *adulteress*. A for *affair*."

What had gotten into Ashley? Had she actually read the book? First spouting off history facts and now a completed English assignment? I made a mental note to take her temperature and make sure she wasn't sick or something.

"Exactly!" Coop said. "A scarlet letter of shame! A physical manifestation of sin! For all the world to see!" Mr. Cooper raised his voice even louder. His whole body trembled as he spoke.

"No A's for Livingston. That's way too good for him! He gets a scarlet *D*—D for *denier*! A climate change denier—the worst kind!"

Evidently Mr. Livingston was one of the folks on Coop's shit list who still didn't believe that humans were the cause of climate change.

"Only God can change the climate," we had once overheard Mr. Livingston say. This did not go down well with our science guru.

Mr. Cooper turned his back to us and began yelling through the wall that separated the two classrooms.

"Do the math, Livingston!" he shouted, pounding on the wall. "No more multiplying the lies! No more subtracting the truth! Add up the facts, Livingston! The wonderful thing about science is that it's still true even if you don't believe it!"

With a final flourish he flung his flosser at the wall and gave it a solid kick.

Even for Coop this was way over the top. To trash another teacher in front of us? None of us could stand Mr. Livingston, but it still seemed a little harsh.

Ashley passed me a note.

"Has Coop lost it?" it read.

Mr. Cooper stopped his rant and, still trembling, walked over to my desk.

"Give it to me," he said. Even in the middle of a mental meltdown there was nothing that escaped that man.

"Give you what?" I asked innocently.

"Give me the note. Now!" He snatched it out of my hands.

"'Has Coop lost it?'" he read out loud to the entire class. Ashley covered her face with her hands and slumped down in her seat.

"'Has Coop lost it?'" he repeated.

Total silence. It was so quiet you could hear crickets.

"Raise your hands if you think I'm crazy," he said.

It was an awkward moment. We all looked around at each other anxiously.

"I'm serious. Hands up if you think I'm crazy."

"Crazy in a good way?" Ashley asked. "Or crazy in a psycho-killer, looney-bin, crystal-meth, whacked-out, get-me-the-hell-out-of-here-right-now kind of way? I'll be the first to put my hand up for the good kind of crazy."

"Me too," I said. Most of the class nodded. A few seemed to be holding back for the second opztion.

That seemed to break the tension. Mr. Cooper sighed, picked up the flosser and put it and the comb back in his front pocket.

"Livingston!" he yelled to the wall. "Get in here!"

The door opened and Mr. Livingston awkwardly shuffled into the front of the classroom.

"Mr. Livingston," Coop began. "I would like to apologize for my unprofessional and disrespectful behavior. For the rest of the period, I will put a capital Q into *Quiet*. And while we may disagree about the facts of climate change, it was inappropriate for me to equate you with an adulterer." Mr. Cooper put particular emphasis on the word *adulterer*.

It was hard to tell whether that was yet another diss or a sincere apology.

Coop held out his hand. "Please accept my heartfelt request for forgiveness."

I wouldn't have been a bit surprised if Mr. Cooper had had one of those buzzers or zappers or mini-Tasers or fake-flower water-squirters or some other bizarre gag thing and had socked it to Livingston yet again.

Mr. Livingston, licking his lips, his eyes nervously scanning the room, seemed to be thinking the same thing. He limply shook Mr. Cooper's hand, mumbled something that sounded like a yes, and, filed silently out of the room.

"Call me crazy," Mr. Cooper said, turning toward us. "Believe me, I've been called worse, that's for damn sure. But, for the record, allow me to tell you what real crazy is."

Mr. Cooper's voice went all soft and quiet—super-spooky. We had never heard him talk like this. It was barely audible, barely above a whisper.

"Real crazy is wildfires burning out of control out West. No rain in California. Torrential flooding around here.

"Real crazy is the glaciers melting and the sea levels rising.

"Real crazy is the millions, or is it billions, of people who live near the coast line, with no way out."

Mr. Cooper's voice began to rise. He had stopped his pacing and was standing stock still in the middle of the room, gazing upwards, his arms out to his side with his palms facing forward. He looked like one of those statues you see in front of some Catholic churches.

The class was mesmerized.

"Real crazy is storm after storm, each one worse than the one before, plowing right on through," he continued.

"Real crazy is cranking up the earth's thermostat, degree after degree, and burning up the very crops we need to survive.

"Real crazy is trying to get out of the hole we're in by digging even deeper. Or in the case of Mount Tom, not digging but blowing it up. Blowing it up and polluting our rivers and making us sick so we can go ahead and burn more of the stuff that's gotten us into this damn mess to begin with.

"You want crazy? That's crazy! I may need a checkup from the neck up. I may be a whacked-out, wigged-out, mondo-bizarro, certifiable crank." His voice became menacing. "But I am nothing, *nothing* compared to that!"

He sat down on the edge of his desk looking somewhat sad and disheveled, blankly staring off into space. The class was quiet. More crickets. Everyone looked at their feet, or out the window—anywhere but at Mr. Cooper.

A minute went by. Then three, or four. No one moved. No one seemed to breathe. We all sat still in awkward silence till the bell rang and then, like Livingston, we filed wordlessly out of the classroom.

20

It's hard when you're fifteen and one of the few adults in your life that you actually like and trust is (a) a borderline lunatic, and (b) convinced that the world is plummeting toward total chaos and catastrophe.

"I don't know," Ashley said. "Maybe going to Coop isn't such a good idea after all. Maybe we should just do it alone. He seems sort of . . ."

"Mentally unbalanced?" I said. "Insane in the membrane?"

"Crazier than a shithouse rat?" Ashley added.

"And that's being kind," I said, laughing. "I don't know, Ash. I mean, obviously he's a bit of a nutcase, but at least he's on our side. Think about it. Think about what American wants to do: cut down all of the trees on Mount Tom. *Our* Mount Tom. And then blow the top off it. I mean, blow up the effin mountain! And once you get the coal, you burn it and fry the planet. Blow up the mountain, pollute the river, burn the coal, and fry the planet. Is that screwed up or what? Like Coop said, who is crazy here?"

Ashley and I had become obsessed with YouTubing mountaintop removal videos. It was absolutely heartbreaking. Beyond tragic. There you saw it. A beautiful mountain. And then, suddenly, *kaboom!* Gone!

The worst kind of magic. Now you see it. Now you don't.

Only it was painfully real.

"God, what a clustermuck," Ashley said, massaging her temples. "It makes my brain hurt. Will you rub my feet? I'm on the verge of a looney tune." Ashley kicked off her shoes and thrust her legs into my lap.

We had abandoned our mini-mine for my bedroom. It was much easier to surf the 'Net that way. Our mine on Mount Tom had yet to go wireless.

"Why is this happening?" Ashley asked. "I don't want to deal. I really don't. I'm tired. My feet hurt. Maybe we've done enough already. I mean, we ripped down the flags, right? Twice. Isn't that enough? It's more than anything anyone else has done. A little more on the left foot. Yeah. Right there. Oh my God, that feels good."

I pressed my thumb deep into that soft spot in the underside of her foot. Her eyes rolled to the back of her head and she went all limp and mushy.

"I agree with you, Ash. About not wanting to deal and all. I mean, it's pretty much a no-brainer. Let's see, a thinkabout with Kevin or a nightmare about climate change. Hmmm. . . Let me get back to you about that."

"Do the other one," Ashley said. "Oh yeah. Right there. Harder."

I pushed my knuckles into the back of her toes. "You know," I said. "One of your feet is bigger than the other."

"What?" Ashley sprang up from the bed. "Oh my God, are you serious?" She sat back down, grabbed her feet and, yoga-like, held them up to her face.

"Relax, Ashley. I'm joking."

Ashley threw a pillow at me.

"You meanie! You almost gave me a heart attack! God, Cyndie, if what's going on with my boobs was contagious and my whole body was becoming unbalanced, I'd lose it. Seriously. I mean, blowing up Mount Tom and climate change and all that crap is bad enough, but this would have totally sent me over the edge!"

"For the five zillionth time Ashley, your boobs are not unbalanced. Your effin brain is. Yours and Mr. Cooper's. But not your boobs."

"Shut up and rub my feet!" Ashley ordered.

"Anyway," I continued. "Here's the point. There's no going back, Ashley. You know there isn't. We're in it for the long haul. And it's not just about us. Think about Sugar Daddy and Bradley Beech and Sadie's Twin and She. Think about Lady Gaga and Jay-Z and Taylor Swift and the Black Crows. I know it sounds like the Disney Channel or some crap TV movie, but we can't let them down, can we? Now that we know what we know we can't exactly un-know it."

"What? Say that again," Ashley demanded.

"No."

I was kind of surprised at myself. Usually it was Ashley all gung-ho full-speed-ahead damn-the-torpedoes, with me cowering in the back seat desperately trying to put the brakes on. Ashley as Belinda the Brave and me as Custard the cowardly dragon.

It was a bit of a role reversal, and I kind of liked it.

"Anyway," I continued, "balanced or unbalanced, certifiable or not, I think we go to Coop. He's pretty much all we've got."

Ashley sighed. A long, painful, drawn-out, why-is-the-world-the-way-that-it-is sigh. "You're right," she said. "Too late to turn back. Speaking of turning, how about a little to the left. Oh yeah. That's it. Right there. Don't stop."

Hmmm, I thought. Rub her feet and I could get Ashley to do anything. With any luck, maybe next time one of those cannons would knock the socks off of Private Kevin.

I cracked my knuckles, flexed my fingers, and practiced on Ashley some more.

21

School assemblies were a good thing.

One: they got us out of class. It was always joy and rapture not to have to sit through high school hell.

Two: I got to hang with my gang. Actually, it wasn't really a gang at all. It was just Ashley. It's not that I didn't have other friends but the Ashley BFF thing had been ratcheted up a notch since the tree-flag escapades. There was a new bond between us, even stronger than before, forged with scissors on Mount Tom. We were, after all, secret agents out to save the world.

Three: we got to witness the drama of high school life unfold right before our very eyes in the auditorium. We watched in anticipation as the Number Ones, Twos, Threes, and Fours strutted their stuff. It was thrilling. Who would sit with whom? Who would wear what? Who was in? Who was out? Who would play the class clown, yelling and leaping and smacking people's rears and making a general ass of himself? Who would be sulking in the back corner, shamed and scarred and seething with rage and anger over some slight or rude comment?

Ashley kept up a running monologue, giving color commentary to every single move every single person made. It was hard to get a word in edgewise.

"Tracy Warner definitely has the hots for Mike Fleming," Ashley said. "Look at the way she stares at him. Somebody give that girl a bib. She's like a drooling machine.

"And Beth Erviti. I mean, seriously, who does their hair like that? She has to bend over to get through the effin doorway. Someone has got to tell that girl it's not the eighties anymore."

In seventh grade Ashley watched an MTV special on hairstyles of the 1980s and ever since then had it in for girls with big hair. It was a pet peeve of hers. No matter what their other outstanding attributes might have been, if their hair was big then it was a definite no-go. You could be the Virgin Mary for God's sake, but if you had big hair Ashley would go off on you.

After finally accepting what a braid spaz I was, she had recently gone into Morgantown and had her hair cut short. Very cute, in a bob style with one side slightly angled and the other pretty steep. She was almost as obsessed with her hair as she was with her boobs. She was constantly surfing the 'Net on different ways to style it. Which products brought a healthy sheen, bounce, and flair. She even used the mirror in our mini-mine to primp and preen appropriately before reemerging into the world.

"Ashley, I don't think the trees will actually care if your hair is a little grubby," I told her.

"Don't be treeist," Ashley replied. "You see how they're always ruffling their branches and dropping leaves. She is more obsessed than I am. She doesn't have a single twig out of place. There is no way I'm going to walk by her not looking my best. Chic and sexy—that's my mantra."

I could never quite figure out what to do with my hair. Growing up momless with a clueless dad and an aunt who was not exactly a fashion icon was not overly helpful in the hairstyle department. I had worn it long most of my life, with Ashley spending hours braiding and unbraiding it. Lately she had been after me to cut it short.

"How about a pixie—you'd look so hot in that," Ashley said. "You'd be like Emma Watson. Kevin's hands would be all over it."

"Looks like Kevin's hands are pretty preoccupied with something else right now," I said, scowling.

Sitting in our seats in the auditorium we had watched Sandra Lewis, a senior, sweep in and practically tackle Kevin, putting her arms around him and flinging her hair all over his face and getting all gooey-eyed and stupid the way girls always seemed to around the popular crew.

Ever since the reenactment incident with the wayward rammer, I had become painfully aware how much I hated Sandra Lewis. Loathed her. Despised her. I knew it was stupid and wrong and made me seem like a silly, petty third grader, but I couldn't seem to help it. I really couldn't.

Not that I knew her from a hole in the wall. I don't think I had ever said a single word to her. But still, I hated her with a passion. If she were trapped in a collapsed, abandoned mine and I was the only one who knew about it, I wouldn't tell a soul. I'd let her claw the walls until her nailless, bleeding fingers were worn to the bone. I'd laugh and laugh as she died the death of a thousand screams. Or so I pictured it, anyway.

And it's not as if they were even going out. Britt had told me that Kevin didn't have a girlfriend. All of Ashley's and my sources, few and far between and as they were, confirmed that he was unattached.

I was well aware that I had as much chance with him as one of Sadie's goats had to sprout wings and start flying. But hey, once you had put anti-itch cream on someone's neck and stared down their shirt and held an ice pack on their enormous head bump, you can never go back to the way things were. Kind of like how it was with cutting down the flags on Tom's trees.

Only not.

And that kiss. That kiss and that handshake that maybe, just maybe, was more than a shake. They both seemed to have gone on forever.

And hadn't he told me I looked hot? And that I'd saved his life?

A girl could dream, couldn't she?

"She's a bitch," Ashley said.

"Who?" I replied, feigning innocence.

Ashley gave me the look.

"Look at her hair. It's like she fell for the old fork-in-the-electric-outlet routine. *Zap!* Frankenstein's bride's got nothing on her. And she's friends with Angie Warton, so she's got to be evil."

Yeowww! Ashley was sharpening her kitty claws.

Angie Warton was the girl who had been throwing herself at Marc Potvin lately. Ashley felt the same way about Angie that I felt about Sandra. Just our luck to have crushes on two popular boys who already had girls hanging all over them.

"Asswipes!" Ashley said.

I nodded my head and contemplated the cruel injustices of the world.

Anyway, back to the assembly.

Mr. Miller, the principal, was a wispy scarecrow of a man with enormous baboon-like eyebrows and a pencil-thin moustache that gave him an old black-and-white-movie kind of look. Not in a mysterious, classic way but more just plain ridiculous. We were convinced he had barely survived his hideous high school years, wasting away as a tormented member of Kingdom Number One (Loser!) and was now gleefully getting his pay backs on all of us at Greenfield High. The vicious cycle where the tortured becomes the torturer, the oppressed the oppressor. Such tragedy.

"I'll have nothing but quiet!" Mr. Miller yelled into the microphone, his words lost in a rising squeal of feedback.

Not a soul stopped talking. No one even looked up.

"There will be silence!" he bellowed again. Even more bedlam.

"If you do not stop your chatter this instant, you will be marched straight back to class!"

That got people's attention. The dull roar subsided to whispers and muffled giggles.

"We have a very important topic to discuss today," Miller continued. "One that is of vital concern to all of us. One that has affected this community of ours in an ongoing and tragic way."

"Oh my God!" Ashley whispered. "Talk about tragic! If this is what I think it is I'm going to blurf right now!"

Mr. Miller droned on. "I would like to introduce two very special guest speakers. Two young men whose lives have been shattered, but through perseverance, hard word, and the grace of God, they have clawed their way back to the land of the living."

Grumbling from the audience.

Tragedy of tragedies, we were to be subjected to yet another dog and pony show on the evils of crystal meth.

Believe me, I've got nothing against recovering addicts doing their community-service gig and preaching the good word to all of us impressionable adolescents. Hooray for them. I mean it. I really do. It must be hard as heck to get up in the front of a bunch of snickering high school students and reveal that your life has been one big clustermuck. It takes guts to tell the world what a complete loser and moron you've been.

It's just that we've heard it so many effin times that I could repeat word for word exactly what those dudes were going to say:

"When I was your age I thought I was invincible."

Or: "I was like, 'Hey, just once or twice, I wasn't going to get hooked.'"

Or: "I thought, what's the problem? I can stop any time I want."

And then they'd drone on and on, recounting the nightmare of debauchery, heartbreak, ripping people off, screwing everyone you knew and everyone you didn't, and not giving a crap about anything but getting high. Winding up in jail and thanking the Lord you were still alive to tell your tale of woe and misery. I once was lost and now I'm found. Blah blah blah.

And that is exactly what they did.

No one made fun of them. No one yelled obnoxious comments. They were just ignored. I'm not sure which was worse.

I know, it sounds cruel and heartless. But by my age, you pretty much either got the message or you didn't. It was too-little-too-late to be trucking out the same-old-same-old "just say no" thing. They needed to start that with Britt's class. Or even earlier. Get at the little dweebs while they were still figuring things out.

Sad but true: you could tell who was getting sucked into the dark side pretty early on. Whose families were so screwed up, who was so neglected, abused, and abandoned, who was so wild and crazy that crystal meth seemed like a step up for them.

Sure, there were exceptions. Good kids gone bad.

Like Jon Buntington.

In ninth grade he was a Three (Friend) with definite Four (Possibility) potential. He was smart, funny, hot, and nice to everyone. And then something happened. Who knows what?

Evil works in mysterious ways. It all went totally wrong and unraveled just like that and he spiraled downhill in an insane way until all was chaos and hell and crystal meth, and before you knew it he was off to live with his uncle in Nebraska who was a retired state cop and was going to knock that crap out of him.

He had returned to school at the end of September. Drug-free, quiet, reserved, but clearly still fighting demons.

But the Jon Buntingtons were few and far between. Most were of the Carl Stenson variety. Dad in jail. Single mom, strung out, on welfare. No money. In fourth grade he burned down his neighbor's barn. In sixth grade he was expelled for punching a substitute teacher in the nose. In eighth grade he did his first fling in juvenile detention for assaulting some girl. Last year he was a bona fide, card-carrying member of the crystal meth club and off in la-la land smoking and then shooting up. Now he was spending the first of Lord knows how many years in juvie for robbing a convenience store outside Greenfield.

Bad kid who stayed bad.

I worried about a lot of things. Fortunately, going off the deep end and doing crystal meth was not one of them.

And, after all, there were other, much more pressing concerns to angst about.

"I don't get what he sees in her," Ashley said.

"Neither do I. She's such a poser," I whispered back.

"Exactly," Ashley said. "And look at her outfit. I mean, Goodwill's fine, but that? Seriously!"

"Wait a minute," I said, confused. "Isn't that the same top that you had on a few days ago?"

"What are you talking about?" Ashley said. Like most everyone else, we had traded in our whispers for a normal conversation. We couldn't hear the meth heads' presentation even if we had tried.

"The beige Urban Outfitter top. The one I said looked so good on you."

"She does not have that top on."

"She does too!"

Ashley squinted her eyes and looked again.

"Cyndie!" Ashley said. "I was talking about Angie. Not Sandra."

Mercifully, the two meth heads eventually had had enough of us, mumbled some final incoherent gobbledygook, and fled the stage.

Mr. Miller returned to the microphone. You could see by his scowls and shaking head he was peeved that we had been such an inattentive audience. Students were getting their backpacks together and shuffling around, ready to bolt for the door.

"I am not done with you yet!" Miller shouted. Oh, the unbridled joy of listening to our fearless leader shriek at us.

"He sounds like one of Sadie's goats when they get screwed by the billy," Ashley said. "*Blaaahhh!*"

I laughed.

"Two important items to note," Mr. Miller continued. "Number one. There will be no grinding at the upcoming school dance this Friday. Absolutely no grinding. Those observed displaying this rude and vulgar act will be escorted out of the cafeteria immediately. Do I make myself clear?"

"What's grinding?" some smart-aleck yelled out.

"You know perfectly well what grinding is, young man!" Mr. Miller answered.

"You mean this?" He and the girl next to him stood up. They turned, back to front, and the guy pressed his man parts against the girl's rear. They starting grinding away.

The crowd went wild. People were hooting and hollering, rebel yelling and rapping it down. A bunch of other kids stood up and started doing the same.

"That is enough!" Mr. Miller yelled. More feedback from the microphone. Teachers intervened and order was restored.

"I have one more announcement to make," Miller thundered.

"First crystal meth. Then grinding. What could possibly top those two?" Ashley asked.

"How about big hair?" I said. "No more crystal meth, grinding, or big hair. The big three. Banished forever. Greenfield High would be such a kinder and gentler place."

"As some of you may know," Mr. Miller continued, "American Coal Company is working on a project on Mount Tom. It will be of tremendous benefit to our local economy and bring additional jobs into town. There is to be a road built to the top of the mountain, where the work will commence. Someone has been removing flagging on trees that are to be cut down. Two young adults have been observed frequenting that site."

Ashley reached out and took my hand. We both held our breath.

"Let there be no mistake. This will be treated as a crime and not some silly prank. If, or shall I say when, the perpetrators are caught, they will be dealt with accordingly."

"What are you going to do, grind them up?" yelled the same kid who had been dancing a minute ago.

"Grind! Grind! Grind!" students starting chanting.

"This is not a joke!" Miller thundered, the feedback squeal continuing. "If you see or know anything about these incidents you will report it to my office immediately. This behavior is not to be tolerated. You are dismissed."

Everybody got up and began grinding their way down the aisles and back to class.

Everybody got up except Ashley and me. We sat glued to our seats. Immobilized. Paralyzed.

What if someone was on to us? What if someone knew?

If we got ratted out there would be hell to pay. The potential punishment was beyond terrifying.

Expelled from school? Sent to jail? Run out of town?

"Bunch of fucking tree huggers," the boy next to us said to his friend. His friend laughed. "Environmentalists! If I caught 'em, I'd shoot 'em."

Oh my God! And now add to the list "murdered"?

For the first time ever I was happy that an assembly was over.

22

"SO MUCH FOR EVEN THINKING about Kevin Malloy and grinding," I said. "If we get caught and we somehow manage to come out of this alive, I'm going to be grounded for life!"

Ashley and I were walking home from school. It was hot and humid as hell. My underarms dripped with sweat. My bra was soaked. My eye shadow had run all the way down to my socks. It was partly from the weather, but mostly it was from worrying about what had gone down in the assembly.

"Look on the bright side," Ashley said. "We're tree huggers! We're environmentalists! We have a name! A label! We're finally somebody!"

"We'll be somebody, all right. How about felons? Convicts? The ones they find in shallow graves ten years from now?" I was still trying to catch my breath from the bombshell Mr. Miller had dropped. Although, truth be told, I did have to admit there was a certain prestige that came with being labeled.

"How could anyone see what we did as a bad thing?" Ashley said. "I mean, saving the environment? Hugging trees? What could possibly be wrong with that? I just don't get it."

"I don't know, Ash," I said. "The more we get into this, the more I think there are a lot of people who just don't get it. We're not exactly short on stupid around here. Or anywhere else for that matter." I was thinking about the news reports

I had watched on television with Britt. West Virginia sure hadn't cornered the market on morons.

Ashley dropped her nail polish and was bending down to pick it up when Bert Stanmere with Michael Mead riding shotgun, the two guys who had almost hit us a few weeks before, came hauling ass around the corner in their beat-up pickup. Bert slammed on his brakes, swerved around us, and honked.

"Oh, yeah, baby!" he yelled. "Bend over some more! Show us what you got!"

Ashley gave them the finger.

"If there was a reality show called *The Stupids*, Bert and Michael would be the stars," Ashley said.

I choose to ignore the fact that Ashley's skirt had flipped up while she was crouching in the middle of a busy road.

"Along with Angie Warton and Sandra Lewis," she continued.

"Exactly," I said. "Anyway, what's our next step?"

"I don't know. Dog poop in their perfume? Hot pepper in their deodorant? We could try . . ."

"Ashley!" I said. "I wasn't talking about Angie and Sandra. I was talking about saving Mount Tom."

"Oh yeah," Ashley said. "That."

"What are we going to do now that we're outlaws?" I asked.

"Be the smartest outlaws we can be!" Ashley said. "What else can we do? And it shouldn't be too hard to pull that one off. After all, we're so effin superior to everyone else!"

I laughed, trying my best to dispel the shadow of fear and dread that Mr. Miller had cast over us. I liked the tree-hugger label. And being called an environmentalist was actually pretty sweet. But outlaws? I needed a little more time to wrap my brain around that one.

But hey, if I was going to be an outlaw at least I wasn't doing it alone. I had my Ashley. We were a gang. So what if we were only a gang of two? That meant there was plenty of room for more.

Giggling in the face of death, grinning at the ugly specter of catastrophe, we locked arms and skipped all the way home.

23

IN THE PAST, if Dad or Auntie Sadie had asked me to go to yet another Civil War reenactment I would have had a hissy fit. Acted like a three-year-old and thrown a tantrum. Refused to go. Barricaded myself in my room.

But times had changed. I had my hoop skirt on an hour and a half before Auntie Sadie had even arrived.

I was totally bummed. This was the last reenactment of the season. My very last time to save Kevin from whatever catastrophe befell him.

"What's gotten into her?" Dad asked Britt.

"She has a boyfriend!" Britt said.

"Shut up, Britt! I do not have a boyfriend."

"Do too!"

"I do not!"

"Whose the guy?" Dad asked.

"There is no guy!" I insisted.

"His name is Kevin Malloy," Britt said. "He's in your division, Dad. He's the one that got stung by the yellow jackets and then got hit by the rammer."

"I'm surprised he's still alive," Dad said. "Must be a glutton for punishment. I didn't even know you were dating, Cyndie. It's good to tell me these things. He seems like a nice-enough boy."

"Dad, I am not dating him!"

"Then who are you dating?" Dad asked.

"No one!"

"Wait. You have a boyfriend that you're not dating?"

"I'll be outside waiting for Sadie!" I yelled, storming out of the living room. "If any of you say one more word about anything to anyone . . ."

"What's gotten into her?" I could hear Dad ask Britt again.

"She has a boyfriend!" Britt said.

•

Miracle of miracles, the reenactment went off without a hitch. Private Kevin did not get stung by yellow jackets. Private Kevin did not experience near-decapitation by a wayward rammer. He did not fall and twist his ankle the way the chief engineer to General Meade did. He did not have a sugar attack and slink away to get an ice cream cone the way the artilleryman on the Union side did. He did not floss his teeth while lying dead on the battlefield and endure taunts of "dead man flossing!" from the spectators the way the Confederate flag bearer did.

He didn't even die. Private Kevin led the charge down the hill that rolled up the Union left flank, taking a dozen prisoners and helping the Confederates win the Battle of Big Bend. Kevin was the hero of the last battle of the year!

I was bummed. I was hoping for some minor injury, at the very least a scrape or a bruise, something that would have sent him to the nurse's tent. I was hoping for some little booboo that would allow my magic fingers to go to work on a sore foot. But, damn, damn, double damn, he had emerged from the battle victorious, without a hair on that handsome head even ruffled. I didn't even get a chance to talk to him!

"I could trip him if you want me to," Britt said. "Or poke him in the eye with the bayonet that Dad didn't need."

I didn't say anything. I knew she was trying to be helpful, but she was still a twit.

I had just finished packing up the nurse's tent into Sadie's pickup and was crouched behind it changing. I had my hoop skirt halfway over my head when, wouldn't you know it, Kevin came limping up.

"Nurse!" he yelled. "Nurse! I've been shot!"

My hoop had become twisted around my boobs and seemed to be stuck there. I could barely breathe.

"Oomph!" I managed to stammer. "Yikes!"

"Are you okay?" Kevin asked. "Can I help?"

"I thought you were dying?" I managed to respond, gasping for breath. I was equal parts mortified that he had caught me in the middle of changing and delighted that he had shown up.

"I was joking," he said. "But you, on the other hand. You . . ."

"Laugh and I'll kill you," I said. I had managed to get the hoop over one of my breasts but it seemed to be wedged in between the two of them in a most awkward position.

"Here," Kevin said. "If I just lift up this side then maybe your boop, I mean your hoop, will just make it over the other one."

Just then Dad and Britt came traipsing around the corner. There I was, halfway undressed, Kevin's hands brushing my boobs, and Dad and Britt show up.

"Oh," Dad said. "Is this the guy you're dating?"

God! Why me? Why do I have to be cursed with a family of such mule heads?

"Good work on the battlefield this afternoon, Private Malloy," my father said, clueless as always.

"Thank you, sir," Kevin answered, saluting him with his free hand. His other hand had a wristband on and somehow it had become caught on the hoop right below my left boob. He couldn't seem to free it. It looked as though he was feeling me up. Not a drive-by but a full-fledged feel-up. With Dad and Britt standing there, staring. Britt's mouth was open wide. At least, thank God, for once she was speechless.

"What's all the fuss about," Auntie Sadie said as she came

around the pickup and joined the growing crowd of gawking onlookers.

This was beyond embarrassing. I was blushing so hard my eye shadow had turned red.

Finally Kevin managed to extract his hand from the hoop/boob and my skirt came tumbling off. I made a beeline into the pickup and somehow managed to get my clothes on, all by myself, without any additional wardrobe malfunctions.

When I emerged, Kevin was still there waiting for me.

"That was fun," he said.

"Yeah, right." I rolled my eyes.

"I came to see if you wanted a ride home?" he asked. "Without the hoop on, you might even fit in my car. I'd hate to have to tow you."

I laughed.

"Let me ask my Dad," I said.

24

"So," I BEGAN. "Why do you do this?"

I had gotten over the humiliation of the hoop hysteria and was trying to get a grip on my situation. I could hardly believe my luck! I was riding in a car with a boy! Not just any boy. The Kevin Malloy boy!

"Why do I do what?" Kevin asked, smiling. "Give cute girls rides home?"

"No," I said, trying to remain blush-free. "Do the Civil War thing. Be a reenactor?"

"I don't know," he said. "There's something about being part of the past that's pretty sweet. You know what I mean? So much simpler. So much less screwed up."

"Are you saying the Civil War wasn't screwed up?"

"No, no, not at all. Totally screwed up. But I'm talking about the past in general. It's like when we have our reenactment camps. We just sit around talking. Build a fire. Cook our food outside. There's no technology. No cell phones. No iPads. None of that crap. I really like that. Can I tell you something funny that happened the other day?"

What a stupid question. He could tell me anything that happened any day. I was hooked. I was like a meth head, addicted after one puff. I could listen to Kevin talk forever.

"Go for it," I said.

"I will. So I help my father out in the hardware store, right? You know the one on Prospect Street?"

"I do."

"Anyway, I do deliveries and stuff. I was bringing a load of lumber to this work site and this guy says he'll text me if he needed some more. I told him I didn't text."

"'You don't text?' the guy asks. I mean his mouth drops open and he takes a step backwards. It was as if I had told him I had an infectious disease or something."

I nodded my head.

Kevin continued. "'Forgive me for prying,' the guy goes, 'but is it arthritis? My grandmother has it. It's a bitch.' He goes on to tell me this sob story about how his grandmother can't seem to get her fingers to move at all anymore and how she has Velcro on her shoes because she can't do laces."

"'Wow' I go. 'I'm sorry. Must be tough.'"

"'It is,' the guy says. 'How do you do deliveries and all?'"

"'What do you mean?' I go. 'With Velcro or laces?'"

Kevin stopped his story for a moment.

"Look," he said, pointing to the side of the road, and slowing the car down. There were seven deer grazing in a farmer's field.

"Cool," I murmured, immersed in the story and relishing the wind in my face and the fact that I was riding in the car with KEVIN MALLOY!

"Way cool," he said. "Anyway, I can't tell you how many times this has happened to me. It's amazing. People immediately assume that because I don't text I must have some debilitating disease, some physical abnormality, some life-threatening emergency, some critical condition they could catch. The idea of choosing not to text blows people's minds. They think I'm a freak or something. I've seen people wash their hands after I've told them. Well, not really, but it's like they're scared of contracting the dreaded no-texting germ."

"Stop the car right now!" I shouted, hunching closer to the passenger door. I opened the window and gasped for breath. "Pull over. I've got to get out! Now!"

Kevin laughed. "Seriously," he said. "Is it that weird?"

"Super weird," I said. "But weird in a good way. A really good way."

Kevin smiled and his face lit up. It wasn't just his mouth that smiled, it was his whole face—his eyes, his eyebrows, his forehead, his cheeks, his ears. Even what was left of the bump on the top of his head smiled. His face was just one big, gigantic smile. It was the cutest thing I had ever seen.

"Anyway," he said. "That's what I like about reenactments. Talking. No texting. Just talking. I'm bummed that it's the last one of the year. I'll miss it. I'll miss doing our camp chores and cleaning our guns and playing music and talking. I'll even miss hanging out with the old farts. Like your father. Who's actually pretty cool, by the way."

I rolled my eyes. "What do you talk about?" I asked.

"With your father? All about you. I know everything about you. Everything."

"Please!" I said, desperately hoping it wasn't true. Or hoping it was true. I couldn't decide which. "Seriously, what do you talk about?"

"A lot about what it was like to be alive back then. Back in the old days. How different it was. How much more people were . . . I don't know, it sounds sort of stupid, but in touch with nature. Part of nature. I mean, soldiering during the Civil War, you were outside all of the time. Living off the land. Hiking around."

"I think they called it 'forced marching,'" I said.

"Hiking, marching, whatever. It's still walking in the woods. They were always doing all sorts of sweet stuff."

"Like killing people. Or getting killed."

Kevin laughed.

"I know, I know, I'm romanticizing the whole thing. I get it. And don't get me wrong, I'm all for modern stuff in most ways. But it's just that we seem to have gone totally overboard. Screwing things up so much. Like the environment. Climate change and all that crap. And have you heard about their plan to blow up Mount Tom? My friend Marc Potvin's father works for American and he was telling me all about it. Plus, it's been in the newspaper and all. Can you believe it? What a bummer. The Civil War was crazy. But all of this seems even crazier."

It was all I could do to nod my head.

We were silent for a few moments.

"Why do *you* do it?" Kevin asked.

"Why do I do what?" I said, regaining my composure. "Accept rides home from cute guys?"

"You know what I'm talking about. Being a Civil War nurse and all."

"My father's been force-marching my sister and me to these things for years. Believe me, I've seen more battles than the real soldiers ever did. And now my aunt's friend who does the fake nursing thing just had a baby, so I'm filling in for her."

There was no way I was going to reveal the truth about my real reason for being there the last two times—that I was totally infatuated.

"Anyway," I added. "It's something to do."

"Something to do? What, like crystal meth? Like grinding? Like cutting the flags off of trees on Mount Tom?"

"I don't do crystal meth," I said. "And I don't grind. At least I never have. Actually, it sounds kind of intriguing. The grinding and all. Not the crystal meth."

Kevin laughed again.

"Speaking of which," Kevin said. "They're having this cotillion in a few weeks. It's a way to close out the reenactment season."

"This what?"

"Cotillion. A Civil War dance."

"You've got to be kidding," I said. "A Civil War dance?"

"You know, they play old-time music. It's like a square dance or something. The guys dress in uniform and the girls wear hoop skirts. I know it sounds pretty lame and all but it might be fun."

"With or without grinding?"

Once more Kevin laughed. I loved his laugh. He laughed the way he smiled, with his whole head.

"Well, it's not at the high school, so I guess anything is possible. Anyway, I'd love to see you grind in that hoop skirt."

I laughed. Laughed and blushed.

"Saturday the 12th," Kevin continued. "At the town hall in Madison."

"Cool," I said.

"Are you going?" Kevin asked.

"It depends," I said. "Are you?"

I could not believe I was actually having this conversation. Where was a flosser and comb when I needed them? I was desperate for something to calm my nerves.

"Only if there are hot nurses in hoop skirts to grind with," Kevin said. "But you have to promise to leave the peg leg at home. Too dangerous!"

"Damn," I said. "I was almost ready to say yes."

We had pulled into the driveway of my house. Britt was sitting on the front step, texting away, waiting for Kevin and me to show up so she could witness the action firsthand.

"By the way," Kevin said. "You said you didn't do crystal meth, right?"

"Duh!" I said.

"And you don't grind but you could be convinced."

"Perhaps."

"But what about the third thing?" Kevin asked.

"What third thing?"

"The cutting down flags thing?'

"What about it?" I asked.

"Would you do that? Would you cut down flags on Mount Tom?"

"Would you?" I asked.

"I asked you first."

"Thanks for the ride," I said, giving him a sly smile. "I'll see you at school."

25

"So . . . ," Britt said.

"So what?" I snapped, looking away so she wouldn't see the color on my face.

"How'd it go?"

"Get a life, Britt."

"Did he ask you out?" she asked.

"Shut up!"

"Are you going to tell me or am I going to have to hit up the text chain?"

"What is the text chain?" I asked.

Britt rolled her eyes.

"Don't you know anything? A text chain is when I text Cassidy who will text Monica who is Kevin's sister Rebecca's best friend. Monica will text Rebecca and she'll force Kevin to tell her everything. Believe me, she has her ways. Everything. And then it will all work its way back up to me."

"Full of lies and misinformation," I said.

"Exactly!"

"Texting is evil, Britt. Don't you know that?"

"Are you going to tell me, or am I going to have to hit up the text chain? Your choice, Cyndie."

"God, I am so stupid!" I said in a ditzy voice, slapping my hand against the side of my head.

"What'd you do now?" Britt asked.

"It's not what I did now, it's what I did then. When you were two, Mom and Dad wanted to sell you. To the highest bidder. Or to the lowest. They didn't give a crap about the money, they just wanted to get rid of you. I was like, 'No, no not my little sister!' And they said, 'But look at her! She's a monster and it's just gonna get worse!' What a mistake I made. We should have sold you way back then. Just like they wanted to. Sold you and gotten rid of you forever. Life would be so much easier!"

I walked up the steps and gave her hair a yank.

"Dad!" Britt yelled. "Cyndie just hit me. Really hard. Like a dozen times!"

Dad poked his head around the corner as I flew on past him.

"What's gotten into her?" he asked Britt.

"She has a . . ."

"I do not!" I yelled down the stairs. Perhaps a little less convincingly this time.

26

We were back in our mini-mine, our hideout, on Mount Tom.

It was going to take a whole lot more than a few intimidating signs or threats from the principal to keep us off our mountain.

In the folk song "This Land Is Your Land" by Woody Guthrie, there is a wonderful verse that most people don't know a thing about:

As I went walking I saw a sign there
And on the sign it said: "No trespassing."
But on the other side it didn't say nothing
That side was made for you and me.

Ashley and I had definitely gone to that side.

We had been extra careful to stash our bikes where they couldn't be seen. Now that we were outlaws, fugitives from justice, criminals on the run, we felt a whole new level of excitement, with a definite dose of paranoia, as we hiked up the trail. We talked more softly, sometimes even in whispers. We listened more intently, trying to read the voices of Lady Gaga and Jay-Z and the Black Crows and all of our other animal allies for word of intruders. We continually looked on both sides of our trail for any sign that the real trespassers had been here since the last flagging.

When we came to our sacred grove we spent a little more time than usual giving She and Sugar Daddy and Bradley Beech and Sadie's Twin extra special long and hard hugs. We caressed their bark with a new intensity. A new tenderness. A new sense of urgency.

We were, after all, flag-cutting, tree-hugging, trespassing environmentalists. Yeah!

I had spent the whole walk up recounting to Ashley word for word my conversation with Kevin in the car. When I finished, Ashley made me tell it all over again.

"I was so pleased with myself!" I said. "I didn't say 's'up' once!"

"Let me get this straight," Ashley said for the fifth time. We were sitting in the mine in our usual positions on our usual cushions. I was holding a candle with one hand, watching the wax drip onto my palm, embracing the heat and the pain, and massaging Ashley's foot with the other. "Colonel Kevin . . ."

"Private Kevin," I said.

"*Private* Kevin asks you out and you say 'Damn, I was almost ready to say yes?'"

"He didn't ask me out."

"Yes he did."

"No he didn't."

"Cynthia. He said he's only going to the dance if there are hot nurses in hoop skirts to grind with! That is so an ask!" When Ashley was being super-serious, she called me by my full name, Cynthia. It was actually kind of cute, in a motherly sort of way.

"He asked if I was going. He didn't ask me *out.*"

"Oh my God, how thick are you? I know we don't have experience with this kind of thing, but you gotta be kidding me. 'I was almost ready to say yes?' 'Almost ready'?"

"It was a joke! I was joking! Anyway, the more important thing was him asking about cutting down the flags."

"Are you serious? More important than getting asked out? Nothing is more important. Not even saving Mount Tom."

"Stop it, Ashley," I said. "Anyway, do you think I did the right thing?"

"No. I don't think you did the right thing! Not at all!"

"You don't?"

"No I don't. You should have said: 'Yes, I'd love to go to the dance with you.' Lame as a Civil War pavilion is."

"Cotillion."

"Whatever. We got asked out by a former Number Two untouchable who has now miraculously, spectacularly, unbelievably risen in rank to not only a Number Four possibility but to a whole brand new previously unthinkable category, a whole new addition to our rating system, the first Number Five of our lives, an actual date. We don't say *no* to that, Cyndie. We just *don't!*"

I loved how Ashley said "we" and "our lives." It was so reassuring.

"Ashley, I'm not asking if I did the right thing about the civilian . . ."

"Cotillion."

"Whatever . . ."

"Which you did not."

"I'm asking if I did the right thing when he asked me about the flags. I mean, I didn't say anything."

"*Qui tacet consentire videtur; ubi loqui debuit ac potuit.*"

"Stop, Ashley! You're scaring me!"

"It's an old Latin proverb: 'He who is silent, when he ought to have spoken and was able to, is taken to agree.' It's what my mother says whenever I refuse to answer her annoying questions."

"Oh my God, I thought you were speaking in tongues! I thought the devil had possessed you!"

Ever since the whole flag-cutting thing I had noticed that Ashley was different. She was paying much more attention in class. She was doing her homework. She was even reading books on her own rather than trash magazines. At least part of the time. It was as if a whole new world had opened up for her and she was making up for lost time. And now here she was spouting Latin, for goodness sake! Amazing!

"So . . . I did the wrong thing?" I asked.

"I didn't say that. But when you go out with him to the gazillion . . ."

"Cotillion."

"Whatever. We're going to have to do your hair differently."

"Who said I'm going to the cotillion? He didn't even ask me." The whole Kevin thing was starting to freak me out. How was I supposed to know how to behave around a boy? With zero experience, I was totally clueless when it came to guys. Sure, I thought I had handled the car ride pretty damn well, but an actual date? That was another kettle of fish entirely.

Ashley crawled over to my cushion, put her arms around me, and snuggled close.

"Criss-cross applesauce!" I said, pouting, weakly pushing her away. For some reason I was annoyed with her.

"In your dreams!" Ashley replied.

We sat in silence for a moment, holding each other and watching the light of the candles flicker patterns across the walls of coal. Shimmery, sparkly, glimmery shadows of light that reflected all of the beauty of black coal right back at us. Beauty and the beast, all wrapped up into one neat little package.

"You really like him, don't you," Ashley said.

"Can you be totally in like with someone if you've never gone out with them?" I asked.

"I'm totally in *love* with Marc Potvin and I've never even talked to him!" Ashley said.

I laughed.

"Then I'm totally in like with him," I said.

"Totally, totally in like?"

"Totally, totally, *totally* in like."

"Cynthia!" Ashley pulled me even closer, if that was humanly possible. "You're going to the cotillion. You are definitely going to the cotillion!"

27

WE DECIDED TO FORM a club at school. Ashley argued that it was committing social suicide, but I convinced her otherwise.

"Clubs are for losers!" Ashley said. "We're just beginning our dating lives and you want to do this? Form an effin *club*? Goodbye, boyfriends. You might as well just sign us up for the nunnery. The only guy we're ever going to snag is Jesus."

But it had to be done. After all, a crusade of two is totally pathetic.

We decided to form a club with Mr. Cooper as our advisor. Every club had to have a teacher as a sponsor. It was another lame school requirement.

We hadn't asked Mr. Cooper yet. But he had to say yes. He just had to.

"We have to have a club name," Ashley said.

"Duh!" I said. "Something catchy. Something cool. Something that will get kids stoked to come to a meeting and join the Great Mount Tom Children's Crusade."

These were the possibilities we came up with:

- No BUTS (No to Blowing up Tom)
- SMUT (Save the Mountain Under Tom)
- PORN (Pupils Organized to Resist this Nonsense)

"I don't know," I said to Ashley. "Maybe we should go with something a little more normal. A little less weird. Something not quite so out there."

Eventually, after six diet cokes and two enormous bags of Cheetos, we decided on KABOOM—Kids Against Blowing Off Our Mountaintops.

We were pleased with ourselves. It was actually pretty witty.

We stayed after school on Monday to pitch our idea to Mr. Cooper.

"A club?" he said. "I thought that was social suicide?"

Ashley poked me.

"KABOOM," I said.

"KABOOM," Coop replied. "Interesting." He took out his flosser and twirled it around in his fingers. He left the comb in the top left pocket of his shirt. Ashley and I looked at each other nervously. The flosser without the comb. We couldn't quite figure out whether or not that was a good thing or a bad thing. We had yet to find a method to his madness. If there was, in fact, a method to be found.

"And you want to form this club, why again?" Mr. Cooper asked.

We had already explained what we had in mind. How we wanted to save Mount Tom. How we thought that getting kids involved would be a good thing. How maybe we could make a difference.

Ashley and I had spent hours surfing the 'Net on moun-taintop removal. Now I launched into the spiel that Ashley and I had practiced fifty times the night before.

"Mountaintop removal is evil," I began. "It just is. It will destroy the mountain. Obviously. And it's a beautiful forest up there. And it'll be gone. Wiped out. Obliterated. Along with all the animals that live there. No trees. No animals. No nothing. What's our state motto again, Ashley?"

"*Montani Semper Liberi*," Ashley said, puffing out her chest.

There she went with that Latin again. I had to smile. She was so proud of herself.

"It means 'Mountaineers Are Always Free,'" I explained. "It's pretty hard to be a mountaineer, free or not, without any mountains, Mr. Cooper."

Coop let the flosser dangle in his mouth. It was just hanging there, half in and half out. He looked at Ashley in amazement.

"And you know the stream that comes down off the mountain?" I continued. "The one that joins up with the Green River? The one that runs right through our town? Right in the back of our school, for crying out loud! Once they blow up the mountain they'll dump tons of rubble and toxic waste into it. It'll be totally polluted. Heavy metals like cadmium and selenium."

"And don't forget arsenic!" Ashley shouted. "There's arsenic, too!"

Ashley and I didn't have a clue as to what exactly cadmium and selenium and arsenic were, but the Internet said they were nothing to mess with.

"Yeah," I said. "Bad stuff, Mr. Cooper. People get really sick from those things."

"Tell him about the air pollution," Ashley said. "Don't forget about the air pollution."

"Yeah," I said. "That too. While they're doing all of their evil up there, it'll pollute the air that we breathe. I mean totally screw it up. People who live around mountaintop removal sites are much more likely to get birth defects, cardiovascular and respiratory disease. They're twice as likely to get cancer. My mother died of cancer, Mr. Cooper. Believe me, it's not a pretty picture."

Mr. Cooper took the flosser out of his mouth and started furiously combing his hair. Ashley and I hardly noticed. We were on a roll.

"And it's not like we're going to get any richer," I said. "American will take the money and run. Yeah, there'll be jobs, but not for miners. Just for the blower-uppers and the truckers. Not many and not for long. And they'll leave us with a blown-up moonscape and a bunch of toxic waste that will last forever. The rich will get richer and we'll stay sick and poor!"

"And that's not even the worst of it!" Ashley said. "There's climate change! Global warming!" She was standing up and pacing the room, with a fire in her eyes.

"We've heard you go off on it, Mr. Cooper. Melting glaciers and rising sea levels and scarier storms and less food. The whole point of American blowing up the mountain is to get at the coal. They'll dig up the coal and they'll burn it to produce electricity and they'll make the planet even hotter. You know what I read, Mr. Cooper? I read that the coal they get from blowing the top off of a mountain is enough energy to last the United States for one hour! One effin hour! Is that worth it? I mean, if they were going to blow the top off of a mountain and do something good it might be one thing. But for *one hour's worth of energy* they're going to blow the top off Mount Tom and fry the planet. Fry the effin planet! Talk about a clustermuck! What could possibly be worse than that?"

Ashley collapsed on the chair next to me. She was trembling. She reached out and I held her hand.

Mr. Cooper looked stunned. Dazed and confused. We knew that he knew all of this stuff, but I don't think he had seen this coming from Ashley and me.

"But here's the good news, Mr. Cooper," I said. We were near the end, wrapping up our rant.

"There's good news?" Coop asked.

"There is. There really is. It's not all gloom and doom. It's not all hopeless. We don't have to destroy the earth to get what we want! We don't have to blow the tops off of mountains to get what we need! We just don't! There's all sorts of cool ways to make electricity that won't screw over the planet!"

"Tell him about wind!" Ashley said, popping out of her chair again.

"Like wind energy. Windmills make electricity, Mr. Cooper! There are big ones going up everywhere! They're putting them out in the ocean and on people's farms and all sorts of places!"

"And solar," Ashley said. "Don't forget about solar!"

"And solar!" I said. "We can make electricity from the sun! We could put up solar panels at school and make our own electricity! Think of it, Mr. Cooper! I mean, which would you rather have? A blown-up moonscape of a mountain or a bunch of solar thingies on the roof? Is that awesome or what?"

"Super-awesome!" Ashley said. "And here's the best news of all, Mr. Cooper!"

"There's even better news?" Coop asked.

"There is!" Ashley said. "Just think of it, Coop—I mean Mr. Cooper: you could be part of something big here. You can be part of something huge. You can be . . ."

"The club advisor!" we both shouted out.

"The club advisor?" Mr. Cooper asked.

"Exactly!"

Mr. Cooper went all quiet on us. He bowed his head and he rubbed his eyes and he took long, deep breaths. He had forgotten about the comb and it was now dangling from the top of his head, twisted around one of his gray hairs, just hanging there. He looked ridiculous, but we didn't care.

"KABOOM?" he asked.

"KABOOM," I replied. "You don't have to do anything. Like extra work. We'll do it all. Seriously. You just have to let us use your room and, like, I don't know, give us the okay and all. It'll be fun."

"KABOOM," Mr. Cooper said again. "And it will be fun?"

"Super-fun!" Ashley said. "And we'll clean up after ourselves."

"Unlike the mine owners," I said.

"We really will. We promise!"

"God, as if I'm not in enough trouble with the administration," he mumbled. "And now I'm going to be the advisor to an anti-coal club in a coal-mining town? That's going to go down really well."

"You mean you'll do it?" Ashley and I both shouted out at the same time.

"Girls, do you know what John Muir once said?"

John Muir was Mr. Cooper's favorite dead environmentalist. His go-to guy.

"No," we replied. "What did John Muir say?"

Mr. Cooper rose up on his tiptoes, plucked the comb from his hair and flung it into the trash can. "John Muir said, 'God has cared for these trees, saved them from drought, disease, avalanches, and a thousand straining, leveling tempests and floods; but he cannot save them from fools!'" Mr. Cooper's voice boomed and he pounded the desk with his fist.

Still holding hands, Ashley and I waited for the punch line.

"And you know what I say?" Mr. Cooper asked, his voice rolling like thunder. "God may not be able to save the trees but you two girls just might. God only knows, but you girls just might."

We sprang out of our seats and gave Mr. Cooper a great big tree-hugging hug.

KABOOM!

28

"You're doing what?" Auntie Sadie asked, putting down her hoe and giving Ashley and me the evil eye.

"We're starting a club at school," I said. "KABOOM. Kids Against Blowing Off Our Mountaintops."

"I thought forming a club was social suicide?" Sadie asked.

We were over at Auntie Sadie's helping her in her garden, and she was in a foul mood. It was the usual weather, hot and humid, and Auntie Sadie had turned into one massive dripping ball of sweat. I had mistaken her fall peas for weeds and had hoed the hell out of them. Ashley had forgotten to latch the goat gate closed and Sadie's goats had gotten loose and wreaked havoc on her fall flowers. One goat had ripped one of Auntie Sadie's bras off her clothesline, snuggled in on top of the winter squash, and was happily munching away on the triple-D cups.

Sadie was the one who put the bop in the wopopaloobops. Her boobs made even Ashley's seem concave. Sadie's bra was bigger than the effin goat, which had refused to turn it loose even after Sadie had hit it in the head with her hoe. And while she was herding it back into its pen, another goat grabbed on to the bra's other cup and now they were having a spirited tug-of-war. All of the other goats had stopped grazing to watch.

Ashley and I laughed so hard that Ashley peed in her shorts.

Not surprisingly, none of this had gone down well with Auntie Sadie.

When Sadie gave you the evil eye you knew it. It was scary. Beyond scary. The lazy left eye went partly closed and sort of shriveled up and quivered, while the right got bigger and bigger until it seemed to migrate into the center of her head, cyclops-like. Now it was staring, unblinking, bearing down right on the two of us.

"What?" I said. "What's wrong? I told you already, I'm sorry about the peas."

"And I'll buy you a new bra," Ashley said. As if that was going to happen. I could just see Ashley going into Macon's Clothing store and custom-ordering a triple-D bra. She'd have to get a shopping cart just to haul it out of there. "I swear, it's for my friend's auntie," she'd say, to the guffaws from the person at the counter. "Yeah, right," they'd snicker back. And then Ashley would go off and klonk them on the head with her purse and all hell would break loose.

"KABOOM," Sadie said.

"Yeah. Don't you think it's a good name? Sort of like the sound it makes when they blow up mountains. Get it?"

"No," Sadie said. "I don't get it. How many times have I told you girls: leave it alone. Coal is the life blood of this town and you know it. Take away the coal and what do we have. Huh? Tell me. What do we have?"

"A mountain?" I said.

"Clean air?" Ashley said.

"Clean water?"

"Healthy people?"

Sadie waved her hoe at us menacingly. She cut quite the figure. A 300-pound, sweat-dripping, red-faced, hoe-twirling cyclops. If some tourists from Washington, D.C., had come driving by at that very moment, they would have U-turned and high-tailed it back across the state line muttering something about inbreeding and the need for forced sterilization.

"I thought you said there was nothing moral about coal?" I told her, reminding her of her story about Bill Mayrose and the mascot scam.

"Moral or not, healthy or not, a working miner is a working man!" Sadie yelled. "A man with a job. A man who can put food on his table. Have you thought about that?"

One look at Sadie and you knew certain people should put a little less food on their table.

"Okay," I said. "I get it. There are jobs when they cut down the trees and blow up the mountain and haul the coal away. I get it, Sadie, I really do.

"But what happens after that? What happens when it's all over? We're left with a moonscape instead of a mountain. We're left with a river unsafe to even look at let alone drink from. We're left living in a town that nobody wants to live in, let alone visit. I thought we were 'Wild Wonderful West

Virginia,' like all the fancy brochures say. I thought we were supposed to become the tourist destination of the nation? Yeah, right, as if that's going to happen. People won't come here to see or to do, Sadie—they'll come here only to see what not to do."

"It's a cruel world, girls," Auntie Sadie said. "Best to face the facts and accept it. Let sleeping dogs lie. You're girls. You're fifteen. There's nothing you can do about it, so there's no use trying. Like it or not, it's a cruel, cruel world."

"It's a beautiful world, Auntie Sadie," I said, my voice rising in intensity. "It's a beautiful, beautiful world. And Ashley and I are going to do everything we can to keep it that way!"

I was facing off with Sadie, both of us with hoes in our hands. Even the two goats had put their tug-of-war on pause and were huddled by the fence, their attention turned expectantly toward us. If this spiraled down into a hillbilly girls' wrestling match then I was sure to get crushed. Literally.

I had never spoken to Auntie Sadie like this. I had never spoken to anyone like this. Except to Britt, of course, but that didn't exactly count.

"Put the hoes down and no one gets hurt!" Ashley said.

Thank God for Ashley. If I had had to stare down that cyclops eye for one more millisecond I was going to lose it.

Relieved, I turned away.

The goat spectators had lost their interest and gone back to grazing. The bra tug-of-war was over. Both sides had won. The bra had snapped in two and both goats were cheerfully munching away, each with a cup of its own. There had been no need to fight over it. There was enough of that bra to keep the whole herd happy for a week.

"Mr. Cooper's going to be the club advisor," I said.

Sadie put the hoe down and ran her fingers through her hair. Her face had morphed back into two eyes. Thank God. The cyclops thing was a bit too much.

"What?" she said. "Come again?"

"Mr. Cooper. The science teacher. He's going to be our advisor. The Big KABOOM."

Sadie collapsed into a chair in the shade and began furiously fanning herself. She reached into her purse and brought out a mirror and lipstick and began beautifying.

"Mr. Cooper," she said. "Mr. Cooper. Well, loddy-doddy. Imagine that." Lipstick done, she reached back into her purse and brought out a hair brush, took the sun hat off her head, and began even more grooming.

"Do you think he needs an assistant?" she asked. "You know, someone to bring snacks to meetings and all? You girls are going to have your work cut out for you." Sadie opened yet another bag of Cheetos.

"It takes fuel to function, girls."

She started fanning herself in even more of a frenzy.

"My goodness," Sadie said. "Is it me or has it just gotten much hotter out here?"

Ashley and I looked at each other in amazement.

•

"I can't believe it," Ashley said. We were riding our bikes home, relieved to feel the breeze in our faces. "Sadie has the hots for Coop."

"Stop it, Ashley," I said.

"Who would have thought?" Ashley continued. "Sadie and Mr. Cooper. Imagine that!"

"No thank you," I said, stifling the gag reflex.

"I mean, oh my God! What if it all works out? What if they hook up? What if they have sex?"

My bike swerved and I almost ran off the road.

"Seriously, Ashley! I'm begging you! For the love of Tom, no more!"

"What position do you think they'd use? Her on top could kill him!"

"That would be horrible!" I said, desperately trying to banish the image from my head.

"Damn right it would be horrible. Worse than horrible! We'd lose the battle. We'd lose everything. If they did the dirty? If they sealed the deal? That beast with two backs would move mountains all right! It would cause an effin earthquake! It would blow the top off Tom! *KABOOM!* Right then and there! No need for dynamite. One shaboink from the two of them, even a bump-nasty quickie and Tom is history!"

I shifted gears and upped my speed and raced ahead to get out of earshot.

29

"I SUGGEST," Mr. Cooper said, looking straight at us, "that you stick with the legal."

We were sitting in Coop's room after school, planning the first meeting of KABOOM for Thursday.

"What are you talking about?" I asked, trying my best to avoid eye contact with Ashley.

Mr. Cooper's eyebrows arched upwards.

"What you two do on your own time is none of my business," he said. "And think carefully, very carefully, about what you choose to divulge to me about those activities. Perhaps the classic 'don't ask, don't tell' strategy might work the best here."

Ashley and I looked at the floor.

"But what goes on in this club of yours must and will remain legal. Do you understand me, girls? Do I make myself perfectly clear?"

We looked at each other and nodded our heads.

"As long as that's settled I have your backs," Coop continued. "I trust you girls to do the right thing. You're smart, you're courageous, and your hearts are in the right place."

I looked over at Ashley and she was beaming. No teacher had ever called her smart before.

"KABOOM is yours," he said. "You can come to me for advice, encouragement, support, whatever. But the club is yours."

Ashley scooted her chair closer to mine.

"You know this is not going to be an easy sell," he said.

We nodded.

"I don't want you to be disappointed at the turnout. It may be a club of two."

"You mean three," I said.

Mr. Cooper smiled.

"You're up against a formidable foe. American's got the odds stacked against you. It's a David versus Goliath thing."

"Yeah," Ashley said. "And David won."

Latin. History. Now Bible trivia? There was nothing out of reach for Ashley's intellect.

Mr. Cooper took out his flosser, twirled it around in his fingers, thought for a moment, and then put it back into his shirt pocket.

"I'll be in the teacher's room if you need me," he said. "Knock on the door when you're done."

•

We had gotten a stash of poster board and markers from the art room to make signs for the meeting.

Ms. Fogg-Willits, the art teacher, was another exception to the "Teachers as Nazis" rule. She was young and pretty and fresh out of college. She hadn't had the time to get jaded and cynical about what artistic morons most of us were. She would jabber nonstop about the "intensity of color" and "the need to blend light and shadow" and how Renoir and Monet and van Gogh were to be worshipped as art gods. No one ever had a clue as to what she was talking about but it was a fun class, and on rare occasions I even brought home something actually worth taping to the refrigerator.

"I just think it's a terrible thing how they want to take the top off that mountain!" Ms. Fogg-Willits told us. "Absolutely terrible. David Hunter Strother would roll over in his grave, poor thing, if he knew what was going on. You take all of the art supplies you need, girls. And you come back anytime for more. My door is always open."

"Who's David Hunter Bother?" I asked Ashley.

"Strother," Ashley said. "Some 1800s illustrator dude. Born across the valley in Martinsburg. I guess he was pretty famous back in the day. Maybe he painted a picture of Mount Tom or something."

Like I told you: Ashley knew everything.

We were going to hang the posters that we made around school to advertise our first meeting. Ashley had drawn a first draft similar to the T-shirt design she had made last spring for the mascot audition. The one with the hillbilly coal miner holding a jug of whiskey.

"That's so overplayed!" I said. "Why not take out the jug and have him smoking crystal meth instead? Much more up-to-date."

"You don't like it?" Ashley said. "You don't think it's a good idea?"

"I like it," I said. "I'm all for stupid West Virginia stereotypes. But it's been done. Maybe we should try for something else? Anyway, the hillbilly looks like he's got a hard-on. And it seems as though he's humping the mountain, not hugging it."

"Details, details!" Ashley said, erasing away.

Eventually we settled on a picture we both liked: still a hillbilly hugging Mount Tom, but Tom didn't look like just a mountain, it looked like the whole earth. Written on the side of the earth-mountain was "Mount Tom." The hugging hillbilly's T-shirt said "Save the Endangered Hillbilly."

Underneath the picture it read:

KABOOM!
Kids Against Blowing Off Our Mountaintops

FIRST MEETING: THURSDAY AT 2:45 ROOM 205
SAVE MOUNT TOM!
SAY NO TO MOUNTAINTOP REMOVAL!

I did the writing. Ashley did the drawing. In an hour and a half we had made six beautiful posters and hung them around the school, one of them conspicuously close to Kevin Malloy's and Marc Potvin's lockers.

We were psyched, ready to roll.

Game on!

30

WEDNESDAY AFTERNOON, Ashley and I were in the middle of science class doing an experiment to see if planarian, a type of flatworm, would move away from light. We couldn't for the life of us figure out why we should actually give a crap, but it was Mr. Cooper's class so we were doing our best to pretend that we actually cared.

Suddenly the classroom phone rang. Mr. Cooper answered.

"Cynthia," he said. "Ashley. To the principal's office. Now."

Mr. Cooper gave us the look as we silently filed out of his classroom.

"Shit!" Ashley whispered, clutching my arm as we waited outside Principal Miller's door.

"Double shit!" I whispered back.

"Do you think he knows about the flags? Do you think he somehow found out? We're screwed, Cyndie. We're totally screwed!"

If there was one way to get the principal's attention in our school it was vandalism. Principal Miller hated it. He hated it with a passion. A year ago kids had broken into the school one weekend and spray-painted lockers and his office door with dirty words. Ever since then he had had it in for vandals. You could come to school loaded, curse out a teacher, or even punch another student now and then and just get a few weeks of detention. But woe to those who vandalized! If capital punishment were legal at Greenfield High School, vandals would have their heads chopped off. Miller would be judge, jury, and executioner all rolled into one. Down would come the guillotine: chop, chop, chop!

Hence the principle's Sermon on the Mount about the flag incident.

We already knew that Miller was not on our side on Mount Tom.

"Coal keeps the lights on!" read the bumper sticker on his car.

"Got a job? Thank a miner!" was proudly displayed on the door of his office.

He was the lead singer in the coal choir. Two years earlier, American had donated money to buy a new scoreboard for the football stadium. A year later they outfitted one of the computer labs with new Macs.

Miller was their lap dog. American would throw and he'd fetch. They'd say the word and he'd sit, shake, and roll on over.

"As much as I hate school I'm going to miss it when we're in prison!" Ashley whispered. "Do you think they'll let us room together?"

Not exactly comforting words.

After what seemed like a forever of math classes, the secretary finally ushered us into the principal's office.

Miller was clearly pissed.

"I am furious!" he thundered, his pencil-thin moustache quivering. "I will not tolerate this type of behavior in my school!"

I could feel the shudders running through Ashley.

"Vandalism is the lowest of crimes. The very lowest of the low!"

All we could do was to look down and wait for the axe to fall.

I felt sorry for my neck. It was going to miss having my head on it. And if, I wondered, I were miraculously spared the guillotine, then what would the punishment be? Suspension? Expulsion? Waterboarding? Doing time with meth heads in juvenile lockup? That would be the hell side of horrible.

Maybe we could say we thought someone was littering. That was it! That was our defense. We removed the flags from Mount Tom because it was litter. Weakest excuse ever but maybe, just maybe, it could work.

"I think, I think, I think I can explain," I managed to stammer. "There is a reason for what happened." Ashley looked up at me with terror in her eyes.

"I don't care what the reason is!" Miller boomed, banging his fist on his office desk and almost knocking his moustache off. "There is never an excuse for vandalism!"

The principal reached down under his desk. Ashley and I flinched. I thought he was reaching for an axe to behead us with.

From behind his desk he brought out the posters we had made. Four were ripped to shreds. The other two had been totally vandalized.

*Kids **For** Blowing Off Our Mountaintops*, one read.

BLOW *UP MOUNT TOM.*

*SAY **YES** TO MOUNTAINTOP REMOVAL.*

The other poster had been altered to have the hillbilly sport a massive erection with the words FUK YOU written across the top.

"I'll be honest with you," Miller said. "I was not happy when you put those posters up. Not happy at all. I think you're naïve, I think you're misguided, and I think you're just plain wrong about this issue. We all owe a tremendous amount of thanks to American for all they've done for our town and our school.

"But as unhappy as I was to see those posters go up, I was even less happy to see them come down.

"I may totally disagree with you about this issue, but, like it or not, it is my job to support your right to free expression. This is, after all, what school is all about. But vandalism! Vandalism! If I catch the people who did this . . ."

Miller's face went all squishy and he furiously licked the bottom of his 'stache. As terrified as I still was it was hard not to laugh.

"Please accept my heartfelt apologies," he said. He held out his hand and, still shaky, we both shook it.

•

"Oh my God," I said as, arm in arm, Ashley and I happily skipped down the hall back to science class. "Miller may be psycho but he's not half bad! And do the yahoos seriously not even know how to spell *fuck*? Could anyone be that stupid?"

"You got to give them credit," Ashley said, laughing. "The 'billy's boner wasn't half bad either."

31

IT HAD BEEN FOUR DAYS since Kevin had given me a ride home from the battlefield. The good thing about Kevin not being into texting was that I didn't have to stare at my phone for hours on end, checking it 500 times a day, thinking that he might just possibly text me. (I only checked my phone 200 times a day, just in case he changed his mind).

Kevin had come up to me in between classes on Monday.

"Hey," he said.

"Hey," I said.

"Have you thought about it?" he asked.

"Thought about what?" I answered, playing dumb. As if I hadn't been thinking about it for days.

"About going to the dance thing. The cotillion. I know it's a ways away. Maybe we could, you know, hang out before that. Do something together."

"Like what? Please don't tell me you want me to lose the hoop skirt, dress like a soldier and march beside you into battle?"

"You know," Kevin said. "Girls really did that."

"Did what?"

"Dressed as men and went off to fight in the Civil War."

"Seriously?"

"Seriously."

"Did any men dress in hoop skirts and stay behind to dance in cotillions?" I asked.

Just then the bell rang and we hustled back to class.

•

"What are you doing?" Ashley asked on our walk home. She stopped, grabbed me my shoulders and shook me. "Are you crazy? Are you nuts? Are you totally and completely insane? The biggest moment of your life and you ask him if he'll dress in a hoop skirt?"

"I didn't ask him that!"

"Whatever! Enough of the stalling, Cyndie! He's going to think you're not into him. He's going to think you're a weirdo! For the love of Tom, just say *yes*!"

"I was *trying* to," I pleaded.

"Don't try, do!"

"We ran out of time!"

"Lead with the yes. *Follow* with the weird shit. You're killing me here!"

Tuesday before lunch Kevin was waiting for me by my locker.

"Yes!" I said before he even had a chance to open his mouth. I had decided to take the goat by the horns and follow Ashley's advice.

"Yes to what?" Kevin asked.

"Yes to whatever you're asking me."

"Ooh-la-la! To whatever?"

"Yes to the cotillion. As long as the hoop skirt stays on I'm good to go."

"But I helped you out of it so nicely last time!" Kevin smiled that sweet smile.

I blushed.

"Promise to leave the peg leg at home?" he asked.

"I promise," I said. "But what about what's-her-name?"

"Who?"

"That girl. The one who's always all over you. Sandra Lewis."

Kevin shook his head and grimaced.

"You can't be serious," he said. "Have you ever seen her in a hoop skirt? Have you ever seen her swing a peg leg? Have you ever seen her resurrect me from the dead?"

"Come to think of it, no."

"My point exactly. Anyway, the cotillion's not for a few weeks. I'll see you before then. And when I pick you up, I'll be the one with the private's hat on."

"Good," I said. "That way I won't confuse you with my father."

Once more the bell.

•

"You're sure you said yes?" Ashley asked, holding my hand as we walked home from school.

"Absolutely positive."

Ashley gave me a monster hug. Which felt so much better than the shakedown did the day before.

"Wow!" Ashley said.

"Double wow!"

"Our first Number Five. A real date. Can you believe it!"

Ashley put her arm around me.

"Next up, Marc Potvin," I said.

Ashley sighed.

"You got an extra hoop skirt?" she asked.

32

WE REALLY DIDN'T HAVE A CLUE as to what to expect for our first KABOOM meeting. Ashley and I had made a list of which kids we were hoping would show up.

Becky: Becky's parents were hippies and she was all about Mother Nature. She was the only vegetarian we knew and the word on the street was that she was a lesbian, although no one had ever seen her with another girl. She was totally out there but had somehow worked the high school scene so that just about everyone liked her, which was practically impossible. She would bring star power to the group. Ashley had asked her to come and she had said she was all over it.

Jason: Jason was a Number Three (friend), and Ashley had threatened to beat the crap out of him if he didn't show. He was a runner on the track team so he'd bring in the jock element.

Sam: Sam was all about fish. It was always fish this and fish that. Sam really didn't seem to give a crap about anything other than fish. He had a bumper sticker on his truck that read "A bad day fishing is better than a good day doing anything else." Sam even had a fish tattooed on his right bicep. I had told him about the threats to the Green River if Mount Tom got blown sky high and he got all bent out of shape.

Frank: Frank was a Jesus Freak. He was active in the Souls' Haven Evangelical Church down on Arlington Street and was a youth leader of the God Squad. Frank was to Jesus what Sam was to fish. Frank had a bumper sticker on his truck that said "What Would Jesus Do?" Ashley had been giving Frank the hard sell about how sacred the Earth was and how pissed Jesus would be to see Mount Tom blown up. Lord only knows, if we could get God on our side we'd be totally good to go!

Piggy: That was his real name. Seriously—Piggy! Can you imagine naming your kid that? His father raised hogs and thought it a name to be proud of. And I thought my dad was weird. We both kind of preferred that Piggy wouldn't show, but he was all goth and punk, and he'd be sure to be there for anything that "stuck it to the man." Anyway, what were we gonna do? No crazies allowed? That would mean Ashley and I would have to bow out.

There were a bunch of other kids who we knew were interested but they had jobs after school. A meeting on a Thursday afternoon just wasn't going to work for them.

"Thank God we're unemployed," Ashley said.

The burning issue that Ashley and I had spent an hour on the phone the night before discussing was the boy question mark. As in Kevin Malloy and Marc Potvin.

"Ashley," I said. "Get real. Marc is the high school mascot, for crying out loud. You can't be Mister Miner and show up at an anti–mountaintop removal thing. It's just not gonna fly. They'd like fire him or something."

"Yeah, but maybe Kevin will show, and Marc's his best bud. They do everything together."

"Who said Kevin's showing?"

"He has the total hots for you. If you're there, he'll be there."

"Please. We haven't even gone out."

"That's the point. He wants to seal the deal early. Work his way into your heart. And the quickest way into a girl's heart is through the top of the mountain!"

"Ashley!" I said. "That makes as much sense as a goat wearing a bra!"

"Mark my words. He'll be there!"

•

It was Thursday at 2:40 and Ashley and I were ready.

Or not.

We'd see soon enough.

Auntie Sadie had stopped by my house before school and dropped off three enormous party-sized bags of Cheetos and some sort of bizarre dip thing that looked suspiciously like composted goat droppings dipped in mayonnaise. I dumped it down the drain as soon as she left.

"Food," Auntie Sadie had said. "The number-one rule for successful meetings." That seemed like her number-one rule for everything.

"I don't suppose," Sadie said, adjusting her bra in my mirror, "you would want me to . . ."

"No thanks," I said. Just as I had expected. She was trying to weasel her way into our meeting so she could sneak a peak at Mr. Cooper. Not on my watch.

By 2:45, those we thought would show had all sauntered on in. Becky the hippie, Jason the friend, Sam the fish, Piggy the punk, and Frank with God as his co-pilot.

Three other kids also came. Tammy and Rich were two juniors who had been going out since the second grade and were big-time outdoorsy and totally into nature. Sharon was this girl who volunteered for an animal rehabilitation center, fixing up wildlife that had been hit by cars or abandoned by their mothers or had flown into windows or gotten tangled up in power lines.

That made ten of us. Ashley and I were thrilled.

And then, trouble.

We were just about ready to get the meeting rolling when in walked the two biggest redneck yahoos in the whole school. Bert Stanmere and his clone, Michael Mead. The same ones we had pissed off in the parking lot. The same ones who had almost run us over when we were walking to school. The two of them had a combined IQ lower than the state speed limit. There was dumb. There was dumber. And then there were Bert and Michael. The very bottom of the barrel of idiots.

"Shit," Ashley muttered under her breath.

And then, to make matters even worse, if that was at all possible, in walked Jon Buntington. He was the ex-friend turned meth head who had been banished to Nebraska to get his act together and had just returned to school. Rumor had it he needed to do community service work for all the trouble he had been in. Maybe this was it.

He looked even scarier than Bert and Michael. Bigger. Stronger. With a Mohawk haircut and a wicked scar on his cheek like he had been exiled from *Survivor*.

"Double shit," I whispered back to Ashley.

The only good news was that Bert and Michael were sitting closest to the door, so to leave the meeting you had to walk right past them. Otherwise the eight other kids who had come would have fled without ever glancing back. Followed quickly by Ashley and me.

Mr. Cooper had already checked in on us and then gone home for the day. We were on our own.

I began.

"So," I said. "I'm super-excited that you all are here. As you know, American Coal Company has plans to log the top of Mount Tom and then blow it up to get at the coal. It's called mountaintop removal."

"Yeah!" Bert yelled. "Go American!"

Michael laughed and then farted really loudly. They high-fived each other.

"There are lots of reasons why mountaintop removal is really bad news," I continued, doing my best not to look at them. "Ashley and I decided to form a club to save Mount Tom. We have some ideas and we'd love to hear from all of you on things we can do."

Michael farted again.

"I've got an idea!" Bert called out.

"And what is that?" Ashley asked in a mocking kind of way. I could tell she was seething.

"Why don't the two of you mind your own damn business?" Bert said. "You don't know shit about this. The only thing you're ever going to know is how to slide down that stripper's pole just like all the other girls, shaking your booty and begging for tips, giving a little head on the side." Bert made blowjob motions with his hand and mouth while Michael laughed hysterically.

"Let the miners do what they do best and stay the fuck out of it," he continued.

"Is that *fuck* with just a 'k'?" Ashley asked, her voice rising a notch.

Bert stood up.

"Listen, bitch," he said.

"No," Ashley replied, standing up and taking a step toward him. "*You* listen, asshole."

The meeting was definitely not going as planned.

Ashley was strong as an ox. Believe me, I knew. Once, when I cracked my head in our mini-mine and was feeling rather woozy, she carried me halfway down the mountain. And once, when some drunken pervert grabbed her while we were on a school field trip to the state capital, she grabbed him back and knocked him flat on his ass.

She was a force to be reckoned with, but she had to face the facts. She was no match for these two thugs. If push came to shove, things were going to get ugly pretty quick. The rest of us were holding our breath, paralyzed with fear, glued to our seats. My inner Custard was rearing its ugly dragon head and I was totally immobilized. No one else seemed to be exactly frothing at the bit to get into it with those two.

Damn, I thought to myself. Why did I put the kibosh on Auntie Sadie coming? She would certainly be useful in a situation like this. All she'd have to do would be to go all cyclops on those two and they'd be history.

But there was Ashley, nose to nose with that bastard Bert. I had visions of her mangled on the floor, beaten to a pulp. I'd be laying flowers on her grave. Best-friendless.

Rescuers come in unlikely places.

Jon Buntington pushed back his chair, cracked his knuckles, took off his baseball cap, and stood up next to Ashley. Somehow, I got my wobbly knees to cooperate and did the same. So did the eight others.

It was turning into a Hallmark Family TV After-school Special.

"Why don't you two go back to your still and let the girls do their thing," Jon said.

"Yeah," Ashley said, taking another step towards them.

"Why don't you back off and smoke some more meth," Bert said.

Jon took a deep breath. The stint in Nebraska had changed him. I don't know what his uncle had him doing out there, hoisting hay bales or tipping over cows or something, 'cause he was one big dude.

"Leave," Jon said, fingering the scar on his face. His voice was soft but menacing. "Leave now!"

"Yeah," Ashley said, taking yet another step towards the two. "Now!"

Just then the door opened and who should parade on in but Kevin Malloy and Marc Potvin.

"Hey!" Kevin said, looking at me and smiling. "Sorry we're late. Did we miss anything?"

Bert and Michael looked at each other, spit on the floor, and left the room. Michael let go one more enormous fart. They both laughed.

"That's *Fuck You* with a *c* and a *k*!" Ashley called out, slamming the door after them.

We all sat back down.

"Well," I said. "That was interesting. Shall we begin again?"

33

"Wow!" I said.

"Double-wow!" Ashley agreed, taking my arm in hers. We were walking home after the first KABOOM meeting.

"I can't believe they showed up!"

"I know!" I said. "They are horrible and I hate them! We need a new category for boys like those. The absolute zeroes! Reserved for the ones even Satan gets annoyed with."

"Jeez, Cyndie, I wasn't talking about them! I was talking about *them*! Kevin and Marc!"

"Oh. Right. *Them*!"

Kevin and Marc! The dynamic duo! The heartthrob boys! In the flesh at our very meeting! I asked Ashley to pinch me one more time to make sure I wasn't dreaming. Who would have thought?

"Do you actually think they really and truly care about the issue, or do they just want to get into our pants?" I asked.

"Does it matter?" Ashley asked. "It's all good!"

Ashley was ecstatic that Marc had showed. The way she was practically frothing at the mouth, I was amazed she had been able to get a single coherent word out during the meeting. Marc, the school mascot, Mister Miner Man himself, taking a stand against mountaintop removal! Wow, wow, and wow again!

Ashley and I were pretty darn pleased with ourselves. Not to brag, but we had done a fab job running the meeting. Everybody had said so. After the boys in the 'hood had been banished, things had gone as smooth as the bark on Bradley Beech.

Kids were psyched. They thought our Children's Crusade was totally awesome. And they had tons more sweet ideas.

The only one who was a little weird was Piggy.

"I say we wait for the logging truck to show up, puncture the tires, smash the windshield, and then put sugar in the gas tank. That'll stop 'em. Assholes."

"Water," Jon Buntington said. Those were the first words he had spoken since shutting down the terrible twosome.

"Water? Water what?" Piggy asked.

"Water. It works better than sugar."

"I suggest," I said, "that we begin with the legal."

Ashley looked at me and grinned.

"Screw the legal," Piggy said. "We got to stick it to the man!"

Piggy had told everyone we had to "stick it to the man" about seven hundred times. He was clearly in love with that phrase. Piggy seemed to be itching for a fight, but at least it was *our* fight. I was glad he was on our side. He and Jon Buntington.

"Somebody's already done the illegal," Kevin said to Piggy, looking right at me. "And you never know, there might be time for more of that later. But for now, I agree with Cyndie. After all, she wears a hoop skirt. She knows these things."

I loved it! Kevin and I actually knew each other well enough to have inside jokes!

Other than Ashley, no one else got it but I laughed and laughed.

Anyway, here was our action plan:

Number One: Get signatures on a petition against blowing up Mount Tom. The more the better. We decided to collect signatures outside Fas Chek (the local supermarket) and the town dump. Those were the two places everyone went to. If you stood there long enough you could meet and greet every single person in Greenfield. Whenever anyone was running for office or collecting money or doing anything at all, you could find them outside Fas Chek or the dump on a Saturday.

Number Two: Write letters. To the mayor, our state representatives, our U.S. congressmen, the Environmental Protection Agency.

Ashley and I didn't have a clue about any of this. I didn't even know there was such a thing as an Environmental Protection Agency. But Becky sure seemed to.

"Wouldn't e-mails be easier?" I asked her.

"No e-mails," Becky said. "They delete them. Handwritten letters they have to open."

"Nobody sends letters," Ashley said. "I don't even know where to buy a stamp."

"That's the point," Becky said. "They get an e-mail and it ends up in the trash can. They get a letter and they're like, 'Whoa, what the heck is this?' And then they actually read it."

"That's genius," Kevin said.

"How do you know all this?" I asked.

"My uncle used to work for a congressman in Washington, D.C.," Becky said.

"Really?" I said. "That's awesome! Is he still there?"

"No," Becky replied. "He got convicted of fraud and embezzlement."

"The congressman?"

"And my uncle."

"Well," I said. "It still seems like a good idea."

"Fraud and embezzlement?" Kevin asked.

"No," I said, laughing. "Sending letters."

Number Three: Get the churches involved. Frank was all over this one.

"Pastors are well respected and listened to," Frank said. "If we get them on board it can only be helpful."

"Yeah," Kevin said. "Having God on our side can't exactly hurt."

"Maybe we could get Him to sign the petition," Ashley suggested.

"Who?" Frank asked.

"God." Ashley said

"Wow," Kevin said. "That would be awesome. Frank, how connected are you? Do you think you could hook us up with that one?"

Even Frank laughed.

Number Four: Look into permits. To blow up a mountain you needed a permit from the state—at least that's what Kevin had said he heard. It was comforting to know that you couldn't, on a whim, just willy-nilly go and blow a mountain sky-high. West Virginia had some sort of say over it.

Kevin told me more about permits when we took a Cheeto break halfway through the meeting and went outside to get some air.

"You know," he said, "if there was any historic stuff up there we could be in luck."

"What do you mean?" I asked.

"Your father told me that West Virginia has a historic preservation law. You can't just randomly go and destroy historic stuff. He thinks there might be a Civil War fortification up there or something. And some sort of cave they stored ammunition in. If there was, it could stop the project. At least for a while."

"Wait a minute," I said. "You talked to my dad?"

"Yeah," Kevin said.

"When?" I asked.

"Last night. You were at Ashley's."

"You called me or him?"

"You. I told you: I don't text. Anyway you weren't there, so I talked to him."

"And you talked about this?"

"Well, we talked about you too."

"You what? What'd you say?"

"I asked for a list of all your ex-boyfriends so I could get inside information on . . ."

"Shut up!" I punched him in the arm.

"I'm kidding," Kevin said. "All I did was ask for your measurements."

"My what?"

"Your measurements. So I can buy you a new hoop skirt. The last one suffered some serious damage after you attacked me with the peg leg. I can't be going to any cotillion with a girl who has a bent hoop in her skirt."

I laughed and punched him again as we headed back into the room to resume the meeting.

Action Plan Number Five: The Great Mount Tom Children's Crusade.

Ashley and I had done the research on this one. We had prepared a mini-presentation for the group.

"In 1963," Ashley began, "at the height of the civil rights movement, hundreds of African American schoolkids marched to the mayor's office in downtown Birmingham, Alabama, to talk to him about the evils of segregation and how it could be ended. As if that was really going to happen. Peaceful, law-abiding kids got blasted with high-pressure fire hoses, attacked by vicious police dogs, clubbed by cops, and dragged off to jail. Fortunately, this pissed off a whole lot of people. Even the president of the United States, John F. Kennedy, shit the bed on that one. Martin Luther King Jr. said that getting kids involved was one of the wisest moves he ever made. It helped pave the way for the mammoth 1963 March on Washington and the passage of the 1964 Civil Rights Act. Both were huge deals.

"In other words," Ashley said, summarizing this pivotal historical event for the group, "it rocked."

"Awesome," Piggy said. "Clubbed, hosed, bitten, and busted. I am totally down for that."

"Does our police department even own a dog?" Becky asked.

"Does our fire department even own a hose?" Kevin asked.

"Here's the point," I said, ignoring their questions. "If we did something like that, we could 'subpoena the conscience of the nation to the judgment seat of morality.'"

"Wow," Kevin said. "Did you just make that up?"

"Yeah," I answered. "And I also made up the 'I Have a Dream' speech. How about Martin Luther King Jr.?"

"And what the heck does it mean?" Sam asked.

"I think," Becky said, "it means that us kids can make a whole lot of difference."

"Yeah," Ashley added. "Maybe the whole country won't be watching, but the mining company sure will."

"And there's something about kids doing stuff that pulls on people's heart strings," I said. "If adults do it, they're like, 'Yeah, whatever.' If kids do it, they're like, 'Hmmm . . . now look at that.'"

"Count me in," Kevin said.

"Me too!" Marc added.

The rest of the group nodded.

So there we had it: five awesome ways to save Mount Tom.

Petitions, permits, pastors, letters, and the Children's Crusade.

Five awesome ways, two awesome guys, and two very scary morons.

•

"Should I have criss-cross applesauced them?" I asked Ashley, referring to the Bert and Michael drama.

"We could have taken them," Ashley said. "Both of them."

"I know we could have," I said, putting my arm through hers.

"I wasn't scared, you know," she said. "I'm not putting up with their shit."

"I know you aren't."

"I was not going to back down," Ashley said.

"You never do."

"We didn't need a guy to defend us. We could have handled them on our own."

"I know we could have," I said.

There was a long pause.

"I'm sure glad Jon Buntington was there," I said, squeezing her arm.

"Me too," Ashley said. "Me too!"

She gave my shoulder a squeeze.

"Overall, though, what'd you think?" I asked.

"I think he's totally hot!" Ashley said, starting to pant again. "And he talked to me! Did you see it? Did you? He actually talked to me!"

"I was talking about the meeting, Ashley. Not Marc!"

"Oh, that. I think it went great. Really great. We done good, girl!"

"We have," I said. "We really have."

34

"DAD," I SAID. Britt and I were sitting at the kitchen table watching him cook. "If a boy calls me, I'd really like to know about it."

Dad looked up from making dinner.

"Oh," he said. "Sorry."

"I told you," Britt said. "She has a boyfriend."

"Kevin is not a boyfriend," I said. "He's a friend who is a boy. Anyway, mind your own effin business."

"Dad!" Britt whined. "Cyndie used the F-word."

"Effin begins with *E*, not *F*, fool face!" I said, threatening her with a serving spoon.

"I always get confused," Dad said, ignoring us. "If the recipe calls for a tablespoon, which I can't seem to find, how many teaspoons would that be."

"Whoa," Britt said. "We're going upscale. Dad's using an actual recipe."

Dinner at our house was not what you would describe as a culinary event. On a good night, *bon appetit* meant unthawing a frozen pizza. By any stretch of the imagination, Dad was not a cook. Britt and I did our best, but with no mom around and a man who thought macaroni and cheese was the pinnacle of a gourmet extravaganza, meals were generally uninspired. Auntie Sadie would occasionally make an appearance, but there are only so many things you can do with Cheetos and goat-turd dressing.

"I'm going to the cotillion with Kevin Malloy," I said to Dad.

"The cotillion?" Dad said. "The Civil War dance?"

"Yeah," I said. "It's not for a few weeks."

Dad stopped cooking, put on his glasses and turned to look at me.

"How old are you again?" he asked.

"Oh my God, Dad! I'm fifteen!"

"I knew that," Dad said. "Isn't fifteen too young to date?"

"Dad!" Britt said, "I've been going out with Taylor since I was nine!"

Britt's definition of going out with someone meant sitting at the lunch table with them. We both ignored her.

"It's the cotillion, Dad. It's no big deal," I said.

"It is too a big deal," Britt said. "It's her first date. You better read her the riot act, Dad. The Three C's."

"The three what?" Dad asked.

"The Three C's. Curfews, cars, and condoms. Please don't make me do the parenting for you."

"Britt," I said. "What part of staying out of my life don't you understand?"

"I told you," Britt said. "She has a boyfriend."

"Tell me again," Dad said, turning back to his cooking.

"She has a boyfriend," Britt said.

"No," Dad said. "Tell me again how many teaspoons make a tablespoon."

•

I woke up with a start in the middle of the night, fragments of a dream still playing themselves out in my head. What had started off as totally hot, Kevin and me dressed in our Civil War garb making out in our mini-mine, had turned into a raging hell. Cannons and cave-ins and our mine collapsing.

KABOOM! The dream faded to black but the idea light-bulb brightly switched on. Epiphany time.

The mine. Our secret mine! How could I have been so dense that I didn't think of this before? That must have been what my father was speculating to Kevin about. If our mine was in fact a *historic* site, if it was part of a Civil War fortification, then Ashley and I could be holding the trump card in our back pocket. American couldn't just go and blow up historic sites to Kingdom Come without some sort of review. If we played our hand right, we just might be able to stop the whole mountaintop-removal project.

But there was a catch. This was our mine. Ours. Ashley and I had vowed never, ever to tell anyone about it. Under penalty of death, we were sworn to secrecy. It was our sacred place. Telling the world meant it wouldn't be our mine anymore. We might be able to save the mountain but we would lose our mountain.

And what if we were able to stop American from blowing up Tom with our other tactics? What if our petitions and pastors and letters and children's crusade actually did the trick? It was possible. It could happen. Then no one would have to know about the mine. It could still be Ashley's and my secret. The mine and the mountain could still be ours.

I could stay quiet, keep the historic card in my back pocket and let it go for now. See how things played out. But then again . . .

Somehow I managed to fall back asleep.

35

AFTER SCHOOL ON FRIDAY, Becky and Ashley came over to work on our Saving Mount Tom Petition. After an hour, this is what we came up with:

We the undersigned urge American Coal Company to immediately cease and desist from its plans for mountaintop removal on Mount Tom.

I loved the "cease and desist" language. It sounded so official. Becky had gotten that one from her parents.

Mountaintop removal will cause irreversible harm to the Green River, put the lives of Greenfield citizens in danger, destroy the biodiversity of one of West Virginia's most spectacular mountains, and contribute to catastrophic climate change. Mount Tom should be left alone and remain forever in its natural state.

"Is Mount Tom really one of West Virginia's most spectacular mountains?" Becky asked.

"It is to us," Ashley and I said in unison.

We were psyched. It was a great petition. Not that I knew a thing about writing one, never having even seen a petition before.

After we finished we sat around eating Cheetos and gossiping.

"You're a senior, right?" Ashley asked Becky.

"I am," Becky said.

"What do you know about Marc Potvin?"

"Get a grip, Ashley," I said. "We're trying to save the world here. Focus."

"I'm just asking," Ashley said. "We can get back to saving the world in a minute."

Becky laughed.

"I don't know," Becky said. "He seems nice. I was amazed he showed. I mean, being the mascot and all. That took balls. It's actually pretty huge that he was there. I think his father works for American."

"Shit," Ashley said.

"What?" I asked.

"What if he's a spy?"

"He's not a spy," I said.

"His father works for American. He's the Greenfield High Miner Mascot. He spells his name with a C and not a CK. Maybe he's a spy."

"Oh my God, Ashley. Don't go paranoid on us. He's not a spy."

"I'm going to call him," Ashley said. "I'm going to call him and ask him if he's a spy."

"Don't be stupid," I said. "You can't go calling someone and asking if they're a spy!"

"Why not?"

"'Cause they're not going to tell you, that's why not!"

"So you think he is one."

"Earth to Ashley: he is not a spy."

"He better not be," Ashley said. "If he is, then I swear to God I'm never talking to him again. No matter how hot he is."

"You're interested in him?" Becky asked.

"Interested!" I answered. "Obsessed is more like it!"

"Boy," Ashley said. "Who would have thought saving the world would be so much easier than finding a boyfriend?"

36

"DID HE SAY ANYTHING ABOUT ME?" Auntie Sadie said.

"Who?" I asked.

"Sammy Cooper. Did he say anything about me at your KABOOM meeting?"

"Sammy? His first name is Sammy?"

"Well, Samuel," Sadie said. "But I called him Sammy when we were dating."

I choked on the Cheetos I had been munching on, spraying them all over my top.

"What? You dated Mr. Cooper?"

"Well, we didn't actually *date* date. But I did ask him to a school dance once."

"Whoa, whoa, whoa, wait a minute," I said, trying to wrap my mind around the impossibility of this. "You were in the same grade as Mr. Cooper? Here? In Greenfield?"

"I was."

"And you asked him out? To a dance?"

"I did," Sadie said. "And I'm thinking of doing it again."

"What are you talking about?" I asked.

"The cotillion. The Civil War dance. The one in a few weeks. I'm thinking of asking him to it."

I inhaled three of the Cheetos without chewing. They shot right back out of my nose in an explosive burst of gooey orange Cheeto grossness.

"Is this a joke?" I asked, sputtering and wheezing. "Are you serious?"

"I am," Sadie said. "I'm thinking of getting back in the game. It's been years since your uncle died. I'm getting antsy. Time for this girl to strut her stuff!"

Auntie Sadie pivoted sideways, pirouetted, and admired herself in the mirror. What she could see of herself. It would take at least three wall-to-wall mirrors to capture her entire image.

"No!" I said. "No! No! No!"

"What do you mean, 'no'?" Sadie asked.

"There is no effin way you are asking Mr. Cooper to the cotillion. Forget about it. Not gonna happen. No!"

"What do you mean it's not going to happen? Why are you so upset?"

"I am not upset!" I said, throwing down the bag of Cheetos, scattering them all over the floor. "You're just not going to the dance. No way, no how!"

"And why is that?" Sadie asked.

"Because Kevin Malloy asked me to the dance, that's why."

"Lovely!" Auntie Sadie said. "We could double date!"

•

"What's up?" I asked Dad. It was later in the day and he was standing at the sink, staring into space.

"What do you mean?" Dad said.

"You look like you're off in la-la land."

"Just thinking," Dad said.

"About what?" I asked.

Dad turned and sat down at the kitchen table and began fiddling with the buttons on his shirt. He looked a little awkward and uncomfortable.

"It's been a long time since your mother died," he said. "Ten years. How would you feel about me going out with someone?"

"Like on a date?" I asked.

"Well, I don't know. Yes. I guess you could call it that. A date."

"With who?" I asked.

"You know Mrs. Yabonowitz? Ilene? She was the husband of Sid who did the reenactments with me?"

"The man who died of cancer a few years ago?" I asked.

"Yeah. Exactly. Well, this morning she asked me out."

"That's awesome Dad," I said, giving his arm a squeeze. "Really great. I'm so happy for you. What'd you say?"

"I said I'd need to talk to my daughters first but, well, yes."

"That is so cool!" I said. "When are you going? And where?"

"It's not for a few weeks. To the cotillion. To the Civil War dance."

I put my head in my hands.

"Something the matter?" Dad asked.

"What could possibly make you think something was the matter?" I said, banging my head against the kitchen table. "I mean, joy of joys, Dad! That's the same dance Kevin and I are going to! I told you that already!"

"Oh." Dad hesitated. "Right. Is that a problem?"

"Problem? How could that possibly be a problem? We can chaperone each other, Dad! Better yet, let's go with Sammy and Sadie and make it a triple whammy. Wait a minute . . . epiphany here!" I got up on my chair, the way Mr. Cooper did in class sometimes, and whacked the side of my head. "Let's invite Britt and Taylor and it could be an eight-date!"

Dad looked confused. "If you think that it might be awkward, then . . ."

"Awkward?" I interrupted. "How could it possibly be awkward? Maybe we could get a few more friends and relatives to sign up and we could march in as an effin brigade! That would be even more romantic!"

"Actually," Dad said, "it would more likely be considered a regiment. You see, during the Civil War a *brigade* consisted of anywhere between two and six regiments, but usually they were made up of . . ."

"Oh my God, Dad!" I yelled, leaping from the chair and storming out of the kitchen.

•

"Wait a minute," Ashley said, dragging me by my arm and making me sit down on the curb next to her. "I have to catch my breath here. Tell me one more time what happened."

For the fiftieth time I explained to her the total shit-show of the cotillion chaos.

"So," Ashley said. "Let me get this straight. On your first date, on your very first date ever, at the same exact place and at the same exact time, your father, some random woman, your aunt, and our favorite teacher will also be having their first dates?"

"It might be Sadie and Coop's second date, separated by a few decades. God only knows. But basically, yes."

Ashley bit her lip. There were tears in her eyes. Her shoulders began shaking.

"Are you okay?" I asked her.

Her whole body began shaking. One big quivering mass of shake. She took a deep breath and then let loose. Not just a normal "ha, ha, ha, that is so funny" laugh but a hyena howl that shook the trees and knocked off leaves and sent birds squawking and scattering to the winds. A full-body take-down, pedal-to-the-metal, hysterical hoot and holler.

"Thanks!" I said, sulking. "So nice to have such a supportive bestie!"

Ashley laughed so hard she got the hiccups. She sat there hiccupping away, gently brushing the leaves out of my hair.

"Criss-cross applesauce!" I said.

"For the millionth time that line does not work with me," Ashley said, scooting even closer. "It never has and it never will. So drop it, girl."

Ashley put her arm around me, her body still jerking from the hiccups.

"You've got to admit," she said softly, squeezing my shoulder and leaning into me. "It's actually pretty funny. Definitely one for the ridiculous jar!"

"Shut up," I said, trying my hardest not to laugh.

37

THE AMERICAN CIVIL WAR began in 1861, when there was no state of West Virginia. Back then we were part of Virginia.

When Virginia voted to secede from the Union in 1861 and join the Confederate States of America, the western counties of the state were pissed. While there was huge support for the South, most of the folks here were just not into the secession thing. They immediately began a movement to split off from Virginia, and in 1863, at the height of the Civil War, the new state of West Virginia was admitted to the Union.

Believe it or not, the two states are still arguing over where the boundary between the two of them should be. Go figure.

West Virginia was the only state to be formed by seceding from a Confederate state. It was originally going to be called Kanawha but everyone realized what a loser name that was and they settled on West Virginia.

"What a waste!" Ashley said when I told her this story. "Think of the names they could have come up with. I mean, really, 'West Virginia'? How lame is that? Totally uninspired. After we stop them from screwing Mount Tom we should work on getting us a new name."

"That would be an excellent use of our time," I said.

"Duh," Ashley said. Then she went quiet for a moment, deep in thought. "How about Crystalmethylvania?" she asked.

"So respectful," I said.

"Or Coalorado."

"That's even better," I laughed.

"Or even Ashleyland after me. Mary got her state. Why can't I have mine?"

"That's just mean!" I said. "It would have to be Cyndieashleyland."

"No way!" Ashley said. "I thought of it first. But because I love you so much I'll settle for Ashleycyndieland."

"Done," I said.

Anyway, back to the Civil War. West Virginia, along with Maryland, Kentucky, and Missouri, was a border state. Border states were Union states that bordered Confederate ones, and, though technically part of the North, were still brutally divided between the North and the South. In those states it was total mayhem. Brother against brother, father versus son. One would be a Yankee, the other one a Rebel, and they'd shoot each other stone-dead at the drop of a hat. Blood ties be damned. It was just blood, blood, and more blood.

And so it was, a century and a half later, as word had gotten out about American's decision to blow the top off of Tom; it was fast becoming the Civil War all over again. *Mountaintop removal* were fighting words. By now everyone knew about American's plans for Mount Tom. Battle lines were being drawn. Opposing camps set up. KABOOM had fired the first shot.

A lot of people still didn't seem to give a crap, but for others, one false word and *boom*, down you went. BFF's were shouting at each other. Inseparables were splitting apart. One anti–mountaintop removal kid got sent to the principal's office and suspended for three days for popping off and punching out his Coal-Is-King best buddy. I had never realized how polarized the school was.

We had another school assembly where a representative from American showed a DVD on mountaintop removal. With American flags waving and patriotic music blaring, the video made it seem as though opposition to mountaintop removal was downright unpatriotic and un-American. Anti-corporation and anti-country. It was God, apple pie, and mountaintop removal.

Halfway through the video, someone (Piggy?) pulled a fire alarm and we got to spend the rest of the assembly standing outside in the pouring rain.

In a coal-mining town there was—surprise, surprise— obviously a ton of support for mountaintop removal. I got that. I really did. So many kids had families involved in mining, including mine. For them, mining wasn't just about jobs, the money that came with those jobs, and the life that that money could buy: a home, food on the table, hope for the future. It was about community and the sense of belonging and identity and purpose. West Virginia had a long and dignified history of mining. It was in our blood; an honorable, noble profession. Also difficult and dangerous as hell. People were proud of their past. It took a heck of a lot of courage to go down into that hole day after day to make a living. Hard-working people had been doing it for generations and our country depended on them.

But, amazingly enough, there was a whole lot of opposition as well. Kids seemed to get it. There was mining, and then there was mountaintop removal. Totally different beasts. West Virginia did not have a long and dignified history of blowing the tops off of mountains. Traditional mining employed miners. Blowing off the top of a mountain employed . . . blower-uppers. It all seemed like a sorry-ass way for the corporate greedheads to make the most money by hiring the fewest people and wreaking the most havoc.

Throw climate change into the mix, with coal as a major culprit, and it changed everything.

Kids I didn't even know were coming up to me and asking about the meeting and what was going on with Mount Tom and did I know about this group in Kentucky that was doing the same thing and had I heard about the big People's Climate March in New York City where 400,000 people rallied against climate change and, can you believe it, mountaintop removal.

Four hundred thousand people! We were not alone! There was a whole world of folks out there freaking out about the same thing!

Wow!

Of course, there was a flip side to all of this newfound fame. Kids I didn't even know were bumping my shoulder as I walked down the hall, giving me the look, flipping me the finger.

And the weirdest thing of all was this: I was no longer some ditzy sophomore whom nobody knew or cared about. I was no longer Cyndie the Invisible.

I was Cyndie the Activist.

Activist! It wasn't that long ago that I didn't know what that word even meant. And now, accidental as it was, here I was fast becoming one.

It was both exhilarating and frightening as hell.

"What's up with this?" Ashley asked. "It is so bizarre. It's like we're celebrities or something."

"Either that or child molesters," I said.

It was true. People who last week didn't even know we existed now, depending on what side of the issue they came down on, either loved us or hated us. The social suicide thing had come true for some. But it was the opposite for others.

"Great work!" some cute senior said, fist bumping me as I fumbled with the lock on my locker.

"Asshole!" some other senior said, stepping hard on my big toe. Truth be told, he was actually pretty cute, too.

Thank God for Jon Buntington. Whenever tempers were rising and fists were clenching and Ashley was about to go off and deck someone, he'd magically appear and the opposition would simply melt away.

Required community service or not, he was like The Enforcer. Our personal body guard.

"Not that we need one," Ashley said, having been saved by Jon yet again from being trounced by the Blow Up Mount Tom gang.

"Of course not," I said, clutching her arm and breathing a sigh of relief.

And then there was Kevin Malloy.

"Are you still going out with me?" Kevin asked as we stood at his locker in between classes.

"What?" I said. "What are you talking about?"

"To the cotillion. To the dance. Are you still going with me?"

"Of course I am! Why would I possibly change my mind?"

"I don't know," Kevin said, smiling. "Now that you're a celebrity and all."

"Stop it." I said.

"You know, ditch the little guy and go with the top dog."

"And that would be . . . who exactly?"

"Jon Buntington," Kevin said.

"Oh my God," I said. "That guy scares the crap out of me."

"You and me both," Kevin said.

"Thank goodness he's on our side."

"Amen to that."

"Anyway, about the cotillion," I said.

"Oh no, here it comes, I knew it. Let the axe fall!" Kevin knelt on the floor, pulled down his collar, and ceremoniously offered up his neck.

"Stop!" I said, dragging him up by his shirt. "There is a possibility for a little awkwardness."

"As in . . ."

"As in my dad, his lady friend, my aunt, and Mr. Cooper are all showing up. Can you believe it? How awkward would that be? My first date and that has to happen?"

"Oh my God!" Kevin exclaimed. "Are you serious?"

"Unfortunately, yes."

"Why unfortunate? I think it's kind of cool!"

"Kind of cool? That all of them are going to be there? What are you, insane?"

"No, no, no," Kevin said, laughing, his longish hair jiggling up and down. "Not that! I meant it's kind of cool that I'm your first."

He walked me to class and gently touched my arm as I turned into the doorway.

38

"I DON'T GET IT," Ashley said. We were back in our mini-mine on top of Mount Tom. Ashley and I had climbed up the mountain a different way this time, one that wound its way up the west rather than the east side of the mountain. It allowed us to sneak in from the rear, making it less likely for someone to see us.

We were mixing it up. Keeping the wolves off our tracks.

Near the entrance to the mine we were able to look down on our usual path. No new trees had been flagged. Nothing marked in any other way. There didn't seem to be any disturbances at all.

A lull in the storm.

"What don't you get?" I asked. She had her feet in my lap and—surprise, surprise—I was painting her toenails. It was a "Green Machine" shade that was guaranteed to have a unique splatter effect with multidimensional glitters. The color wasn't exactly my fave, but the name was awesome.

"Evil," Ashley said. "I don't *get* evil."

"You and me both," I said.

"I mean, could you imagine if your job was to blow the top off of mountains? Seriously. If your job was to push the button to blast away."

"No," I said. "I can't imagine that!"

"You'd be, like, at a party and everyone would be introducing themselves and one person would say, 'Oh, I'm a nurse, I take care of sick people,' and another person would say, 'Gee, that sounds nice, I'm a special-ed teacher, I work with some amazing children,' and then another person would say, 'I work in a grocery store, I order the food to put on your table,' and then they'd all be like, 'What do you do?' And you'd say, 'I blow the top off of mountains so they can dig stuff up to fry the planet,' and they'd say 'What? No way!' And you'd say, 'Yup,' and they'd say, 'Holy cow!' and you'd just nod your head and watch them all back off like you had the plague or something.

"I mean, how could you live with yourself? How could you wake up in the morning and look at yourself in the mirror without hurling a brick through it? Or just plain hurling?"

"I don't know," I said. "If you think about it, what choice do the button-pushers have? They must look at it as just a job. They need the paycheck and they're just clocking in and clocking out. Doing as they're told. I mean, what are they going to do? Say no and get fired? What other kind of work can you get around here? And it's not like they're the ones who made the decision to go with the blow. Somebody else is calling the shots. I think the dudes who came up with the idea are the real bastards. They're the evil-doers. The workers are just caught between a rock and a hard place."

Ashley paused for a moment and wiggled her big toe.

"Can you do that one again?" she asked. "It doesn't seem to be glittering as much as the others."

I brushed on another coat.

"Here's another thing," I continued. "I think the problem is that a shit-ton of people at that party wouldn't back away. They'd do the opposite. They'd all be like, 'Wow, that's awesome,' and then all the guys, and girls, or whoever, would want to do you because you were the one who blew the tops off of the effin mountains. It's not just the people who are thinking it up who are evil. It's the people who are letting them get away with it. And when you get right down to it, we're not exactly blame-free either. After all, who are the ones using all of the electricity from the coal-fired plant? I don't see us just saying no."

Ashley looked like she was about to cry. I put the top on the nail polish and snuggled up close. She wiggled her toes.

"I'm not sure how multidimensional they look," she said.

"I'm not sure what *multidimensional* even means," I said, blowing on her toes.

Ashley put her head on my shoulder.

"When Kevin's your boyfriend are you going to spend all of your time with him and never want to hang with me again?' she asked.

I pinched the underside of her foot.

"If, and it's a huge if, Kevin becomes my boyfriend, then I will make it clear from the get-go, that nothing, absolutely nothing, stands between me and my Ashley. And if I have to whack him again with that peg leg to get the point across, then whack him I will."

"Promise?" she said.

"Promise!" I said.

"You know what?" she said.

"What?"

"I'm glad we're doing what we're doing."

"Me too," I said.

"Even if it's not all that glittery."

"Oh, it's glittery all right," I said. "And something tells me it's going to get glitterier before it's all over."

I blew on her toes one more time. She put on her socks and shoes and we walked hand in hand down the west side of the mountain, the sun casting shadows on the oaks and the maples, and the mountain so incredibly beautiful.

39

"ARE YOU AWAKE?" I whispered to Ashley. It was three in the morning on a Friday night and she was sleeping over at my house.

"No," she said, turning over and putting a pillow over her head.

"Then how are you talking?" I asked, taking the pillow off.

"I'm sleep-talking. Leave me alone. Go back to bed."

"I'm in bed. I need to talk to you. I need to tell you my dream."

Ashley sat up, kicked the covers off, and threw her legs over the side of the bed.

"So much for my beauty sleep!" she said, yawning. "Let me pee first."

I knew I had her. Ashley loved dreams. She loved hearing my dreams and trying to interpret them. She considered herself a mini-Freudina and boasted that she could psychoanalyze with the best of them.

Over the summer we had gone online and attempted to order this herb from Peru called *Calea zacatechichi*, also known as the Dream Herb and the Leaf of God. The site promised us we could obtain "divine messages through dreaming" and experience "intense and unusually lucid dream sequences with profound meaning," which sounded totally awesome and which made Ashley bounce up and down in her chair. Halfway through ordering we left to get a snack and Britt came snooping in to spy on our 'Net surfing and ratted us out to Dad, who had a shit-fit. He assumed it was another name for crystal meth or something. The fact that you were supposed to smoke the stuff got his knickers all in a twist and, needless to say, that was the end of that. So, damn it all, we were left to dream on our own.

Occasionally though, even without the Leaf of God, I'd dream a doozy. And Ashley loved it when I did.

She came back from peeing, climbed back into bed, and got into child's pose, a yoga position we had learned in gym class. Ashley was convinced that it brought more blood to her head and made her think deeper thoughts.

"So," I began, "I was wearing my hoop skirt . . ."

"Round," Ashley said. "Symbol of fertility. Coming into womanhood."

"Shut up," I said. "Anyway, we were at a dance."

"'We' as in 'you and me'?"

"No. 'We' as in 'Kevin and me.'"

"See?" Ashley said. "There you go! Abandoning me already!"

"Ashley, relax! It's a dream, for crying out loud!"

"Meanie!"

"May I please continue?"

"Humph!"

"So. It's not the Civil War cotillion thing but the school dance. Everybody's grinding away and it's hot as hell."

"'Hot' like in 'sexually hot'?" Ashley asked. "'Hot' like in a thinkabout hot?"

"No," I said. "'Hot' as in 'temperature hot.' 'Hot' as in 'I'm burning up.'"

"Is everybody hot? Or just you."

I thought for a moment, the dream beginning to slip away even as I spoke.

"I can't remember. All I know is that I'm sweating up a storm, so I rip the fabric off, and there I am in front of everyone with only the hoop and not the skirt, and they're all laughing and pointing and I'm yelling, 'See! See! Is this what you want the world to come to? Hoops with no skirts? Is this really what you want?'"

Ashley sat up and stared at me intensely.

"Then what?" she asked.

"That's it." I said.

"What do you mean 'that's it'? What about Kevin? What did Kevin do?"

"I don't know. The dream was over. I woke up and gave you a poke."

"Oh my God," Ashley said.

"What do you think?" I asked.

"I don't know," Ashley said. "It can't be good. Hot as heck and hoops with no skirts? Sounds like the world's going to hell in a handbasket!"

"But what does it mean?"

Ashley got back into child's pose and remained in position, silent for a minute. Finally, she sat up.

"The hoop," she said, "is Mount Tom. The skirt is life on the mountain. A skirtless hoop is a lifeless Mount Tom."

"Wow!" I said, pretty impressed.

"The hoop," she said, "is Mother Earth. The hot is climate change. Global warming. A skirtless hoop is a lifeless deep-fried Mother Earth."

"Double wow!" I said. I had to admit, that was pretty inspired.

"The hoop," she continued, "is your virginity. A skirtless hoop is a deflowered virgin. The heat is your passion, your raw sensuality, your budding sexual desire, your craving to do it with Kevin Malloy!"

"Shut up!" I said, throwing the pillow at her.

Although, come to think of it . . .

•

"You know," Ashley said as we were eating breakfast the following morning. "I was thinking about this skirtless hoop thing."

"Oh no!" I said. "Here we go again. Please, not in front of Britt!'

"What?" Britt said, looking up from her *Teen Vogue* magazine. "What not in front of me?"

Ashley ignored her. "If we took a video of you grinding away with a skirtless hoop and put it on YouTube, that thing could go viral. We could get advertisers and make millions and buy Mount Tom back from American! We'd save the mountain and you'd be a fashion diva, a skirtless hoop goddess. What do you think?"

"I think you've been smoking a little too much of the Leaf of God," I said.

40

PETITION DAY! Our first big (legal) activity!

Saturday after breakfast we headed over to the dump with Kevin, Marc, Becky, and Frank to get signatures on our petition.

> *We the undersigned urge American Coal Company to immediately cease and desist from its plans for mountaintop removal on Mount Tom. Mountaintop removal will cause irreversible harm to the Green River, put the lives of Greenfield citizens in danger, destroy the biodiversity of one of West Virginia's most spectacular mountains, and contribute to catastrophic climate change. Mount Tom should be left alone and remain forever in its natural state.*

Tammy, Rich, Sharon, and Piggy were over at Fas Chek doing the same thing. Jason ran track and had an away meet, and Sam was off fishing somewhere. It was unclear what the heck Jon Buntington was up to, but Ashley and I were way too intimidated by him to ask.

Ashley was ecstatic that Marc Potvin was going to be there. She spent an hour and a half doing her hair and choosing her outfit.

"Earth to Ashley!" I said. "We're going to the dump. It stinks. There's shit everywhere. Literally shit, like dirty-diaper shit. I'm afraid your sexy shampoo smell is going to get a little lost in the sauce. It'll be more like shampoop!"

"No way!" Ashley said, rearranging the angle of her bob for the fiftieth time. "Mine has a calming mix of twenty-five pure flower and plant essences. It's infused with an original aroma. Guaranteed to get the guys flocking to my hair."

"Great, Ashley. That's just what we want. All the old perverts in town shuffling on over to stick their snotty noses into your hair."

"Sign first, sniff after," Ashley said. "It's my secret plan. We'll have the petition pages filled with signatures in no time. Anyway, I don't see you skimping on the perfume. And when was the last time you actually wore a hoopless skirt?"

It was true. The fact that Kevin was picking us up had ratcheted up my heart rate by more than a few beats.

"This isn't a date, right?" Kevin had asked, when we made our made plans for petitioning. "I don't have to wear my Confederate uniform or anything, do I?"

"Oh my God, Kevin!" I said. "We're collecting signatures for the petition. It is not a date."

"Good," Kevin said. "It would be weird having our first date be at the dump."

"As if a first date at a Civil War dance isn't weird enough," I said, laughing.

"Exactly," Kevin said. "Anyway, it would be way too awkward going out with you without your entire extended family showing up to supervise."

"Shut up!" I said, punching him in the arm.

The dump opened at ten and we got there shortly after. Becky, who knew a lot about these things from her activist parents, had called Scott Adams, the town dumpmaster, and gotten permission for us to collect signatures.

It was hot. Bone-wringing hot. My armpits were already drenched from the stifling humidity. Not exactly the most attractive thing in the world.

The heat, the humidity, the sticky, gooey pavement, and the smell of incoming dump made for a less-than-romantic atmosphere, but standing next to Kevin collecting signatures was a wondrous thing.

Kevin was remarkable. He had a way about him that drew people in. He was like a dump magnet. Charming, but not annoyingly so. And he was great with the old folks, complimenting them on their hair or their ability to haul out their own trash.

"Step right up!" he'd yell when another carful pulled in. "Save Mount Tom. Save the world. Smell Ashley's hair!"

It was going great. Sure, there were grumbles here and there and we got ignored by more than a few, but there were also boatloads of people signing the petition. Even the miners. They were pissed because mountaintop removal was taking the miner out of mining. The blasters, the scooper-uppers, the trucker-awayers would all be from out of town. There weren't going to be nearly the jobs there would be if there were a traditional mine on the mountain.

"Thanks for doing this," they'd say.

"Great job."

"Good for you."

One toothless old lady came tottering up, dragging her trash bag behind her, and shouted to us, "That's right, kids. It's good to see someone getting off their asses and raising hell! Let them bastards have it! Sons of bitches!" Then she hocked a loogie, a big, ol' juicy one, right behind us, and shuffled away.

"Just think," Ashley said. "That'll be us in seventy years."

"I can't wait," I said.

Other than the shit smell, the morning was coming up peaches and cream. Frank had gotten into a long discussion with some old geezer about God's desire to save His creation, and you would have thought he was preaching the Sermon on the Mount. A bunch of other folks had clustered around to listen. Becky was nothing short of inspirational in her Save the Mountain pitch, plus she had the flirt gene and drew the old folks in like flies on garbage. Ash was grinning from ear to ear while continuing to flick her hair in the hopes of sending the twenty-five-flower-and-plant-scented wafts Marc's way. Kevin and I stuck together and were reeling the dump-goers in big time. Before we knew it, we had almost fourteen pages filled with signatures. Way over a hundred people.

Good times couldn't last forever. Just when we were thinking about packing it in, trouble showed up in a muscle pickup truck.

Surprise, surprise: Bert Stanmere and Michael Mead.

"And I thought dirty diapers stank!" Ashley muttered.

"Shhh . . ." I whispered. "Let's just go. The dump closes in a few minutes anyway."

"Hey!" Bert shouted, walking towards us. "Look who's here. It's my favorite dykes. The tree-hugging homos!"

"Hey!" Ashley shouted back. "I had almost forgotten the two of you lived here. Now I know where that lovely smell of shit comes from. Welcome home!"

Bert snarled and spat—spot-on, smack-dab in the very same place as the crusty old lady's.

"Stop, Ashley!" I whispered, this time a little more urgently. "Please. Let's just go."

Becky and Frank had already left and Kevin and Marc were behind the recycling bins, helping some old folks empty out their car. We were left to fend for ourselves.

"Whatcha doing, girlies?" Bert asked, making a grab for the petition. Ashley was too quick and hid it behind her back.

"Nothing that concerns you," she said. "It's paper. With words. You'd have to be able to read to understand."

"Don't fuck with me!" Bert said, spitting again.

"You've got to be kidding!" Ashley said, with an exaggerated grimace. "Anyone who would do it with you would have to be clinically insane. Or is there some dump rat here that you get it on with?" Ashley made little rat-like noises, stuck out her front teeth, and moved her hips in a humping motion.

"Bitch!" Bert yelled, reaching out to grab her arm.

Ashley twisted away and slapped him across his face. Not just a dinky, mild, tentative slap, but a full-fledged slap-whap that twisted his head and sent him reeling a couple of steps backward. A Civil War–cannonshot slap.

Kevin and Marc stopped what they were doing and came hustling over. The dumpmaster also joined us.

"Dump closes in two minutes," he said, glaring at Bert and Michael. The look he gave them made it seem as though he had made their acquaintance previously. "I suggest you finish your business and get on out of here."

Bert stood still, rubbing his face, and squinting his eyes at Ashley.

Ashley took a step towards him but I grabbed her arm and held her back.

"Thanks, kids," the dumpmaster said. "You done good. Anytime you want to come back, feel free. My dump is yours!"

"Thank you," I said. "We really appreciate it. You've been awesome."

"We'll be back, too!" Bert said, still rubbing his face. "You better believe it, bitch. We will be back!"

I took hold of Ashley and steered her away before she could go for his jugular.

•

"You guys want to grab something to eat?" Kevin asked.

"Duh!" we all said.

Ashley, Marc, Kevin, and I were headed back to town from the dump. Kevin was driving and I was riding shotgun. Even with the windows wide open, the residual dump smell, combined with Ashley's twenty-five plant essences, was still a tad overwhelming.

We parked in front of Casey's Diner, the go-to breakfast joint in town with a blueberry waffle thingamabob to die for and milkshakes the size of my thighs.

"Ashley," I said, as we had all sat down and ordered. "I love you. I really and truly do."

"I love you, too," she said.

"I honestly think that you'll be my best friend forever. I cannot imagine life without you."

"Right back at you," she said.

"But damn it if there aren't times when you could really learn to keep your mouth shut!"

"What?" she said. "And let those assholes run all over us? No effin way! I'm standing my ground!"

"I know you are," I said, stabbing a fork full of waffle and blueberries and popping it into Kevin's open mouth. We hadn't even gone on an official date and I was already feeding him! "And we have your back. You know we do. I'm just saying you don't have to go off on them the way that you do."

"That bastard Bert started it!"

"Tell the part about humping the rat again," Kevin said.

I poked Kevin with my fork.

"Stop it!" I said. "Don't encourage her!"

"I think she did the right thing," Marc said. "I mean, those guys needed a smackdown."

Ashley beamed.

"Let me channel Frank for a moment with the 'What Would Jesus Do' thing," I said. "After all, we're trying to take the moral high ground here, right? What with saving the mountain and all? Wouldn't turning the other cheek have been more appropriate?"

"I'll turn his other cheek any day!" Ashley said. "Slap it down! Boom! He won't need to shave for weeks!"

"Bastard!" Marc said, fist-bumping her.

"Asshole," Kevin said, reaching over and wiping a blueberry blob off of my chin. "Not you. Him."

"Thanks," I said. "All I'm saying is that we need to . . ."

"I know, I know," Ashley said. "Jesus, Gandhi, Martin Luther King Jr. I get it, Cyndie, I really do. It's just that I get so damn mad sometimes!"

"I know you do," I said forking another waffle bite into Kevin's mouth. He was like a baby bird. As soon as I'd pop one piece in he'd open his mouth wide and start panting for another one.

"Do you actually chew or do you just inhale?" I asked.

"Mumph!" he mumbled.

"Anyway," I continued. "If we're going to do this Children's Crusade thing we can't have you going off all the time. We just can't. Think if all the black kids had done that down in Alabama in 1963. John F. Kennedy wouldn't have turned the other cheek, he would have just turned away. Let them get what they got. Hosed and bitten and beaten and busted. Things would have turned out a lot differently. And not in a good way."

"But we need people to get mad," Marc said. "There's so much to be mad about. I mean, the damn coal company wants to come in and blow up the mountain." This spoken by the boy whose father worked for American and was the high school miner. Amazing!

"*Our* mountain," Kevin added, looking at me.

God, he was cute!

"People need to get off their asses and into the streets," Marc continued, sounding a lot like Piggy. "Mad works."

"I think Cyndie's point is that there's mad and then there's *mad*," Kevin said. "Ashley you were awesome today. You really were. Of course, if you needed backup I could easily have taken him down." Kevin rolled up his sleeve and flexed his biceps. "Boulders," he said. "Rock-solid. Feel them!"

I rolled my eyes

"But Cyndie's right," he continued. "We're on stage now. Up front and center. People are going to be watching our every move. We screw this up and the whole thing goes down. We blow our tops, they'll blow off Tom's. We're just going to have to chill."

"I'll chill after I pee," Ashley said, turning to me. "Are you coming?" We headed off to the girl's room.

"Oh my God!" Ashley said from the stall next to mine. "Did you see how he rushed to my defense? Did you see that?"

"I did," I said.

"Do you think he likes me?"

"I do. I really do. Do you still think he's a spy?"

"I couldn't care less! And Kevin! Oh my God. He can't keep his eyes off of you! And you're actually feeding him! That is so hot! Can you believe this is happening to us?"

"Pinch me again."

Ashley laughed.

"Maybe I'll ask Marc if he wants to walk me home after lunch," she said. "Is that too weird? Is that too forward?"

"No," I said. "Not at all. One bit of advice, though."

"What?" Ashley said. "Tell me."

"One smackdown is enough for the day. Unless absolutely necessary, keep your hands to yourself."

"What? That's no fun! I can think of a certain place I'd love to be putting my hands!"

"Ashley!"

"Just kidding!" Ashley said. "Not!"

41

"YOU SURE THIS WASN'T A DATE?" Kevin asked as he drove me home. Ashley and Marc had left us and walked. "I mean, we did go out to lunch and all."

"We did," I said.

"And, you know, I picked you up and now I'm dropping you off."

"You are."

"And we've been doing a lot of stuff together. You know, between the Civil War battles, the hoop-skirt take-off, hanging out between classes, KABOOM meetings, and now this whole dump and lunch thing." With the car windows wide open, Kevin's hair was blowing into his face and he kept having to flick it out of his eyes. Again, I noticed those girly-girl eyelashes, long and curly, the ones that Ashley and I could only dream of having. Lavish lashes you'd spend big bucks on in a spa trying to replicate.

"Dump and a diner!" I said. "I gotta admit, Kevin, it doesn't get much more romantic than that!"

Kevin laughed.

"Anyway, why are you so obsessed with whether or not it's a date?" I asked.

We had pulled into my driveway and parked the car. Kevin drummed his fingers on the steering wheel.

"I'm not obsessed. I'm just . . ." He drew in a deep breath and let it out slowly, continuing to drum away. Once more he flicked his hair out of his eyes. "You know when I kissed you after the flying rammer thing? Do you remember that?"

Did I remember the kiss? Was he kidding? It would be lodged in the mainframe of my brain's hall of fame for eternity!

"I have a rather vague memory of it," I answered.

"Well, I'd really like to do that again. For real this time, without an audience. Just the two of us. And if we're just friends, then I can't. I mean, we're not just friends. Well, we are, but, if it's a date, then . . ."

Kevin did the deep breath thing again and then turned and looked right at me. Not just looked but really *looked*. It wasn't the way you look at someone you know and they're interesting and all but they're not *that* interesting and you've got other things on your mind like school or your zit goatee or what's for dinner and you're listening to them but not really looking. He looked at me and it made me feel like I was the most important thing in the whole world, more important than school or dinner or the Civil War or even Mount Tom. No one had ever looked at me that way before.

I looked at him and I didn't blush. At least I think I didn't. I looked right back at him and I thought: *Wow. So this is what it feels like! So this is what all of the songs and books and movies are all about. The first look. The first real look!*

"So," I said, trying to catch my breath. "Let me get this straight. If it's a date, we get to kiss? If it's not, we don't?"

"Exactly," Kevin said. "Call me old-fashioned but that's the way I feel. Is that weird?"

"Super-weird," I said. "It makes lame sound tame."

"Thanks," Kevin said.

"You're welcome. I mean, seriously Kevin, think about it. You've put me in a bit of a pickle here, haven't you? We could call it a date, we get to kiss, but I spend the rest of my life living with the fact that my first date was at the town dump. I'd be scarred for life. That's a really tough burden to carry, you know. Or, we don't call it a date, we don't kiss, and I spend the rest of the weekend flogging myself with my peg leg cursing my stupidity, my body bruised and bloodied and battered and totally unattractive, so when I see you at school on Monday you run away shrieking and screaming and want nothing to do with me ever again and I spend my entire life sad and lonely and heartbroken, a shattered, cold, cold remnant of the totally hot sex goddess I once was."

"Crap!" Kevin said. "I hadn't thought of that. This really is a tough one."

"It is. It totally is."

"Maybe if we get your father, your sister, your auntie, and Coop out here, we could sit down and figure this whole thing out together."

"Can Ashley and Marc come too?" I asked.

"Absolutely!" Kevin said, laughing. "The more the merrier!"

"I don't know," I said. "That's sort of asking a lot of them. I mean, it could take hours to round them all up. And God only knows what Ashley and Marc are up to. Maybe, just maybe, we could work this out ourselves."

"Wait!" Kevin said stopping his drumming and reaching out to grab my hand. "I've got it!"

"What?" I said, feeling his fingers encircling mine, hardly believing this was happening.

"Compromise!" Kevin said, squeezing my hand. "We can call this something other than a 'date' and I'll bend on the first-kiss rule."

"A take-out?" I said, squeezing back.

"Too fast-foody."

"A courtship?

"Too back-in-the-day."

"A thingamabob!" I said, grabbing his other hand in mind.

"Super-strange!" Kevin cried. "But perfect! I could definitely see kissing you after a thingamabob!"

"Damn!" I said, letting go of his hands.

"What's the matter?"

"What do I do about the dump thing? I'm still stuck on that one. I'm sorry, Kevin, but I just can't have my first thingamabob be at the town dump. Call me old-fashioned but I just can't!" I was hoping I wasn't dragging out this long tease for too long. We were almost there. I could practically taste his lips on mine.

Kevin bent forward and closed his eyes. I reached over and pulled a strand of hair out of his face and rearranged it behind his ears.

Suddenly he bolted upright.

"I've got it!" he cried, once more grabbing my hands and squeezing tight.

"Tell me!" I said, squeezing back, even tighter this time.

"It's not a dump!"

"It's not?"

"No!"

"Then what is it?"

"It's a recycling station! An environmental transfer site!"

"Fantastic!" I said. "My first thingamabob at the recycling station! I am totally down with that!"

"Kissable?" Kevin asked. He had taken off his seat belt and scooted closer to me.

"Totally kissable!" I answered. Kevin turned and took me into his arms.

42

"How'd it go with Marc?" I asked Ashley. It was later that night and she was over at my house.

"Oh my God!" she said.

"Oh my God good?"

"Oh my God!" Ashley said again.

"I'm dying here Ashley. Tell me. Tell me!"

"I am in *like*. I am in total *like*!"

"What happened?"

"Well," Ashley said. "It started off a little awkward. I was demonstrating the smackdown move I made on that bastard Bert, but I accidentally let poor Marc have it across his face. I meant to hold back but, spaz that I am, that didn't exactly happen."

"I warned you!" I said.

"And then, I sorta said I had a boyfriend who went to another school, so Marc would think I was experienced and knew how to be around boys and all. But then he asked me what school and I got all tongue tied and said it wasn't really a boyfriend just some random guy off the Internet."

"Smooth move!"

"Yeah, I thought so. And then I was walking backwards so I could face to face him and he'd catch what was left of my twenty-five calming flower and plant essences, but I backed right into a stop sign and smacked my head and fell over backwards. I scratched the crap out of my knee and was bleeding all over, so we had to go to Fas Chek and get a Band-aid and it was super-embarrassing."

"Nice!" I said, trying not to laugh. "It sounds like things went really well!"

"They did, they really did!" Ashley said, taking off her shoes and socks and, as always, sticking her feet in my lap. "I thought, *Yeah, he's a guy. He'll want to walk me home just to get a closer look at my gorgeous boobs.* But he didn't even bring them up!"

"No!" I said.

"Yes! He was interested in *me.* I figured it was just because I was hot but it's not. Guys can want hot *and* smart! We can be both!"

"And you certainly showed him the smart part," I said, continuing to rub her feet.

Ashley, caught up in the throes of Marc-mania, was completely oblivious to my sarcasm.

"And you know what's weird? Really weird?"

"That your feet smell like Cheetos?" I said.

Ashley took a toe whiff. "God, they do. They really do! That is weird. But let me tell you something even weirder, and don't go off on me. I'm glad they're trying to blow the top off of Tom!"

"You're *what*?"

"I feel like a total shit saying this, but in a really selfish way I'm glad they're trying to blow up the mountain."

"You've got to be kidding me!" I angrily flipped her feet off of my lap.

"Stop!" she said, putting her feet back on me. "Listen to me. I mean, of course I feel horrible that those assholes want to blow up our mountain. I hate them. I really do. I think I hate them more than I've ever hated anyone in my life other than that creepy circus clown that was stalking us when we went to the carnival the summer before last."

I put my hands over my ears. "*Ahhh* . . ." I yelled. "Don't talk about the clown! Not the clown! Anything but the clown!"

"Sorry," Ashley said. "The point is I hate them. I hate them *almost as much* as the scary circus clown. And that says a lot. But ever since we found what they're trying to do, it's like a whole new world has opened up for us. We're like different people, Cyndie. You and me. People want to hear what we have to say. People want to do what we want to do."

"Well," I said. "*Some* people. Don't forget about Bert and Michael, the dipshit duo."

"The good people do. I mean, this is seriously awesome. Let's face it, at the start of school we weren't exactly tearing it up around here. We were like, Ashley and Cyndie who? If someone had told us then that in October we'd be leading the charge on a hot political issue and that Number Twos would be asking us out, I'd have said, 'Get off the crystal meth, dude!'"

"Marc asked you out?"

"He asked me out!"

"Oh my God!" I yelled.

"He did! He seriously did! I mean, look what's happening to us, Cyndie! We collected over a hundred signatures today. Strangers at the dump told us we were awesome. I slapped down one of the biggest shitheads in school. And to top it off, we're on the verge of crossing into Boyfriendland. Scoring Number Fives! I'm like, thank you, American! Don't hate me for it. That's just how I feel!"

"I'm past the verge," I said.

"What? Of hating me? No! You can't be."

I laughed.

"I will never, ever hate you. But I think I've crossed."

"Criss-crossed? Apple sauced?"

"No! Cross-crossed. Into Boyfriendland!"

"What?"

"He kissed me! Kevin kissed me!"

"Oh my God!" Ashley yelled, jumping up and down. "He kissed you?"

"He did!"

"Oh my God!" Ashley yelled again, leaping up on to my bed and then bouncing into my arms.

"Do you see what I mean?" she said, hugging me tight and twirling me around in circles. "Do you see what I'm saying? Thank you, American Coal Company! *Thank you!*"

43

"DID YOU SEE MY BACKPACK?" Ashley asked me at lunch. "I swear I left it right here when I went to pee."

"No," I said. "I can barely keep track of my own junk. Did you leave it in the girl's room?"

"I didn't take it in with me. I left it right here."

"I haven't seen it," I told her. Actually, I hadn't seen anything. All during lunch I had been doodling. First the word KEVIN drawn endlessly in elaborate loops, curves, spirals, and wavy lines. Then TOM, with the O in TOM becoming the Earth, or a snake chasing its tail, or the yin/yang symbol, or the peace sign. Who knew how many things you could do with the letter O. To the casual observer, it might have looked as if I were desperately torn between two boys. Lovesick and too confused to choose. As if somehow writing their names over and over would make the answer magically appear.

"Damn. Where would I have put it?" Ashley looked around the lunchroom.

Most kids had backpacks that looked pretty much the same. Boring, functional, run-of-the-mill blah backpacks. Not Ashley. Ashley had been using this hot-pink backpack ever since elementary school, with ribbons and stickers and an "I Love Justin Bieber" patch. No one else would be caught dead with a backpack like that. Ashley didn't give a flying frig.

The best thing about it was that you could spot her from a mile away with that thing on. It was like a glowing beacon, a backpack lighthouse. If you looked at it long enough you could go blind. Mr. Cooper made her hide it in the closet during class because he thought it might bring on a seizure.

"I know I had it right here," Ashley said. "Are you sure you didn't see anyone . . ." She stopped talking in midsentence and opened her mouth wide.

There was Jon Buntington, strolling down the cafeteria isle, whistling Dixie, and swinging Ashley's backpack. All eyes in the cafeteria were on him.

"This yours?" he said, sitting down next to us and flinging the pack on the table. A zipper was open and the contents spewed out. Lip balm, half opened gum, two tampons, her pack of pills, and a plastic baggie full of something.

"Dude, why do you have my backpack?" Ashley asked, hurriedly stuffing things back in. "And what the hell is this?"

She held up the baggie for Jon to look at. The rest of the cafeteria was looking just as hard.

Jon snatched it out of her hand and put it in his pocket.

"What are you doing?" Ashley asked. "What's going on?"

"The Bert and Michael show," Jon said. "Assholes."

"What are you talking about?" Ashley said.

"I saw them walk off with your backpack. They were putting shit into it. Crystal meth. That's what's in the baggie. They were setting you up. They're trying to get you busted."

Mr. Livingston, the evil math teacher, came bustling up to the table. "Jon, Cyndie, Ashley. To the principal's office. Now."

•

It was, as they say, a total shit show. Some tattletale freshman had told Mr. Livingston that Ashley had sold Jon Buntington a bag of crystal meth, and now we were seated in the principal's office being read the riot act. I could barely believe it was happening.

"Let's cut to the quick," Principal Miller asked. "Are you dealing?"

"What?" Ashley answered, rising out of her chair, steam coming out of her ears.

"Are you dealing crystal meth? Were you selling Jon crystal meth?"

"Are you kidding me?"

I was terrified that Ashley was going to go off on the principal. Take him down. Grab her backpack and start whacking him on his head, branding him for life with the "I Love Justin Bieber" insignia. I was scared to death that just when I was finally becoming girlfriend material I'd have to throw it all away and spend the rest of my life on the run with Jon Buntington and Ashley, flitting from town to town, always looking over my shoulder for the sirens and the handcuffs. The FBI's Three Most Wanted. The Justin Bieber gang.

But Jon Buntington coolly and calmly explained what went down and somehow, miraculously, Ashley kept her cool. Jon had watched Bert Stanmere and Michael Mead snatch Ashley's backpack from the cafeteria table while she was peeing and I was off in la-la land, lost in my doodles. He followed them out to the hall and watched them put a baggie in her backpack. When Bert and Michael saw Jon they dropped the pack and ran like hell. Jon came back to the cafeteria, flipped the backpack to Ash, and that's when the baggie came out.

"Why would Bert and Michael do such a thing?" the principal asked.

"Because they're out to get us," I answered. "You know how we're trying to save Mount Tom? That's what has pissed them off so much. They're beyond pissed off. They're totally nutso on the issue. They can't stand the fact that we don't want the mountain blown sky high. They'll stop at nothing to try to stop us."

"Look," Ashley said. "Bert and Michael are the ones that vandalized our KABOOM posters, the thing you got so upset over."

"How do you know that?" the Principal asked.

"Because we do," I said. "We're sure of it. Who else could possibly drop the C from the F-word. Then they crashed our meeting, talking trash. We're on the opposite sides of the mountaintop issue here. And that's okay. But it's not okay when they're playing dirty and going at it the way they are."

Boy, something had happened. Belinda the Brave had nothing on me. Even the principal didn't scare me anymore.

"And then," Ashley said, "on Saturday we were collecting signatures at the dump and they showed up again. I mean, this is a democracy. We have our rights. There we are being responsible and engaged and involved in issues the way we're supposed to, and they're trying to grab our petitions and be a bunch of big bastard bullies!"

Ashley conveniently left out the slap part.

"And now this," I said. "They're trying to get us in trouble so we'll stop doing what we're doing. But it's gonna take a heck of a lot more than those two losers to shut us down. We will not be silenced!"

"And anyway," Ashley added, "why the heck would Jon walk down the aisle flashing my backpack if we were going to do something like that? Do you really think we're that stupid? Do you really think I'd hold a bag of crystal meth up to his face for all the kids to see if I had any clue as to what was even in it? They were out to frame us!"

The principal sighed that principal kind of sigh, a prolonged *whoosh* of a sigh that seemed to indicate that he wasn't paid nearly enough to deal with this kind of bullshit. We sat in silence until Mr. Livingston came back into the office.

"Gone," he said. "Flew the coop. Can't find them anywhere."

"See?" Ashley said. "We're not lying. None of us would ever do something like this. Ever. Well, Jon did, but not anymore. Right Jon?"

Jon, who had been uncomfortably fidgeting throughout the ordeal, nodded his head.

"Back to class," the principal said. "All three of you. But I want to see you here in my office at 2:35 sharp this afternoon. Do you understand me?"

The three of us nodded.

•

"Did you really slap the principal?" Marc asked Ashley. Marc and Kevin were walking us to Miller's office after school.

"Oh my God, Marc!" Ashley said, giving him the staredown.

"I knew you didn't. But that's what kids are saying."

"The legend grows," Kevin said. "Never a dull moment with you two. Pretty soon you're going to be like goddesses. Untouchables."

Ashley looked at me with a quizzical expression on her face. I had neglected to tell her how I had divulged our boy rating system to Kevin.

"That's the last thing I want to be," I said, reaching out and holding Kevin's hand. "Well, maybe the goddess part would work."

"As Alice in Wonderland said, 'Things just get curiouser and curiouser.'" Kevin squeezed my hand.

"Welcome to Wild, Wonderland West Virginia," I added.

"Good luck," Marc said. "May the Force be with you."

Kevin leaned over, brushed back my hair, and kissed me. A wild and wonderful kiss. "We'll be here for backup. Give a shout if you need us."

"A shout," Marc added. "Not a slap."

•

"So it wasn't even crystal meth?" Kevin asked. He was driving me home after our meeting with the principal. Marc was walking Ashley home.

"No. It was baking soda, for goodness sake. Baking soda! And, get this, Bert and Michael had gotten it from the cafeteria lady. Somehow she heard what was going down and told the principal. They said it was for a science experiment."

"What a couple of yahoos."

"Totally."

"What's going to happen to them?" Kevin asked.

"I guess they were stupid enough to come back to school after fifth period and Miller dragged their sorry asses down to his office. He confronted them with our version and along with the cafeteria lady's story, and they ended up confessing."

"Morons."

"Here's the worst part. They told him it was meant as a joke. A stupid prank. Not to be taken seriously."

"And Miller believed them?"

"I don't know. He was pretty cool when he met with us. Anyway, he was pissed enough to suspend them for a day, but that's it. Just a day. Something tells me we haven't seen the last of them."

"Should I be jealous?" Kevin asked.

"Of the two of them? Totally jealous," I said. "I've always had the hots for bad boys. And I'm such a masochist. I totally love it when guys say crap about me."

Kevin laughed.

"No!" he said. "Jealous of Jon Buntington. He always seems to be riding to your rescue just in the nick of time."

I put my hand on Kevin's knee and smiled at him. "This jealousy thing rocks. It really does."

"I'm serious," Kevin said, putting his hand over mine.

"Then you're a moron," I said.

"Good," Kevin said.

"Good that you're a moron?"

"Shut up," Kevin said.

"Only if you kiss me."

Kevin pulled the car over.

"Done," he said.

44

"Cynthia," Dad said. "We have something to discuss."

I hated when Dad called me "Cynthia." When Ashley did it, it was kind of cute. When Dad did it, it meant I was in trouble. The last time he referred to me by my full name was when I had barricaded Britt in her closet for three hours because she was by far and away the most annoying person in the entire universe, and then she somehow broke free and came sobbing to Dad, telling him that she was a shattered person and scarred for life—and I got called "Cynthia."

"Britt, why don't you go upstairs and do your homework," Dad said.

"I don't have any homework," Britt said. "Anyway, I think I should be part of this."

"Part of what?" I asked.

"The discussion we're going to have about your recent behavior," Britt replied. "The incident at school today, with the principal. What happened at the dump on Saturday. You're doing it with Kevin Malloy."

"What are you talking about!" I yelled. "And how do you know all of this?"

"See?" Britt said, with that awful little smirk on her hideous dweeb face. "I told you she was doing it with him!"

"Shut *up*!" I threw a pillow from the couch at her. "Dad!"

"Britt!" Dad said. "To your room. Now!"

"You can run but you can't hide!" Britt sneered, as she ever-so-slowly inched her way out of the living room.

"Oh my God! You are such a . . ."

"Girls!" Dad said, his voice rising a notch. He waited for Britt to exit. "Cynthia, we need to talk about . . ."

"Britt, I know you're sitting at the top of the stairs!" I yelled. "Dad said go to your damn room!"

Dad let out a long sigh, similar to the sigh Principal Miller had let loose when I was in his office earlier in the day. It wasn't even dinnertime and it had already been a two-adult-sigh day.

"I'm not doing it with Kevin Malloy," I said. "Seriously, Dad, we've only had one date. What kind of a girl do you think I am?"

"You've gone on a date with him?" Dad asked.

"Well, it was more like a thingamabob."

Dad looked confused. "And where was this?"

"At the recycling station."

"At the recycling station? We have a recycling station?"

"She means the dump!" Britt yelled from the top of the stairs.

"Shut up, Britt!" I yelled back. "I'm not doing it with him, Dad. I like him. I like him a lot. But give me a little credit here."

"I saw you making out with him in the driveway after school," Britt yelled.

"*Oh my God, Britt!*" I screamed. "You're spying on me? Really? Are you serious?"

"It was impossible not to!" Britt yelled back. "I could hear the slurping noises even with the television on!"

"What did I say about watching TV after school!" Dad yelled.

"Good God, Dad, just let her come down. The whole neighborhood can hear us. And we're going to get hoarse from yelling."

Before Dad could sigh again Britt was back on the couch, wide-eyed and bushy-tailed.

"I just don't know how comfortable I am with this," Dad continued. "You're fifteen years old. Fifteen. I'm not sure that you should be making out with boys in the driveway at fifteen."

"Dad. Please. It's not *boys*. It's *a* boy. Kevin Malloy. You know him. I'm not going to do anything stupid. There have been two girls in my grade who have already dropped out this year because they're pregnant."

"Soon to be three," Britt added.

"Who else?" I asked.

"Nancy Garlock. She just found out."

"Terrific!" Dad said. "How reassuring. I feel so much better now."

"Dad!" I said. "Relax. The point is this. Number one: I am not doing it with him. Making out is not doing it. Number two: I don't plan on doing it with him anytime soon. Number three: if or when I do, you can bet I'm going to be using protection. I know how it works, Dad. I know about birth control. I'm not stupid."

"Of course you're not," Dad said. "I just worry. Boys are boys and, well, boys are . . ."

"Horny," Britt said.

I put my hands over my eyes. I could not believe I was having this conversation.

"Enough of this," I said. "On to the next subject."

"I just worry that . . ."

"I get it, Dad. I really do. If and when I decide, and it will be me not him deciding, that I am ready, I'll be careful. Can we please change the subject?"

"Why don't you just sext him?" Britt asked.

"Britt!" I said. "How do you know all of this stuff? She's the one you're going to have to worry about, Dad. Not me. Just wait till she gets her period. You'll be totally screwed then!"

Dad slumped over, put his face in his hands, and scrunched his knuckles into his eyes.

"This is, like, the most awkward conversation ever," I said, curling into the fetal position on the couch. "Can we please move on!"

"No way!" Britt said. "We're nowhere near done!"

Dad sighed yet again as he straightened back up. "I got a call from Principal Miller today. Looks like you've made some pretty nasty enemies out there. Those two boys seem like very scary individuals."

"Assholes. Bastards."

"And I also heard about what happened at the dump on Saturday."

"Wow, Dad, is there anything you don't know about me?"

"I know you care very deeply about this mountaintop removal issue, Cyndie."

Thank God he was calling me "Cyndie" again. The "Cynthia" thing was creeping me out.

"And I'm proud of you for that," he continued. "I really am. But I honestly think you need to reconsider this whole thing, given some of the recent events that have happened. I will not have you putting yourself into dangerous situations. You know and I know that there are people in this town who are not very happy with your activism. *Environmentalism* is a dirty word around here."

"Too bad *mountaintop removal* isn't."

"Well, it is what it is. Whether you like it or not."

"What are you saying, Dad? What are you telling me?"

"I'm saying that it makes sense to tone it down a little. You're fifteen. You don't need to move so quickly. Let the adults deal with this. It's a complicated issue, sweetheart."

"Oh, *nowww* I get it. Let the adults deal with it. That makes so much sense, Dad. What a relief. That is such good advice!"

Dad looked confused again.

"Well," he stammered. "I'm glad you think so." Dad was like Ashley, completely clueless when it came to sarcasm.

"I totally think so, Dad. I mean, look at the wonderful job you adults have done with this so far. You've blown the tops off of, what is it, 500 mountains? Blown them up, Dad. *KABOOM!* They're gone forever and they're not coming back. Wow! What an awesome job. And you've polluted how many rivers with toxic waste? How many new cases of cancer? Mom would be so pleased to know about that one, wouldn't she? I bet she's up in heaven right now, sitting in the cloud bleachers, yelling, 'Go, guys, go! Blow up another one for me!' You shut down drinking water for the entire state capital in Charleston for how many days when the slurry dam broke? The water is *still* probably unsafe to drink! And all of this so we can burn the effin coal to fry the planet? You're right, Dad. You are so right! I'm so happy with how you adults are running things. I really am. I'm so pumped about my future! Killer storms. Rising sea levels. Drought. Wildfires. Less food. More terrorism. And my favorite place in the whole world turned into a wasteland! Wow, Dad, thank God for the adults. You're doing such an awesome job handling the effin world the way that you are."

I had emerged from the fetal position and had been pacing the room the entire time while I went off like this. All the while, Dad had sat there in stunned silence. Even Britt was quiet.

Totally spent, I collapsed on the couch and brought my voice back to normal.

"No offense, Dad. By *adults* I didn't mean you."

"Is that a compliment?" he asked.

"Yeah," I said.

"Damn," Dad said.

"Damn what?"

"Damn it. I'm never going to be able to retire, now."

"What are talking about?" I asked.

"The way you argue I'm going to have send you to law school. That's four years of college, then three more years to get your legal degree. Think of the cost. I don't want you burdened with a huge debt, so I'll never be able to retire."

"Is that a compliment?" I asked, snuggling up next to him, putting my arms around him, and resting my head on his shoulder.

"Yeah," he said. "But I still think . . ."

"Dad," I interrupted. "I will be careful. I promise. About boys and about mountaintops. But I am going to do what I have to do. And you'll know everything that's going on because somehow, the snoopity-snoop that she is, Britt will find out and I'm sure she'll tell you."

"She's right," Britt said. "I will."

"You could tell me, too," Dad said.

"I could," I said.

"Not everything, but some of the stuff I would like to know. I really would."

"Deal. Are you ready?"

"Ready for what?" Dad asked.

"Kevin Malloy and I are getting married. I'm going to be a child bride!"

"What?" Dad leapt up.

"Chill, Dad! I'm kidding!"

Not for the last time, Dad breathed in deep and sighed even deeper.

45

FRANK'S EVANGELICAL YOUTH GROUP was having a meeting at his church on Sunday night, and Kevin and I were going to back him up. It was two weeks since the fake-crystal meth incident, and Ashley and Marc were off to the movies. Date night trumped doing God's work.

We were there to get the group's endorsement for the Save Mount Tom campaign, collect more signatures for our petition, and see if we could use the church as our staging area and starting point for the Children's Crusade.

"Do I have to behave myself in church?" Kevin asked. It was Sunday morning and I had been talking on the phone with him for two hours. We had gone miniature golfing the night before and I had walloped him. I had three holes-in-one. It was awesome.

"You better behave yourself everywhere," I told him.

"That's no fun," he said. "If I hold your hand while we're there, will they damn us to the raging fires of hell, start casting stones at our privates, and drive us out like rats from of a flooded mine onto the street?"

"They might," I said. "But I kind of doubt it. Frank has a girlfriend and I've seen him holding hands at school with her."

"But while we're there I should probably keep my tongue in my own mouth," Kevin said making slurping sounds over the phone.

"Probably a good idea," I said. "But only while we're actually in the church itself. Before and after don't hold back."

"Excellent. I'm looking forward to it."

"Me too."

"You know, Cyndie," Kevin said. "We sure go on the weirdest dates."

"They're not dates, Kevin! They're thingamabobs! Remember?"

"Oh yeah, my bad. Just imagine what it's going to be like once we really start going out!"

It wasn't hard for me to imagine at all.

•

On Sunday night the church meeting room was full with kids from middle through high school. Not just from our town but others as well. Kevin had picked me up early, and after a glorious session of oh-so-fun tongues in mouths in the church parking lot we had gone inside to meet Frank and company. There were a few awkward moments as I kept trying to strategically position my hair, with no success. There was just no way to conceal the hickey on my neck courtesy of Kevin, aka The Human Vacuum Cleaner.

Frank was a youth pastor and the designated leader of the evening Bible study group. He began the meeting with prayers and testimonials to Christ and a song about how Jesus loved us. Then we got down to business.

I had not been raised as a churchgoer. After all, attending service on Sundays got in the way of my family observing way more important things, i.e., the never-ending Civil War. As previously noted, the only church we were involved in was the Church of the Holy Reenactment, which held weekend services on Civil War battlefields.

To be honest, I hadn't ever really thought all that much about God. I could see how the idea of Him and heaven could be comforting and reassuring, but it seemed to me that so much of the hatred and war and trouble and strife in the world was over whose religion was right. Whose God was the true one. Whose faith the chosen one. If there was a God, would He really have anything to do with all of that baloney? I didn't think so. If God was love, then killing in the name of Jesus or Jehovah or Mohammad, or whomever it was you worshipped, made about as much sense as blowing up Mount Tom.

It was clear, however, that these kids were true believers and that their support of our Save Mount Tom Campaign could make a huge difference.

So there we were, sitting in church, surrounded by evangelicals and making our pleas for them to be the saviors. The saviors of Mount Tom.

Frank and Kevin and I spoke about the evils of mountaintop removal, the plans we had made, and the work we were doing. The group was totally into it. They asked good questions. We gave good answers. After an hour we were getting to the end of the meeting.

"Did you watch TV this afternoon?" I asked the group. "The discovery they made in Egypt on Mount Sinai? It's all over the news."

"What did they find?" one of the more gullible, younger kids asked.

"There were actually eleven commandments. Not ten," I said.

"Really?" the kid asked.

"Really. Evidently Moses tripped on his way down the mountain and broke the third stone tablet that the eleventh one was on. They just found it yesterday. Under some Pizza Hut or something."

"No!" the same kid said, his eyes as big as pizzas.

"Yes. And do you know what the Eleventh Commandant is?"

"What?"

"'Thou shalt not blow the tops off of mountains.' There it is. Clear as day. Written with the finger of God!"

"Wow!" the little kid said. "Awesome."

"She's joking!" Frank said, looking at me askance. Apparently this line of humor was perhaps a little over-the-top for him.

"He's right," I said. "I wish I weren't, but I am."

The kid looked disappointed.

"It should have been the tenth," Kevin added. "I mean, really. Doesn't that one say something about not coveting your neighbor's ox or donkey? I wouldn't even think that would make the top fifty."

Everybody laughed, including Frank.

"In all seriousness," I said. "Can you imagine God giving his blessing to blow the mountain sky high? All in the name of the Almighty Dollar? *Boom!* Take that, Creation!'"

"But shouldn't we just trust in God, knowing that the Earth is in His good hands?" one of the kids asked.

"Trust in God, but tether your camel," Frank replied.

"You guys are the biblical scholars," I said. "You guys are the experts. What's the Bible say about protecting creation?"

Frank opened his Bible and read aloud. "*Isaiah 11:9: They will neither harm nor destroy on all my holy mountain, for the earth will be full of the knowledge of the LORD as the waters cover the sea.*"

"Exactly," I said. "It doesn't get much clearer than that, does it? Read it again, Frank."

"*They will neither harm nor destroy on all my holy mountain.*"

"There you have it," I said. "There's not a whole lot of room for interpretation is there? God's pretty much telling it like it is. No ifs, ands, or buts. No tiny fine print at the bottom of the page stating 'Not applicable to West Virginia,' or, 'Exception granted to American Coal Company.'"

"And I don't see a sign anywhere in front of the church," Kevin said.

"A sign?" one of the kids asked. "Saying what?"

"'*God was wrong. Support mountaintop removal.*'"

Everybody laughed again.

I reached over and gave Kevin's hand a squeeze. "And Frank, doesn't the Bible go on and on about how pissed God will be if we screw the whole thing up? I mean, not in those exact words, but you get my point."

Frank opened his Bible and read again. We hadn't rehearsed beforehand but we were like a well-oiled machine. I'd talk. He'd quote. We were on a roll. There's nothing like the Bible to back you up.

"Revelation 11:18," he read. "'The nations were angry; and your wrath has come. The time has come for judging the dead, and for rewarding your servants the prophets and your saints and those who reverence your name, both small and great—and for destroying those who destroy the earth.'"

"Oh yeah!" Kevin said, pumping his fist in the air. "Payback time's a bitch, dude! What goes around comes around. *Boom!*"

I poked Kevin. "Sorry," he said.

"As Christians we're called upon to protect God's creation," Frank said, shooting Kevin a friendly scowl. Frank had a wonderful speaking voice, soothing and gentle and convincing as hell. And, to add to the package, he was eye candy, too. Not nearly as hot as Kevin but still pretty sweet. I'd even think of making an occasional appearance in church if he was the one spouting off the word of the Lord.

"We have that opportunity," Frank continued. "Right here. Right now. To be stewards of creation in our very own backyard. To protect Mount Tom and all of the critters that God has put upon it. Mount Tom is our holy mountain. At this moment, in this place, we can make a difference. We can be the word of the Lord. Let us pray together."

Everyone bowed their heads and closed their eyes while Frank did his thing and Kevin put his hand on my thigh.

46

"THAT MEETING WAS SOMETHING!" Kevin said, as we came up for air after fifteen fabulous minutes of making out. We had left the church but were still sitting in his car in the parking lot. I was snuggled up close and he had his arm around me.

"It sure was," I said. "I think it went well, don't you?"

"I think it went great! I mean, you were totally locked in. You had them eating out of the palm of your hand. It was awesome!"

"Stop," I said, snuggling closer.

"No. I'm serious. I bet most of those kids started off the meeting not giving a rat's ass about mountaintop removal. But after seeing you in action they're completely on board. I can really relate."

"What are you talking about?" I asked.

"I'm just saying I get where they're coming from. I mean, after all, that's how I got into this whole Mount Tom thing."

"By not giving a rat's ass about mountaintop removal?" I asked.

Kevin looked flustered. "No, no, no. It's not that I didn't care, it's just that, well, you know . . ."

"No," I said. "I don't know. Tell me."

"I hardly knew anything about mountaintop removal when I first met you. Just like the kids in church. And then you came along and, well . . ."

"Well what?"

"I wanted to be with you."

I should have been flattered. I should have been pumped with pride. Here I was in this fairy-tale romance, making out with a former Untouchable who tells me he joined KABOOM just to be with me! What could be more of an ego boost than that?

But for some reason I was getting super-annoyed with Kevin. I just couldn't help it. Maybe it was fallout from the meeting at the church. Maybe the whole "holier-than-thou, what would Jesus do" thing had rubbed off on me a little too much. I wanted Kevin's motives to be pure and noble, beyond reproach. I hadn't gotten into the mountaintop removal fight so I could hook up with boys! Why should he get into it just to hook up with me? It didn't seem right. It seemed cheap and shallow and stupid. I wanted everything to be perfect—and this wasn't.

"So you don't give a rat's ass about saving Mount Tom!" I told him, this new bitchy side of me rearing its ugly head.

"Of course I do!" he said.

"That's not what you're saying."

"It is what I'm saying. Because you care, I care. That's my whole point!"

"Oh, I get it," I said, scooting away from him. "You want to save Mount Tom so you can get into my pants."

"Your hoop skirt. I want to get into your hoop skirt!"

"Oh my God, Kevin. That's really lame. Sad and lame. I really thought there was more to you than that."

"Chill, Cyndie. I'm joking. It's a joke." Kevin reached out and tried to hold my hand but I folded my arms tight, locking them away.

"Criss-cross applesauce," I said.

"What?"

"Never mind. You don't get it."

"I do too get it. And anyway, who cares how I get into it as long as I'm into it? What difference does it make?"

"I care," I said. "And it does make a difference."

"Why? Why does it make a difference?"

"Remember what Frank said? '*They will neither harm nor destroy on all my holy mountain.*' Do you think Jesus was doing God's will just so he could get with Mary Magdalene?"

Kevin burst out laughing, which only served to piss me off even more.

"You can't be serious?" he said.

"Listen, Kevin. If the only reason you care about saving Mount Tom is because you want to get with me . . ."

"That is not what I said, and you know it! Don't twist my words."

"Then what are you saying?"

"I'm saying people get active in issues for different reasons. Look at Frank. He does it for God. Look at Piggy. He does it to be bad-ass and rebellious. Look at you. You do it because it's your special place and you were born with the do-good gene. I'm doing it because I'm totally into you. What's wrong with that? We're active, aren't we? Isn't that what matters?"

"So, if you go and dump me for some girl like Sandra Lewis who's onboard with the whole blowing-up-the-mountain thing, then you'll jump on her bandwagon?"

"Wait a minute," Kevin said. "Are we fighting?"

"No, we are not fighting!" I said. "You're just being an idiot!"

But we were fighting. We were. And now that we were going at it, I couldn't stop. The rational voice inside my head that was pleading for calm and sanity was being drowned out by the annoying, bitchy, whining voice that just wouldn't shut up.

Why was I acting like this? Maybe God was to blame! Maybe God really was like Santa and watched our every move and was pissed that I was making out in the church parking lot and was now punishing me by making me such a bitch. That was it! I could blame God!

"Will you chill?" Kevin said, clearly now getting annoyed with me as well. "All I'm saying, for the five millionth time, is that that's how I got into it. Because of you. It's a compliment, Cyndie. It's a total prop. And now that I'm into it I totally care. I really do."

"It doesn't sound like it."

"Get a grip, Cyndie! If you start playing gatekeeper and devising some sort of litmus test that decides who gets to be active and who doesn't based on how pure their motives are, then that's just plain stupid."

"Now you're telling me I'm stupid?"

"Oh my God! What's gotten into you? Do you have a bug up your butt or something?"

That was it. I had had enough. I opened the car door, jumped out, and slammed it shut.

I knew I was overreacting, but I felt possessed, which, coming out of church, was really weird. It was like I was having an out-of-body experience where I was floating above the church, looking down on Kevin and me in the car in the parking lot, witnessing the whole damn thing playing out it a way that was not going down well. It was like in the movies, when the silly, stupid girl has a silly, stupid hissy fit because everything wasn't going exactly the silly, stupid way she wanted it to. And you know that the end of the scene will just not be pretty.

"What are you doing?" Kevin asked.

"Leave me alone. I'm walking home."

"You can't be serious. This is ridiculous."

"Really?" I shouted. A few kids from the meeting who were hanging around the front steps of the church turned to look at us. "Really? So let me get this straight. You don't give a rat's ass about Saving Mount Tom. I've got a bug up my butt. I'm stupid. And I'm ridiculous. Is there anything else you'd like to tell me?"

Kevin looked like he was in shock. His mouth was wide open and he had that deer-in-the-headlights, what-the-hell-is-happening expression on his face.

"I'm sorry," he said. "Will you just get back in the car? Please?"

"No," I said, loud enough for the whole neighborhood to hear. "I'm going to save you the trouble of dumping me for Sandra Lewis!"

"What?" Kevin asked, putting his arms up in the air as if to surrender. "What are you talking about?"

"*I'm* dumping *you*!"

"Don't be ridiculous! You can't dump me!"

"Why not?"

"Because we haven't even gone on a date yet!"

I stamped my feet, turned my back and marched away.

•

"You did what?" Ashley asked. The first thing I had done when I got home and had finally stopped crying was to call her. She had just gotten back from the movies. I didn't even ask about her date.

"I broke up with him," I said, still choking back tears and desperately trying to catch my breath.

"You broke up with Kevin?"

"I broke up with Kevin."

"Are you kidding me? When?"

"An hour ago."

"Oh my God, that's like three days in relationship time!" After just a few dates Ashley had already become the world's foremost authority on relationships.

Through the sobs, I somehow managed to give her the lowdown on what went down.

"Are you completely insane?" she asked. "Are you totally nuts? Have you had a massive mental meltdown?"

"Ashley!" I yelled, starting to cry again. "You're supposed to take my side on this! I told you what he said about me!"

"Your side? There is no 'your side,' Cyndie. There's the right side and the stupid, ridiculous, girl-with-the-bug-up-her-butt, totally wrong side."

I tried to say something in my defense but all I could do was cry.

"Let me get this straight," Ashley went on. "He tells you how wonderful you were at the church meeting. Then he tells you you're like a magnet that draws people into the issue.

Sort of like, I don't know, a girl Jesus or something. And then finally, to top it off, he tells you that you're so awesome, that he's so into you, that now he's totally stoked about saving Mount Tom. All because of you. That he was blind and now he can see! Am I getting this right?"

Tears, tears, and more tears.

"And then," Ashley continued, "because of all of those cruel horrible things he's said, you go and dump him?"

"No!" I sobbed. "Yes! I don't know!"

"My God, Cyndie, you're acting like you've lost your mind!"

I cried some more.

"You've got to get off that high horse of yours and cut down on the holier-than-thou crap. That might play well in church but it's not gonna go down in real life. It's just not. Otherwise it's going to be you and me against the world, and the odds are already stacked against us. And can I say one more thing?"

I managed a muffled "Yes" through the tears.

"If that stupid, ridiculous girl doesn't march herself over to Kevin's house right now and beg for forgiveness, I'm going to have to go over to American Coal Company's headquarters, break in, steal a stick of dynamite, and blow that bug out of your butt myself! And that is not, I repeat, not something I am looking forward to! Do you understand me?"

"Yes, ma'am," I meekly replied.

"Now get off the phone!" Ashley yelled. "Now! Go!"

•

"Whoa, whoa, whoa," Dad called out as I tore down the stairs. "Where are you off to at this late hour, young lady?"

"She just broke up with Kevin and now she's going to make up," Britt said. When I burst out of my room I had whacked Britt in the head with the door. She had been kneeling outside listening to every word of my conversation with Ashley. I didn't even bother to give her a dirty look.

"It's Sunday night!" Dad called after me. "It's a school night!"

"Don't worry, Dad," Britt said. "She's not going far. Kevin's parked in the driveway."

•

I opened the car door, slid in next to Kevin, and rested my head on his shoulder. We were quiet for a while. Not an awkward quiet. More like a "whew, am I glad that's over" kind of quiet. A comfortable quiet. I just snuggled up close and took comfort in his breath.

"That was the worst hour of my entire life," I finally said.

"Actually, it was only 57 minutes and 23 seconds," Kevin said, putting his arm around me. "But who's counting?"

"How long were you going to sit here?" I asked.

"I don't know. Forever? Actually, I was thinking of going home and swiping my dad's boom box and bringing it back so I could blast some really lame love song over and over until all of the neighbors started screaming and you were forced to come out and make up with me."

"Just like in the movies."

"Just like in the movies," Kevin said, pulling me tighter.

"Should I go back inside so you can do it? It actually sounds pretty romantic."

"Nah. This will work. Anyway, I was yanking a blank on which song to use. I was going to go with Peter Gabriel's 'In Your Eyes' but . . ."

"Already been done."

"Exactly."

We sat in silence for another minute while he caressed my shoulder.

"I was a bitch, wasn't I," I said. "I'm sorry. I don't know what got into me."

Kevin's hands moved from my shoulder to my neck.

"You know one thing I really like about you?" he asked.

"Besides the bug up my butt?"

"Actually, I find your butt totally hot, with or without the hoop skirt on. But I could live without the bug."

"Good to know," I said.

"One thing I really like about you is how un-boring you are. You are far and away the most interesting girl I've ever met. I mean, seriously, there's never a dull moment with you. Never."

"Just stupid and ridiculous ones."

"Exactly! And you know the really good news?"

"Tell me," I said.

"Now that we've had our breakup and makeup we can be done with all of that crap. Get the drama out of the way early on before we even officially start dating. Been there, done that, good riddance. It will make things so much easier. Now we can start going out. No more thingamabobs, but actual, real dates, and not get sidetracked. It's a good thing."

"I like how you think," I said, putting my knee in his lap and my hand on his thigh. "So, just to be sure, you're not just trying to get into my hoop skirt?"

"I am not *just* trying to get into your hoop skirt," Kevin said, turning towards me and stroking my hair. "I'm trying to get into other things as well. Like saving Mount Tom. It's possible to multi-task, you know."

"It is," I agreed. "It really is." I pressed my lips up against his neck.

"And you're not going to dump me for Sandra Lewis?" I asked.

Kevin laughed and shook his head. "There's that bug again! I promise: I will never ever dump you for big-haired Sandra Lewis."

"That's not the only big things she has," I said.

"You know what they say?"

"No. What do they say?

"Quality over quantity. I like yours much better! I like everything about you much better! You promise not to leave me for Jon Buntington?"

I shuddered. We were quiet again.

"I'm so sorry I overreacted," I finally said.

"You did overreact."

"And I'm so sorry I was such a jerk."

"You weren't a jerk. You are just so into doing the right thing. I mean, it's totally awesome and all, but it can be awfully hard for us mortals to keep up with you sometimes. All of this activism stuff is totally new to me. I'm doing the best that I can. I really am. Maybe you can cut me a little bit of slack. That's all. Just a little bit." Kevin kissed both my cheeks, soft butterfly kisses.

"You know what?" I said to him.

"What?"

"I really like you."

"I know," Kevin said. "And I really like you. Really, *really* like. And, this probably sounds stupid, but, now that you're back, I could easily spend the rest of my entire life parked out here in your driveway with you."

"It does sound stupid," I said. "Stupid and wonderful!"

47

"ROAD TRIP!" Kevin yelled, leaping out of his car, picking me up, and twirling me around.

Fall wasn't just around the corner anymore. We were smack-dab in the middle of it. The oppressive summer heat was gone and the trees had changed into their fall wardrobe. Some had already stripped naked and, lucky them, snuggled into a deep sleep. The weather was perfect. Late fall in West Virginia. A great reminder of why I loved living here.

"Kevin?" Britt asked, tugging on his arm. "Can I go with you? Please? I really, really, *really* want to go? Please?"

"Shut up, Britt!" I said. "You're not going. Get out of his face and leave us alone!"

"Why can't she go?" Kevin asked. "Everyone should see this."

"Yes, yes, yes!" Britt squealed.

"Oh my God, Kevin," I said. "She's not anyone. She's my little sister!"

"I swear," Britt said, "I'll turn my back and close my eyes if the two of you want to hook up! And I won't tell Dad anything! I promise! These lips are sealed!" Britt zippered her mouth shut.

"Britt!" I yelled. "What part of *get lost* don't you understand!"

Britt went running into the house. "Dad!" she yelled, her mouth unzipped already. "Kevin said I could go! Kevin said I could go!" Britt came tearing back with her backpack and her stuffed bunny. She was twelve years old but, depending on the moment, she was twelve going on twenty or twelve going on four.

"I call shotgun!" she yelled.

"In your dreams!" I yelled back.

•

We were off to Kayford Mountain, seventy miles away. One of the many West Virginia mountains whose top had already been blown off by a coal company. We were joining a group that was taking a tour of the mountaintop removal site.

At the last KABOOM meeting we had watched YouTube videos of mountaintop removal. It was hard to watch them and think they were actually real. It was hard to watch them and not think, *Yeah, right, as if that could actually happen.* You'd look at those videos and you'd think, *No way! People wouldn't do something like that to a mountain. They just wouldn't.*

It was almost too horrible to believe.

So we decided to go and see for ourselves. Up close and personal. Take a . . .

"Road trip!" Kevin yelled again, picking me up, and hurling me upside down into the front seat while Britt, laughing and screaming, tumbled into the back.

"Bunny stays up front with us, or we ain't going nowhere!" Kevin said.

"Mister Wiggins," Britt said, giggling. "Her name is Mister Wiggins."

"Whoa, it's a chick bunny with a dude's name?" Kevin asked.

"Don't let her age fool you," I said. "She's got a twelve-year-old body but a four-year-old brain."

"The bunny's twelve years old?" Kevin asked.

"Oh my God!" I said, "I'm surrounded by morons!"

I had to admit there was something totally sweet about how Kevin dealt with my family. He was super-nice to my father and all big-brother, palsy-walsy around Britt. And it wasn't fake. It was genuine. It was who Kevin was. And, in return, they liked him. They liked him a lot. After all, what was not to like?

Depending on calculations, I had been going out with Kevin for 63 days (if you defined clubbing him with a peg leg as "going out with him"), 56 days (from the time I saved his life from the wayward rammer), or 35 days (the thingamabob at the recycling center and the oh-so-yummy first real kiss). We had gone to the movies, bowling, miniature golf, football games to see Marc the Mascot make a complete ass out of himself, walks on Mount Tom, out to eat, and lots of awesome fooling around whenever and wherever we could. We still hadn't gone dancing. The Civil War cotillion thing had been postponed to the end of November due to the fiddler in the old-time band breaking his finger.

Wonder of all wonders, Kevin was now my official boyfriend!

I loved how the word sounded. I said it over and over again in my head.

My boyfriend!

I know it sounds pathetic, but I had a permanent bruise from pinching myself so many times.

Anyway, back to the road trip.

Kevin, Britt and I swung around town to pick up Ashley and Marc (also totally a couple) and then drove over to Fas Chek to meet up and caravan with our fellow KABOOMers. Becky was driving Piggy, Frank, Tammy, and Rich. Sam was off fishing, Jason was running track, Shannon was working, and Jon Buntington was, well, who knows where.

We had asked Mr. Cooper if he wanted to come but he made up some lame excuse about needing weekend alone time away from us teenagers lest he wind up in the lunatic asylum. Anyway, he said, he had seen mountaintop removal sites before and, at his age, his heart was fragile enough as it was. One more look might just break it.

"Look at Piggy!" Ashley whispered.

We stuck our necks out of the car windows, trying not to be too obvious but gawking anyway.

"He's dressed like a human being!" I whispered back to Ashley. "What happened to the spikes in his hair?"

"Do you think he's hitting on Becky?" Ashley asked.

"I thought Becky was a lesbian?" Britt said.

"Maybe he's hitting on Frank." Ashley said.

"Frank has a girlfriend," Britt said. "It must be Becky. Look at him looking at her!"

I was rubbernecking so far into Kevin that I knocked up against the steering wheel and the car horn blared. Piggy and Becky jumped. I scrunched down behind the seat.

"Hey!" Kevin called out to Piggy. "Nice hair!"

And then off we went to Kayford Mountain.

•

Kevin had become obsessed with the old John Prine song "Paradise." It was the perfect soundtrack for a mountaintop removal road trip. After the fifth time around on his car's CD player, we were all screaming the lyrics, tragic as they were:

When I was a child my family would travel
Down to western Kentucky where my parents were born
And there's a backwards old town that's often remembered
So many times that my memories are worn.

And Daddy won't you take me back to Muhlenberg County
Down by the Green River where Paradise lay
Well, I'm sorry, my son, but you're too late in asking
Mister Peabody's coal train has hauled it away.

Of course, what's a road trip without getting totally and completely lost. We had pulled off the interstate and could not for the life of us figure out which way to go. Kevin was sure it was to the right; I was convinced it was to the left. No one in the back seat had been paying any attention at all.

"Let Mister Wiggins decide!" Britt said.

Just then we saw this old-timer walking down the road.

He was a picture-perfect hillbilly, straight out of a Saturday morning cartoon. He had his hillbilly swag on: patched overalls, crazy-ass hat, and a beard that exploded out of his face. And, for the love of God, he was carrying a jug. A jug! It was like we had gone back in time a hundred years ago to the good ol' moonshining days and here, walking among us, was the chief moonshiner himself.

Kevin stopped the car and rolled down the window. "Excuse me, sir?" he asked. "Do you know how to get to Old County Road?"

The reek of a lifetime of frequent drinking and infrequent bathing drifted into the car. I stifled back a gag.

'Billy scratched his beard, picked his nose, and thought for a moment.

"Turn your car around, take a left at that barn over there, and go three sees," he said. "At the third see take another left. One more see and that's Old County."

Kevin looked confused.

"I'm sorry?" Kevin said. "Can you say that again?"

"Turn your car around, take a left at that barn over there, and go three sees. At the third see take another left. One more see and that's Old County."

"Three C's?" Britt whispered. "Cars, condoms, and curfews? How are those even directions?"

"Shhh!" I shushed, both to Britt and to Ashley. Ashley had her fist in her mouth, biting back giggles.

"Ummm," Kevin said. "What exactly is a 'see'?"

The old-timer sighed and looked longingly at his jug.

"Turn your car around, take a left at the barn over there and go as far as you can see. Then go as far as you can see again. Do it one more time and take another left. One more see and that's Old County."

"Thank you, sir," Kevin said. "Have a great day."

So that was it! Three sees! And we thought we needed a GPS!

Just lucky it wasn't nighttime.

Then the coal company came with the world's largest shovel
And they tortured the timber and stripped all the land
Well, they dug for their coal till the land was forsaken
Then they wrote it all down as the progress of man.

And Daddy won't you take me back to Muhlenberg County
Down by the Green River where Paradise lay
Well, I'm sorry, my son, but you're too late in asking
Mister Peabody's coal train has hauled it away.

Finally, hoarse voices and all, we pulled into the parking lot to meet the tour group, barely on time. We would have been there an hour earlier but Ashley had to stop to pee every thirty seconds.

"Are you pregnant?" Britt asked her.

"Shut up, Britt," I told her.

"I'm not pregnant," Ashley said.

"When you're pregnant you pee a lot," Britt said.

"I said shut up, Britt. She's not pregnant."

"I'm just saying . . ."

"Don't say anything!"

"I'm not pregnant," Ashley said. "I just drank, like, five gallons of coffee before we started this morning. Sorry."

"I guess when you're pregnant," Britt continued, clearly not getting the keep-your-mouth-closed memo, "the baby, like, kicks you in the bladder all of the time, which makes you have to . . ."

I whacked Britt in the arm. "What part of *zip it* don't you get! Earth to Britt: you're twelve years old! You do know that you have to have sex to get pregnant!"

I turned to the back seat for confirmation from Ashley.

"I'm not pregnant, Britt," Ashley said, giving me a look that I had never seen before. A look that moved mountains. Marc turned away, his blush a beet red. "I'm on the pill. Unless you're like, totally unlucky, you don't get pregnant when you're on the pill."

•

We were walking down an old dirt logging road heading toward Hell's Gate, the entrance to Kayford Mountain. There were fifteen of us in the tour group. Nine of us from KABOOM, Britt, a couple of old hippies from Massachusetts, two stoners with dreadlocks, and our tour guide, a local activist from the group Keeper of the Mountains.

I had had no idea that there were so many groups fighting mountaintop removal in Appalachia. When Ashley and I first started KABOOM we thought we were the only ones. That no one cared but us.

Come to find out there was a swarm of like-minded groups fighting the good fight. We were not alone!

As we walked, Elise, the activist, gave us her talk about mountaintop removal. She had lived here all of her life. Born and bred in the holler the next town over.

"They are blowing the mountains out of the mountains," she said, her wonderful West Virginia drawl making her words come alive. "They are destroying the most diverse forest in the United States. When I was a little girl there were more species of plants and animals here than you could shake a stick at. And now they're gone. Gone! I thought the mountains would be here forever, but I was wrong. They're gone and they aren't coming back."

Ashley was walking a step behind me and I felt her tap me on my shoulder.

"Don't be mad," Ashley whispered. "I was going to tell you."

"Shhh!" I shushed. There was a time and a place to talk about losing your virginity, and this was neither.

"They dump the debris into the hollers, and it destroys the headwaters of the streams," Elise continued, walking backwards, tour guide–style, while she continued to talk. "You can't begin to believe how polluted the water is. It makes a skunk smell sweet."

"Wednesday night was the first time," Ashley whispered. "Oh my God. It was unreal!"

"Shhh!"

"Logging is one thing. When you log, trees come back. When you blow the top off a mountain, there is no place for them to come back to. Without trees to hold in the water, when it rains it does more than pour. We all live downstream. The river rises and people's homes get flooded. Businesses close. It is an absolute nightmare. People watch the weather channel and pray to God for sunshine."

"He was so gentle," Ashley whispered. "So nice."

"Ashley, please, not now!"

"When they set off the explosions," Elise said, "it was like living in a war zone. You'd have thought you were in Baghdad or Gaza. It cracked the foundation of my mama's house. It brought the chimney down at my auntie's."

Ashley just couldn't contain herself. "I thought it would hurt a lot. You know, the first time and all, but it didn't that much. It really didn't."

I tried the ignore routine.

Elise continued, "I don't know a single family where people haven't gotten sick. I am so, so tired of going to visit people in the hospital. Seems as though the only businesses booming around here are the florists and the funeral homes."

"Are you listening to me?" Ashley whispered.

"No!" I said, a little too loudly. The group stopped and looked at me.

"Sorry," I said. "I'm just getting a little emotional."

"Not to worry, darling," Elise said, coming over and putting her hand gently on my shoulder. "That's what we need around here. A little more emotion!"

I glared at Ashley.

This was totally crazy! Here we were walking towards Armageddon and Ashley couldn't stop talking about doing it for the first time. It was more than a little weird.

"This whole mountaintop removal business has taken the coal miner right out of mining," Elise continued. "Instead of going under the mountain they just blow it up. It's one big job suck. What took a whole union to do now takes a single machine. And the guys they brought in to do the dirty work were all from out of town. Not a single soul from Kayford."

"Don't be mad!" Ashley whispered again. "I was going to tell you!"

"So it's not like the buck stops here," Elise went on. "Amazing as it is, people still buy the coal company lies. About jobs and economic growth and the good times to come. The truth is that the companies take the money and run. Extracting the greatest wealth from one of the most impoverished places in our country. Leaving us even poorer than before, and with a shattered moonscape of a mountain."

Elise stopped talking and we walked in silence for the last few minutes. Finally we rounded the last bend, looked ahead, and stopped dead in our tracks. Immobilized. Stunned.

Hell's Gate.

There wasn't a place on Earth more appropriately named.

The work of the devil in all his infinite horror stretched out before us. An absolute nightmare. The mother of all shit-shows. Hell on Earth.

The YouTube videos were nothing compared to this.

Even Ashley was speechless.

There was not a living thing in sight. Nothing. Just a desolate, dug up, blown-up, alien shitscape stretching on and on, see after see after see. What used to be the height of nature's glory, the pinnacle of creation, was now reduced to ruin. An absence of color: no green in sight. Just the dull, endless monotony of flattened, gray, dusty, pulverized rock.

It was like before there was life on the planet, when everything was nothing and the world was desolate and raw and scary and formless. It was like after the apocalypse, when the world has gone crazy and beauty has turned ugly and good is evil and none of it makes any sense. It was like another planet, absent of the beauty, the joy, the miracle of life. It was like an alternate universe where a sickly gray was the only color.

They say seeing is believing, but I could not believe what I saw. I just couldn't. I closed my eyes. I opened them again. I closed and opened, closed and opened. But the topless mountain, the ghostly grave of Kayford, would not go away.

The haunting words of John Muir that Coop had quoted came roaring back to me:

God has cared for these trees, saved them from drought, disease, avalanches, and a thousand straining, leveling tempests and floods; but he cannot save them from fools!

If this was not the work of fools then there was no such thing as foolishness.

John Prine's "Paradise" was still locked in my brain:

Then the coal company came with the world's largest shovel
And they tortured the timber and stripped all the land
Well, they dug for their coal till the land was forsaken
Then they wrote it all down as the progress of man.

Progress? If this was "progress," then . . .

Britt started crying and held my hand. I started crying and held Kevin's hand. Kevin looked like he was ready to kill someone. Ashley had turned away into Marc's arms and Frank had closed his eyes as if in prayer. Next to seeing my mother dead, next to seeing her lovely body withered and lifeless and spent in the hospital room, this was the worst moment of my life. The absolute worst.

No one said anything. There was nothing that could be said. Words would only screw it up even more.

So we just stared and cried and cried and stared and then, when we couldn't take it anymore, we turned and walked away.

48

WE WERE BACK IN OUR MINI-MINE, Ashley and me, just the two of us. It was the day after our road trip to Kayford and I was still in recovery from the nightmare we had witnessed. The morning had been chilly and the leaves had turned. One final fling of color and then *boom*, down they went. Just like that.

"Sometimes I wish I were a tree," I said to Ashley. "Life would be so much simpler."

"Until some yahoo with a chainsaw comes and knocks you on your ass."

"Hmmm . . ." I said. "Good point."

"Anyway, if you were a tree you wouldn't get to have sex," Ashley added.

"Trees have sex."

"They do not."

"They do, too," I said. "It's just not like people sex. You know, they use the bees and the wind and stuff like that."

"Good God," Ashley said. "Imagine that. Imagine if we had sex like trees do. We'd have to have the insect express come on over and deliver the packet of your boyfriend's stuff right inside you. You'd be like, 'whoa, whoa, whoa, dude, not that oaf of an oak's! Gimme that hot sugar daddy's over there, the one twiddling his twigs at me! Come on now, buzz to it!' It would kind of take the fun right out of it."

"I guess," I said.

"And think about this one," she went on. "Imagine if trees had sex like we do."

"Like *you* do," I said.

Ashley smiled.

"Imagine Bradley Beech giving the come-on to She. 'Hey baby, why don't you brush that beautiful white ash of yours against my hunk trunk. Oh yeah. Feel how hard my nuts are? You know I'll make you bark for more!'"

"Is that the line Marc used on you?" I asked, laughing.

"You mean the line *I* used on *him*," Ashley said. "He was like, 'No rush, we can wait, I don't want to pressure you,' and I'm like, 'Dude, I don't want to wait, let's do it!'"

"It was good?" I asked.

"Well, it hurt a little," Ashley said. "But I was still really into it."

"How'd you know what to do?" I asked.

"I didn't have a clue. It just happened. And half the fun was trying to figure it out!"

"And it wasn't, like, awkward or anything?"

"It was totally awkward. But awkward in a really exciting way. Marc had done it before with one other girl last year, so he sort of knew what was going on. But not really. And anyway, since I'm on the pill, and he had, you know, only done it with a girl who hadn't done it before, I wasn't worried about getting anything so we didn't have to fool around with one of those thingamabobs."

"Call them 'condoms.' 'Thingamabobs' has already been taken."

"How about 'thingamamarc'?"

"More like 'thing*on*amarc'!"

We both laughed.

"Anyway," Ashley said. "It made it easier."

Ashley had been on the pill ever since she had first gotten her period. Up until now it had had nothing to do with sex. Her periods had been really crampy and bloody and one big horrible yuck that would keep her home from school and in bed and full of blah. The pill had been a lifesaver for her. Thanks to it her PC's (period crummies) had all but disappeared.

"Do you love him?" I asked.

Ashley looked at herself in the mirror hanging on the wall of coal. She twisted her bob and she wrinkled her brow.

"No," she finally said. "I don't. At least not yet. I like him. I really like him. But I'm not in love with him. Do you think that's wrong?"

"Do I think what's wrong?"

"That I'm having sex with him but I'm not in love with him."

I paused for a moment. There was no way I would have sex without making love. I just couldn't do it. And, as grown up as I thought I was, fifteen was still fifteen. It seemed young to be doing something that intense. But I was me and Ashley was Ashley. I wasn't going to judge.

"No," I said. "I don't think it's wrong. Marc is an awesome guy. And I know he really likes you. I mean, you two are a couple and all."

"We are."

"You're on the pill, so you've got that covered."

"Thank God for the pill!"

"If it was a one-night thing, if you weren't going out, if he was using you, if you weren't on birth control then, yeah, I'd say it was wrong. But that's not the case."

Ashley came over and hugged me.

"You know the really weird thing?" Ashley said.

"No, tell me."

"I bet half the people in this town would have me roasting in the fires of hell for having sex, whether I was in love or not, when I'm only fifteen. Even though they probably all did it themselves. And I bet a whole bunch of those very same folks are the ones praising to high heaven the bastards who want to bomb and bury Mount Tom. Which makes about as much sense as a cow's meow."

"Exactly."

"It's just so weird. I mean, in the same week that I had sex for the first time we went and saw Kayford's Mountain."

"What was left of Kayford's Mountain."

"Between Wednesday and Saturday I witnessed the very best and the very worst of what the world has to offer. It's enough to make my head explode!"

"I thought you said it hurt?" I asked.

"You know what I mean," Ashley replied.

"Anyway," I said, "I'd say you did a tad bit more than 'witness' the very best part."

"Truth," Ashley said. "But think about it: making love, or like, or whatever you want to call it, versus rape. Creation versus destruction. Heaven versus hell. Pretty weird, huh?"

"Very weird. Although let's hope you didn't create anything."

Ashley snuggled over and took my hands in hers.

"Are you thinking about it?" she asked.

"Thinking about what?"

"About *it*!"

"Duh! But I know I'm not ready yet. I'm definitely going to wait a while."

"You should get on the pill. Or at least get a bunch of thingamakevins. Gotta be prepared."

"It was worth it?" I asked again.

"It was sick!"

We sat there, quiet for a moment.

I thought about what a different world it was from the end of the summer. So much had changed. I had thought I'd never have a boyfriend—and I was wrong. I had thought good girls didn't give it up at fifteen—and I was wrong. I had thought the mountains would be here forever—and I was wrong.

"You know what is really, really, really weird?" Ashley asked.

"What?"

"With all of the bad out there. With all of the evil. With all of the mountaintop destroyers and the crazies and the meth heads and the clustermucks that go on and on—even with all of that—I am so happy right now. I really am. I have Marc. I have you. We have a mountain to fight for."

"What's the opposite of criss-cross applesauce?" I asked, snuggling closer.

49

"YOU KNOW," Becky said. "I'm not sure mountaintop removal quite does the trick."

"What do you mean?" I asked. It was Thursday after school and we KABOOMers were meeting again.

"The words: *mountaintop removal*. They just don't cut it. It sounds so, I don't know, clean. Nice. Sanitized. Almost normal. Like going to the dentist or something. This won't hurt a bit. You'll feel a little pinch and then we'll remove the mountaintop."

"Or getting a Brazilian wax," Ashley added. "I'd like my mountaintop removed, please."

All the girls laughed. I'm not quite sure the boys got it.

"Words matter," Becky said. "It really does change how people think about things."

"My uncle just got back from Afghanistan," Jon Buntington said. Everybody looked up when he talked. He so rarely spoke that when he did, everyone was all ears. "When our troops kill women and children over there they call it *collateral damage*. Not *murder*. Not even *death*. But *collateral damage*. Takes the blood right out of it."

"It sure does," I said.

"And when our troops accidentally kill one of our own they call it *friendly fire*. Can you believe that bullshit? There, there, ma'am, no need to cry. Your son was killed by friendly fire."

"That sucks," Piggy said.

"You said it, bro." Jon frowned and shook his head.

We were all amazed. Jon had never put together so many words in his life!

"It's like what we were talking about in English class," Kevin said. "We had to read *1984* a few weeks ago. George Orwell. I thought I'd hate it but he's, like, the bomb. It was all about making lies sound truthful and murder respectable. 'War is peace, hate is love, slavery is freedom.' That kind of stuff. Dude, they're out to keep us in line."

"Orwellian coal-speak," Becky said. "*Mountaintop removal* makes it seem like you can stitch it all right back together again when they're done. No need to ask questions. It'll all be good as new. Trust us."

"I'm surprised American hasn't come up with another name for it," Ashley said. "Something kinder and gentler. Like, I don't know, *mountaintop enhancement*. Like something you'd do to your boobs."

"It's like what Elise at Kayford's Mountain was telling us," I said. "The lies the company spews about turning a ragged, good-for-nothing mountaintop into a beautiful garden meadow. American should call it *garden-top placement*."

"Or *mountaintop gardening*," Kevin said.

Jon spoke and all listened. "My uncle said in Afghanistan when they blow up a village and burn down all the houses and bring on the shit-show, they call it *pacification*. They could call this *gardenication*."

We all laughed at the absurdity of it all.

"Screw this *mountaintop removal* bullshit," Piggy said. "Let's come up with a better name for it. Something closer to the truth."

"I like what you called it the other day," I said to Ashley.

"What was that?" Ashley asked.

"'Bomb and bury.'"

"That's a good one," Marc agreed.

"How about 'dig and destroy'?" Kevin said.

Everybody starting chiming in. Phrases came fast and furious.

"'Wreck and ruin.'"

"'Burn and bulldoze.'"

"'Pillage and rape.'"

"'Chank and whack.'"

"'Bang up and bust.'"

"Let's just call it like it is," Piggy said, wrapping things up. "No need to mince words. It's an AFU."

"AFU?" I asked.

"Yeah," Piggy said. "All Fucked Up. They don't remove the mountaintop. They fuck it up."

"It's as close to accurate as we're probably going to get," I said.

So there we had it. In one short meeting we managed to put *mountaintop removal* to rest forever. *AFU* it was.

All fucked up.

Truer words had never been spoken.

50

MY DAY HAD BEGUN in the usual fog with my alarm clock blasting me out of yummy dreamland and into reality. It had turned cold overnight and my bedroom floor was freezing. Desperate to pee, struggling to make it to the bathroom before letting loose all over the floor, I went to sit on the toilet seat and *voilà*: Yuck! Total and complete grossness.

"Dad!" I yelled. "How many times do I have to tell you! You've got to put the seat down." I had plopped right on into the seat-less bowl and gotten Dad's pee splatter all over me. It was the height of disgusting. No way to start the day!

Things went downhill from there.

Ashley and I were walking to school when Bert and Michael come hauling around the corner in their truck.

"Hey, darlin's," Bert says, drooling and leering at us. "How's about we give the twos of you a ride to paradise?"

"Hey, assholes," Ashley said. "How's about I kick the twos of you in your effin balls? Oh no! Can't do that! You don't have any, now, do you?"

I picked up a rock and threatened to throw it at them. They both grinned, spat in our direction, and sped away in a muffler-less roar.

School was even worse.

Mr. Livingston, the world's worst math teacher, was attempting to explain in his usual crap way a fairly basic formula that could project income growth into the future.

"This is important," Livingston said. "Some of you gentlemen might find this incredibly useful for a business you might eventually become involved in."

I raised my hand.

"Mightn't us ladies need it to?" I asked, in as mocking a voice as I could muster, dialing up my good ol' holler-girl West Virginia drawl. "You know, for figuring how many diapers my nine kids might need?"

I was glad I still didn't have that rock in my hand. I was seething.

A few months earlier, a comment like that from Livingston would have soared right over my head, totally unnoticed. Not now. Those days were over. The mountain-top removal issue was opening my eyes to all sorts of other social injustices that flooded our holler. And once your eyes are open, there is no closing.

Mr. Livingston made some weak, squirmish response and quickly moved on.

But the worst had been saved for the afternoon.

After school I went to buy tampons at Fas Chek. Not exactly my favorite thing in the world to do, particularly when Mr. Potter was at the register. Mr. Potter had been at the register forever. Mr. Potter had probably been at the register when West Virginia split from Virginia at the height of the Civil War. Mr. Potter was the reason some girls hitched rides to the next town over to buy tampons, just so they didn't have to deal with his stinky eye.

Even the word *menstruation* had exacerbated my pissy mood. I mean, come on—*men*struation? Jeez, the one thing we have that guys don't and they still have to name it after themselves?

I hated buying tampons from Mr. Potter. I absolutely hated it. It was one of the things that distressed me the most about not having a mother. Mom would definitely have done this most embarrassing of tasks for me.

I put it in the back of my brain to be the tampon buyer for Britt when her time came. As annoying as she was, I didn't want her to have to go through Potter hell.

But have blood, must buy. No matter what slime lurks behind the counter.

"Hello, sweetheart," Potter says, licking his lips. I'm buying tampons and the old fart calls me "sweetheart"? Yuck. Beyond yuck. Really creepy yuck.

"I hear you've gone all anti-coal on us, huh?" he continued. "Leading the charge in the War on Coal now, are we?" Oh, the joy of living in a small town where everyone knew everyone's business.

"It's called saving Mount Tom," I said. "I'm not against the Number 3 Mine. That's where my uncle and my granddaddy worked. What I am against is blowing up Mount Tom. If they ruin the mountain it could very well ruin our town, which would put you, Mister Potter, out of business."

"Well, well, well," he said, not even bothering to hide his smirk. "Aren't you a feisty little thing. Sounds like you've been listening a little too much to those outsiders. Those elitist college kids. Those environmentalists." The way he spat out the word *environmentalists* was the same way you'd spit out the words *Pittsburgh Panthers*, the University of West Virginia Mountaineers' chief football rival.

Those were the three worst things you could be called around here: An *outsider*. An *elitist*. An *environmentalist*. The terrible trio. The triple whammy. To be labeled one was harsh enough. Three strikes and you were totally out.

For some people, an outsider meant you hadn't lived in West Virginia your whole life. And I mean your whole life! Over the summer there had been an obituary in the paper for a ninety-three-year-old West Virginia woman who had moved here from Pennsylvania when she was three, nine decades ago. The obit read "though not originally from around here, she nonetheless managed to make this holler her home." She had moved to her holler in 1925! She had lived in the same valley for ninety effin years! Yet she was still tainted! She was still an *outsider*. You couldn't even go to Charlestown for the weekend and not come home to raised eyebrows.

An *elitist* meant you had an education. For some people it even meant you had finished high school. "Now," folks would say. "I might not be as educated as you are, but . . ." The implication being that whatever that educated person said was suspect. Not to be believed. Probably an outright lie. Why? Because they had gone to college? Hello!

The more schooling you had the less likely you were to know anything? Go figure!

And then there was *environmentalist*. I was proud of the title, but when people labeled you as that, it was *boom*! The ultimate smackdown. You could be a child molester, a wife beater, a meth addict, a thief, and a down-and-out no-good—but as long as you weren't an environmentalist there was hope. There was at least a chance for redemption. A good chunk of the population considered environmentalists worse than black widow spiders. They ate human babies for breakfast.

"No need to worry your pretty little head about any of that stuff," Mr. Potter continued. "Don't be like your mama.

You just be a good girl and let those coal boys do what they do best."

"My mama?" I was confused. "What are you talking about?"

"Sweetie," Potter continued, ignoring my question. "With looks like yours, you're never going to have to worry about a thing." Potter was leering at me, spittle forming at the corner of his mouth. He was practically fondling the box of tampons, stroking them as he put them in a bag. It was all I could do to keep my lunch down.

I was pissed. Really pissed.

"Mr. Potter," I cooed. "Haven't you heard? It's the twenty-first century. Us holler girls can work the corner and still shut down the mountaintop removers. We can do two things at once, Mr. Potter! Isn't that special?"

Mr. Potter looked confused. He stopped fingering the tampon box and handed me the bag.

"I think you best mind your own business, missy," he said. "Stay out of the way of the big boys."

"I think you should shut the hell up, Mr. Potter," I said. "And stay out of the way of *me*!" I shot him the most evil eye I could muster, gave him the finger, and stormed out.

•

"You better watch it," I said to Kevin. I had just finished telling him, for the third time, the drama of my day. We were parked in my driveway after going to the movies. Usual guy-movie plot. Spoiler alert: everyone killed everyone else and then blew everything up in the end. Kevin, of course, thought it was awesome.

It had done nothing to raise my opinion of humans with penises.

"Uh oh," he asked. "What did I do now?"

"It has not been a good day," I said. "One wrong word from you and I'm liable to bite your head off."

"Ooh-la-la," Kevin said, reaching over and stroking my hair. "Just like the black widow spider. Except I think she does that after they get it on." His hand slid off my hair, down to my shoulder, and began to creep further south.

"Sometimes they eat them first!" I said, slapping away his hand and putting it back on the steering wheel.

"Yum. That could be fun too."

"I'm serious!" I said. "You better watch it!"

"I am watching," he said, turning to me and staring at my boobs. "I can't keep my eyes off of them."

"Ahhh!" I yelled, arching my head back and clenching my fists. "Guys!"

"Uh oh," Kevin said. "What did we do now?"

"There are days that I wish I lived on a planet of just girls. No penises. No testosterone. Just girls."

"But then there'd be no me!" Kevin said, his fingers walking their way back into my hair.

"Humph!" I said. One of the things about Kevin was that he was so damn cute. Try as I might, it could be incredibly hard to stay in a bad mood around him for long.

But I was so right. A guyless world (well, okay, with one exception—Kevin . . . and maybe Marc for Ashley) would make life a whole lot easier in so many ways.

"Why do guys do this stuff?" I asked.

"Do what stuff?" Kevin asked.

"Don't play dumb with me," I scolded. "You know what I'm talking about."

Kevin sighed. "You know, Cyndie," he said. "Think how much better it would be if you'd just tell me what I did wrong. It would make it so much easier to apologize that way."

"You didn't do anything wrong!" I snarled.

"Okay. So you're mad at me because . . ."

"I am not mad at you at all! Oh my God, Kevin. Haven't you been listening to a word I said? Ugh! You can be so thick sometimes!"

Kevin leaned into me and let out another sigh. An exaggerated one, loud and long, his breath blowing softly in my ear. "There are days when I wish I lived on a planet of just guys," he whispered, his fingers tracing the shape of a heart on my back, the tingling in my ears spreading down to my neck and beyond. "No vaginas. No estrogen. Just guys."

"Yeah, right," I said, turning back into his arms and trying not to laugh. "We'd see how long that world would last. I'd give it three days max!"

"You know the biggest problem with that world?" he asked.

"No one to go out and buy you more beer and nachos during halftime?"

"The biggest problem with that world is that there'd be no you!" Kevin said, his fingers walking their way back into my hair, down to my shoulder, and then, gloriously, further south. This time I did not move them away.

•

It was close to midnight, my curfew. We had been fooling around for half an hour. I had drawn the line at my belly button. Anything above was fair game. Anything below, off-limits.

It had been the most thrilling half hour of my life.

I had just put my bra and my top back on and was resting my head on Kevin's shoulder.

"You know," he said. "I do get it."

"What *it* are we talking about?" I asked.

"It. The *it* of your day. All the screwed-up-guy-stuff it. I mean, I'll be honest, I had never really thought about it before. How hard it must be for you. To be a girl and so beautiful."

Boy, could Kevin make my insides melt.

"How you have to deal with all of the bullshit. Like what a moron Mr. Livingston is. And that dickhead Potter. He had you sliding down the pole right there in the drug store!"

I momentarily stopped melting to refreeze at the thought.

"I mean, I had always thought that every girl just wanted to be pretty, but around here all that seems to get you is a load of crap. So many guys must just look at you with one thing in mind. And one thing only."

He kissed the top of my head.

"And not only are you so pretty but you're so smart. And you're out there 'sticking it to the man,' as Piggy likes to say with this whole Mount Tom thing. I mean, you're the whole package. The real deal. And I never realized how hard that must be. It must really suck sometimes."

There was nothing left to melt. I was one big puddle on the car floor. I fought off the urge to rip off all of my clothes, and his, and go at it right then and there. In the front seat. In the back. In the middle of the lawn. Anywhere.

"I'm sorry," Kevin said.

"You're sorry? For what?"

"I don't know. For being a guy. For being a part of the whole penised race."

I laughed.

"I forgive you," I said, snuggling closer.

"You do?" he asked.

"I do. Penis and all."

I kissed him one more time and walked to my house and let myself in. I could feel him watching me. I could feel his eyes on my body. I could still feel his hands and his mouth and his glorious kisses all over me from the belly button on up.

But I could also feel something else.

He had called me the real deal. The whole package.

He had got it.

For the first time I could feel the L-word beginning to take shape. Not all four letters. Just the first. Just the L.

But it was a hell of a capital L.

51

"YOU KNOW," Auntie Sadie said. "You are all piss and vinegar. One feisty little girl."

"Sadie," I said. "I'm fifteen years old. Not so little anymore. But I'll take the piss and vinegar part as a compliment, even though I don't have a clue as to what you're talking about."

Auntie Sadie put down her pitchfork, waddled on over, and enveloped me in her massive arms.

"You'll always be my little girl," she said.

"And you'll always be my big auntie." I held my breath and clenched my fists, in a desperate attempt not to be smothered to death by the hugeness of her hug.

"How's that beau of yours?" she asked, mercifully releasing me and going back to her digging. We were working her garden, bringing in late-fall potatoes. She pitchforked, and I followed on my hands and knees, rooting through the earth and digging them up. The potatoes were enormous. Bigger than my fists. Even bigger than Sadie's fists.

There was a certain magical quality about potato harvesting. It was like treasure hunting, only better. You can't eat gold.

"Kevin?" I said. "He's great. More than great."

Sadie stopped digging, leaned on her pitchfork, and stared at me. Try as I might, I had never quite gotten comfortable with her lazy eye. It just sort of floated there, not really looking but wanting to, while the other eye bored right into me. After all these years it still creeped me out.

"Are you keeping him in line?" she asked.

"What are you talking about?"

"You know damn well what I'm talking about!" Both eyes managed to focus in on me for that comment.

I blushed.

"Yeah," I replied, reaching down and fiddling with my belly button. "I'm keeping him in line."

"Let me tell you something," she said. "A pretty little girl like you has got to watch it."

My hand wrapped around a monster of a potato and I resisted the urge to hurl it at her. Put to rest that lazy little eye forever.

"Sadie!" I said, trying to keep my voice in check. "No offense, but if anyone tells me again how pretty little girls like me have to watch it, then I'm going to take these potatoes, or, better yet, that pitchfork, and do some serious damage!"

Sadie took the tool and held it in front of her like a multipronged sword. "Bring it on, baby," she laughed. "Give me what you got!"

I lobbed a potato up in the air and, miraculously, she stuck it! Caught it right at the end of the pitchfork!

"Oh yeah!" she cried. "Am I good or what?"

"Or what," I replied.

"Look darling, I'm just trying to watch out for you. I promised your mother that I would, and I'm damn well going to do it."

"I'm fifteen years old, Sadie. I can watch out for myself."

Sadie laughed in a grimacing kind of way.

"Don't go biting my head off for worrying about you. That's part of my job. To worry. About you and boys. About you and all your shenanigans with the coal company. There's a big ol' world out there to worry about."

"Well, don't," I said. "I'm on it."

"That's what I'm afraid of!" Sadie said.

I blushed again.

"The boy thing I get," Sadie continued. "Whew! You should have seen me in high school."

"Please," I said. "Spare me the details."

"There was this one time when I was about your age, at a party, and there were these two guys and I . . ." Sadie's lazy eye started twirling in fast motion.

I took two potatoes and stuck one in each ear. "La la la la la la la! I can't hear you!"

"All right, Mrs. Potato Head. Anyway, boys are one thing. But do you have to go after the coal company as well? Can't you just drop that one? You know, like a hot potato. Just let it be. What happens will happen."

"Not if I can help it."

"It's the coal company, honey. This is not a game."

"Never underestimate what us pretty little girls can do," I said.

Sadie sighed. "Lordy," she said. "Why can't you just be like all the other girls?"

I took a potato, cocked my arm back to throw, but thought better and let it drop harmlessly in front of me.

"Like Ashley?" I asked.

"No. Not like Ashley. Like the *normal* other girls."

"Oh, yeah. The normal girls. Now I get it. So, what exactly should I be doing, Sadie? Getting pregnant? Dropping out of high school? Making sure my hair is big and my brain is tiny? Is that what you want?"

"No. Of course not."

"Then what is it?"

"It's just that . . ." Sadie leaned on the fork and looked a little lost. I felt kind of bad for her, but a proud kind of bad. I was pretty pleased with the not-so-normal label.

"You know who you remind me of?" she asked.

"Who?"

"A younger version of Widow Combs."

"Widow what?"

"Widow Combs. You've never heard of her?"

"Never."

Sadie plopped herself down in the dirt and opened up a bag of Cheetos, emptied most of the bag into her lap, and tossed the rest over to me.

"Widow Combs," she said. "Now *that* was one feisty old lady."

Sadie rearranged her bulk, stretched her arms, and settled into storytelling mode. She closed one eye (the lazy one, thank goodness), so as not to let it distract from the story.

Ever since I could remember I loved to listen to Sadie tell her stories. She could take a classic fairy tale like Cinderella and put a West Virginia coal-country spin on it. Cinderella living in the holler and working in the coal mine, the prince the son of the mine owner. Cinderella losing her miner's helmet rather than her glass slipper.

Sadie would talk with her hands, pulling words out of the air and flicking them over to me. During the scary parts of a story she'd open both eyes, the lazy one flopping around until your goose bumps were liable to burst.

She was a great storyteller.

"In 1965," she began "way, way back in the day, there was a woman who lived in a holler across the border in Kentucky named Ollie Combs. Her husband had gone and died, and, from that day on, everyone just called her Widow. Widow Combs. I met her once before she died. I heard her speak. She was quite the woman.

"Anyway, the coal company come to strip-mine her land. Back then, if you had sold away the mineral rights, you didn't have no more say 'bout how they could come and get that coal off your land than a goat had wings. They could strip-mine your own land till it was as naked as the day you was born. You couldn't do jack about it. No way, no how, no nothing."

When Sadie got into the storytelling zone she'd let her language slip into mountain talk, and her West Virginia accent would drift even farther south, back to the hills of Georgia where my grandfather's grandfather had been born. I lay in the cool grass next to the potato patch and listened.

"So ol' Widow Combs was not so pleased with how this strip-mining thing was going down. Got her knickers all in a kink, it did. When them coal boys come with their big ol' bulldozers and their coal company trucks, she was more pissed than a sober drunk. 'We live hard,' she said. 'I don't bother nobody, but you have invaded my home. I don't want my home destroyed, its all I got left.' She was a frail little thing, Widow Combs was. Didn't weigh no more than the beard on a billy. And she was over sixty years old as I recall. Old and frail but fearless."

"What happened then?" I asked.

"Well, the dozers come and Widow Combs sits on a boulder right in front of them and refuses to move. 'I have never been in trouble,' she said. 'I just want to live my life in my holler and be left alone.' That old woman was something else."

"And then?"

"Well, you can imagine that didn't go down so well with them bulldoze boys. They had a job to do and they were damn well going to do it. Widow or not. So the police come and they dragged that woman right off her boulder and arrested her. Sent her on down to the county jail, where she spent Thanksgiving Day 1965 eating chicken dumplings. She and her two boys. One was twenty, the other seventeen."

"Seventeen?"

"Seventeen. Just like that beau of yours."

"Wow," I said, hanging on to every word.

"Wow is not the half of it."

"Did it work? Did she stop them?"

"Well, here's the amazing thing. There was a photographer from the local newspaper who had come to see what all of the hullabaloo was about, and he snapped a picture of the widow getting carried down the mountainside by the Kentucky State Police. She had refused to walk so they just dragged her sorry ass. Dragged her down the mountain. Wouldn't you know it but that picture went . . . how do you call it?

"Viral?" I said.

"That's it. Viral. And this was before the Internet. Widow Combs was all over the news, not just in Kentucky and West Virginia but everywhere. Folks was so used to the coal company getting what the coal company wanted. No questions asked. And then along comes this tired old widow who just says no. It shook things up it did. And damn if something actually didn't happen."

"What?" I asked. I was totally stoked by the story. "What happened?"

"The very next year the Kentucky politicians, the very same ones the coal company bosses thought they had in their pockets, went out and rewrote the strip-mining laws. Made them much more strict. Ten years later, the big boys in Washington gone and done the same thing. Heck, I do believe she was even invited to the White House."

"Awesome," I said. "Totally awesome."

Sadie looked at me sternly. "Don't go getting any grand ideas into that pretty little head of yours, young lady. She was over sixty. You're fifteen."

"Almost sixteen," I said.

"Like I said, fifteen."

"How do you know all this?" I asked.

"Well," she said, tilting her head back, her lazy eye doing its thing. "Your mama."

"My mama? What about my mama?"

"When your mama was younger she was all about saving these mountains from the strip-miners. If it wasn't for your mama they might have mined that old mountain of yours a long time ago. She brought Widow Combs out here sometime, oh, I don't know, must have been the late 1980s, to do a talk to the group your mama was involved in. Come to think of it, you remind me a lot of your mama, too."

"What?" My jaw dropped. So this was what Potter had been referring to. "My mother? My mother was an environmentalist? Like me? Doing this kind of stuff? Why didn't anyone tell me?"

"You never asked," Sadie said, looking a little uncomfortable.

"What did she do?"

"What didn't she do is more like it. Same kinds of things as you. Marches and petitions and harassing the politicians. You name it, she did it. Anything to stop the strip-mining."

"Oh my God, Sadie. I'm out here putting myself on the line and you never told me this? Dad never told me? Why?"

Sadie let out a long sigh.

"It was hard on your mama. People don't always like those who rock the boat. Too many waves. Your mama took a boatload of crap. People were pretty mean to her. As I recall, really mean. She lost a lot of her friends. Couldn't get a job in town or nothing. It was hard on your daddy, too."

"But why didn't you tell me?"

"We didn't want it to happen to you. Me and your dad. Like I said, I told your mama before she died that I would watch out for you. And that's what I'm doing!"

"By lying to me?" I was practically screaming.

"I never lied to you, sugar."

"You never told me the truth!"

"Not telling is different from lying."

"It's still wrong."

"You never asked. I never told."

"How am I supposed to ask if I don't know the questions?" I was furious.

"Calm down, sweetheart."

"Calm down? Calm down so they can do their dirty work without anyone raising a stink? Calm down so it can be business as usual? Calm down so they can blow up my mountain, *our* mountain, poison *our* land, and pollute *our* water? Calm down so they can fry the effin planet? These are the same damn issues that Widow Coombs and my mama were active with. It doesn't seem like my mama was calm at all, Sadie! 'Calm down,' my ass. I'm ramping it up!"

I leapt up, kicked over the basket of potatoes, and stormed home.

•

"Dad!" I yelled. "We need to talk! Now!"

Dad was hunched over the pot in the kitchen, making—surprise, surprise—macaroni and cheese for dinner. I burst into the room like a billy goat to a nanny in heat.

"I can't believe that you didn't tell me about Mom!"

Dad turned down the burner on the stove and sat at the table.

"Tell you what about your mother?" he asked. His shoulders were slumped. He looked tired. For the first time I noticed shades of gray in his hair.

"You know what!" I spat. I was pissed. "Sadie told me about how when Mom was younger she went at it with the strip-miners. Why didn't you tell me? How dare you not tell me!"

I could see Dad tense up. His shoulders rose and his brow furrowed and he drummed on the table with the stirring spoon.

His voice was soft. "I was planning on telling you. I was. It's just that . . ."

"It's just that *what*, Dad? What? I don't get it, I really don't."

"I didn't want what your mother did to influence you. I know how much you, I don't know, worship her. If I told you about all of the activities she was involved in against strip-mining then, I thought that you might . . ."

"Do the same? Oh my God, Dad! Mom was doing the right thing and you didn't tell me because you didn't want me doing it? That makes about as much sense as nothing!"

"I was worried about you. I didn't want you to go through the same heartache and pain and trouble that your mother did. It was very difficult for her, Cyndie. Going up against coal when Coal Is King is not easy. You know that. People can be very, very ugly, and do very mean things. Particularly if you're a girl. It's hard enough being a girl around here. And a girl who's an activist? I did not want those ugly things happening to you."

"I am fifteen years old, Dad. You're treating me like I'm Britt's age."

Dad put the spoon down and rubbed hard at the space between his eyes.

"What?" I said. "What is it?"

"You know Britt's little friend Taylor?"

"You mean her so-called boyfriend? Yeah, what about him?"

"He broke up with her."

"Dad. They weren't even dating. What's the big deal? And don't change the subject."

"It is a big deal, Cyndie. It's a big deal to Britt. She's really hurt. And I'm telling you this because it has everything to do with what we were just talking about!"

"How? How does it have anything to do with it?"

"She may not act like it, Cyndie, but Britt is so proud of you. She idolizes you. She really does. She was talking it up at school about how her big sister is going to stop mountain-top removal. About how her big sister is going to save Mount Tom. Well, I guess Taylor's parents work for American, so he doesn't quite see things the same way you and Britt do."

"And that's why he dumped her?" I quietly asked.

"That's why he dumped her. And not in a very nice way, either."

"The macaroni's boiling over," I said.

Dad got up and took the pot off the stove.

"Where's Britt now?" I asked.

"Upstairs. In her room. Crying her eyes out."

•

"Hey, Britt," I called, knocking on her door. "Can I come in?"

"No!" she said. I could hear her sobs. "Go away!"

I opened the door and went on in.

Britt was lying on her bed, a pillow over her head, clutching tightly to Mister Wiggins, her bunny. I sat down on the edge of her bed.

"I said go away!" Britt's voice was muffled by the pillow.

I put my hand on her back.

"Dad told me about Taylor. That really sucks. I am so sorry. I really am."

Britt sobbed even louder.

I remembered how, when I was little and I was sad, my mama would rub my back. She didn't tell me not to be sad. She didn't tell me everything would be all right. She would just sit on the side of my bed and rub my back and listen.

So that's what I did. I sat on the edge of Britt's bed and I rubbed her back.

"What happened?" I finally asked.

Britt took the pillow off of her head.

"He is such a jerk! He dumped me because I want to save Mount Tom. Can you believe that? That's what happened. He's an idiot and a jerk and I hate him. He called me a slut! A slut! For wanting to save Mount Tom!"

I thought about all that Dad and Sadie had said, and I closed my eyes and let out a long sigh.

"Asshole!" I said tenderly.

"Whatever. I can't believe I was ever even going out with him!"

I had to turn my head to hide my smile. Britt's definition of "going out" had been sitting with Taylor at the lunch table.

"He is such a loser," she went on. "And you know what?"

"What?"

"He chews with his mouth open!"

"Gross!" I said. "Who wants a boyfriend who does that!"

"Yeah," Britt said. "I was going to break up with him anyway. He's like a total poser. Anyway, I want a boyfriend just like Kevin."

"Better watch it, Sister!" I smiled, continuing to rub her back. "You steal him away from me and that old Mister Wiggins of yours is history!"

Britt sat up, made the peace sign, pointed the two fingers at her eyes and then pointed them at me.

"I'll be watching you," she said. "One false move and that boy is mine!"

We both laughed.

"Want to know something really awesome?" I asked.

"What?"

"I guess Mom was really active in saving mountains, too," I told her.

"Really?" Britt sat up.

"Really." I told her everything that Sadie and Dad had told me. Everything.

"Wow!" Britt said. "That is so cool. Not the stuff about people being mean to her and all, but the other stuff. And the Widow Combs thing. That's totally awesome! Maybe we can do that."

"I hope we don't have to," I said.

I looked at Britt. Really looked at her. At how young and innocent and fragile she was. And how pretty. Not just cute pretty but beautiful pretty.

I was finding out that pretty had its downside. That pretty was definitely a double-edged sword. I wanted to be pretty. I wanted Britt to be pretty. But I definitely didn't want all of the bullshit that seemed to come with it.

I looked at Britt again. I noticed little bumps on her chest. Bumps I swear were not there a week ago. Just the beginnings.

"Wow!" I said. "What's going on here? It won't be long and I'm going to have to go with you to buy bras."

"Really?" Britt asked, perking up considerably and touching her boobs. "When?"

"I don't know," I said. "Soon. Things are really starting to . . ."

"Grow. I know!" Britt said, smiling. "And I'm getting hair down there too. Just a few. Want to see?" Britt squirmed out of her pants and showed me.

Awkward!

But hey, I remembered this. It wasn't that long ago that my body had started going through the same thing. I remembered the Gettysburg fiasco and not having a clue as to what was going on.

"Here's another thing," I said. "It won't be that much longer and you're going to get your period. Don't freak out like I did when you start to bleed down there for the first time. We should get you pads now. Better to be prepared."

"Cool," Britt said.

I shuddered at the thought of another visit with Potter the Perv at Fas Chek.

"Maybe we can get Kevin to drive us to Charlestown where we can go to some bigger stores. You know, get a better selection and all."

"Yeah!" Britt said. "This weekend? Can we? Please?"

"Sure," I said. "Why not? Kevin will be thrilled to go with us to buy bras and pads for you!" Once again I hid my smile. "But Mister Wiggins is definitely not invited. It's just too much for her little bunny brain. She's torn and tattered enough as it is. Buying bras and pads would totally send her over the edge. Right down the rabbit hole!"

Britt laughed and threw her arms around me.

"Thank you!" she said, burying her face in my breasts and breathing in deeply. She held me for quite a while.

"I love you!" she finally said.

Wow, I thought. She really wasn't so bad after all.

"I love you too," I said.

52

"So what does it actually feel like?" I asked Ashley. We were back on our mountain, in our sacred grove of trees, bowling with acorns. We had set up little alleys in the dirt with pins made of hemlock cones and we were happily bowling away, all the while serenaded by Jay-Z, the red squirrel. Hyper chatterbox that he was, it was hard to tell whether he was cheering us on or just pissed because we had stolen his lunch.

I was crushing her, 79–43. I loved beating Ashley in games.

"How do you *think* it feels?" Ashley answered. "Terrible. Don't rub it in."

I had just gotten a strike. It was now 89–43. First to 100 won.

"Terrible?" I said. "I thought you said it was awesome?"

Ashley stopped in mid-throw, looking confused.

"I'm definitely not on my game. I'm down almost fifty points. How can getting my ass kicked possibly feel awesome?"

I laughed and flung an acorn at her.

"Ashley! I'm talking about sex, not bowling."

Ashley laughed so hard she started to choke. She was gasping for breath. I was scared I was going to have to do the Heimlich maneuver on her. I had a vague memory of it from ninth-grade health class. I knew it had something to do with whacking her boobs but the details were a little fuzzy. It took nearly a minute before she could even speak.

"Seriously," I said. "What's it feel like, you know, to have Marc inside of you?" I had asked her this a bunch of times before but I was still so curious. I just couldn't seem to wrap my brain around how the whole thing went down.

Ashley wiped the laughter tears from her eyes.

"It's kind of like bowling," she said. "Real bowling. You have these two big balls. You have this one even bigger pin. And then you . . ."

"Stop!" I said. "I'm being serious, Ash. I want to know."

Jay-Z had quit his incessant chattering and was now staring at us in his little dweeby rodent way, all buggy eyes and twitchy ears.

"Are you old enough to hear this, Jay-Z?" Ashley yelled. "Do you need a permission slip from your mama?" The red squirrel raced over to Bradley Beech, acrobatically leapt up to the first limb, and chatter-answered what we took to be a yes.

"I mean, it's great," Ashley said. "Particularly after the first couple of times, which kind of hurt. But now that I know what's going on it's much better. We've only done it, like, five times. It's really fun. I do kind of wish he'd last a little longer though."

"What do you mean 'last longer'?" I asked.

"I mean, as soon as he's inside of me, you know, as soon as we're going at it and I'm starting to figure out what to do, he's already done."

"Done?"

"Yeah, done. He, you know, does his guy thing and that's pretty much it. I've barely opened the door and he's already in and out."

"Like, how long?' I asked.

"Not long."

"Like, minutes not long?"

"Are you kidding me? That would be awesome! It's like, I don't know, half a minute at the most. Quickie is way too long a word for it."

"Have you told him that?"

"What? Are you crazy, Cyndie? What am I supposed to say? 'Hey Marc, do you mind lasting a little longer here?' Seriously, it still feels good and all. It feels great. I'm just, you know, not getting off."

"And he is."

"He sure is."

"How do you know?"

"What do you mean how do I know?"

"I mean, can you, like, feel it."

"Big time! Afterwards it's like totally drippy down there."

"What do you mean, 'drippy'?" I asked.

"You know, goopy. Gooey."

"No, I don't know. I don't know anything, Ashley. Tell me. You have to tell me everything."

"After he's done it's just drippy down there. I don't how else to describe it."

"Oh my God!" I said. "I never thought of that. Where does it all go?"

"I don't know. It just kind of drips out I guess."

Thank goodness Ashley was the first one to do it. If I hadn't known these essential facts when the time came for me, I think I would have totally freaked out. I would have thought that, I don't know, my insides were falling out or something. Goopiness was definitely not something they taught us in ninth-grade health class.

"But you don't, like, you know, get off or anything?"

"Not totally. Don't get me wrong. I really like it. But he hasn't gotten me all the way there yet."

"Does he touch you before he goes in? Like, down there?" I asked.

"Of course. And that's really fun, too. But he hasn't quite figured out where my thingamabob is."

"Your thingamabob?"

"Yeah."

I was confused. *Thingamabob* was coming to mean so many different things.

"You know what I'm talking about," Ashley continued. "The thinkabout thing. That little button down there. The spot that feels so good. I'm yanking a blank here. What's it called?"

"The clitoris?"

"That's it. The clit."

She laughed again.

"Have you asked him to, you know, pay attention to that?"

"Oh my God, Cyndie! That would be, like, totally embarrassing. It's much easier to do it than it is to talk about it. Much easier."

"So let me get this straight," I said. "He's hardly in before he's out. He can't seem to find your thingamabob. And then, when it's all over, you're the one that gets stuck with all of the goopiness?"

"Exactly!" Ashley said. She started to laugh again. Big-time laughter. She laughed so hard she began to choke again. And, even if I had remembered, I was laughing way too hard to do the Heimlich maneuver.

53

"LIFE IS LIKE A FERRIS WHEEL," Auntie Sadie was fond of saying. "Sometimes you're riding on top, holding hands with your honey, eating fried dough and cotton candy with the whole wide world stretched crystal-clear before you as far as the eye can see.

"And other times, you're not so lucky. Other times you're plummeting down, free-falling, terrified and dizzy, your stomach doing somersaults and your bowels ready to explode."

Sadie was right about the ups and the downs. And today, unfortunately, was a hurtling-down day. After I'd been on top for so long, the plummet, just like Sadie had said, was horrifying.

I had kept the idea about our mini-mine as a possible historic preservation site secret from Ashley, Kevin, and the rest of the KABOOMers. Ashley hadn't been in on the conversation with Kevin about the permitting process, and it hadn't come up again in KABOOM meetings. She still didn't realize the possibility of using our mine as a way to stop the mountaintop removal project. What if our mine really was a historic site? Or, better yet, part of a Civil War fortification? It *was* possible.

It wasn't though I hadn't wrestled with the to-tell-or-not-to-tell dilemma. But I knew that telling Ashley and then everyone in KABOOM meant that it wouldn't be our mine anymore. Having a secret place just for the two of us meant everything to me. I was so into Kevin, and Ashley was so glued to Marc, that we were spending less and less time just with each other. But the mine was still our sacred, secret place. We had grown up there. Giving that up, going public with it, would be almost too much to bear.

I had asked Kevin to talk more about historic preservation sites and the permitting process at the meeting in order to see how Ashley reacted. Then we could take it from there. Maybe one of these days we would have to share our mine with the rest of the world. But I wanted to put that day off for as long as possible.

We had just begun our Thursday after-school KABOOM meeting when Principal Miller walked into the room. He didn't sit down, but instead stood awkwardly by the door, one hand on the knob, nervously licking his moustache. He declined Ashley's offer of Cheetos.

"I'm here to inform you," he began, "that this is to be the last meeting of your group."

"What are you talking about?" I asked.

"I'm quite sure that there are other more appropriate places for you to meet, outside of school." Miller's moustache was nervously twitching. "And with Mr. Cooper no longer your advisor, you have no choice. You will have to go elsewhere."

"What?" Ashley asked. "Mr. Cooper is no longer our advisor?"

"I have requested that Mr. Cooper step down, and he has agreed. Without an advisor, there can be no club."

"Whoa," I said. "He hasn't even come to a meeting! He's had nothing to do with our group."

"It doesn't matter. My decision is final. No advisor, no club."

"Is this because of American's donation? Are they the ones making you do this?" We had heard the rumor that American Coal was all set to make another large contribution to the high school, this time funding new bleachers for the football field.

Principal Miller was silent.

"I thought you were all about our right to free expression!" Ashley said. "I thought you were all gung ho over 'this is what school is all about.' And now we can't even meet here?"

"The case is closed," Miller said. "This meeting is your last." He turned and left the room.

We were pissed.

"Son of a bitch!" Piggy said. "We've been betrayed. Coop has grassed on us."

"I'm sure there's an explanation," I said. "Coop would never do something like this."

"He would if his job was at stake!" Kevin said.

"They wouldn't do that to him, would they?" I asked.

"Don't forget who we're up against," Becky said. "They're American, remember? They run the show. Even here at the high school. They tell Miller to jump and he says, 'How high?' He'll do whatever they say."

"But to stop a dinky little group like ours? Seriously?"

"I guess that's the good news," Frank said. "They must not think of us that way."

"Son of a bitch!" Piggy said again.

We sat there in stunned silence.

"And where the heck is Marc?" Ashley asked. "Why isn't he here?"

Kevin let go of my hand, twirled his hair, and stared at the floor.

"What?" Ashley asked, staring at him. "What's going on?"

Kevin squirmed in his chair.

"Kevin!" Ashley demanded. "What the heck is going on?"

"He told me not to say anything," Kevin said. "He told me he'd tell you later."

"Tell me what?" Ashley asked, her voice rising a notch. The rest of the group looked away in awkward silence.

I turned toward Kevin and gave him the look. Kevin sighed and twirled his hair even faster.

"I guess Marc isn't going to come anymore," he said, still not looking up.

"What do you mean 'he's not coming anymore'?" Ashley asked, getting out of her chair.

"Mr. Miller gave him an ultimatum, too. Keep being the mascot or stay in KABOOM. His choice."

"And he chose the mascot?" Ashley was practically shrieking. "Over us? Over me?"

Kevin didn't answer.

Ashley burst into tears and fled the room. I gave Kevin the look one more time and went out after her.

•

It was the evening after the last meeting and Ashley was over at my house. Dinner had yet to be served, and she was already on the second box of Kleenex and halfway through the third bag of Cheetos.

"I can't believe this," she kept repeating through the tears. "I can't believe he did this to me!"

"He didn't do it to you," I said. "Think of what an honor it is to be the mascot. For Marc to give that up was asking a lot."

"I don't give a shit about the stupid mascot!" Ashley yelled. "It's lame and I hate it!"

"I know," I said. "I hate it too. But put yourself in his shoes. It was a tough choice."

"Choice? What kind of choice was it? You either do the right thing or you don't. You either stand by your principles or you cave. And he caved! And he didn't even have the guts to tell me! Maybe he really was a spy. Maybe this whole thing was just one big joke to him."

"You know that's not true!" I said. "He was going to tell you. Kevin said so. And, anyway, it doesn't mean you have to be done with him."

"Oh, I am done with him, all right. I am so done with him. I wouldn't get back together if he came crawling, begging, pleading. I told him so. 'Don't call me,' I said. 'Don't text. Don't Facebook. Don't even look at me in the hallway. It is so over!'"

"Don't you think you might be overreacting?" I asked.

"Overreacting?" Ashley shouted. She hadn't even noticed that she had mistakenly wiped her eyes with a Cheeto and begun munching on a Kleenex. "Overreacting was when you dumped Kevin. That was just stupid. I mean, seriously, if he's going to choose the damn mascot over me then I am done! Finished! Out of there! I will never, ever talk to him again!"

I wiped the Cheeto crumbs out of her eyes while she spit out the wad of Kleenex.

"So what do we do now?" Ashley asked.

"Well," I said. "I could get Kevin to talk to him. You know how much Marc likes you. I bet he'll come around."

"Stop!" Ashley said. "I meant what do we do about Mr. Cooper and KABOOM? About finding a place to meet?"

"We can do it at my house," I said. "Or at Frank's church. We'll think of something."

Ashley sighed and put her head on my shoulder.

"Goddamn Ferris wheel," she said.

"Yeah," I agreed. "It kind of sucks, doesn't it."

•

School was awkward. The no-contact rule was in full force. In between classes I'd post up at the end of the hallway, scan the field for he-who-shall-not-be named, and give Ashley the thumbs-up signal when the coast was clear. She would race from class to class with her eyes on the floor, desperate to reduce the chance of any inadvertent sightings. Given that

Marc was Kevin's best friend, it was doubly awkward when the two of them were together. Since I wasn't allowed to talk to Marc, I'd have to use hand signals to get Kevin's attention. It was all super-complicated.

And then there was Mr. Cooper. Oh my God, the man was a wreck! A total basket case. He was so out of it that he had quit combing or flossing. His hair was a mess and there were green things growing between his teeth. Thin as he was, he seemed to be losing weight. You could practically see right through him.

Rather than demand an explanation from him immediately, we decided to give him the silent treatment. In fact, we ignored him completely. We could see that it was killing him.

After a few days of this, Frank convinced us of the virtue of forgiveness. "'For if you forgive men when they sin against you,'" he quoted, "'your heavenly Father will also forgive you.'"

Fortunately for Mr. Cooper, Ashley and I were so exhausted from devoting all of our mad vibes at Marc that we didn't have much left in the wrath department for Coop.

After school, a bunch of us KABOOMers converged on Mr. Cooper's classroom to offer up the olive branch. Minus Piggy. Piggy was still in a rage. He wanted to burn down the school. "It's us versus them!" Piggy ranted. "The line has been crossed. He's either with us or against!"

Piggy was not exactly one to forgive and forget.

But it was awfully hard to stay mad at Mr. Cooper for long. He was so pathetic in his remorse.

"You must think I am an evil, evil man!" Coop said, his head in his hands. "I have totally let you down. But I was told by Principal Miller that I had to quit KABOOM. I did not take it lightly. I ranted. I raved. You have got to believe me."

"We believe you," I said.

"Miller's cut me a lot of slack before, but he wasn't going to budge on this one. American was going to withhold their latest donation if the school continued to sanction this club. Miller gave me a choice: stop being the advisor or stop teaching. What was I to do?"

Mr. Cooper looked like he was ready to cry. It was super-awkward.

"It's okay, Mr. Cooper," Ashley said. "We'll meet somewhere else. We'll still do our thing. It's not like you did anything anyway."

"Ashley" I said. "Don't make this worse."

"You must hate me!" Mr. Cooper said, his voice low and trembling.

"We don't hate you," I said. "We could never hate you."

"'Woe to that man by whom the Son of Man is betrayed!'" Coop said. "'It would have been good for that man if he had not been born.'"

"What are you talking about?" I asked.

"It's what Jesus said about Judas," Frank said. "That's a little over the top, Mr. Cooper. I don't think what you did to us is quite that bad. I wouldn't floss—I mean, fret too much over it."

"Anyway, we get it," Ashley said. "You had to do what you had to do. And, seriously, what kind of a job could you possibly get other than in this shithole?"

"Ashley!" I scolded.

"I just meant he's so old and all."

"Thanks," Mr. Cooper said. To our great relief, he had brought out his flosser again. The in-between green-tooth thingies were creeping me out. "You've made me feel so much better."

54

"Look at this girl," Ashley said. We were back in my room, supposedly writing a letter to the Environmental Protection Agency about how horrible mountaintop removal was. Ashley had insisted on taking a break from saving Tom and was flipping through the pages of *Teen Vogue*, dissing all the anorexic models, laughing at their hairstyles. She still wasn't over the breakup with Marc, but at least she was laughing again.

Given the disaster that was the last KABOOM meeting combined with Ashley's heartbreak, I still hadn't broached the idea that the mine just might be a historic site. But now it seemed time to tell her. Probably way past time.

"It's like that day you stuck a spoon in the light socket in second grade," Ashley continued. "The Frankenstein's bride look, remember? Even Mr. Cooper on a bad hair day doesn't look this wack. Could you imagine a photo shoot with your hair in this clustermuck? I'd sue the magazine!"

"Seriously, Ashley," I said. "Enough of the monster 'dos. I've been thinking. Kevin and my father were looking into possible Civil War historic sites on the mountain and it just may be that our mine is part of one. Can you believe it? If that's the case, then we may be on to something big, Ashley. Something really big! I mean, we might be able to use historic preservation as a way to stop American! And don't go biting my head off over this, but maybe we should bring KABOOMers to our mine and have a meeting there. Think how dramatic that would be? They'd all flip! I know we made a pact never to tell anyone about it, but maybe now's the time. It feels right to me."

Ashley ignored me.

"Wait, wait, how about her?" Ashley flipped to a particularly frightening image. "Is this like the Halloween issue or what? Scary, that's what it is. I mean, total zombie. Just look at her."

I grabbed the magazine and threw it under the bed.

"Stop, Ash! Are you even listening to me? We need to figure out what to do. We may not have that much time. American has been quiet for way too long. There have been articles in the paper and they did that assembly thingy but other than that they've been eerily silent. They're probably trying to keep it all hush-hush and then, *bam*, bring the hammer down. Just like that. I know they're up to something, Ashley. There's no way a bunch of ripped-down flags are going to stop a big company project like that. It just isn't. They're going to be back. I can feel it. Sooner rather than later."

"Whoa, whoa, slow down. If you're saying saving Mount Tom is more important than trashing the teen vogueies, then I'm out of here!"

This time I ignored her.

"What do you think?" I asked. "About telling everyone and then meeting in the mine? It would get people pumped. We swore it would be our secret forever but . . ."

Ashley looked away.

"What?" I asked. "What's the matter?"

Ashley sat up, swung her legs onto the side of the bed, began to say something but looked down and stopped herself.

"I get it," I said. "I know how much it means to you. To both of us. The mine is our place. Our secret place. I know what you're thinking. But saving Tom is bigger than the two of us, Ashley. As hard as it is, we're going to have to give it up. I should have told you about the permitting thing a while ago. I'm sorry. It was just that I was afraid you'd want to tell everyone and then, you know, the mine wouldn't be ours anymore. And that sucks. It really sucks. But I think that the time has come to . . ."

"I took Marc there," Ashley said, still not looking at me.

"You *what?*"

"I took Marc there. Ugh! A few days before we broke up."

"You took him . . . ?"

"Yeah. To the mine. We did it there."

"You took Marc? To *our* mine? Without asking me?"

Ashley didn't answer. She had begun to cry.

"And you did it there?"

I was furious!

"You had no right!" I yelled. "You had no right to bring him there without asking me. That was *our* mine! That was our secret and we made a pact in the seventh grade and we swore that come hell or high water we would never tell anyone about it. Never! I didn't even tell Kevin about it when he brought up the whole historic preservation thing. And you brought Marc there? *Him?* And you did it there?"

Ashley fell back into my bed, her tears soaking the sheets.

"Now it's not our place," I said, my voice buckling. "And it never will be again!"

I wished I was over at Ashley's. I wished I was in her bedroom so I could stomp out and slam her door and run home and go to my bedroom and slam my door and be in my place where no one could come in. And if she called I wouldn't answer the phone. And if she came over I wouldn't let her in.

"*You're* crying?" I said. "*I* should be the one crying. That was our sacred place on our sacred mountain and you threw it all away. You've ruined everything!"

Ashley put a pillow on her head in a fruitless attempt to muffle her sobs.

"And now that you've broken up with him he'll probably go out and tell all of his friends about how he did it with you up there and they'll go up and spray graffiti and trash it with beer bottles and before you know it they'll turn it into an effin crystal meth lab! And if it was a historic site they'll screw it all up so bad that it will be useless to us. Useless! Marc betrayed you once. He'll do it again!"

I started to cry even louder than Ashley.

Shit, shit, and triple shit.

Britt opened my bedroom door.

"What's up, ladies?" Britt asked. "Boy trouble?"

"Get out!" I yelled, taking the pillow off of Ashley's head and throwing it at Britt.

"Jeez!" Britt said "Excuse me for breathing." She turned and made a hasty retreat.

Everything was going to shit. All of the bad stuff that was happening came crashing down on me at once. Miller had kicked our group out of school. Coop had turned Judas. Taylor had dumped Britt. Marc had chosen the mascot over KABOOM. Ashley had dumped Marc. And now this.

I thought about what Sadie and Dad had said about Mom. About how mean people could be. About how unfair it all was. Maybe they were right. Maybe it was all just too much for me. Maybe I should throw in the towel and just give up.

"It doesn't even matter anyway," I continued, my voice breaking. "They're just going in there with their death machines and they're going to cut down all of the trees and they're going to blow the top off the mountain, and it's all going to be SHIT! I don't even care about it anymore. None of it matters!"

Ashley was having trouble breathing she was crying so hard.

I'd seen her cry before. I'd seen her cry more times than I could count. Once she had climbed way up high on Bradley Beech and a limb broke and she fell and dislocated her shoulder and cried so hard she threw up.

But I'd never seen her cry like this.

"If you're going to throw up, go to the bathroom," I said. "Don't barf my bed."

"Woof, woof," Ashley mumbled through her tears.

"Barf, not bark, you idiot!"

"I was going to tell you before," she said, tears still streaming.

"Yeah, right," I said. "Why did you do it?"

"I don't know. I just wanted to share it with him. God, I wish I hadn't. The jerk."

"I want to share it with Kevin and I haven't!"

"I'm sorry. I am so sorry."

Ashley caught her breath, composed herself and scooted closer to me.

I wanted to criss-cross applesauce her. I wanted to kick her out of my room. I wanted to make her go home and cry herself to sleep in her own bed.

But it's awfully hard to do that when your best friend in the whole universe is lying in your bed and holding your hand, crying her eyes out, and apologizing over and over again.

"You really did it with him there?" I asked.

Ashley perked up.

"We did. It was fun. A little creepy. A little kinky. But really fun. Afterwards my hair looked like zombie girl's, but other than that. . . And here's the tragedy. Just when he finally figured out where my you-know-what is I've gone and dumped him."

"Humph," I said, still mad as hell.

Ashley had finally toned it down to sniffles.

"I am so sorry for not asking you. I really am. But we were going out and we were looking for a place to fool around and it just sort of happened. I'm sorry."

"Humph!" I said again.

Ashley reached over to my bedside table and pulled out two Kleenexes. She handed one of them to me.

"You know," Ashley continued, "everything you just said was totally right. Everything except for one thing."

"I've never said anything wrong in my life," I replied.

"Well, there's always a first time. And this was it."

"Okay. Tell me."

"You said it doesn't matter. You said they're just going to go in with their death machines and cut down all of the trees and blow the top off of Tom and turn it all to shit."

"Yeah," I said. "What's your point?"

"You're wrong. They aren't going to do it. It's not going to happen, Cyndie. And do you know why?"

"No. Tell me why."

"Because of you. You're going to stop them. You're going to think of something, just like you've done with this whole historic preservation thing. I knew you would. Everyone in KABOOM knew you would. That's why everyone keeps showing up to meetings. That's why everyone's so stoked. That is so awesome about our mine maybe being a Civil War site! I can't believe I didn't think of that before! I mean, I always just assumed it was Hillbilly Tom's mine. Those kinds of places are a dime a dozen around here. But if it isn't . . .

"You know, Cyndie, the tree cutters and the mountaintop blower-uppers may be incredibly powerful. They may have all the equipment. They may have all the money. But we've got a secret weapon that they don't have."

"What's that?" I asked.

"We've got you!" Ashley said.

It's awfully hard to stay mad at your best friend in the whole universe, even though they screwed up royally, when they go and say stuff like that. Even if it is a crock of crap.

I tried my best to humph again but all that came out was a sigh.

"I'm right, aren't I?" Ashley asked.

I took a deep breath and held it. Difficult as it was, I got a sudden jolt that this wasn't just about me. I could picture Widow Combs and Mom and Elise from Kayford's Mountain and all those who came before me and all those who would come after holding their breaths as well. As imperfect as we all were, we were fighting the good fight. And there could be no letting up.

I let my breath out, scooted closer to Ashley, and gave her a forgiving hug.

"Actually," I said, "you're wrong. *We're* going to stop them, Ashley. Not *me*. *We*."

"We are," Ashley said, squeezing my hand.

We lay there holding hands, our heads touching.

"Did your hair really look like zombie girl's?" I asked.

"Worse!" Ashley giggled. "Even worse."

55

I WAS NEATLY FOLDED into Kevin's lap on my living room couch while we waited for Britt and Dad to come home from an ice cream run. I had ordered chocolate chip cookie dough. Kevin, for some godforsaken reason, was getting boring old vanilla.

What was wrong with that boy?

The four of us were spending an awesome evening watching a really stupid movie.

I loved how perfectly I fit into Kevin's lap. I was scrunched up with my head tucked into his shoulder and my knees folded into his legs. With Britt and Dad gone we were all over the map. I had one hand inching a few degrees south of his belt buckle. He had one hand drifting north of my inner thigh while his other hand slid east to west in delightful circling motions under my top.

I was hoping Dad's car would break down. Or maybe the ice cream store would get robbed and Britt and Dad would have to be interrogated as witnesses. Or at the very least, the two of them would be abducted by aliens and whisked off to another planet to get prodded and probed and poked for at least another hour or two. Anything to delay their coming home. Anything to allow Kevin to continue doing exactly what he was doing.

And then, suddenly, Kevin stopped kissing me. He looked into my eyes.

"You know what?" he said, this time circling my lips with his fingers. His voice was trembling.

"What?" I asked, twirling his hair. I loved to twirl his hair. He had been all set to get it cut the day before but I had convinced him to leave it long for at least one more week. Longer was so much more twirlable.

"I really, really, *really* like you," he said.

"I am so, so, so glad."

"And you know what else?"

"Tell me," I said, twirling away.

"That's as high as it goes."

"High as what goes?"

"Reallies on the likeability scale. Three of them. It doesn't go any higher than that."

"So you can't really, really, really, *really* like me?"

"Nope. Can't do it. Against the rules. Three reallies is the max."

"That doesn't seem fair," I said, faking a frown. Kevin put his fingers on my lips and pushed them up into a smile

"I'm not so sure," Kevin said. "Maybe it *is* fair. Maybe it's even better than fair! This is, like, uncharted territory for me, but I'm kind of thinking that if you do one more really cute thing, or even look at me one more time in that way that you do, then we may have to switch it up."

"Switch it up?" I asked. "What do you mean?"

Kevin kissed me. One kiss on each of my eyes, on each of my cheeks, one on my chin, and then a long, slow yummy mouth kiss.

Once more he pulled away and looked at me.

"Switch it up," he whispered. "Begin a brand new scale. You know, upgrade. Move on to something beyond *like*."

"Beyond *like*," I murmured. I could barely breathe.

"Yeah," he said. "Beyond *like*."

I took his face in my hands and kissed him hard.

Kevin sat up. "That's it!" he said. "That's what I was talking about. Now you've gone and done it! There's no turning back!"

"Gone and done what?"

"That one more really cute thing. Just like I said. Do you know what that means?" He took both my hands in his and looked right into my eyes. I held my breath.

"Tell me," I whispered.

"That means that I am totally and completely . . ."

The door opened and Britt came crashing in.

"I scream! You scream! We all scream for ice cream!" she sang. "Never fear, ice cream is here!" She flung herself over the top of the couch, plopped down next to us, and slung her legs onto mine, which were still draped over Kevin's.

"You didn't watch any more of the movie did you?" she asked. "It's like the worst thing ever, but I kind of like it." Britt stopped and stared at the two of us.

"What?" she asked. "What's going on? What did I miss?"

I nestled my head back onto Kevin's shoulder, reached around him, and held him as tight as I possibly could.

•

"Wow!" Ashley said. "He was going to say it! He was going to come right out and say it!"

"Are you sure?" I asked.

"Are you kidding me? He was! He definitely was! What else could it possibly have been?"

I had given Ashley the blow-by-blow of last night's episode, and she was right. At least, I hoped she was.

Kevin had almost said it! He was that close! That close!

I could have killed that half-wit twit of a Britt!

Sisters! Achh!

"What would you have said?" Ashley asked. "He was going to drop the L-bomb. You know he was! What were you going to say?"

What *was* I going to say? I probably wouldn't have been able to move my tongue at all. It would have just flopped there, hanging out and rolling around dripping pools of saliva like someone in the middle of a seizure, for goodness sake.

Maybe, just maybe, I might have spit out some such incoherent spaz gobbledygook that would have left poor Kevin wondering what part of Planet Ditz I came from.

"*Plumph!*" I would have sputtered. Or maybe "*Blurph!*" Or something equally insane.

Either that or I would have just passed out.

It wasn't that I hadn't been thinking about this forever.

I had liked Kevin from the get go. And then really liked him. And then really, really, *really* liked him.

And now?

I knew I loved my father. But that's because he took care of me and gave me things and got all misty-eyed whenever I brought home good grades and, well, he was my father. I was supposed to love him.

I knew I loved Auntie Sadie, because she was a lioness and I was her cub and she would have faced a herd of charging hippos and kicked their asses to save mine.

I knew I loved my sister, even though she was a royal pain in my butt and was always into my things and driving me crazy, and had totally blown Kevin's big moment. But she was, after all, my little sister. What else was I supposed to do? It's not like I really had a choice.

I knew I loved Ashley, because she was my Ashley and I would always love her, even when she screwed up. And she would always love me, and that was just the way that it always had been and always would be.

I knew I loved Mount Tom and his trees and his animals, because the thought of the bastards blowing his top off made me so totally crazy that I was ready to do just about anything, anything, to stop them.

And then there was Kevin. Just like he had said, this was uncharted territory.

One thing that made me nuts was when kids said they loved someone and adults pooh-poohed it and got all dismissive and stupid and said crap like "You don't even know what love is." As if adults have cornered the market on love, with so many of them blowing it big time and screwing around and breaking up and getting divorced and generally making mayhem and mockery out of the whole love thing.

The way I see it, if someone says that they're in love, then they're in love. No questions asked. I mean, who am I, who is anyone, to tell them that they aren't?

"What would you have said?" Ashley asked again.

I had spent a sleepless night, eyes wide open, replaying the conversation over and over in my head and thinking up the most awesome reply had Kevin actually come out with it. An Academy Award–winning reply. A reply that would be the title of the number-one hit song by Beyonce or Taylor Swift or whoever was the hottest star of the moment. A reply that would go viral and be on the lips of every teenage girl in the entire world. A reply that would have completely blown Kevin away and made him get down on bended knee, weeping with joy, and ask me to marry him on the spot even though I was a few weeks shy of sixteen and he was less than two years older.

"And you would have said what again?" Ashley asked for the third time.

"*Plumph!*"

"Excuse me?" she asked.

"*Blurph!*"

"Ahhh. . . Now I get it. Weird-girl-speak for totally and completely!"

Ashley hugged me.

56

It was Friday afternoon, the day before the Great Mount Tom Children's Crusade. KABOOM had nominated (more like forced!) me to be the speaker and, flattered as I was, I was nervous as hell.

Ever since we had been kicked out of the high school, KABOOM had been meeting at my house. We had put a lot of time and effort into organizing the crusade. We had it all over Facebook and other social media. We had sent out a press release to the local paper and to TV and radio stations. We had plastered posters up, not just at our school, but also at two other schools in the towns nearby.

THE TIME TO MARCH IS NOW!!!!!

KEEP THE TOP ON TOM!

JUST SAY NO TO MOUNTAINTOP REMOVAL!

SATURDAY, NOVEMBER 18

NOON

SOULS' HAVEN EVANGELICAL CHURCH

SHOW THE WORLD YOU CARE!

KABOOM

KIDS AGAINST BLOWING OFF OUR MOUNTAINTOPS

A few of the cooler teachers like Ms. Fogg-Willits, the art teacher, had disregarded Principal Miller's directive and allowed us to come into their classes to give a plug for the march. Even Diaper Lady, the English teacher—surprise surprise—let us do our thing. She had even gone so far as to require her classes to write an essay on mountaintop removal. Mr. Cooper, while still not entirely in our good graces, had somewhat redeemed himself by allowing extra credit for all those kids who showed up at the march. We had even finagled our way into the middle school to drum up support, and we had Britt's posse on board.

Talking in front of those classes at school had been hard enough. Just the thought of standing in front of a crusade of kids and giving a real speech scared the crap out of me. The old angst-filled Custard of storybook-dragon fame was crawling back into her cage again, her spiked dragon tail tucked meekly beneath her belly. Belinda was nowhere to be seen.

"Please, will you do it?" I begged Ashley for the millionth time. "Please?"

"Unh uh! You're the go-to girl. And if there were any hecklers out there I'd go off and start pounding them. You know me. Anyway, you're way better at this sort of thing!"

"I am not!"

"You are too!"

"I'm fifteen, for goodness sake!" I said. "What do I know?"

"You're two weeks older than I am," Ashley said. "And you know a lot!"

"I do not!"

"You do too!"

"We sure aren't sounding like we're fifteen," I said.

"We are too!" Ashley said.

"We are not!"

I was stuck with being the speaker.

Kevin had assured me I'd do great.

"Chill!" he said. "You're going to kill it!"

"How do you know?" I asked.

"'Cause I know! You always say the right thing."

I reminded him of our mini-breakup.

"Well," Kevin said, smiling. "Almost always."

"And what if I don't?" I asked. "What if I do something really stupid instead? What if I trip going up the church stairs? What if my voice goes all wavery and weird? What if I make a complete and total ass of myself? What if I run out of things to say?"

"You? Run out of things to say? Fat chance of that happening!"

I poked him.

"Don't sweat it," Kevin continued. "All the girls will be jealous because you're the center of attention. All the boys will be checking you out. And most kids won't be listening to a word you say anyway. They'll all be way too busy scoping out who's there!"

"Thanks, Kev," I said, poking him again. "That's just great. Really great! I've been in agony for days working on my little speech thingy—and now you tell me it doesn't even matter?"

"It matters to me!" he said. "I'll be listening."

"You better be!" I told him.

To make matters even scarier, we found out that our press releases had actually worked. A Charlestown television station was sending a camera crew down to make a news story out of the crusade. They would have their cameras rolling while I spoke!

I had a tizzy in my tummy and a hunk of lumps in my throat.

•

"Can I lead the parade?" Britt asked.

"It's not a parade," I told her. "It's a march. There's a big difference."

"Whatever!" she said. "But think how fun it would be if the Twirling Tweens led the charge? Not just us baton-twirlers but clowns and stilt-walkers too. It would be awesome!"

"No clowns!" I said, covering my ears. "Please! No clowns!"

Britt and a bunch of her friends had been taking a circus arts class in the downtown community center and they were dying to strut their stuff.

"Any dancing bears?" I asked.

"How'd you know?" Britt said. "It was supposed to be a secret!"

Britt's best friend Patty had a sister in the second grade and she was helping some of the little elementary school dweebs make polar bear puppets.

"Polar bears?" I asked Britt. "And the point of that is . . ."

"Oh my God, Cyndie, don't you know anything?" Britt rolled her eyes. "You blow up the mountain and you get the coal. You burn the coal and you warm the earth. You warm the earth and you melt the icebergs. You melt the icebergs and you drown the polar bears. And polar bears are *sooo* cute!"

Who could argue with that?

Kevin told me that some of the rowdier seniors were planning on having a party down by the river in Heaver's Holler on Friday night. The theme was "Throw Up—Don't Blow Up!" Evidently vast quantities of alcohol were to be consumed. As in: what else was new.

He asked me if I wanted to go.

"Wow!" I said, "That sounds like so much fun! Should I wear a trash bag for splatter control over my hoop skirt? I hope it's BYOT."

"BYOT?" Kevin asked.

"Bring your own toilet! Or do you just hurl away all over Mother Nature?"

"I just asked," Kevin said sheepishly. "Jeez, at least they're with us!"

He had a point. But we (as in I) decided we'd go to the movies instead. And a chick flick at that! I had had quite enough of things getting blown up and thrown up, thank you very much.

Frank had gotten his evangelical youth group totally pumped and they had promised to show up en masse. It was reassuring to know that we would have God, the circus, polar bears, and a bunch of totally hungover seniors on our side.

After a sleepless night, Saturday, thank goodness, finally came. It was warmish and beautiful. Good cause or not, there were a lot of fair-weather friends out there who were probably not going to show if the mid-November weekend weather sucked.

We had no idea what the turnout would be. Twenty kids? Fifty? A hundred? We were hoping for lots, but we really didn't have a clue.

The members of KABOOM met at the church at eleven o'clock to go over last-minute details. Sam, to everyone's shock, had given up fishing for the day in order to show. Even Jon Buntington was there, which made me feel much better. Not that Kevin wasn't a certifiable hunk, but no one messed with Jon. It was good to have a little more visible muscle. You never knew what might happen.

Ashley was still not over Marc's betrayal, but at least she had progressed to the point where she wasn't looking over her shoulder every fifteen seconds. She had even, gasp, begun chatting it up with Sam in a pretty flirtatious way.

"You think he'll show?" I asked her.

"Sam?" Ashley replied. "He's already here."

"Ashley!" I said. "You know who I'm talking about."

"What do I care?" Ashley said, lying through her teeth. "He's history!"

So there we were, standing on top of the church steps, not knowing what to expect, and a crowd began to gather. Big kids. Little kids. Kids we knew. Kids we didn't. Kids from other schools in other towns who had somehow heard about the crusade and had managed to make it to the church on time. Kids eight to eighteen, with a few toddlers thrown in for good measure. One of the tenth-grade girls who had dropped out because she was pregnant even showed up with her baby in tow.

"Wow!" Ashley said.

"Double wow!" I said, clinging tightly to Kevin.

"Who would have thought? It's like a real crusade!"

"Only better! No water cannons or attack dogs in sight!"

"Damn!" Piggy said, borrowing Britt's baton and twirling it menacingly. "I was hoping for a little more drama!"

Kids were crazy creative. There were hand-painted signs and outfits galore.

Tammy and Rich had come dressed as Uncle Sam and Auntie Sammie, all decked out in red, white, and blue. Rich was waving an American flag. Tammy had a sign with the words to "America the Beautiful" written on it:

O beautiful for spacious skies,
For amber waves of grain,
For purple mountain majesties
Above the fruited plain!
America! America! God shed His grace on thee,
And crown thy good with brotherhood
From sea to shining sea!

On the other side of the sign it said:

KEEP AMERICA BEAUTIFUL
AND
THE MOUNTAINS MAJESTIC:
STOP MOUNTAINTOP REMOVAL!

Sam was dressed in his fisherman outfit, lures and flies and hooks sticking out every which way. He had his fishing pole in one hand and in the other a sign that read *Mountaintop Removal's Awfully Fishy!*

Becky had a sign with a picture of a mountaintop blowing up, volcano-like, with rocks raining down on a cute little farm and terrified baby farm critters scattering in every direction. *Chicken Little Was Right!* the caption read. *The Sky Really Is Falling! Save Mount Tom!*

Sharon, whose parents owned the Tasty Top soft-serve ice cream parlor, had made a huge cardboard cutout of an ice cream cone. The scoop of ice cream was drawn to look like a mountaintop and was drooping precariously. *If the Top Falls Off It's Ruined!* the caption read. In smaller letters it said, *Tammy's Tasty Top—Say you saw this sign and get a free kiddie cone.*

You know you're doing something right when you've got the local ice cream shop on board!

Not only were there kids and signs and outfits and props, but the TV station from Charlestown had shown up and there was a reporter from the newspaper as well. It was surreal: interviewers, cameras, lights, and action. One of the camera crew shoved a microphone into my face and I blathered on about the evils of mountaintop removal while crowds of kids continued to gather.

"Promise again you won't dump me, now that you're famous?" Kevin whispered in my ear.

"No chance!" I whispered back, giving his hand a squeeze. "Like it or not you're stuck with me!"

"I like it!" he said, squeezing back.

I was not exactly looking my best. Ashley had spent over an hour on my hair but the wind had picked up and whipped it into a frenzied faceful. My damn chin had erupted again and two zits the size of Mount Tom had reared their hideous heads. Even without dynamite, they were threatening to blow their tops off and spew grossness all over the crowd. My throat still had a tangled knot in it and I was paranoid that nothing would come out.

I turned to Ashley and tried desperately to untangle my tongue.

"I can't do this!" I whimpered.

"There are things a girl has got to do, and this is one of them," Ashley said firmly.

"I wrote the speech!" I said. "You read it!"

"You're going to be great!"

"I have to pee!"

"Hold it!"

The time had come. Channeling Widow Combs and Mom and Elise, I turned to face the crowd.

I had practiced my speech in front of Kevin and Ashley and Britt. It was maybe three minutes at the most. Three minutes. That wasn't long. I could do three minutes.

I breathed in, letting my hair and my zits and my voice and the butterflies in my stomach do what they were going to do.

"I'm super-excited to be here!" I began. "And it's so awesome to see so many of you out there!"

The church parking lot was overflowing with kids, and they hooted and hollered.

"We are here today to save Mount Tom! We are here today because mountaintop removal destroys the environment! Pollutes our water! Leaves us poorer! Makes us sick! We are here today because we care! We are here today because we are going to stop this madness!"

With every other word I said, all the kids in the crowd, way more than a hundred by now, would clap and cheer and stomp their feet. Some boy had even brought along an air horn, which he blew every fifteen seconds.

I'd say something and they'd all yell it back.

It was sick!

"Blowing the top off the mountain is wrong!" I yelled.

"It's wrong!" they yelled back.

"It's stupid!" I yelled.

"It's stupid!" they yelled back.

"Are we going to let them do it?"

"NO!" they yelled back.

"What are we going to do?"

"Save Mount Tom!"

Three minutes? Who was I kidding? The speech took me fifteen minutes to get through! I had the crowd whipped into a frenzy. Even in my wildest dreams I hadn't thought it would go down as well as it did. It was such a rush!

The plan was that as soon as I had finished we would begin the march, but suddenly, to my total shock, who should bound up the church steps but Marc Potvin. Marc the betrayer! Coming back to haunt us. He was dressed in his mascot outfit, the Greenfield High School Miner, his miner's helmet, oversized overalls, inflatable shovel, and all.

"Shit!" I thought. If he was here to disrupt the march, things could get ugly pretty quickly.

"My name is Marc Potvin," he yelled to the crowd, not even looking in my direction, "and I am the Greenfield High School Miner!"

Kids pumped their fists in the air.

"Miner! Miner! Miner!" they chanted.

Ashley was standing in the front row, her mouth open, stunned, frozen. I didn't know whether to try to stop Marc from speaking or let it play out. I turned to Kevin for support but he was smiling. Smiling!

"I'm here today," Marc boomed, "to tell you that mountaintop removal's got nothing to do with regular mining. Nothing! American Coal Company wants to blow up the mountain *and* they want to take the miner out of the mine. No miners mean more money for them. And it seems to me that that's all they really care about. Not you. Not me. Not our dads and moms and uncles and granddaddies who work the mines. Not about Greenfield. And definitely not about Mount Tom. They only care about their bottom line: Money! I mean no disrespect for the hard-working coal miners out there, but, after a hell of a lot of thought"—he winked at Ashley—"I'm here today to tell you that I can no longer, in good conscience, go out with this getup! If American wants to get rid of the miner, then they'll have to get rid of me!"

And then, with a dramatic gesture, Marc flung off his miner's helmet, stripped out of his overalls, and then, for the grand finale, took a pin out of his pocket and popped the inflatable shovel.

The crowd roared. One of the girls yelled, "Keep on going! Take it all off!"

"Coal may be king but I refuse to be the jester!" he yelled to the crowd. "Is there anything funny about mountaintop removal?"

"No!" the kids yelled.

"Is there anything funny about blowing the top off of Tom?"

"No!"

"Then I'm telling you right here, right now, Greenfield High School needs a new mascot!"

Kevin came scooting up the stairs and helped Marc squeeze into a tight T-shirt.

Kevin was in on it! This was well rehearsed!

"*KABOOM!*" the shirt read, with a picture drawn of Mount Tom. Underneath was written "*SAVE THE MOUNTAIN!*" It had the look of Kevin's art, infantile and pretty pathetic, definitely not one of Ashley's masterpieces. But *boy*, did it work.

Marc continued, his voice growing even stronger.

"From this day forward!" he yelled. "I am the Greenfield High School *Mountain!*"

Ashley's face was ready to split in two from the size of her smile.

Marc went into body-building pose, sucking in his stomach, puffing out his chest, raising his arms and flexing his biceps to make them look like mountain peaks. He roared at the crowd and, once again, they roared right back at him!

"Mountain! Mountain! Mountain!" they chanted. The girls who had yelled for him to take it all off were jumping up and down and screaming.

"Wow!" I said to Ashley, who had joined me at the top of the steps. "I did not see that one coming! Double, no, *triple* wow!"

Ashley was speechless.

"Let's march!" Marc ordered, turning to Ashley and leaping into her arms.

KABOOM! Off we went!

•

As promised, the circus led the charge. Marc, betrayer turned hero, was right: none of this was a laughing matter, but there was certainly nothing wrong with adding a little joy to the struggle.

Britt and her fellow tween twirlers were whirling and twirling away, all in sync until one of them would drop her baton and they'd all giggle like crazy. It was hard not to notice Britt giggling even louder whenever the stilt-walker, a boy in her grade, was anywhere within earshot.

"Looks like Britt has gotten over Taylor," Kevin said.

"Looks like Marc never got over Ashley," I said, putting my arm around him.

One of the circus girls was doing backward somersaults. One boy was walking on his hands. The stilt-walker was tottering on his stilts, precariously leaning this way and that, one pothole away from catastrophe. Two goofball clowns (fortunately not nearly as frightening as I had feared) were hamming it up and, courtesy of Auntie Sadie, handing out fistfuls of Cheetos. There was even a kid on a tiny, souped-up bike doing wheelies and jumps and ringing his three little bicycle bells like a car alarm on crystal meth.

Behind them came a mini–marching band with four kids from the high school playing the tuba, trombone, banjo, and ukulele. They were wildly out of tune and it was unclear whether the sound was actual songs or just plain noise. But what they lacked in musical ability they certainly made up for in exuberant enthusiasm, so it was all good.

They were followed by the polar bear contingent. The little ones had their puppets on their arms and they were waving them around and doing a little Texas two-step and it was the cutest thing you'd ever seen.

"Watch and learn," Kevin said to me. "That'll be us at the cotillion next weekend!"

One of the kids had a hand-drawn sign with two polar bears sitting on a mountaintop hugging each other. The caption, in little-kid scrawl, read "*Blow Kisses Not Mountains.*" It made me want to cry.

Then came the God Squad.

Piggy had suggested that Frank dress in a loincloth, put a crown of thorns on his head, drag a wooden cross behind him, and have a sign draped across his chest reading *Mount Tom*. Piggy had volunteered to dress like a Roman gladiator with a sign that said *American Coal Company*, and he would whip Frank with his chains as they walked.

Frank was aghast.

"That," he had told Piggy, "is the most sacrilegious, offensive, stupid idea I've ever heard of."

Piggy mumbled something about "sticking it to the man," but he hadn't brought it up again.

So instead, the church kids had made a banner that read *Souls' Haven Evangelical Youth Group Says No to Mountaintop Removal* and they all marched under that. Not quite as theatrical, but overall probably a much better idea.

The rest of us followed behind, holding our signs and chanting our slogans, with the high school hungovers sluggishly dragging their sorry asses in the rear. And the way they were all over each other, it was hard to tell where Ashley ended and Marc began.

Between the circus freaks, the cutesy polar bears, the marching band, and the colorful signs and banners, the TV camera crew was in seventh heaven, frantically eating it all up.

> *What do we want?*
> *To Save Mount Tom!*
> *When will we do it?*
> *Now!*

"This is classic!" Kevin said, his arm around me, his hand straying down to caress my butt. I had finally stopped hyperventilating from my speech and the Marc shocker, and I was actually becoming calm enough to enjoy myself.

"You were awesome!" he said. "Just like I knew you'd be! I am so proud of you!"

"I am so proud of us!" I said, snuggling closer. "And can you believe what Marc just did? You were holding back on me! You knew!"

"I told you he'd come around," Kevin said, smiling. "There was only so long he could stay away from Ashley."

I sighed. All was right in the universe.

Whose Mountain?
Our Mountain!
Whose Mountain?
Our Mountain!

The chanting continued. Townsfolk were lining the street watching the crusade go by. Some clapped and cheered, others frowned and jeered. There were a few shouts of "Go back to your mamas!" or "Environmentalists suck!" but the overwhelming response was as good as you could expect. Way more fist pumps than middle fingers.

It was revealing to see which side people came down on. It was like a window into their politics. Some of the townsfolk I thought would be hostile and pissed were welcoming us with open arms. Others I had assumed sympathetic had their backs turned. A town divided.

We were almost to the coal company headquarters when we stopped and, on cue, stood in silence with our hands in the air and our faces looking down for two whole minutes.

During my speech I had prepared the marchers for this moment.

I had told kids to think about why we were here.

To think about the 500 mountains that had already had their tops blown off.

To think about the thousands of people whose lives were devastated by cancer and birth defects and sickness.

To think about the trees and the plants and the wildlife whose homes were no longer and whose wildness was disappearing.

To think about the planet that was warming and the climate that was changing and the need for all of us to take action now.

Kevin is the one who had come up with the idea for the two minutes of silence. I had thought that it sounded a little hokey and lame. I had thought that kids, particularly the littler ones, would wiggle and giggle their way through it.

But it worked. It really worked.

For two solid minutes you could have heard a mosquito fart. Total and complete silence. Some of the hungovers had made it to the front and were holding the puppeteers, who nestled, silent, in their arms. I got goose bumps.

And then, at exactly the end of two minutes, Kevin let out his rebel yell, the air horn answered, the marching band kicked it up, the polar bears roared, everyone hooted and hollered, and on we marched.

It was absolutely unreal!

I loved it. I loved everything about it!

I loved being surrounded by my people who felt the same way that I did.

I loved being in a crowd of kids who really and truly cared.

I loved being part of something way, way bigger than myself.

I loved walking with Kevin. I loved showing the world that I had a hottie boyfriend with his hands all over me. I loved that Marc and Ashley were back together and that other girls and guys were checking us out. I loved that little kids were looking up to us.

I loved being young and strong and pretty and smart and doing the right thing in the right place at the right time.

I loved it all. I pinched myself yet again to make sure this wasn't some fantastical-orgasmic-thinkabout-walking-day-dream thingy and that it was really and truly happening.

Who would have thought life could be so good?

And then, wouldn't you know it, life's Ferris wheel took a downward turn and the shit-show started.

We were almost to the center of town, walking under an overpass, when we were ambushed. Flat out, middle of the day, totally out-of-nowhere ambushed.

Okay. It wasn't Syria in 2015 or Iraq in 2005. It wasn't Birmingham, Alabama, in 1963. There were no suicide bombers or drone strikes or AK47s or tanks or attack dogs or rabid police.

But there *were* water balloons. Big ones. From the top of the overpass we were being bombarded by effin water bombs! Not just a few. Hundreds!

"Shit!" Ashley yelled. "It's those bastards! Bert and Michael and their dickhead posse. Look, I can see them!"

Sure enough, there on top of the bridge were the terrible twosome and their gang wreaking havoc on our heads. Balloon after balloon came splattering down.

The Children's Crusade stopped dead in its tracks. Everyone turned to look to me and Ashley for direction. Jon Buntington was twitching by my side like a pit bull on fire. Piggy, with his chains around his neck, was, as always, itching for a fight. One nod of my head would turn them loose and the dickhead posse would feel their wrath.

I recalled the YouTube clips of the 1963 Civil Rights Children's Crusade. Kids our age getting pummeled by police, ripped apart by dogs, turned end over end by fire hoses. And they didn't fight back. Not one of them. Unimaginable violence, unthinkable horror, met with nonviolent resistance. With the whole world watching, those kids had shown the whole world who was the most powerful. That might does not make right. That good can triumph over evil.

I didn't think for a moment that this was 1963. But I did think that if the kids back then could endure dogs and fire hoses and police batons, then we sure as heck could endure a bunch of stupid, lame water bombs.

"Sit!" I yelled. "Everybody sit!"

Kevin and I scooted over to the polar bear brigade, sat down, and folded a couple of the little ones under our arms, doing our best to shield them from further soaking. Other big kids followed suit, with the hungovers forming protective pyramids around the little dweebs. Everyone sat, except for the God Squad, who knelt in prayer.

We didn't run. We didn't cry. We didn't fight back. We just sat right down where we were, criss-crossing and apple saucing. We sat and started to sing the old civil rights anthem from that other Children's Crusade so long ago:

We shall not
We shall not be moved.
We shall not
We shall not be moved.
Just like a tree that's standing by the water.
We shall not be moved.

"We're sitting like a mountain!" I yelled.
"We shall not be moved!" kids sang back.
We're sitting like a mountain
We shall not be moved.
Just like a tree that's standing by the water.
We shall not be moved.
And the TV camera kept on rolling.

One of the hungovers, drenched to the core, reached into her purse and brought out a tube of face wash. She stood up, washed her face, and yelled to the top of the overpass "Hello! How's about one more, please! I'm waiting for a rinse here!"

Three of the polar bears stood up and starting roaring like bears. And dancing. Roaring and dancing and giggling like crazy.

Britt and her buddies went back into circus mode, baton twirling, somersaulting, hand walking, clowning, and stilting away, to much applause and whistling from the amazed onlookers.

The band started playing again.

The Great Mount Tom Children's Crusade, drenched, undaunted, and happy as could be, stood, rose, and marched onward.

57

THAT EVENING we were gathered in my living room, glued to the television. Britt, Dad, Kevin, a very happy Ashley, Marc (who couldn't stop grinning), me, and a boatload of popcorn. I was tucked into Kevin's arms, Ashley into Marc's, and Britt into Dad's. As always, Ashley had her feet in my lap.

"The middle toe," Ashley sighed. "Do that one. Do it harder."

"Ashley!" I told her, faking a frown. "I thought that's why you got back together with Marc. So I could retire from chief foot rubber. Marc the Mountain, you're dropping the ball here. You got to step it up!"

"No way!" Ashley said. "No one does it better than you! That's why you'll always be my best friend. My tootsies would shrivel up and wither away without that magic touch of yours. Anyway, Marc needs to pay attention to more important things." Ashley snuggled closer to him and kissed his neck.

"Cover your eyes, Dad," Britt said, putting her hands over Dad's face. "These teenagers and their hormones. It's like a minefield out there. Anything can happen."

"How old are you again?" Dad asked Britt.

"Twelve going on twenty," Kevin said. "But not a tween much longer—right, Britt? Don't you turn thirteen the same week Cyndie hits the sweet one-six?"

Dad let out a long sigh. "Two teens," he said. "What am I going to do then? How am I going to survive?"

"No worries!" Kevin said. "I'll be here to keep Cyndie in line."

"Yeah, right!" Ashley said, whacking him with a pillow. "Without us girls to watch over the two of you slackers, the place would go to holy hell!"

"You mean the three of them," Britt said. "Don't leave out poor old Dad. He may be old but he's still just a clueless guy."

"Shhh!" I shushed. "We're on!"

It was 6:00. Time for the local news.

If the camera crew hadn't been sympathetic to the Children's Crusade before the ambush they certainly were after. I got that they were supposed to be unbiased, present the news as it happened, and keep their own feelings in check. But the fact that the newswoman's enormously high mountain of a hairdo had been drenched flat by a water bomb had most certainly helped our cause.

"Look!" Britt yelled. "There I am!"

Sure enough, the segment opened with Britt and the Twirling Tweens leading the Crusade, twirling their batons and grinning away.

"I'm famous!" Britt screamed. "Do you see me? I'm on TV! I'm famous!"

"Shhh!" I told her.

There I was, addressing the crowd, sounding reasonably intelligent. The way the camera framed it, you couldn't tell whether there were two hundred kids or two thousand. It was awesome.

There was Marc, flinging down his miner's helmet, popping his shovel, and strutting his stuff.

"I still cannot believe you did that!" Ashley sighed, snuggling even closer to him. "And I am so happy you did!"

There was the march, zooming in on the cutest little ones waving their polar bears. Zooming out on the God Squad with their *What Would Jesus Do?* signs.

There was the ambush, with a water bomb exploding in the middle of the camera lens. *Boom!*

There was KABOOM duct taping the Save Mount Tom petitions to the door of the American Coal Company office.

There was a brief clip of a mountaintop removal site in another part of West Virginia, a bombed-out, moonscaped crater of total devastation. Then there was a scene from afar of *our* mountain: beautiful, green, glowing, sacred Mount Tom.

"Whether you agree with them or not," concluded the newscaster with her mountaintop hair flattened, water still dripping down her collar, "these kids have certainly shown they're out to make a difference."

End of story.

We all applauded. Kevin hugged me and fist-bumped Marc. Britt was bouncing up and down on the couch and couldn't stop screaming.

"I'm famous! Did you see me? I was on TV! I'm famous!"

58

DANCE TIME! The Civil War Cotillion! After months of anticipation the big night had finally arrived!

For all of its total and utter lameness, I was actually pretty psyched.

Number one: I got to be with Kevin. A date with Kevin, no matter how bizarre the setting, was the absolute best. It seemed like ages ago that he had first asked me out and I had bumbled my way into a yes. It was hard to believe the cotillion was supposed to have been our first date. Our very first! And now, by the time we were finally going, we were inseparable.

Number two: It was a dance. I loved to dance and, other than spinning around with Ashley in my room, I hardly ever got to. This would be my first dance with Kevin.

"It's jigs and reels and quadrilles," he said. "It's going to be a blast. Just no grinding! I think that's the only rule."

"If we can't grind, then why are we going?" I asked.

"We do get to swing, if that's any consolation. And promenade."

"Jumpin' gee willikers! And do-si-do? Please tell me we get to do-si-do!"

"Behave yourself and there might even be a little sashaying," he said.

"Ooh-la-la. Be still my heart!"

Number three: I got to do my hair in the 1860s way: two braided pigtails pinned in the back, and two more braids from the front swooped and tucked into them. Ashley and I watched a YouTube tutorial on hairstyles of the 1860s, and Ash was pumped to experiment on me. Of course, what should have taken a mere fifteen minutes lasted an hour and a half, with numerous near-death experiences. Hair spray in my eyes. Bobby pins twisted deep into my skull. And, horror of horrors, way too many little wispies sticking out of my braids.

"Twist, pin, and tuck," I ordered. "Twist, pin, and—ouch! Stop! If you stab me one more time, I'm going to . . ."

"No pain, no gain," Ashley said.

"Said by the one not bleeding profusely from the gushing wounds on her head."

"Fashion over comfort, darling. Beauty is pain. And God, you look so cute!"

"Yeah, right. Do you think he'll even notice?"

"He better. You've lost way too much blood for this to go unrecognized."

The only problem with the braided pigtails was that they were tucked against my ears so tightly that it made it kind of hard to hear. But I figured it was a dance so it wouldn't matter.

Number four: I got to wear my hoop skirt again. I hadn't put it on since the reenactments were over for the season, and I'd grown super-fond of it ever since Kevin had made the hotness comment. Sadie's reenactment friend, knowing how attached I had become, had actually gone and given it to me. It was now my absolute fave outfit.

"How do you go to the bathroom in that thing?" Ashley asked. Not only had she done my hair but she had also shoe-horned me into my hoop skirt and frock and slip and all of my assorted Civil War getup. "I don't see how you'd even fit into the stall."

"I don't go," I said.

"What do you mean you 'don't go'?"

"I don't go to the bathroom."

"How do you not go the bathroom? What if you have to pee?"

"I stopped drinking three hours ago," I said.

"Oh my God, Cyndie, that's just weird. You should wear one of those adult diaper thingies."

"I am not going on a date with Kevin wearing an effin diaper!"

"It's way better than pissing yourself!"

"Stop! You're making me laugh. And when I laugh I have to—"

"Pee," she cut in. "My point exactly! How are you going to possibly keep a straight face with people sashaying, prome-nading, and do-si-doeing around like a bunch of lunatics? I'm telling you, there's going to be a puddle on the floor before you're done, and it's not going to be pretty."

"Thanks, Ash. Thanks a lot. That's really helpful."

Of course, when Kevin came to pick me up I couldn't fit into his car, which meant I had to start the whole shebang all over again. Ashley gave Kevin a quick reminder on how to put me back together.

"I totally remember how to take it off," Kevin said, grinning at me. "Isn't that good enough?"

"Are you sure you don't want me to come?" Ashley asked. "I'd hate for the fire department to have to roar up mid-dance with the jaws of life and rescue you from the mess that Kevin's made."

"Thanks for the offer," I said, "but I think we'll survive. Anyway, with Dad, Mrs. Yabonowitz, Sadie, and Mr. Cooper, I think I'll have all the help I need." I rolled my eyes.

All I could think was: *Thank God it wasn't my first date!* If it had been my first time out with Kevin and I had to share the dance floor with those four adults, I'm not sure I could have handled it. Dad was as nervous as a gawky teenager, and God only knows what was going through Auntie Sadie's mind. Kevin thought the whole thing was hysterical. I just thought it was embarrassing.

The dance was held in the old Grange Hall in the town next to ours. I don't know what I was expecting but the sheer number of folks waltzing in was mind-numbing.

"I thought this was, like, a little dance or something," I said to Kevin as he began corkscrewing me back into my hoop. "I swear, there are more people here than fought in the actual Civil War!"

It was a definite time warp—1863 and not a moment later.

The guys were dazzling in their Civil War uniforms, both Blue and Gray. Polished buttons, waxed moustaches, feathers in their caps. There wasn't a slacker in sight. Even Dad and Mr. Cooper looked pretty sweet. Of course, Kevin was the most dazzling of all.

And the women. Oh my God! Scarlett O'Hara had nothing on these belles. There wasn't a stitch out of line. Hoops galore. And the hair! Whew!

Kevin preened one more time in his car's side-view mirror and put on his cap. We were finally ready to make our grand entrance.

"Does my hair look all right?" he asked.

"Dashing!" I said. "To die for! How about mine?" I did a little twirl and an awkward curtsy.

"Fine," he replied. "Let's go."

"'Fine'?" I said. "'Fine'? I come this close to bleeding to death and all I get is a 'fine'?"

Kevin gathered me in his arms (as much as he could given that my hoop stretched close to the Kentucky border), swung me around, and kissed me.

"*Fine* is Civil War slang for 'awesome'! Completely awesome!"

Arm in arm, we entered the hall.

After all the time it had taken me to hop in and out and then back into the hoop, the dance was already in full swing when we got there. The hall was huge and it was filled to the max. There was a stage with an old-time band strumming and plucking and sawing away: fiddle and guitar and mandolin and stand-up bass. Other than electric lights and the neon exit signs, we were back in the middle of the nineteenth century.

There were three long lines of dancers running the length of the hall. Guys on one side, ladies on the other. Kevin and I walked in and immediately got swept into the closest line.

Late as we were we were stuck at the end.

The musicians had stopped playing and the caller stepped onto the stage. Civil War dance that it was, this was no ordinary dance caller. Lo and behold, it was Robert E. Lee, Commander of the Army of Northern Virginia. One of the greatest generals in American history! Calling our dances!

"Who's ready for the Virginia Reel, *West* Virginia style?" he shouted.

The dancers exploded with rebel yells, hoots, and hollers.

"Lead couple, raise your hands!"

Kevin and I looked around while everybody else in our line stared at us.

"Dang," I whispered, "we're the effin lead couple!"

Timidly, we raised our hands.

"We're going to begin with a forward and a bow. Forward two and a three and a bow, backward six, and a stop right there."

I didn't mind being the center of attention. In fact, I had kind of grown to like it. Leading the KABOOM meetings. Speaking at the Children's Crusade. Standing up to Sadie and the principal. Who would have thought I'd enjoy having all eyes on me? But not now. Not here. Here, everyone seemed to know exactly what they were doing. Everyone except Kevin and me.

To further complicate matters, my tightly wrapped braids made everything sound somewhat muffled and distant.

"What?" I asked Kevin.

"I didn't say anything," Kevin said.

Somehow I managed to forward, curtsey, and stagger back in place.

"Right elbows and then left elbows," the general called. "Ready, swing! Around, two, three, four, five, six, and a left elbow. Back and a two and a three and a four, and then stop right there!"

I consider myself pretty bright, but I've always had issues around right and left, as in which was which. Plus, I could hardly hear what the caller was calling. I gave Kevin my left elbow, he gave me his right, which somehow made us twist around so that I ended up on the guys' side, and Kevin on the ladies'.

"Two hands and we go clockwise," General Lee called out.

Clockwise! God help me! That was even worse than right and left. I lost valuable seconds trying to figure out which way the hands went, and in a Virginia reel, seconds were everything.

"Ready, go. Two hands and circle four, five, six, seven, and eight."

The good news was that somehow I ended up back with the ladies.

"Next comes a do-si-do with a right shoulder."

"Goodie!" I whispered to Kevin. "The do-si-do!"

Kevin laughed.

"Right shoulder, three, and four. And, then, stop right there."

Once again I was in the guys' line. We had been dancing for all of one minute and I had already changed gender three times.

"Left shoulder, see saw, back to back, and a back in place."

"See saw"? Had I heard that right? Was this a joke?

"Head couple take two hands in an elongated position and you're going to slide down the set for eight, and everybody claps. Slide and two and three and four, five and six and back the other way."

A hoop skirt is hard enough to walk in, let alone slide down the line, whatever the heck that meant. It took my total and complete concentration not to topple over. Form be damned. I just wanted to remain upright.

"Next the head couple will reel down the set. Right elbows with your own partner, left elbows with the opposite down the line. Left to the outside. Meet your own couple with the right. Always right to your own, left to the opposite. And keep going down the line. Slide back down the set and then we're going to peel the banana."

"Reel down the set"? "Left to the opposite"? "Peel the banana"? Was he serious? I gave a tug at my braids to loosen them and free up my ears. I hadn't a clue as to one word of what General Lee was saying.

"Let's go ahead and try this with the music."

Oh my God! I gave Kevin the "man the lifeboats—this ship is going down!" look.

There are people who dance for fun and there are people who dance because they honestly believe they are God's gift to the Virginia Reel. We were in the line with the latter. They seemed to take everything *way* too seriously.

Try as I might, it was too late to bow, or even curtsy, out now.

Every single step, I screwed up. If we were supposed to lead with the left, I went with the right. I moved forward instead of backward, counterclockwise instead of clockwise. There was not one single instance when I did the right thing. And Kevin, if you can believe it, was even worse than I was. I could at least keep time with the music, but he was totally dancing to the beat of a way-too-distant drummer.

We swung instead of do-si-doed. We slid instead of circled. We see-sawed instead of peeled the banana. It was a total and complete disaster.

I had never had so much fun in my life!

"Let's do it again!" I said to Kevin when the music stopped.

"We better switch lines. These folks are ready to kill us!"

By about the fifth time around we had gotten it halfway down so we only screwed up every other move. One of the older dancers, a guy in his seventies dressed like a colonel whom I vaguely remembered from one of the reenactments, went so far as to give me a wink and a nod.

"Is he hitting on you?" Kevin asked, hand on his sword.

"Don't worry," I said. "I only fall for privates."

After about an hour of Virginia reeling, just when I had finally figured out my right from my left, we took a break and headed to the back of the hall for a breather.

"Oh my God," Kevin said, grasping my arm.

"What?"

"Look! In the corner! It's Abraham Lincoln."

Sure enough. There, drink in hand, was the president of the United States, at least the northern ones. Abraham Lincoln. In the flesh.

He didn't just look like Abraham Lincoln with his stovepipe hat, slumped shoulders, gnarly wrinkled face, and that mustache-less beard. He really was the president.

Everybody else simply dressed the part. This guy really *was* the part. He was holding forth as if it were actually 1863, waxing eloquently about the Emancipation Proclamation, about the evils of slavery, about the ineptitude of the Union generals.

"Bad news," I whispered to Kevin.

"I know," Kevin said. "Someone's going to shoot the president. We've got to tell him! We've got to warn him not to go to Ford's Theatre!"

"No, not that!" I tugged on Kevin's sleeve. "Even worse!"

"What could be worse than President Lincoln being assassinated?"

"I have to pee!"

"You're kidding me!"

"I wish. You have to help me. You have to help me *now*."

"But I thought . . ."

"Now!"

As previously noted, getting me in and out of the hoop skirt required the skills of a Civil War surgeon and more hands than I had. And I didn't have a second to lose. The Virginia Reel had rattled things up inside. I had to pee. Bad. Really bad.

"You should have worn the diaper!" Kevin said.

"Shut up. Come with me into the bathroom."

"No way! I'm not going into the women's room. They'll think I'm a pervert."

"I don't care what people think! I have to pee!"

"Then we'll go the men's room," Kevin said.

Desperate times called for desperate measures. Off we went into the men's room.

Kevin and I snuck into the farthest stall so he could help me out of the skirt. I was standing on the toilet with my hoop halfway off when who should come bursting in the bathroom but Abraham Lincoln. I could see him through the slit in the stall door.

He rushed into the stall next to ours, unbuttoned his pants, grunted, farted loudly, and sat down to do his business.

Just my luck. The only time in my life that I'm in the men's room and the president of the United States has to take a dump!

Then two other men came in. One of them was Robert E. Lee, the caller of the dances. The other one looked like a general, too. They perched themselves in front of the mirror and began re-waxing their moustaches, while Kevin and I held our breath in the stall.

"You see who's here?" Lee asked the other guy.

"No. Who?"

"That spaz girl who couldn't dance worth shit. She's the same one leading the anti–mountaintop removal charge. She goes to the high school. The one we saw on TV."

"Seriously? That little dweeb?"

"The very one. She needs to mind her own goddamn business. Environmentalist!" General Lee frowned, spat into the sink, and continued waxing away.

"You got that right!" the other officer nodded.

"She's a hot little thing though," Lee continued.

Needless to say, this conversation did not go down well with Kevin. As long as I could be free of the effin hoop and blissfully pee I was willing to turn the other cheek. After all, fame had its downside. But not so with Kevin. He was pissed. Really pissed.

I had the hoop halfway off with my arms pinned to my side, unable to hold my nose from the presidential stench, when Kevin, desperate to defend my honor, flung open the stall door and came flying out.

"How dare you!" he shouted, taking off his cap and flinging it to the floor. "Dissing my girl! Trashing my cause! I demand satisfaction!"

The two generals were totally taken aback. They looked into the stall and there I was, dress halfway off, arms in the air, bladder about to burst.

"What the hell?" General Lee said.

Kevin took his sword out of his scabbard, flicked the general's hat off of his head and stomped on it.

"Son of a bitch!" Lee yelled, taking his sword out of his scabbard and waving it in the air.

Holy Mother of a Mountaintop! They were going to have a sword fight! In the middle of the men's room! Over me!

Just as sword was about to clash with sword, Abraham Lincoln flew out of his stall, pants at his knees, toilet paper trailing from his shoes, still farting away.

"The boy is right!" Lincoln shouted. "You are nothing but a lowlife and a scoundrel!" Holding a roll of toilet paper as a weapon, Lincoln whacked the sword out of General Lee's hands and then tripped over a trash can, knocking open the bathroom door before falling flat on his ass, half in and half out of the bathroom.

At that very moment with mayhem imminent, who should walk into the men's room but Mr. Cooper, all decked out like a Union cavalry officer. And standing outside was Auntie Sadie in her nurse's garb. I could even see Dad and Mrs. Yabonowitz peering in from around the corner.

"Gentlemen!" Mr. Cooper roared. "And woman! Criss-cross applesauce! How dare you interrupt this night of pleasure with your fisticuffs!" Coop helped President Lincoln to his feet. We all stared meekly at the floor. Twenty-five years teaching high school hooligans had certainly honed Mr. Cooper's disciplinary skills. When Coop yelled, folks listened. Even outranked as he was by the President of the United States and General Robert E. Lee, Mr. Cooper was still the man.

"Cyndie! Kevin!" Cooper lectured. "I expected better of you. And Mr. President, with all due respect . . ." Coop only glared at the two older Confederates.

Presided over by the president himself, General Lee apologized to me, we all shook hands, the guys re-sheathed their testosterone and their swords, bowed, and saluted each other. Then we all marched out of the bathroom with all of the dignity we could muster.

"Cyndie," my father said, still waiting by the door. "This is Mrs. Yabonowitz. Mrs. Yabonowitz, my daughter Cyndie."

"Very nice to meet you," I said, standing there in my underwear and holding my hoop skirt, my bladder ready to rupture.

"Well," Kevin said. "It's nice to know we have Lincoln on our side."

"Oh my God! The polar bears, the circus, Tammy's Tasty Top, and now Lincoln!" I exclaimed. "Who would have thought?"

We were on our way back home after the dance. After the incident in the men's room we had managed to squeeze in a few more Virginia reels, and our last dance had been perfect. We had peeled the banana with the best of them. Hooray for us!

During a break, one of the younger dancers had even snuck in with a boom box and managed to put on a rap reel. We got in a few awesome minutes of new-fangled grinding, though dirty dancing with a hoop skirt on was challenging at best. A handful of the old-timers even came out to strut their stuff. Before Robert E. Lee got too pissed we had scooted out the side door and headed for home.

"Now it belongs to the ages," I said.

"Wasn't that some dude's line when Lincoln died?" Kevin asked.

"Something like that, only I don't think he was talking about dancing."

"Probably not," Kevin agreed.

"And Kev," I cooed, "you were my knight in shining armor. Rescuing his damsel in distress!" I put my arms around him.

"I thought I was your private in shining buttons," Kevin said. "Anyway, it was probably a good thing that Coop walked in when he did. Assaulting Robert E. Lee in a bathroom, no matter how much of a jerk he might be, doesn't play well in these parts."

"Was I really such a spaz?" I asked.

"In the men's room?" Kevin asked. "Well, standing on the toilet seat, stuck in your hoop, with your . . ."

"No," I laughed. "On the dance floor!"

"Yeah, pretty much," Kevin said. "But don't sweat it, I was even worse. And here's the good news."

"Tell me."

"You might be a spaz, but you're *my* spaz."

Kevin turned and kissed me.

There are times in life when I get a sudden jolt, an electrical shock, a bolt of lightning, and an enormous flashing neon sign lights up the entire sky: LIFE IS GOOD! Not just good but *great*! An awesome dance! Ridiculous reels! A not-very-civil war in the men's room! Grinding away, hoop skirt and all! And now, here I was, somebody's one and only spaz.

I squeezed Kevin's thigh and nestled my head on his shoulder.

59

AS BOTH MOUNT TOM and Kevin heated up, the pressure to do well in school seemed to increase, too. Teachers were paying more attention to me, and expecting more out of me than ever before. Whether they were for or against mountaintop removal was irrelevant. Teachers and even other kids seemed to think that somehow I now knew something about everything.

"What are your thoughts about the Articles of Confederation?" Ms. Fydenkevitz asked in history, seemingly interested in my opinion.

"What kind of atmosphere do you think Steinbeck is trying to create in *Of Mice and Men*?" Diaper Lady asked me in English class. Thank goodness I had read it.

Even Mister Livingston was calling on me in math class.

As much as Tom and Kevin were doing their best to distract me, I felt like I had to be on my academic game. It was all becoming pretty intense.

•

It was fifth period, right after lunch, and I was sitting in science, trying to make sense of cellular respiration when, wouldn't you know, Kevin's face appeared at the window of the classroom door. He motioned for me to come out.

I couldn't help but smile. I had just spent my entire lunch with him and now, here he was, skipping class to see me again.

I had that boy right where I wanted him!

I shuffled up to Coop's desk, clutched my stomach, and asked for a hall pass. He gave me the look.

"Girl stuff!" I said, waving my backpack and making a yucky face. "Gotta deal."

The only good thing about getting your period was that you could use it to get away with so much stuff.

"Can't get enough of me, huh?" I asked, putting my arms around Kevin and nuzzling his neck as soon as the door shut behind us.

For the first time ever, he took my arms off of him.

"Bad news," he said. "Really bad."

"What?" I asked, startled by the look in his eyes. "What happened?"

"It's started. They're there."

"What started? Who's where?"

"The logging trucks are at the foot of Tom. They're good to go."

"Are you serious?" I asked. I felt my breath stick in my throat.

"I am. I really am!"

"How do you know?" I asked.

"Marc's dad texted him." Good for Ashley, I thought. She had trained that boy well.

"What do we do?" Kevin asked.

It was such a surreal moment. It was hard to take in all that Kevin had just said, hard to believe that it was actually true. After all the months of focusing on Tom, after all the letters and the petitions and the meetings and the march, after all the hard work we had put into KABOOM, I had never actually pictured how it would all go down. I hadn't ever let myself go there.

But now, here we were, Kevin and I, standing outside Mr. Cooper's classroom, reality jumping down our throats.

The logging trucks were at the foot of Mount Tom. The mountaintop destroyers were all set to do the devil's work. The nightmare was beginning!

"What do we do?" Kevin asked again.

I nestled my way back into his arms, feeling him wrap them tight around me, feeling his heart beating nearly as fast as mine, feeling so close to him it made me want to burst. I wanted to freeze time and stay that way forever. I wanted to lose the horror and the pain and the tragedy of the real world and just be in Kevin's arms. Kevin and me. Just the two of us. Nobody else. Nobody. Forever.

I breathed him in. In and out and in again.

"Take me there," I said. "Drop me off. Come back and rally the troops. Let's go."

"Are you sure?" Kevin asked.

"Let's go!" I said, not sure at all.

We ran to Kevin's car.

On the way I made a brief pit stop and unlocked Ashley's and my bikes, stuffing the locks and chains into my backpack.

"What are you doing?" Kevin asked.

"I don't know," I said. "But they may come in handy."

We leapt into his car and, just the way they do in the movies, Kevin backed up, and peeled out of the driveway.

"I don't want to leave you there," Kevin said. "Alone. I don't think it's a good idea."

"You have to," I said. "You have to come back and tell everyone. Like Paul Revere. Except you have to yell, 'American is coming! American is coming!' Not 'the British.'"

"I don't want to be away from you," Kevin said.

"I know," I said, reaching out and taking his hand.

Kevin was driving crazy fast. At one point we almost went off the road and into a ditch. But finally, we sped around the corner and there we were.

Ground zero. The heart of darkness.

There were a whole mess of guys standing next to the logging trucks drinking coffee and eating donuts with their hard hats on and chain saws in hand. Waiting for the word. Ready to go. Ready to log the road to the top of Tom so they could blow the mountain sky high. Ready to destroy the temple of the gods.

And it would all start with the very first cut of the very first tree.

The beginning of the end.

Kevin slammed on his brakes next to a huge timber harvester with claws and saws like something from the apocalypse. A death machine that could gobble up Sugar Daddy, Bradley Beech, Sadie's Twin, and She, take them down with one whack, and spit out logs like tooth picks.

I took my seat belt off and opened the door. Kevin scooped me in his arms, hugged me, and then, holding my face in his hands, kissed me. Kissed me hard.

"If anything happens to you . . ."

"Go!" I said. "You're Paul Revere, remember? Go! Now!"

Kevin kept my face in his hands, taking me deep into his eyes.

"I love you," he said. "I love you so much!"

"I know," I said, fighting back tears. "I know! And I am so in love with you."

"If anything happens . . ."

"Go!" I shouted.

60

I DIDN'T HAVE MUCH TIME TO THINK. I just acted. Before any of the temple destroyers had time to stop me, I grabbed the two bicycle chains out of my backpack, tightly wound them around each of my thighs and locked them tight to the timber harvester.

"What the fuck!" the logging supervisor roared. He was pissed. *Really* pissed.

I had chosen my quarry well. The harvesting machine was the go-to gal, the one to get the ball rolling, the mother of the tree cutters.

Locked in tight, I had shut it down. There was no way to cut down the trees with me mucking up the works. No harvester, no trees.

Trees they could tackle. But evidently my thighs were, thank goodness, off-limits.

I assumed I'd be scared half to death, but a surreal feeling of calm enveloped me like a soothing quilt. I looked out at the scowling cluster of men huddling with their chainsaws and their hardhats as if were all a dream, and I realized that there was nothing else I would rather be doing, that there was nowhere else I would rather be. I knew I belonged right here, right now, chained to the tree harvester. It was as if I had been made for this very moment. As if this were my chosen place in the universe.

It wasn't long before the police arrived with bolt cutters, cut me lose, and carried me to the police car. I refused to walk. Just like the Widow Combs back in the day. And, wouldn't you know it, just in the nick of time a television news crew arrived with the same reporter who had been at the Children's Crusade, and they got the whole thing on camera.

"Stop mountaintop removal!" I shouted as they carried me away. "Save Mount Tom!"

The police put me in the back of the cruiser and drove me to the county jail.

•

I watched the hands of the clock tick ever so slowly, minute by minute, hour by hour, till it was almost 8:00 p.m. I had been in jail for almost six hours. Six effin hours. And nothing had happened. Other than bleeding all over my underwear, absolutely nothing.

The jailer dude called my house repeatedly but there was no answer. He even called Ashley's and Kevin's and got the same response. Nothing.

So I just sat there in jail. All by my lonesome. Well, me and the jailer dude, who kept getting phone call after phone call that, try as I might, I could not manage to overhear.

I figured that by now someone would have come and rescued me. Bailed me out. Sprung me loose. Helped me fly the coop. Whatever it was they called it.

Where was my dad? Where was Kevin? Where was everyone?

Maybe Kevin had gotten in an accident on the way back to school, and no one knew I was here. Maybe he was lying in some hospital bed somewhere. Maybe he was dying. The love of my life, and maybe he was dying. Maybe he was dead!

I lay on the hard concrete jailhouse floor and desperately tried not to let my mind wander to the dark side.

Instead, I replayed the scene over and over in my head. Not the one of me chaining myself to the harvester. Not the one of me being carried away by the police. There would be plenty of time for those reruns.

It was the closing scene with Kevin that was running rampant through my brain.

"I love you," he had said. "I love you so much!"

I could handle the cops. I could handle jail. But if anything happened to that boy . . .

After what seemed like an eternity, two police officers finally came in and unlocked the cell door.

"Cyndie," the heavier one said. It was the same one who had cut through my bicycle chains and carried me to the police car. "Let's go."

"Where?" I asked. "Go where?"

"To the gymnasium. At the high school. It's where we're holding everybody."

"Everybody?" I asked. "What are you talking about? What do you mean, 'everybody'?"

"You tell me," the cop said. "You're the one that started this whole damn mess."

"Tell you what?" I asked, confused at best.

"What's going on," he said. "We must have arrested close to a hundred people. No way they could all fit in this dump. So we're putting them in the gymnasium. You're going to join them."

"Arrested them for . . ."

"Don't go playing dumb on me," the cop said. "They were doing the same damn thing you were doing and you know it. Blockading the mountain. Stopping the loggers. And now a bunch of them have all gone and dressed up in Union blue and Confederate gray and they're occupying the place. Who would have thought the Rebels and the Yanks would ever agree about anything. Somebody told me that Stonewall Jackson and Abraham Lincoln are sitting up in the same tree! Abraham Lincoln, for God's sake! I've been on the force for twenty-three years and I've never seen anything like this."

I sat up on the floor and stared, wide-eyed, at the officers.

"Come on, Cyndie," the heavy-set one continued, mopping his brow. "It's been a helluva long day. Please don't make us carry you. My back is killing me."

I got up and walked out the jailhouse door.

Epilogue

IT'S HARD TO BELIEVE I'm the same person as the girl I was a few months ago.

I look back on the me who started her sophomore year in high school, on the me with her drive-bys and her kingdoms of boys and her ridiculous jar and her utterly lame life, and I think to myself, *Wow! Not bad, girl. Not bad at all!*

I know it sounds like bragging. I know it sounds like I've turned into this big-headed bitch with all this swag. It's not like that. It really isn't.

But, truth be told, I feel pretty good about myself.

People ask me how I did this. People ask me how I helped organize the group that shut down the mountaintop removers. That saved Mount Tom. That helped spark new groups all over Appalachia.

And I tell them this: If I can do it, then anyone can!

It's not like I had signed up for this. It had fallen in my lap. I was an accidental activist.

But accidents can be good things. No—great things! I wouldn't have missed this accident for the world!

When you're right, when you have truth on your side, when the stakes are so high, then it's not that hard to be the one to step up. I mean, don't get me wrong, this was no cake-walk. But it was also fun as hell.

In fact, when they took me from the jailhouse to the gym it was heaven. People clapped and cheered and hugged me. It was beyond awesome! Too many wows to even list!

Kids in the gymnasium jail! Arrested! Just like the real Children's Crusade of 1963. Martin Luther King Jr. would be proud. And so would my mother. I just knew it.

"I got arrested!" Britt said, leaping into my arms. "Just like you! I got arrested!"

Sure enough, Britt and half of the circus (including her new heartthrob stilt boy) had joined the blockade and ended up in the makeshift gymnasium jail.

Ashley (who, along with Marc, was also a jailbird) filled me in on the news. Kevin had played the role of Paul Revere to a T. He had even burst into the front office at school, switched on the microphone, and announced to the entire student body what was going down. A little more high-tech than the lanterns in the Old North Church steeple, but, hey, he done good.

With all of the KABOOMers leading the charge, kids came to the rescue! Piggy had removed the chains from his wardrobe and locked himself to a tree, finally scoring that sweet opportunity to truly "stick it the man." Sam the Fisherman had woven a web of fishing line through trunks of trees that even chainsaws might have a hard time cutting their way through. Frank had knelt in the middle of the road with his Bible open and his lips moving in silent prayer until he was hauled away. Jon Buntington, lying in front of a tree harvester, had actually been smiling. And Ashley and Marc the Mountain, handcuffed hand in hand, refused to be separated even when they were arrested.

And they say all we teenagers care about are our Facebook status and how we look and what we wear. Ha! Take that one and shove it up your logging machine!

Kevin, aka Private Paul Revere, had also called my father, and the news spread like wildfire to the reenactors. Just a few nights earlier Ashley and I, bidding a bittersweet farewell to our beloved secret, had told Dad about our mini-mine, and he had done some research at his college library and was convinced that the mine really was part of a long-forgotten Civil War fortification. The Army of Northern Virginia and the Army of the Potomac joined forces and transformed themselves into Revolutionary Minutemen and swarmed the mountain in a moment. Kevin and my father, both of whom had quickly changed into their Confederate uniforms, occupied the tree that was to be the first one cut.

"I never dreamed," my father said after the dust had settled and we were home again, "that the proudest moment of my life would be having both of my daughters wind up in jail. Up in heaven Mom is smiling!"

There were lots of arrests for trespassing that afternoon. That's what they charged us with: trespassing. You could blow up the top off an effin mountain and call it business as usual, but if you tried to save the very same mountain you got busted for trespassing.

Go figure.

The papers and the TV had a field day. We were splashed all over the news. Front page, even. Not just in West Virginia but in other states as well. Just like Widow Combs. Afterwards, Ashley and I brought the KABOOMers to our mini-mine and Piggy found an old Civil War–era canteen in the stonework above it. The newscaster who had covered the story when I was getting hauled away returned to do a lengthy piece on KABOOM featuring us KABOOMers at the mine and focusing in on the Civil War connection. The State Historical Preservation Office came marching in and demanded that the whole project be put on hold while they surveyed the site. American Coal Company, reeling from bad publicity particularly after the press revealed that they had known all along about a historic site on the mountain, was forced to put their mountaintop removal plan on hold. There was even a rumor floating around that American was going to donate the land to our town for a historical and natural preserve.

We had won!

Mount Tom, at least for the moment, was safe.

Who would have thought?

•

I've always loved stories where good triumphs over evil and truth wins out in the end. That's pretty much what happened here, except that good got a restraining order over evil and it's all tied up in court and a bit muddled over what will happen to Mount Tom next. But hey, you've got to celebrate life's victories, permanent or not.

There's a full-fledged archeological dig taking place at our mine and the stonework above it. All sorts of awesome artifacts have been found, including Civil War guns, bayonets, and even the barrels of three cannons. Ashley and I have been helping out at the dig after school, and Ashley is now convinced she wants to become a Civil War reenactor.

"No offense," she told me, "but no lame nurse thingy for me. I want to be a Union general or something. On a horse."

Kevin has gotten word that he's been promoted to a captain among the reenactors, which means he'll now outrank my father. Dad couldn't care less. He's head over heels with Mrs. Yabonowitz, and the two of them have been double-dating with Auntie Sadie and Mr. Cooper.

And speaking of couples, the dipshit duo, Bert and Michael, got caught breaking into a liquor store after they somehow managed to lock themselves in the freezer overnight. Just when I thought they couldn't get any stupider they went off and did that.

And Kevin, now Captain Kevin, and me?

Quadruple wow!

For my sixteenth birthday, he took me out to dinner in a really fancy restaurant. He told me that, next fall when he graduates, he wants to go to West Virginia University in Morgantown because it's not that far from me. He told me that he doesn't ever want to be far from me. He told me that if it was 1863, at the height of the Civil War, he'd desert the army and take me with him out to the West and we'd get a farm and we'd raise goats and we'd grow peaches and bananas.

"You can't grow bananas out West, you idiot!" I told him, squeezing his thigh under the table.

"*You* could!" Kevin said. "You can do anything."

I blushed.

"You could!" Kevin repeated. "After what you've done with Mount Tom, growing bananas out West would be a piece of cake."

"I've got an idea," I said. "Why don't we just stay here and save mountains instead?"

"Deal!" Kevin said, taking my face in his hands and kissing me.

Acknowledgments

MANY THANKS to all of those wonderful people who gave me such valuable feedback during the writing of this novel. Thanks to Julia Sullivan and to my teen readers Gretchen Saveson, Mairead Blatner and Lucy Norton who were invaluable in helping me refine the teen voices. They also pointed out how totally "pathetic" and "pointless" certain sections of the draft were, which considerably helped me (I hope!) in crafting a better book. Thanks to Taylor Adams (my son) and Casey Adams (my daughter) for their edits and their kind words of support and encouragement. They are the two best children this dad could ever hope to have. Thanks to all of the unnamed Civil War reenactors who shared their stories and experiences with me. Battle on, people, battle on. Thanks to the Hatfield Historical Society and particularly Kathie Gow for opening up their collection and letting me actually touch a real hoop skirt. Thanks to Elise Keaton for her insights into West Virginia activism and her fabulous work in Keepers of the Mountain. Thanks to my Green Writers Press intern, Kaitlyn Plukas from Bennington College, for her outstanding editorial insights and her untiring marketing and promotional efforts. Thanks to my editor Mike Fleming who is the BEST and reminded me that I could greatly broaden the appeal of the book by refraining from pissing off and offending practically everyone in the universe and that I could do so without compromising the integrity of the novel. May his three legged dog stay fat and happy. Thanks to my fabulous publisher Dede Cummings and her vision of the Green Writers Press, which incorporates and facilitates the gift of words to help foster a sustainable environment. Thanks to my wonderful wife Morey Phippen who somehow has managed to stay married to me for thirty-four years without completely losing her mind, who is my number one cheerleader, and whom I love so much. Most of all thanks to all of the amazing, dedicated, tireless activists in Appalachia and elsewhere who are drawing attention to the tragedy of mountaintop removal and the devastating impact it has on local communities and the environment. The time to stop mountaintop removal is NOW!

KABOOM!
Reader's Guide

SPOILER ALERT:
Do NOT read this until AFTER you read the book*

*I know after reading this, you will want to read all of these
questions, but for goodness sake, DON'T!

1. How does Cyndie's character change throughout the book?
Does she change for the better or for the worse? Why? Use
examples from the text to support your answer.

2. Why does American Coal Company want to blow the top
off of Mount Tom? Why do Cyndie and Ashley think this
is bad? Use examples from the text and your own outside
research to support your answer.

3. Why does Mr. Cooper get so angry at people who ignore
climate change? Is his anger justified? Why or Why not?

4. Does Cyndie's family influence her decisions around activism? Why do Cyndie's dad and Aunt Sadie decide to not tell her about her mom's activism? If you were a parent, would you have told Cyndie? Why or Why not?

5. Compare and contrast Cyndie and Ashley. How do they approach their respective relationships with Kevin and Marc? Do these relationships change throughout the book?

6. Why is Cyndie upset at Kevin after the meeting at the church? Is her reaction justified? Why or Why not? What's more important: one's intentions or one's actions?

7. Is activism important? Why or Why not? How do people become active in environmental and social issues? What are some important qualities in an activist? Do Cyndie and Ashley have those qualities? Is Cyndie and Ashley's conversion to activism realistic?

8. Cyndie and Ashley's first act of activism (cutting down the flags marking the trees) is technically illegal. Are illegal activities such as this one and Cyndie's actions at the end of the novel (chaining herself to the logging truck) justified? Consider the "necessity defense" popularized by MLK and other examples from history in your response.

9. How do you define courage? Can Marc's actions, specifically when he renounces his coveted job as mascot, be considered courageous? Who else in KABOOM! would you consider to be courageous and why?

10. What is one environmental issue that affects your community? Name at least two different ways you can work to make the situation better. Are your strategies plausible? Why or Why not?